***Books by Fran Stewart***

<u>The Biscuit McKee Mystery Series</u>:

> *Orange as Marmalade*
> *Yellow as Legal Pads*
> *Green as a Garden Hose*
> *Blue as Blue Jeans*
> *Indigo as an Iris*
> *Violet as an Amethyst*
> *Gray as Ashes*
>
> *Red as a Rooster*
> *Black as Soot*
> *Pink as a Peony*
> *White as Ice*

*A Slaying Song Tonight*

<u>The ScotShop Mysteries</u>:

> *A Wee Murder in My Shop*
> *A Wee Dose of Death*
> *A Wee Homicide in the Hotel*

Poetry:

> *Resolution*

For Children:

> *As Orange As Marmalade/*
> *Tan naranja como Mermelada*
> (a bilingual book)

Non-Fiction:

> *From The Tip of My Pen: a workbook for writers*
> *BeesKnees #1: A Beekeeping Memoir (#1 of 6 volumes)*
> *BeesKnees #2: A Beekeeping Memoir (#2 of 6 volumes)*
> *BeesKnees #3: A Beekeeping Memoir (#3 of 6 volumes)*
> *BeesKnees #4: A Beekeeping Memoir (#4 of 6 volumes)*
> *BeesKnees #5: A Beekeeping Memoir (#5 of 6 volumes)*
> *BeesKnees #6: A Beekeeping Memoir (#6 of 6 volumes)*
> Coming Soon - *Clear as Mud*

# Red as a Rooster

## Fran Stewart

My Own Ship Press

Red as a Rooster
the 8th Biscuit McKee Mystery
Fran Stewart



ISBN:  978-1-951368-18-0

This is a work of fiction. Any resemblance to any person living or dead is purely coincidental.

This book was printed in the United States of America.


Published by
My Own Ship Press
PO Box 490153
Lawrenceville GA 30049

myownship@icloud.com
franstewart.com

*For Diana, Eli, and Veronica*

The final four books of the Biscuit McKee Mystery Series were written as one complete book and are meant to be read as such. I make no attempt to "bring the reader up to speed" at the beginning of each of the three later books, for I assume you will read them in order.

It is not absolutely necessary that you read the first seven books of the Biscuit McKee Series before you begin reading these, but please note this SPOILER ALERT: There are references in these last four books to some of the problems Biscuit and her friends encounter in the preceding seven books.

Beginning on Page 344, you will find information on the geneology of the families in this story as well as historical and chronological information on the following topics:

Original Families on the Trek
Children of Beechnut House
Martinsville Town Council Chairmen
Chronological listing of Owners of Beechnut House

Who's in Biscuit & Bob's House (present day)
Latecomers
Who's in Matthew's House

Finally, the 2020 revised versions of the Biscuit McKee Mysteries (published now by My Own Ship Press) have allowed me to clear up various inconsistencies that careful readers have pointed out over the years. My thanks to each of you. You know who you are because I replied to your emails.

# The Beginning
## The Year - 1692
## The Place - Brandtburg, in the Green Mountains
## of the Northern Colonies

**LUCELIA SABRISS LOOKED** like a bedraggled owl after a particularly violent rainstorm. Her wet, heavy woolen cloak in dappled shades of gray, brown, and white adhered to her shoulders as she rode into town in the dilapidated wagon. Those eyes of hers, luminous as the owl she resembled, took in everything, missed nothing.

It was only later that Albion Martin found out that Gilbert Sabriss, the man driving the wagon, was the father of the owl woman. Albion had not truly noticed him that first day and barely acknowledged him from then on until the day in 1693 when he asked Mister Sabriss for permission to court Lucelia.

"Before you begin the courting," Mister Sabriss said in his quiet voice, "you should know that we lived outside Salem."

"Salem?"

"In the Massachusetts Bay Colony."

Albion wondered what this had to do with courting. "Yes?"

"My daughter was known to the women of the town. She is a healer. She sewed with many of the women. She birthed babies and treated wounds. She used herbs and simples that she concocted, and many times the women of Salem came to her for counsels."

"Yes?" By this point Albion was thoroughly confused. Why was Lucelia's father telling him these things?

"We came away, leaving in the middle of the night with little but the clothing on our backs soon after the first troubles started."

"Troubles?"

"Accusations."

"Accusations?" Albion could not help repeating the words he heard. He had no idea what the old man was talking about.

They were alone in the room, but Mister Sabriss looked around as if afraid someone might be listening through the very walls. "Witchcraft," he whispered. "There was talk of witchcraft."

Albion thought of Lucelia's gentleness, her kindness, which seemed to be balanced equally by strength, decisiveness, and her fortitude in the face of the ills she combatted on a daily basis. Had she not tended Albion's mother through the wracking cough that had beset her for months? Had she not administered teas and poultices day and night? Had she not rejoiced with the entire family when Mother recovered?

From that first vision of her the previous year, with her soaked bonnet limp around her head, Albion had scarcely noticed another person in all of Brandtburg. If his horse had not had such sense, Albion would have ridden straight into the side of the tavern that first day. So now, when Mister Sabriss said his daughter might have been accused as a witch had they not escaped when they did, Albion refused to believe it.

It was not long, though, before the Brandt men in the town began to say that Albion had been bewitched by the large-eyed woman. If Albion was bewitched, though, so must have been his parents, for they both approved of Lucelia. The elder Mister and Mistress Martin liked her father well enough, too, although Mister Sabriss was an unassuming man who seldom spoke above a breathy whisper.

It was only after William, the first child of Albion and Lucelia, was born in 1694 with a white birth caul clinging to his body so tight it looked like a shroud, that the rumors began to grow. None of the midwives had ever seen a caul birth before, but of course they had all heard that such a child would have a lifetime affinity for water. One had been born in the neighboring valley some years before, and word was that the child grew to be happier in a boat on the nearby lake than on the shore with the other children. It was not natural.

After Lucelia's next children were all daughters, one a year for five years, and all of them born with the sac-like caul, the Brandts began to question the right of the Martin family and all their near kin to be there in the Brandt family's valley. After all, Albion Martin and his parents had not lived long in Brandtburg. It was but Albion's grandsire who had first come this way and married a local woman. The Brandts had lived there for more generations than anyone could remember, unlike those newcomer Martins.

When tinker-borne rumors of what happened in far away Salem finally filtered into the Green Mountains, the Brandt men began to shun the Martin who had married the wide-eyed refugee, the one who had come into their quiet valley so soon after the Salem witch trials began. With the shunning came the Brandts' disapproval of Albion's parents as well, for had they not welcomed the witch woman and her father into their family?

It was only after the shunning that Albion and Lucelia moved, in 1700, with his parents, her father, and the six children away from the center of Brandtburg to a cluster of cabins they built well to the east of the town, on the west-facing slope of the nearest mountain, where the land was filled with rocks, but was fertile indeed. The rocks were useful for marking the boundaries of the fields, and the work of removing the rocks made for strong young men.

So, amid the newly cleared and fertile fields, they raised their children and accumulated around themselves the beginnings of the Martin clan.

Albion's father thought the move was a fine idea, for he had never been comfortable around the Brandts. Albion's mother missed her women friends, but had, of course, been raised to believe the scripture that commanded "whither thou goest," never realizing that the woman in that story had been going, not with her husband, but with her dearly beloved mother-in-law.

**WHEN THE BRUISED** and battered bodies of Albion and Lucelia Martin were found in a roadside ditch three years after they moved away from the center of Brandtburg, it was Albion's mother who took over the raising of William and his five sisters. Nothing was ever proved as to whose hands had done the deed. No one ever stepped forward to claim responsibility for the murders, although there was rejoicing among the Brandt men that evening after the word had spread that the witch and her husband were no more.

Eventually, Albion and Lucelia's only son William Martin, the first child who had been born with a caul, married and had but two children, both of them boys. He named his sons Homer and Silas.

Lucelia and Albion's five girls, raised with firm but loving discipline by their grandparents, grew to marriageable age and were soon wed to men who came to the valley from other parts of the colonies. So began the growth of the community on the mountainside to the east of Brandtburg, as the Garners, the Breetons, the Hastings family, the Russells, and the Surratts had children of their own.

Richard Hastings founded a public house in the center of Brandtburg; Haverill Breeton caused havoc among the Martin community and the Brandts as well when he built his house in Brandtburg next door to a Brandt; and Reverend Russell caused a church to be built toward the eastern edge of the town to service all those who were kin to the Martins.

The Martin women gradually formed deep and trusting friendships with the Brandt women, particularly after Mistress Breeton invited them to a quilting bee at her house, one that was attended by her next-door neighbor and numerous other Brandt women as well. The Brandts came as much to satisfy their curiosity as to do their quilting.

But most of the men of the Martin clan kept to themselves, even when they sat long evening hours in the Hastings tavern.

## Forty-Nine Years Later
## Friday, 17 April 1741

**SILAS MARTIN AND** his elder brother ambled down the gentle lower slope of the mountain through the gathering dusk to Robert Hastings' public house in the center of Brandtburg. "You will be married on the day after the morrow," Silas said, curtailing his stride to match that of his much shorter brother, "and then you will spend all your days and nights with your wife, and there will be none of your time for me." Silas cuffed his brother's arm in good humor. "So tonight, I will buy you your last drink as an unmarried man."

"I accept your offer of the drink." Homer elbowed Silas in the ribs a little harder than absolutely necessary. "We may have to imbibe once again tomorrow eve, and I will let you buy me that one as well. And then on the Sunday night, you will buy me my first drink as a married man."

"Not so!" Silas knew Myra Sue Russell well enough to know that she would think poorly of a new husband who went drinking on his first night of marriage. And Homer must have forgotten—how could he?—that the tavern would be closed as it always was on Sundays. "You will be more than busy Sunday evening." Silas elbowed Homer back, and it might have devolved into one of their good-natured brotherly tussles if Homer had not, uncharacteristically, turned solemn.

"You will find a woman of your own on our long road, and then I will buy you *your* last drink."

"I will hold you to that promise, brother."

Silas knew tonight's ale would not be the last of Homer's drinking, despite how much they joked about it. The man loved spirits far too much to give them up just because he was getting married. Silas only hoped he could keep Homer on his feet the day of the wedding. It would not do to have him fall flat on his face at the altar.

They approached the tavern from the fertile land to the east, as always. As they passed Reverend Russell's church, Silas slowed his steps, gazing at the sunken grave where his father, William Martin, had lain for three years and at the fresher earth, still mounded up, that held his mother. Homer had not slowed at all, and Silas soon trotted to catch him up.

Silas could not help but look to his right before entering the crossroads where the tavern sat, to where Gore Mountain towered in the distance, visible between two of the intervening smaller mounts. He loved that sight, particularly now in the waning light of a spring evening, while what was left of the sun shone on the snow-covered tip. Within moments, though, his view of Gore Mountain was obscured by the spreading beechnut tree that stood almost like a sentinel before the inn.

As they entered the small tavern, they ignored the group of Brandt men gathered at the far end of the room around a dark, wax-stained table beside the fireplace. Instead, they walked to an empty bench in the corner closest to the bar.

Ira Brandt, drunk as he had frequently been since the death of his wife, hoisted himself to his feet. One of his compatriots reached out to prevent the large candlestick in the center of the table from toppling as Ira steadied himself none too gracefully and raised his pewter mug of ale. "Behold, the grandsons of cowards!" he shouted to the assembled men. His words may have been slurred, but his voice carried easily across the length of the room.

Silas looked at his elder brother. He tended to defer to Homer, simply because Homer was the older of the two, but sometimes—often—Silas thought he himself had better sense. On an occasion such as this one, he knew without a doubt he had much better sense. They both were men, but Silas, at nineteen, felt himself to be far more grown in many ways than his twenty-one-year-old brother.

Homer hardly paused a heartbeat before he said, "What we fear in ourselves, we accuse in others."

Ira snarled, and Silas could see Homer tense his arms.

Silas quietly counted the men encircling the table. *Seven of them. Two of us.* He did not like the odds. Ira's brother, Hubbard Brandt, the most sensible of the Brandts so far as Silas knew, was not among those seven. Why could Homer not keep his mouth shut?

"Your meaning, sir?" Ira asked, none too pleasantly.

Silas thought Homer's meaning had been perfectly plain, but perhaps the reasoning was too obscure for Ira's muddled brain. Silas had been a bit surprised that Homer had stated his case so well. Homer's remark had been almost literary, but since Homer could not read and was not usually that philosophical, Silas decided it had been only a fortuitous happenstance. Perhaps Homer had heard some such comment from Myra Sue Russell, Homer's intended. If so, Silas was equally surprised that Homer had remembered it.

Homer's voice cut across the room as sharply as a thrown knife. "Our grandsire's father sent yours howling to the west like a whipped cur."

*Now he has done it,* Silas thought, inwardly cursing his brother for his impetuous anger.

"A lie! That is a lie! It was the Martin who ran, the Martin who left to go east!" Ira had appeared red-faced before, possibly just a trick of the light from the fire, but now his face darkened as his bulbous eyes frogged even farther out in anger. For the first time, Silas saw that Ira believed what he said. What, he thought, if the lie had indeed been on the Martin side?


**THE INNKEEPER, ROBERT** Hastings, was a man well accustomed to stopping disruptions before they went too far. It was good business sense. Despite the fact that he was leaving with all the other Martin descendants within two days, he could not allow a brawl in his tavern. He had arranged to sell the public house to a man newly come to the valley. He could not afford to deliver damaged goods to the new owner.

The new owner was prepared to pay in ready cash, which Robert Hastings needed, for he had agreed to finance the company as they traveled, knowing that barter was not always possible. He would be well repaid once they reached their destination, wherever that was.

Before the two angry men could approach each other, Hastings stepped between them and held up his wide fleshy hands. "Gentlemen, gentlemen! We will have peace in this room. It is a common room, where all are welcome so long as they leave their contentions outside."

Hastings may have been a part of the Martin clan, but his ale, brewed by Chauncey Endicott, was the finest known in the valley and beyond. While most of the Martins lived to the east, and most of the Brandts lived to the west, men of both families met almost nightly in the middle. It was usually peaceful. Robert Hastings intended to keep it that way until the very last moment before he started on the trail out of town Monday morning.

Such was the respect of the community for the portly, good-natured publican that the men stopped advancing and slowly unclenched their fists. Neither was willing, though, to be the first to turn away. Knowing this, Mister Hastings offered them each a free flagon of ale.

"I will accept happily," Ira Brandt bellowed.

"I thank you for your generosity, sir," Homer said without taking his eyes off Ira, "but my brother will buy my drink, in celebration of my upcoming marriage." He eyed Ira Brandt from head to foot and added, "I prefer to drink with my own kind."

Robert Hastings felt the wrath of the Brandts even before he heard their murmurs of anger at the obvious insult. He raised his voice to an ebullient tone. "In that case, Mister Martin, I will provide your *second* pot of ale." It was just enough to lessen the tension. To be sure of the effect, Robert Hastings laughed aloud. His father, Richard Hastings, the original innkeeper, had taught him early how a good loud laugh that sounded genuine was one of the best ways to alleviate a dangerous situation. Father had made young Robert practice his chuckles over and over and over again, until it was almost impossible for someone hearing his hearty jollity not to join in.

As Robert grew older, his girth had increased to such a degree—almost as round as his bulbous nose—that when he laughed, his belly trembled and heaved, doing a dance all its own, and Robert had perfected a way of patting it that for some reason added to the mirth of those around him. The overall effect of joviality never failed to infect the surrounding men.

In the ensuing merriment, indulged in by all present, even the two near-combatants, Robert Hastings smiled and smiled as he served the ale. Behind his twinkling eyes, however, he thought, 'Homer Martin is like to get himself killed with such a stubborn, unyielding bullhead-edness. I hope he does not bring down the wrath of Ira Brandt on all of us.' At the same time, he knew that Ira was as obstinate as Homer. Not a good combination to have together in a public house. Or anywhere else for that matter.


**FOR AT LEAST** six months out of every year, snows howled around the cabins and came near to cutting each family off from the others in the valley. This forced isolation helped to soften the brawling. But come springtime, the tensions would rise again, and fights broke out with little provocation—usually over mistaken matters of family pride, although what fights did happen were often resolved when all the men repaired to the tavern to nurse their cut lips and bruised knuckles with a pint of Chauncey Endicott's fine ale.

Still, there were fights. The valley where they all lived had become too crowded. It was harder and harder for the two family groups to avoid each other. It was harder, too, for the younger sons who would not inherit land from their fathers to find room for themselves.

The Brandt houses still tended to cluster at the western side of the valley. The Martins, who had come later to the valley, had all settled on the eastern side, except for a few, like the minister who lived beside his church, the Hastings family who lived above the tavern, and the Breetons who lived in the middle of the town, surrounded by willow trees next to a small brook. And next to a family of Brandts. All the rest of the Martin clan lived in homes clustered partway up the mountainside.

Some months ago, before the harvest, Homer Martin had addressed the assembled men of the Martin clan who had gathered in Reverend Russell's church at Homer's behest. "I will not be able to hold my wrath for long," he told the men.

Silas Martin wondered at that. Considering the number of fights Homer had instigated, Silas thought his brother's choice of words a poor one. He had held back nothing, as far as Silas could see.

For the most part, the two groups coexisted fairly amicably. When there were fights, it was usually Ira Brandt or Homer Martin who started them. As far as Silas knew, the women of the two clans enjoyed each other's company. Only a few held to the strait-laced old enmities.

The men had heard much from travelers, and from the constantly peripatetic tinkers who visited several times a year, about the lands to the south, where the winters were less severe, where the livestock had ample grass year-round. "Why can we not leave these Green Mountains," Call Surratt proposed that evening in response to Homer's statement, "and take our families to a place where they will no longer live in dread of retribution?"

"Do you fear the fighting, cousin?" Willem Breeton's raspy voice cut through the mutterings of the crowded assembly.

Silas was not surprised that Willem Breeton wanted to stay, for his wife of many years was sickly and very well might not survive a long journey.

"Never!" Call sputtered. "I am no coward, but I wish to raise my family where I can spend my hours working, and not defending myself and them from the cowardly Brandts and their kin."

Eventually Willem Breeton came to believe that his wife might benefit from milder weather. He committed himself to the journey, and when his wife died that autumn, he convinced himself that leaving would be better for his four living children.

Gradually the men worked out a plan. They spent the ensuing winter gathering their gear, repairing their wagons, and rigging canvas covers and tents for the rains they were bound to meet along the upcoming journey. Their womenfolk saved and stored, quilted and sewed, preserved foods and organized the household goods. In the spring, they would leave.

Silas Martin did not want to leave, although he admitted—only to himself—that life would be somewhat easier without Sophrona Blanchard swooning around him. She would be left behind with no regrets on his part whatsoever. In fact, his only regret was the month he had wasted when he first thought he might want to court her. Thankfully, he had come to his senses. Not that he had been unwise to have been attracted to a plump, curly-haired Brandt, but he had been ill-advised to feel even a passing interest in so vacuous a young woman. She seemed not to have a thought that was truly her own.

He loved these green hills and mountains, though, and hated to leave them. He knew he would miss the sight of Gore Mountain towering to the north, and surely the blazing autumn glory of these hills could not be matched anywhere else in the colonies. But the people, the ones preparing for the journey, were his family, his kin. He and his brother were the only direct male descendants of the first Martin to come into these parts of the northern colonies, while it was still wilderness indeed, before it even had a name. That first Martin had sired one son and twelve daughters. The second Martin, Albion, had sired one son and five daughters.

Now the eleven family heads who had gathered in Reverend Russell's church were linked together not only by the bonds of blood but joined in intention as well. They were the great-grandsons of that first generation. Besides Homer and his nineteen-year-old brother Silas, the extended Martin clan—all those who had chosen to leave—included almost ninety people. By the time they left Brandtburg the following spring, there would be more, but the men that September night in 1740 had not considered the needs of the women who were with child. Why should they? Women always adapted. And anyway, did not the Good Book say, "Whither thou goest I will go"? It was a woman's lot to follow her husband.

The men made their plans, not striving to keep them secret. There were arguments around the various family fireplaces, of course. The women raised valid questions, and the men often as not adjusted their plans to deal with the women's objections—as if the changes had been their own idea. Gradually the mood of the people as a whole swung about in favor of the exodus.

The Brandt men accused them of cowardice in leaving, and privately boasted of their own prowess in driving off the evil Martins.

The men who had chosen to leave congratulated themselves on their foresightedness.

The women simply planned and packed and took private moments to say farewell to their dear friends among the Brandt women.

# Wednesday December 6, 2000
# Martinsville, Georgia

**I LOOKED ACROSS** the breakfast table into the eyes of my husband, Bob Sheffield. "This is probably as good a time as any to tackle the attic," I said.

"Why do I think that won't happen?" He stroked his dark luxuriant mustache—the one I'd talked him into growing. Years ago, I'd read a sign somewhere or other that said 'Kissing a man without a mustache is like eating eggs without salt.' I couldn't agree more. I'd always had a soft spot for a thick mustache, although I drew the line at full beards until I found out how soft Bob's beard was. My late husband had grown a beard for a short time—a very short time. His had felt extremely scratchy.

"You've been putting that job off ever since we moved in here," Bob said, drawing me back into the present. "Why would you start it today?"

*I could help you.*

Why indeed, I wondered, as my orange and white tabby cat jumped up into my lap, meowed, and kneaded my stomach gently. She adopted me five years ago when I moved here to become the librarian in this small town in northeast Georgia. That was the year I found a dead body on the library stairs.

*Excuse me?*

"What's wrong, Marmalade? Why are you squawking like that?"

*Squawking? I am the one who found the body.*

Well, truthfully, Marmalade here was the one who found it. That was the morning I'd met my Bob, who at that time was the town's only cop. My name is Bisque McKee. My nickname since childhood has been Biscuit. And when Bob and I married, I kept my birth name, as I had done with my first husband, Solomon Brandy. Sol's and my three children took a while to accept Bob completely, especially the two girls. They didn't want to seem unfaithful to the memory of their dead father, I guess, but Bob's common sense, good humor, integrity, and downright kindness eventually won them over.

*SoftFoot is a very nice human.*

When Bob and I bought this huge old house, we found its attic stuffed with the debris of generations of inhabitants. I swear, every single one of them must have added to the assortment of unwanted paraphernalia in the cavernous space at the head of the creaky old stairs. Come to think of it, I'd left a number of 'no longer wanted but too good to throw away' bins in the attic of my former house in Braetonburg, the next town north of Martinsville, but it wasn't as if I were abandoning all those items to strangers. My younger daughter and her family lived there now—and I supposed that some day she'd be asking herself why on earth Mom had left behind all that junk for her to clear up.

I've been promising myself ever since that first April when I moved into this old house, that I would sort through everything *someday*. So why indeed did I want to do today what I'd been putting off for years?

"Because the weather looks like it's closing in," I said. "The radio says the ice storm of the century is on its way." I paused to look out the bay window at the ice-encrusted gardens. "I'd say it's here already."

*You are right, Widelap. All the squirrels and birds have been chattering about it for several days. We knew it was coming.*

"I suppose you're right," Bob admitted. "The storm's already here, although I wish this were a weekend so fewer people will be out on the roads."

I blew out my breath. "Nobody's going to be on those roads with this much ice."

He raised one of his dark eyebrows at me. "You have more faith than I have in the common sense of the drivers around here."

Luckily our town was small enough that most of us walked wherever we wanted to go. Except for Sadie Russell Masters, who drove her bright yellow Chevy every time she had a chance.

"If the storm holds up for very long, we'll have to cancel tap dance lessons next Tuesday." Then I remembered and swore under my breath. Since I generally never do that, even quietly, Bob looked a question at me. "The library board meeting," I said. "We scheduled it a week early because of the holidays coming up."

"Look on the bright side. You might miss tap dance, but you'll also miss that meeting."

I could tell he was laughing at me, but I didn't mind. After all, he was right. I'd had a sneaky feeling for the past three months that Clara deliberately scheduled the monthly library board meetings on Tuesdays just so I'd have to miss my class. What on earth did that woman have against me anyway?

"Tonight's council meeting's been postponed," he said.

"Good. You never enjoyed attending those anyway. Was anything important on the agenda?"

"Are you kidding?" The laughter left his face, though.

"What's wrong?"

He let out a deep, noisy breath. "Last night, just before I left the station, we had one of those hunter-finds-an-unidentifiable-body faxes come in."

*Another body? Where?*

Marmalade squawked and jumped from my lap into Bob's lap.

"You didn't mention it."

"It wasn't here in Keagan County. South a ways."

"So why would they fax you the notice?"

"Probably somebody decided to look into cold cases and threw out a net to every station in a hundred mile radius to see if they could catch anything."

"Seems like quite a long shot."

He took off his glasses and rubbed the bridge of his nose. "You never know. They had a femur, so they could make a pretty good estimate of the person's height, and one of the other bones had evidence of a fairly serious old break."

"Then, they could just search medical records, right?"

He looked at me with what seemed to be compassion for my naiveté. "They'd have to know which records to look through. Old X-rays can verify an identity after the fact, but aren't much help during the initial trace."

"Could it have been a hunter who shot himself by accident?"

"Herself. They had enough bones to tell it was an adult female."

"Any teeth?" I knew dental records could help.

"Nope. No teeth. The neck vertebrae were still there, most of them. Enough to show it was probably murder. The fax included a couple of photos, and it was pretty obvious, but the skull was missing."

"Ewww! The body was beheaded?"

"It's much more likely," he assured me, "that a bear or a dog carted off the skull."

"Could they check DNA?"

"Not if they don't have the missing person's DNA already in the system. Anyway, DNA tests take forever, and this case would be pretty far down on the totem pole. They had some hair, too, but no indication whether it was from the victim or somebody else."

"You think it might have been somebody from here?"

"We don't have anybody missing, but I set Reebok to searching through old files just in case. You know how he loves to do stuff like that."

I set my tea aside. It didn't seem quite so soothing at the moment. "So it wasn't a recent body?"

"It wasn't a body really. Just some bones. And a few short hairs, wound around one of the finger bones."

Why was I so worried about this?

When my children were little, I used to have nightmares that one of them would go missing. I wondered if my daughters ever had the same fears now that they were mothers themselves. At the moment, I couldn't imagine anything worse than losing a child. But then I thought about some of the things Bob had had to investigate over the past few years—someone's murdered sister, fiancé, wife, son, mother, and even a dear friend of ours. I picked my tea back up and cradled the warm cup between my cold hands. Any death, any loss, took a toll.

I looked across the table again and felt inexpressible comfort when Bob met my gaze.

I was so lucky to have him in my life. Even after five years with him, we could still find new topics to talk about. Just last night, we were snuggling before going to sleep. He'd said something about the beehives he'd gotten from Sadie Masters, my favorite eighty-something person in the whole world.

"Sadie's amazing," I said.

"You have no idea."

"What do you mean?"

"Did you know she was one of the original Rosies during the second world war?"

"Rosie the Riveter?"

It was too dark for me to see his nod, but I felt it against my hair.

"Really? I had no idea. She never mentioned it."

"She wasn't the woman on the poster, but she definitely worked as a riveter."

This didn't sound right. "They had heavy industry around here back then?"

"No," Bob said. "If I remember correctly, when Wallace shipped out overseas, Sadie traveled to Omaha to stay with Wallace's war-widow sister. You'll have to ask her for the rest of the details."

"That woman probably has stories that could fill years." I yawned. "I'll ask her the next time I see her. In the meantime, I think she's the wisest person I know—except for maybe my mom. And your mom."

"A function of advanced age, maybe?" I could hear the laughter in his tone. "Think we'll ever get there?"

"If we keep learning from Sadie, we just might."

"I'll be sure to do that."

"Bob? Why didn't you ever tell me that before? About Sadie, I mean."

He brushed a stray lock of my hair back away from my face. "You never asked me about it."

He had a point there. "Okay. So what other interesting stories have you never told me about"—I let out an enormous yawn—"about people here in your hometown?"

"I'll think of some more to tell you. Tomorrow." And he'd given me the sweetest goodnight kiss.

*Look!*

Marmalade let out a loud yowl that interrupted my reverie. She jumped onto the wide windowsill and seemed to inspect the backyard. I couldn't see anything in particular. Bob turned his head to follow my gaze. Marmalade swiveled her head back and forth, almost as if she were watching something fly by her. A bug, maybe? Although what any self-respecting bug was doing out and about in frigid weather like this was anybody's guess.

*There is much to see if only you would open your eyes.*

## 1978

**"MOMMY? SEE THE ..."** Three-year-old Charlie Ellis paused because she didn't know the word. She made wavy motions with her hands. She loved the way colors looked brighter when the ... the special things fluttered around her head.

"There aren't any butterflies this time of year, honey. It's winter. Once the cold goes away and the sun warms up the trees and the flowers, the butterflies will come back. You'll be able to see them then."

Charlie tilted her head to one side and watched the flutteries for a while. She remembered butterflies. At least she thought she did, but that had been a very long time ago before the air got so cold outside. These weren't butterflies.

Every time she tried to talk to Mommy about the flutteries, Mommy thought she was saying something different.

One fluttery brushed the end of Charlie's nose and she laughed.

"What's funny, sweetheart?"

"Tickles."

"You want me to tickle you? Okay!" Mommy swooped in and scooped her up into a big laughy tickly hug.

One of the flutteries wavered right next to Mommy's cheek, but Mommy didn't act like she even felt it.

Maybe she didn't?


**BY THE TIME** Charlie was five, she'd learned the word for angels. Her flutteries didn't look like any of the angel pictures in books, but maybe everybody else had different angels.

In kindergarten, she tried to draw pictures of her flutteries, but they never looked as bright and as beautiful as what she saw around her.

"Are those butterflies, Charlie? They're very bright."

Charlie studied her teacher before answering. "Yes," she finally said. "Butterflies."

Just to be sure, though, she took the picture home.

"I love your pictures, darling. They're the prettiest butterflies I've ever seen." Mommy stuck the picture on the fridge with a big red magnet and then knelt to hug Charlie.

This is good enough, Charlie thought as she hugged her mommy. I just won't say anything about the flutteries anymore. She planted a big kiss on Mommy's neck, right where a fluttery had been a moment before.

**BY THE TIME** Charlie was in second grade, she never saw the flutteries anymore.

Whenever she felt a soft wisp against her nose or her cheek, she brushed it away. It was probably just a mosquito. Or her imagination. Mommy had talked a lot about imagination. She said Charlie had a very big one.

## 2000

**FROM A BLOCK** up the street we heard Doodle-Doo, Maggie Pontiac's rooster, issue a loud complaint about the cold. At least, that was what it sounded like to me. I took another big sip of licorice root tea, savoring the sweetness of it. Then I had to shuffle my mug as Marmalade jumped from the windowsill onto my lap.

*Your lap is warmer than the window.*

"So," Bob asked, "you really are going to tackle the attic?"

"Why not? It's way too hot in the summer, but now seems perfect. The wood stove is cranking out enough heat to warm the upstairs without a bit of a problem, so I won't freeze. In fact, I think it'll be cozy. Do you want to help?"

*I will spend the time with you.*

I patted idly along Marmalade's back as she kneaded my lap and purred loudly, and I watched Bob run a hand through his silver-sprinkled black hair. "Let me see…" He peered at me over the rim of his reading glasses. "I need to think about this. Do I want to spend hours in a crowded attic," he asked, "nosing through old trunks and organizing hatboxes and rummaging around broken hobby horses that may have been up there ever since the esteemed Homer Martin founded this town in 1745?"

I nudged his shin under the table. "Why," I asked with a laugh, "do I think your answer is *no*? And anyway, that hobbyhorse isn't broken. At least I don't think it is. It's just old and faded. And it couldn't have been just Homer. I'm sure his wife Mary Frances had a lot to do with the founding as well."

"If you say so, my love."

The words might have been sarcastic coming from any other man, but Bob's tone was agreeable. One thing I really like about my husband is that he's so fair. All the time.

He turned his attention back to his chicken, mushroom, and onion omelet, and I munched idly on a piece of stove toast—buttered bread that I'd browned in one of my cast iron skillets. I'd made toast that way for years. Who needed a toaster when it tasted so much better like this? I inhaled that unforgettable smell of yeasty homemade dill bread. The dill was some I had harvested and dried in the late summer. Yum. My garden, thank goodness, had finally recovered from all the disruptions of a few years ago.

All the extra loaves I'd baked yesterday were wrapped and tucked into the freezer. No sense trying to bake bread only one loaf at a time. Occasionally, I double the already-generous recipe. For some unfathomable reason, this time I had quadrupled it. When it rose, it almost overflowed my largest mixing bowl, and I was thankful I had enough bread pans to handle it all.

*I prefer my own food. You could give me some of that chicken in the white coldbox.*

I felt a surge of optimism, probably prompted by Marmalade's extra-loud purr. I *could* tackle the attic. The good thing about a heavy snowstorm was that it prevented anyone from going anywhere. At least, it did in here in the south. Nobody knows how to drive on the ice because we almost never get any to practice on. And the incline of the Martinsville streets as they slant up from the Metoochie River makes driving even more treacherous. A good day to stay inside and eat soup, since my library would have to be closed anyway.

The pot of chicken stock simmered on the stove, filling the kitchen with that aura of yummy that happens whenever you combine water, a couple of picked-over chicken carcasses, carrots, onions, celery, and whatever else I'd thrown in. I sure hoped the power wouldn't go out. Of course, I'd already strained out the bones and soggy vegetables and skimmed off the excess fat, so what was left was good chicken broth. All I'd have to do would be to add meat and veggies, maybe some quinoa too, and we'd have a feast for lunch. And plenty for our supper as well. Probably enough for another week and plenty to freeze, too. It was a huge pot, and it always seemed a shame not to fill it right up. I was very glad Bob liked soup and homemade bread.

*I like chicken.*

Marmalade meowed, and I figured she was asking to go outside. "Not now. You'll have to stay inside for a couple of days."

*Mouse droppings!*

"Why?"

"Not you," I told him. "Marmalade. I don't want her freezing her little paws. Especially if she's sneezing like that."

We'd installed a cat flap in the back door but had decided to close it up last night to help keep out the cold air. She could use her litter box, and I wouldn't have to worry about her.

I didn't have to worry about any of my children, either. Scott and his new wife Pumpkin had a wood burning stove in the Healthy Self herb store—they lived in the small apartment above it. And Sandra, along with her husband and the two girls, would probably retreat to her sister's house in Braetonburg, so Sally would end up with quite a houseful.

"Have you checked our supply of lanterns?" I pushed a small mound of omelet onto my toast and took a bite, wondering what else I needed to do before the power went out, as I was fairly sure would happen. Georgia ice storms are absolutely treacherous, and the main power station north of here had needed upgrading for some time.

*You could give me some chicken.*

Bob looked at me over the rim of his glasses.

"Never mind," I said. "I know you did." Bob was a cop. Bob was always prepared for any emergency. I took a silent inventory of all our hard-weather arrangements. Candles, lanterns with plenty of fuel, a gas-powered generator to keep the fridge and water pump running, a composting toilet, a whole lot of five-gallon jugs of filtered water in case the pump froze, which Bob swore wouldn't happen. I hoped he was right. We even had an old-fashioned percolator for brewing coffee over a campfire. We'd tried it out—and it worked just fine—on the wood stove we'd bought last year.

There had been a particularly persuasive salesman at an Atlanta store we'd visited, who'd told us if we could convince at least five other families to purchase similar stoves, he'd arrange for Bob and me to get free delivery and installation. With a deal like that, how could we go wrong?

I'd picked a bright red Defiant from Vermont Castings Company. It was redder than Doodle-Doo, Maggie Pontiac's rooster.

We'd done even better than five, and the salesman had been delighted with us. So now, a dozen other Martinsville families—as well as my parents and my younger daughter up in Braetonburg—had the stoves. The Johnsons, Margaret and Sam Casperson, Carl and Sharon Armitage, Pumpkin, and our next-door neighbor Matthew Olsen had been among the first to accept the offer.

My friend Melissa Tarkington, who owns *Azalea House Bed & Breakfast*, had refused, though. "If the power fails some night," she'd told me, "I'll just come camp out at your house."

*I could guide you. I see very well in the dark.*

"Leaving your B&B guests, I suppose," I'd said, and Marmalade had gurgled happily beside me.

*Gurgled?*

"Oh no. I'll bring them along with me. Your house is big enough for a small army."

"Well, if you do, bring lots of food. You know I don't like to cook."

*GoodCook loves to cook.*

I couldn't understand how anyone could have said no to the wood stove deal. Bob and I couldn't pass up a chance to be self-sufficient. We didn't get many winter power outages—in fact something about the configuration of our deep dead-end valley gave Martinsville a relatively mild climate year-round—but when the power did occasionally go off—usually the fault of that less-than-dependable sub-station a ways up the valley—I hated to hole up in one room trying to conserve heat.

Sadie Masters, one of my elderly library volunteers, the one who drove her yellow car everywhere, had declined the stove offer as well. "I have my old pot-bellied stove in the parlor. It will keep me warm enough." I was surprised she'd kept it, since it was the only thing in her house that wasn't yellow, but then again, her parlor was closed off most of the time, and I supposed it wouldn't have been safe to paint a wood stove. "Bob, does Sadie have a good supply of firewood inside?"

"Of course."

Of course. Why had I even asked? He'd been so good about doing extra chores for her after her husband died. In fact, he'd been an angel of mercy for them ever since Wallace had that first stroke a number of years ago. But of course, that was what folks here in Martinsville did. We cared for each other. Especially people as sweet as Sadie.

A sudden gust of wind shook the house and the lights flickered. Oh dear. I wondered if Melissa's teasing might become a reality. "I'm going to call Mom and be sure she and Dad are okay."

"No reason why they wouldn't be," Bob said, although I thought I detected an undercurrent of some sort in his voice. He was a cop. Cops knew so much about what could go wrong, I wondered how Bob ever managed to consistently see the good all around him. "They bought a wood stove, remember?"

"I know, but I'll feel better if I touch base. It'll only take a minute."

I knew that *minute* to be true, quite literally. My mother has never been one to chat on the phone. Even this early in the morning, she would have already finished breakfast and would be heading into her studio to throw a pot or work on a new glaze. I caught her just before she left the kitchen.

"Your father already called Mark," she told me. "He said Blue was packing a suitcase and they'd be over here within an hour."

"I hope they remembered to float a log in their swimming pool to give the ice a way to expand safely." My Auntie Blue—short for Beulah—swam every day she possibly could, even when the temp was down near freezing, but this time around, there was a good chance her pool was going to be frozen solid. At least with the wood floating in the center, the expansion of the ice would push up on the log and prevent the sides of the pool from being forced apart.

"Don't worry," Mom said. "She added salt to lower the freezing point several degrees, and Mark dumped four big logs in there. Gotta go. My new glaze won't wait."

Auntie Blue was a hoot. Once her pool melted—as eventually it must—she'd haul out the logs and swim in salt water. I could almost hear her. *Just like swimming in the ocean, but without the sharks*, she'd say.

*I cannot hear her. She is not here.*

While I was at it, I called my daughters Sandra and Sally. Sandra's two girls were happy to be facing at least several days out of school, but they began squabbling loudly and Sandra excused herself "to be sure there isn't any blood."

"You're kidding, right?" But she'd already hung up.

Sally's toddler, my second grandson, was the exact opposite of his placid older brother. He always seemed to be fractious, rather like his father, my less-than-favorite son-in-law. I sincerely hoped he'd grow out of it. "Gotta run, Mom," Sally said after only a few seconds of greeting. "He's hollering so loud I can barely hear myself think."

"Wait," I said. "Did you invite Sandra over in case the power goes off?"

"Yes, Mother." Sally sounded even more sarcastic than usual. I had hoped that having children of her own would help soften her a bit. We'd had a rocky relationship for years—although some years were better than others. And some were worse.

Then there was my son Scott, who had married Pumpkin, the owner of the local herb shop, just a month ago. They were still in the honeymoon stage, of course, but I thought they might not mind a phone call at this early hour.

"We're fine, Mom," Scott told me. "Remember that wood stove you sold Pumpkin?"

"Of course I remember it."

"It's churning out the heat even as we speak."

"Well, take care."

"Don't worry about us. With the shop closed, we'll spend the whole day in bed—uh, I mean we'll be staying inside."

I just bet they would. Newlyweds. At least they'd keep each other warm. I hung up the phone and returned to the table just as Bob downed the last of his coffee, picked up our dirty dishes, and headed for the sink.

"We may have an army descending on us soon," I told him.

"Your parents and daughters?"

I guess he hadn't been able to tell too much from hearing only my side of the conversations. "No. They're all doing fine. But if the electricity goes out, I'd be willing to bet Melissa's going to turn up."

I glanced out into the backyard where our new storage shed was filled with head-high stacks of well-seasoned wood. And only yesterday Bob had brought in a huge load of it, filling the large firewood rack we had in the living room. Why on earth had we bought such a capacious contraption, though? Surely we wouldn't go through that much wood. Luckily, our living room was expansive enough to handle such a big piece of—what do you call a wood rack? Furniture? Accessory?

The story I'd heard shortly after we bought this rambling old house was that it had served as a public house and inn from way back near the beginning of Martinsville. Although we had no way of knowing for sure, we had come up with an educated guess. The living room must have been originally used as the inn's main gathering and eating area. I could imagine tankards of ale, straw strewn all over the wide-planked floor to absorb the inevitable spills, and a merry fire in the enormous fireplace—which we'd bricked up when the wood stove was installed.

On the second floor there were loads of small bedrooms, none of which we used, but I did keep clean sheets folded and ready on each bed—well, on most of them. I didn't have nearly that many sheets. There must have been families with eight, ten, twelve children living here in the past. I wondered briefly how the mothers ever managed that many. I'd sometimes felt overwhelmed with only three. Of course, each child back then would have had numerous tasks, and the older girls, from what I'd read, always helped to tend the younger children. I thought back to my abbreviated conversation with Sandra. Her two girls could make more noise than a freight train coming through. Now multiply that noise by four or five. I shuddered. The mind boggled to think of a dozen children running through this house.

"At least you're completely ready if they come," Bob said, interrupting my thought process. He plopped both our plates in the sink and ran hot water into the basin.

"How so?"

He nodded toward the big walk-in storeroom. "That pantry is stuffed to the gills."

*I told you to store extra food. Especially chicken.*

Marmalade wound between my legs, purring loudly. I set my

mug of tea back down and pulled some cooked chicken from the fridge to place in her bowl.

*Thank you.*

"We do have a lot of food on hand." Especially soup and bread, I thought. "Maybe Melissa won't have to bring quite so much with her."

"Huh?"

"Melissa has guests this week, so if she comes, she'll bring them with her."

He grinned. "I thought maybe you were talking to Marmalade."

Dear Bob. He understands when I talk to my cat.

*Mouse droppings! You and SoftFoot are <u>my</u> people.*

Bob studied Marmalade as she sneezed. I know sometimes he talks to her too. Too bad she doesn't understand us.

*Humans. Will they ever learn?*

"This ice can't last more than a day or two, wouldn't you say?"

He raised an eyebrow.

"It has to be melted by tomorrow night," I added. "Or at least by noon or so on Friday."

"Why would that be?"

"Glaze and Tom are getting married on Friday, as you know quite well, and if you think I'm going to miss my sister's wedding just because of an ice storm, you've got another think coming."

"I know that."

"But if the storm lasts, nobody will be able to get to the church, including the bride and groom."

"These storms seldom last more than a day or two," he assured me. But then he ruined this reassuring declaration by saying, "But the ice takes forever to melt afterwards, and the weather report said—"

"You know as well as I do you can't rely on Radio Ralph's weather reports."

"Not WRRT," Bob said, referring to our Keagan County radio station. "It was on NPR. I listened while you were taking your shower last night." He turned back to the sink.

If we were in for a day or two without power, at least I'd have clean hair. I'd brushed it dry beside the wood stove—loved that process. It's so much more … more elemental than using a hair dryer.

I hated the thought that Glaze and Tom might have to delay their wedding, though. "Bob?"

He rinsed off a plate and placed it on the drain board. "Yeah?"

I picked up a drying towel. "Are you going to turn off the water now?"

"I already winterized the pipes leading to the outside faucets. The ones inside here should be fine as long as we keep the wood stove cranked up. We'll probably need to leave the cabinet doors open so the heat can get to the drains under the sinks, especially for the bathrooms upstairs where the sink is against an outside wall, but"—he lifted his hands from the soapy water—"this one's in the middle of the room, so it should be fine."

"Just in case, how about if we fill the bathtubs with water?"

He raised an eyebrow yet again.

"If Melissa shows up—and I know she has three guests staying with her, the Pontiacs and somebody else, a professor of some sort—our composting toilet might not handle that many people. We could put a bucket in each tub so people can flush the regular toilets if the water does happen to freeze."

"It won't freeze, but if you're that worried about it, filling the tubs won't hurt anything." He dried his hands and grabbed three plastic buckets from the utility room. "These should work."

We filled the tubs and left a plastic pail next to each one. If we didn't need this, it would be a terrible waste of our good well water, but if we *did* need it, I'd be awfully glad I'd thought about it before we had a problem. Melissa and her three guests, my sister Glaze and her house-mate Madeleine Ames. That would be six extra people.

Almost as soon as we finished filling the tubs—we used hot water, to add a bit more heat to the house, at least until it cooled off—the lights flickered again. We were prepared, though, so the flickering didn't seem quite so ominous. We opened all the cabinet doors beneath the sinks just to be on the safe side.

Before we went downstairs again, I detoured into the bedroom and picked up my heavy fleecy vest. I'd read once that if you can keep your head covered and your chest insulated, then you'll stay warmer. Well, even with the wood stove churning out the heat, if the power went out I wanted to be as warm as I possibly could. I didn't want to put on a hat and end up with flat hat-hair, but just for good measure, I went ahead and put the vest on over my bulky sweater. Might as well be fully prepared.

Downstairs, I pulled a box of heavy knitted slipper socks out of the closet. If we had an influx of people, I didn't want them tromping around in their boots, and they probably wouldn't want to freeze their feet. Even through winter socks, the wide plank floors would be cold.

### *Azalea House*
### Martinsville

**C. C. MELLINGER, Ph.D.** was used to snow and ice in Vermont, but hadn't expected it in northeast Georgia. The wind had cranked itself up to a screaming fit, and showed no sign of moderating its tone of hysteria. She could still see out the window of *Azalea House*, the bed and breakfast place she'd chosen as much for its name as anything else, but didn't hold any hope of the visibility lasting for long, since the ice seemed to be building up on everything in sight, including the windowpane itself. In the distance, she heard a rooster crow raucously. "If I were you," she muttered, "I'd stop crowing and nestle down in a warm pile of straw out of the wind."

She shifted her pencil to her other hand and used her fingertip to trace her initials on the frosty glass. Then she laughed at herself. Such a homely, normal reaction to a fogged up window. This house wasn't a new one by any means, and she wondered how many other fingers over the years had reached out to trace their own initials. That was just one of those things that everybody did, yet people seldom left any record of having done it. In all her research, she'd never found an old letter or a diary that said, "I traced my initials in the window fog this morning."

She'd thought a winter sabbatical in Georgia would be a welcome change from the six months of Vermont winter and the month-long, near zero bouts that her home state was prone to. As it was, she'd been lucky last night to get her rental car all the way down the winding river valley in the dark. The drive from the Atlanta airport hadn't been too bad—although she would have been hard-put to find her way if Melissa hadn't sent her such detailed driving directions. Once she left Interstate 85 and headed north on 441, dusk had descended. That hadn't been too bad, but as soon as she eased through the cliff-sided pass into the town of Russell Gap, she'd been hit with a nearly blinding barrage of sleet, backed up by a wind that raged up the valley from the south. Thank goodness there had been little other traffic on the road.

A gentle knock on her door broke into her reverie, and the welcome voice of Melissa Tarkington asked, "Would you like some coffee, Dr. Mellinger? I just brewed a new pot."

"Yes, I'm coming!" She strode across the room, tucking her pencil into the top of her thick braid of russet hair. It wasn't that long past breakfast, but she longed for a hot cup of coffee, more to warm her cold fingers than to fill her sated stomach, although the breakfast coffee itself had tasted like a dessert. Melissa had told her that she used only shade-grown coffee.

When she opened her door, she found Melissa, dressed warmly in black sweatpants and a bulky red sweater, just turning away. Melissa looked back at her newest B & B guest and smiled. "I know it's a little early for a mid-morning snack, but there's some coffee cake, too."

"Sounds heaven-sent right now." Probably loads of calories, but with this weather, she had a feeling she'd appreciate the extra fuel. "And please call me Carol. I was beginning to wonder at my sanity for having subjected myself to this weather. In fact, at home we'd be gearing up for the January thaw in a few weeks."

"I hate to bear bad news, but I just listened to the weather report on National Public Radio, and they said this looks like the ice storm of the century."

"That doesn't sound encouraging, but I shouldn't be surprised after what I had to drive through to get here last night. At least I have one cold-weather outfit with me." Actually, the only warm clothes she had were the ones she'd worn from her house to the airport the previous day. The same ones she had put on this morning as soon as she looked out the window. They were a bit rumpled, but she'd rather be warm than fashionable any day. She'd assumed December in Georgia would be mild, and her suitcase contained a lovely complement of summer slacks and lightweight tops. Carol Mellinger wasn't used to the South.

Melissa paused at the head of the stairs and looked her guest up and down. "We're about the same size. If need be, you're welcome to borrow some of my clothes."

"Thanks. I appreciate that. What I'm wearing will get old—and odiferous—fairly soon."

"We don't usually get this much winter down here," Melissa said over her shoulder as she led the way downstairs to the snug kitchen, "especially in this long narrow dead-end valley. The bad heat of summer always seems to pass us by, and the winter ice storms hardly ever happen here. I guess this is our lucky year for a little excitement in the way of weather." She bypassed the dining room. "I hope you don't mind sitting in the kitchen. It's cozier in there."

Carol followed Melissa, sniffing appreciatively at the smell of freshly baked coffee cake, interlaced with the comforting aroma of freshly brewed coffee. She settled into one of the carved chairs that surrounded the sturdy old maple table. The blue and white checked tablecloth and the white-painted cabinetry exuded old-fashioned warmth. If she had to be caught in an ice storm, at least she was cozy and comfortable, sitting on a well-padded chair, and getting ready to enjoy some superb coffee. Her first breakfast here had been superlative, although she'd had to think a while about those cheese grits before she tried them out. Research. That was what it was. Research. They'd been quite tasty, in fact. She idly wondered if she could whip some up for a faculty get-together when she returned to Vermont. She wondered if the grocery stores in Vermont even carried something as southern as grits. Maybe Melissa would give her the recipe?

Meanwhile, a midmorning snack sounded like a great idea. She studied Melissa's warm clothing. "You said you don't usually get much winter weather, but you certainly seem to be prepared for it."

Melissa smoothed her sweater over her hips. "This Georgian is absolutely terrified of snow. Most of us have down parkas and long johns and enough sweaters to outfit a polar expedition. Once the temp drops to sixty-five degrees, we haul them out."

"Sixty-five degrees would be considered a heat wave in Vermont this time of year."

"I'm really sorry about this weather. There are so many interesting little shops in town, all within a block or two, and most of my guests enjoy walking around." She looked out the window. "It'll be a while yet before that's possible."

"Well, the storm can't last too long, can it?" Without waiting for an answer, Carol asked, "Which shops are your favorites?"

Melissa screwed up her mouth as she thought. "I'd have a hard time picking. The deli is wonderful. My friend Biscuit and I go there for coffee—or hot chocolate—on a regular basis. It's up near the end of town on Main Street. Closer to home, there's the Healthy Self Herb Shop. It's run by a young woman who came to town a few years ago. Her name's Pumpkin, but she never told anybody her last name. Now she's married to Biscuit's son, Scott, so I guess Pumpkin is a Brandy now."

Carol noticed that Melissa seemed sad somehow. She waited.

"Pumpkin took over the store after Annie McGill died. Annie was … was pretty special."

Carol clasped her hands together on the table.

"Annie loved organic everything, and she was such a generous-hearted person. She was … she was murdered several years ago, and Pumpkin took over the shop." Melissa shook herself. "Pumpkin's delightful. She used to be a manicurist at the Beauty Shop, our local hair salon. She got the owner to start using environmentally friendly nail products."

"Sounds like my kind of person. And I love herbs and such stuff. Maybe I'll drop by, once the storm abates."

Melissa filled a heavy mug and passed it across the table. "Cream's in the little blue pitcher. Pat and Dave Pontiac, the other two guests here, should be down shortly. They skipped breakfast this morning, but Dave never misses a chance at coffee cake, so now you'll get a chance to meet them. They're old Martinsville natives who sold their house and went out west when Dave's company opened a new headquarters out there. He retired this past summer. Well, actually, he sold off his company, so they came back to Martinsville. Eventually, I guess they'll buy a house."

"Sounds like it took them a long time to pack up."

"What do you mean?"

"If he retired last summer and they just made it here?"

"Oh, no. They like to stay at *Azalea House*. In fact, they've been here since August."

"No family to stay with?" Carol asked, setting her mug back down. Damn, that was good coffee.

Melissa laughed. "Yes," she said. "They *do* have family. Two married daughters and one married son, with a total of six grandchildren between them. They stay at *Azalea House* so they can have some rest and quiet, as I'm sure they'll tell you, since they've announced it to everyone in town they've seen over the past four months."

Carol rotated her coffee cup slowly, admiring the subtle shifts in the color of the glaze. "Handmade?"

"Absolutely. Over the years I've gotten all my dishes from a potter who lives in the next town up the valley."

"I have to admit I looked underneath the plate you served my breakfast on."

Melissa chuckled. "A lot of people do that—the ones who like fine pottery."

"It said I M M. Initials?"

"That's right. Ivy Martelson McKee. Two of her daughters live here in town." She glanced out the window. "Once the storm is over, you might enjoy meeting them."

Carol nodded, but her heart wasn't in it. Neither Martelson nor McKee was on her list of families to be investigated. That was all right, though, she could always invent some sort of excuse to get out of it. Or meet them quickly and then leave.

"One of them, who's turned out to be a very dear friend, stayed with me, here at Azalea House, for the first year after she moved to Martinsville five years ago."

"I know this won't sound very diplomatic, Melissa, but I can't help wondering, how on earth do you survive? How do people find you? This place isn't exactly a hotbed for tourism."

"You're right. It's not, but I have a lot of repeat customers. Once people find me the first time, they seem to keep coming back. And I give a special rate to folks who move here—if I like them—so they can have a comfortable place to stay for a few months until they find something more permanent." She poured herself a cup and sat across from Carol. "You may have noticed, there aren't any motels. Not in this end of the valley. Only in Russell Gap."

"I get a few months, but you said your friend stayed a year."

"That was an unusual case. She'd just been hired as the town's librarian, and somehow or other it just all worked out. She and I liked each other right from the start."

The windows rattled in a particularly vicious burst of wind. Melissa shivered. "There've been some who came and stayed for a while and then, for whatever reason, left and never came back."

Carol thought for a bit. "I imagine it takes a particular type of person who likes to live in a small town."

Melissa guffawed. "A small town hidden in the middle of nowhere?"

"I didn't say that."

Melissa dropped the laugh. "You didn't have to. I've always thought Martinsville was sort of like Shangri-La. The kind of place that you can't find unless you really need it."

"Are you saying people don't stay here unless they're born here?"

"Well, no. Biscuit McKee—that's the librarian—fit right in, and there've been a few others who stayed, like—" Melissa searched her memory. She didn't have to look very far. "Like Charlotte Ellis. She lived here when she was a kid. Not here in Azalea House, but in Martinsville. She and her mom moved away when she was eight or ten, and she finally came back about three years ago and stayed with me for a couple of months until she found a place of her own. Nice woman, although she's awfully quiet. She lives just down the street." She nodded toward the window.

"Why'd she come back?"

Melissa shrugged. "Who knows? Missed it, I guess. She was never one to talk too much about herself."

The wind moaned again, and they both settled into serious coffee drinking.


## June 1983


**CHARLIE ELLIS LOOKED** a question at her mommy. "Why do we have to go away?"

Mommy's eyes scrunched up in a way Charlie didn't like. "Charlotte honey, you have to understand." She looked away, out the window, and Charlie wondered what she was looking at. "Actually," Mommy said in a real soft voice, "you don't have to understand it, but we just need to go." Mommy kept staring out the window. "I've stood this town for twenty-seven years, and I can't stand it any more."

"But I like it here."

"I'm sorry honey, but I don't. I can't live in this house anymore, and now that your grandma's dead, I can leave. She's the only reason I had to stay here."

Charlie didn't really miss Grandma. Grandma never hugged her or loved her or baked cookies for her the way other kids' grandmas did. And Grandma only pretended to need that cane. Charlie knew. She'd seen Grandma hop right up out of her chair a bunch of times when she thought nobody was looking.

"I have a new job down in Atlanta, and I start next Monday."

"Where will I go to school?"

"There's a real nice school just a block from the house, and two blocks from where I'll be working. You'll like it."

"Will you walk me to school each morning?"

"Absolutely. Then I'll go on to work from there."

"I won't have any friends."

"You'll make friends." Mommy smoothed back Charlie's bright red hair. "Anybody as nice as you can make friends real easy. Anyway, making friends is easy in third grade."

Charlie wasn't sure she believed it. Mommy was very nice, but she didn't seem to have many friends, except for Grandma Masters across the street. "Where will we live?"

Mommy let out a big sigh. "It's time you met your daddy, honey. We're gonna live with him."

Charlie's eyes scrunched up just like Mommy's had. "Will I like him?"

"You'll have to. What I mean is, of course you will. He's a very nice man. He's the one who got me this job. It's …" Mommy paused a long time, almost like she'd forgotten what she was going to say. "It's time for you to meet your daddy." Then Mommy kind of shook herself and said, "When we get to Atlanta, I don't want you to mention Martinsville at all."

"Huh?"

"Ever. To anybody."

"Why not?"

"You'll need to trust your mommy about this one, honey. I don't want anybody to know where we came from."

"Not even my new daddy?"

"He already knows, sweetheart, but he's the only one."

Charlie sure didn't understand. She'd obey her mom but she didn't see why she couldn't talk about Martinsville to any of her new friends, if she ever made any.

"Can I tell people about making cookies with Grandma Masters?"

Mom looked at her for a long time. "Sure you can, sweetheart. Just don't say Martinsville."

"Can I tell about the cliffs?"

"No, dear. Nothing about the hills or the cliffs or the name."

"That's okay, I guess." Charlie and Mommy hadn't taken any long hikes in a long time, not since Charlie's arm got broken two years ago.

"When will I get to bake cookies with Mrs. Masters again?"

Mommy gathered Charlie onto her lap. "Oh, sweetie, it may be a very long time. Maybe someday you'll come back here. After all, you call her Grandma, so you'll have to come back sometime."

Charlie patted Mommy's cheek. "Of course I will, silly. Grandma Masters will miss me, too."

## 2000
### Azalea House

**READY FOR SOME** coffee cake?" Melissa asked.

Right on cue, Pat Pontiac walked in, followed by her husband Dave, who was rubbing his hands in anticipation. "That's my favorite coffee cake you're talking about, right?" He nodded absentmindedly toward the newcomer.

"Have a seat, Dave," Melissa instructed him. She stood and picked up a cake-laden wooden platter from the counter behind her. "Say hello to Dr. C. C. Mellinger, who's here on sabbatical from the University of Vermont. She's a history professor. Drove in late last night."

Dave extended his hand. "Dave Pontiac. Retired. My wife, Pat. We stay here with Melissa to escape our noisy grandchildren."

Melissa winked at Carol, handed her the plate of coffee cake, and distributed plates and forks all around. Pat rolled her eyes, then laughed and nodded. "We tried staying with Maggie and Norm just once. Between the goats bleating to be fed and the rooster crowing—"

"Well before dawn," Dave said.

"We didn't get much sleep."

Carol smiled. "That must have been the rooster I heard a little while ago, but it wasn't before dawn."

Dave hunched his shoulders. "Doodle-Doo crows any time he feels like it, whether it's day or night."

"Then there are the children," Pat said, rubbing her hands over her arms.

Carol couldn't help but notice that Pat's sweater was cashmere.

"We love our grandchildren to pieces, but we also treasure occasional silence. You get the six of them together and the chaos is unimaginable."

Carol thought of her own childhood. "I can imagine it would be," she said. "My sister and I argued constantly. All I have to do is multiply that by three."

"The funny thing," Pat said, "is that they're loud and boisterous, but they don't really squabble. Our daughter Maggie and her husband adopted a little boy recently. Willie hardly talked at all for the longest time, but once he started, he turned into a natural-born diplomat. Something about his very presence seems to keep the other children calm."

"Yep," Dave said, "not quiet, but calm. He's only five, but he's the most diplomatic person I've ever met."

Pat smiled fondly at her husband. "He's a treasure all right."

Melissa tried not to shiver when she remembered how they'd almost lost Willie during that horrible week when Annie McGill was murdered. Willie's mother's car had been struck by a hit-and-run driver. It plunged over an embankment, killing the mother and leaving Willie, who was just a toddler at the time, strapped in his car seat. He was stuck there for several days until the crash scene was discovered almost by accident. Another day and he probably would have died from dehydration.

She looked up and met Pat's eyes. She could tell Pat was remembering the same thing.

Dave settled back and accepted the mug Melissa handed him.

Pat straightened a bit in her chair and stirred cream into her own mug. "So, how did you end up in Martinsville, Dr. Mellinger?"

"Call me Carol, please. That's my middle name, but it's what I go by." She took a bite of the coffee cake. "Wow! This is even better than the coffee. This trip's worth the lousy weather if the food's going to be this good."

She seemed suddenly to remember what Pat had asked her. "I'm researching a number of related families that left a valley south of Gore Mountain in Vermont a little more than two hundred and fifty years ago. I have reason to believe they ended up in this area. I've been tracking them as part of a history project. They did a good job of covering their trail, but I think I might have found them at last."

"Who were they?" Melissa asked, as Pat echoed her question.

Dave chimed in. "Why are you tracking them?"

Carol leaned back in her chair. "This is the part of history I en-joy—surprising people." She waited until three sets of eyes tracked in her direction, three forks were laid back on their plates, and three cof-fee cups were set down. "I want to resolve a blood feud that started in Vermont over three hundred years ago, between my mother's family and the Martin family."

Dave and Pat spoke at the same time. "Martin?"

"As in Martinsville?" Melissa asked.


**"I CAN'T REMEMBER** many true ice storms," I mentioned once Bob and I had finished feeding the birds. He poured himself a fresh mug of coffee and I lifted the teapot to fill my own. I usually make a whole pot-full at a time. With the double-thickness tea cozy I'd knitted, it stays piping hot for hours. "Maybe a couple when I was a kid up in Braeton-burg, but that's about it, and they weren't nearly this bad. Oh, and one when Sally and Sandra were one and two. That one was worse than the other two, but maybe it was just that I was an adult and was more aware of the possible repercussions. I was pregnant with Scott, and I remem-ber thinking that if anything happened and I had to get the kids out of the house, I'd freeze to death because by that time I couldn't get my coat fastened around my truly enormous girth."

*What is a gurth?*

"I remember that one," Bob said as Marmalade meowed. "My dad was worried about how he'd get out to help people if he got an emergency call."

"Did he have many emergencies?"

"None that I remember. But that didn't keep him from worrying."

I waited for a moment until a particularly nasty wind gust quit slamming ice crystals against the window. "Do you think you'll have any this time around?" Before he could answer, I said, "Dumb question. There's no way to know, is there?"

"Well, Reebok's at the station. I'm sure he'd be delighted if some hardened criminal came to town and he had to brave the ice and snow to arrest the guy."

Bob's assistant police chief had a yearning for adventure—cops and robbers type. "I hope he doesn't get a single call," I said, "because then you'd feel like you had to go out to back him up." I set down my mug, wrapped my arms around his waist, and leaned my head against his chest. Even through his heavy sweater I could hear the reassuring thump of his heart. "I'd rather have you here, safe and warm with me."

*And with me, too.*

Marmalade insinuated herself between our ankles, purring mightily.

*I am saying something to you and SoftFoot, but you do not listen, Widelap.*


**"THE MARTIN FAMILY?** As in Martinsville?" Melissa repeated. "Why here?"

Carol looked around the table, assessing the interest level. "It's a long story, but I can shorten it to a bare outline if you like."

Dave waved his short, blunt fingers toward the frosty window. "Why bother to tell it faster? Does it look like we're going anyplace soon?"

"I guess not. Well then," she stretched her arms wide, not even trying to stifle a grin, "here goes. It all went back to some early research for my doctoral dissertation, although I was denied that topic, so my dissertation ended up being about something else altogether. Still, I was interested and kept up the research on the side. As I said, I'm trying to resolve that blood feud between my mother's family and the Martins. Not that it's bloody now, but in the distant past it certainly was. The research is an ongoing project with me, and I plan to write a book about it—if I can solve the problem."

"What problem would that be?" Pat had just taken an enormous bite of coffee cake, and she held her hand over her mouth as she spoke.

"The problem? Where the Martins and their relatives disappeared to when they left Vermont."

Melissa picked up the coffee carafe and circled the table to refill the large mugs. "Are you saying they came here?"

"Well, they covered their tracks really well. If you're used to looking through historical documents, it's possible to find a great deal of information about the expansion of families throughout this country." She paused to add a dollop more cream to her cup.

"You mean through census figures," Dave suggested.

Carol shook her head. "I mean newspapers and letters and tax records, as well as wills, deeds, court minutes, and voter lists. The Martins left Vermont in 1741, although it wasn't called Vermont at the time. That name was officially adopted on the fourth of July in 1777, when the newly formed Independent Republic of Vermont ratified a constitution. It was the first written constitution in North America to abolish slavery, give the vote to men who did not own land, and establish public schools. At first, they wanted to called it *New Connecticut*, but the name *Vermont* finally won out." She gave a rueful grin. "But all that's beside the point. That's the problem with being a historian. We keep getting sidetracked by interesting historical notes. Where was I leading with all this?"

"Dave asked you about the census," Melissa reminded her.

"Oh, right. I couldn't track them easily in Vermont because there simply weren't any census records in the 1740s. In fact, the first national census wasn't until 1790. Of course, Vermont wasn't included in that census, since it didn't become the fourteenth state until 1791, so the first census records for Vermont are from 1800." She twisted her lips into a grimace. "I sound like I'm lecturing again. As to finding the names here on this end of the trail, the federal government lost the first three census records for the state of Georgia. The census from 1820 has been reconstructed, but there aren't any official census records until 1830, at which point all of the family names I researched showed up."

"So if you don't have any records," Pat waved her hand as if wiping a slate clean, "how do you find out things from way back then?"

"Normally people who left one area would write home sporadically to family members, sending the letters back by any means they could find."

Pat nodded sagely. "The pony express."

Again, Carol shook her head. "That didn't start until the time of the Civil War, the 1860s, and primarily covered the west." Her voice took on a tone of awe. "Sometimes those pony express riders traveled 250 miles in a day."

Dave guffawed. "I can do five, six hundred a day easily."

Melissa rolled her eyes.

"I'm sure you can," Carol said. "In a car. On interstate highways."

"Oh, yeah."

"The Pony Express operated for less than two years. Once the telegraph lines were completed, there wasn't any need for the riders."

"The post office, then," Pat said. "That's been around a long time."

"Not quite long enough. Ben Franklin was the first postmaster. In 1775."

"So," Melissa asked, "what did they do before there was a post office?"

"Letters were often entrusted to someone who was simply traveling in the general direction the letter was intended to go. If that traveler veered in a different direction, he'd pass it on to someone else, and so on, until the letter or package arrived, sometimes after an interval of only a few weeks—but more often after months."

"And sometimes never, I would guess," Melissa said.

Carol shrugged. "Those are the instances we never find out about. But in this case, even if there had been willing couriers headed in the right direction, there weren't any remaining families to write home to. Homer Martin took the whole extended clan with him, all the descendants of the first Martin who settled in that mountain valley."

"Well," Dave said, "it was a man named Homer Martin who founded Martinsville back in 1745, but other than the coincidence of his name, what makes you think they came here?"

"That's the fun part of historical research. Sometimes it's like a bolt out of the blue." She paused. "That sounds trite, doesn't it?"

Melissa nodded, but Pat said, "Don't leave us hanging like that. What happened?"

"For a number of years—I told you this started when I was working on my doctorate, but I couldn't find enough evidence to make it the subject of my dissertation. Still, I never dropped it. Every time I've seen or heard the name *Martin*, I've looked into it as much as possible. And then, just a couple of months ago, I happened to hear a radio news spot about how Hubbard Mar…" Her voice trailed off, for she was suddenly aware that some of these people might have been related to the principals in the story that had been reported on the national news.

Dave cleared his throat. "Don't worry about it," he said. "He wouldn't have been much of a loss."

Pat pursed her lips. "I wouldn't have wished *that* on anybody, though, no matter how much I dislike him."

"If you knew him as well as I do," Dave said, "you'd change your tune."

His wife snorted. "He's gotten better over the years."

This time, he was the one who snorted.

"That was a great news story," Melissa said. "I loved the way Marmalade kept making noises in the background. She has a really loud meow."

Carol laughed to herself. It had been a particularly entertaining piece of reporting.

# Wednesday, September 27, 2000
### Transcript of Broadcast Interview by "Radio Ralph" Towers, WRRT
### Picked up by National Public Radio as a human interest story and re-broadcast on WVMT, Vermont Public Radio

RRT: Your WRRT reporter on the scene, Radio Ralph Towers here, re-

porting from the fire station in Martinsville, Georgia. I'm inter-
viewing Martinsville firefighter Hal Quincy Cartwright, known
to his colleagues as Hoss, who was first on the scene to discover
a badly injured Hubbard Martin, who is the Chair of the Martinsville Town Council.

[Background: cat meows]

HQC: I'd say I was the second on the scene. The first one was the cat.

RRT: [laughter] Please tell us how you found Hubbard, uh, Mr. Martin.

HQC: It was the darnedest thing I ever saw. I drove to the station from
my house in Garner Creek early this morning. I was putting on
my gear—you know, two-way radio and stuff like that—when
Marmalade, this cat here, the one meowing at you—she showed
up, all yowling like she had a real problem. She'd run out toward
the street and then she'd come back, holler at us some more and
run right out there again. All of us at the station, we've known
Marmalade for quite a while, and she doesn't ever act like that.
She usually just purrs a good morning, checks out whether we
have any food available, and then goes on her way. Sometimes
she sits and visits for a while, watches us clean the station or
tend the hoses, things like that.

[Background: cat meows]

RRT: So, would you say her activity this morning was out of character?

HQC: Sure was!

RRT: What was your response to her unusual behavior?

HQC: Well, I figured something was up. I still had a few minutes before my shift officially started, so I told the others I was going to
follow her and see what she'd do.

RRT: And did she lead you somewhere?

[Background: cat meows]

HQC: She sure did. I even had to climb over a couple of backyard pick-
et fences. I guess cats don't have to stick to sidewalks [laughter].
Anyway, she leads me right up to the base of the cliff.

RRT: The high cliff that bounds Martinsville on the west side?

HQC: That's right. And I find Hubbard all bunched up in a tight ball.

RRT: Did you determine the extent of his injuries at that time?

HQC: I could tell he was hurt bad, so I called on the two-way and
they got the med unit there right away—it wasn't but a couple

of blocks. [Background: cat meows] And I called the town cop, too, just in case.

RRT: Why do you suppose nobody else had responded to Mr. Martin's injury?

HQC: I doubt anybody else was up that early. [Background: cat meows] Except for Marmalade. It wasn't hardly even dawn yet. And Hubbard might not have cried out.

RRT: You say he didn't cry out. Could you tell what had happened?

HQC: He wasn't in any shape to give us any information [Background: cat meows]. Even if he had been, we don't talk about our patients.

RRT: Do you have any theory about what might have transpired?

HQC: Nope.

RRT: Could he have fallen from the cliff?

HQC: Possibly, but I can't say one way or the other.

RRT: The cliff there is about sixty feet high. Were his injuries consistent with someone who had fallen that far?

HQC: C'mon, Ralph, you know I can't talk about Hubbard's injuries.

[Background: cat meows]

RRT: Gimme a break, Hoss. This is important news.

HQC: Maybe, but you won't get it from me.

RRT: Uh …the cliff farther down the valley is more than twice that tall. If he'd fallen down there, would you say we'd probably be having a funeral?

HQC: No comment.

[Background: cat meows]

RRT: It's too bad this noisy cat can't give us any information. [Cat meows again]

HQC: I'm sure she would if she could.

RRT: Was the site where Mr. Martin fell close to any houses?

HQC: [Pause] Naw. There're houses all along Fifth Street, and I guess you could say their back yards extend right to the cliff, but none of the houses got built anywhere close to it. Falling rocks, you know.

RRT: Or falling bodies?

HQC: Uh … I wouldn't put it like that.

RRT: Did you transport Mr. Martin via ambulance?

HQC: Yep. Well, not me personally. The medics on shift are the ones who took him up to the hospital in Russell Gap, and they're not back yet. We decided the Montrose Clinic in Garner Creek wouldn't have extensive enough facilities to take care of the seriousness of his injuries.

RRT: Just how extensive were they? Could Mr. Martin have been pushed?

HQC: Cut it out, Ralph.

RRT: Uh … thank you, Firefighter Cartwright.

HQC: You're welcome. [Background: cat meows] Aren't you going to thank Marmalade, too?

RRT: Oh … of course. Thank you. [Background: cat meows] This is Radio Ralph Towers, reporting from Martinsville, Georgia, for WRRT, where you get all the news almost as soon as it happens.

## December 2000
## Azalea House

**"I NEVER HEARD** any sort of follow-up," Carol said. "How is Hubbard doing?"

Melissa leaned her forehead into her right hand. "Not very well. I'm sure you can tell, I don't like Hubbard very much. In fact, not at all, but ever since somebody pushed him over the cliff, he can't communicate. It's like his mind just isn't there anymore."

Carol reached impulsively to touch Melissa's arm. "Oh, I'm so sorry."

"It wasn't your fault," Dave said.

Melissa gave a sideway grimace at Dave before she said, "Thank you, Carol."

"Do you know for certain he was pushed? Did they catch whoever did it?"

"It could have been suicide, I guess—"

Dave interrupted her. "Of course it was suicide."

"You could be right, Dave, but I happen to think he was pushed. Nobody's been charged, though. I'm not even sure whether Bob and Reebok have any suspects."

"Reebok?"

"That's his name." Melissa smiled. "His parents knew about the antelope, but not about the running shoes." She waited a moment for Carol's appreciative chuckle. "Bob Sheffield is the town cop and Reebok Garner's the only other officer, although he does prefer to be called a deputy."

"Wild West Syndrome?"

Melissa nodded.

So did Pat.

"I wonder if Clara did it?"

"Dave! Why would you say that?"

"Don't tell me you haven't thought the same thing."

"Well," Melissa mused, "I can think of plenty of other people besides his wife who might have considered it as well."

"If he's so unpopular," Carol said, "why do you keep electing him to be the council chair?"

"It's not like that," Melissa said. "The position is sort of inherited."

"Be that as it may," Carol said, "the name Martinsville caught my eye. And then that firefighter named Hoss mentioned Garner Creek and Russell Gap." She sat back, as if that pronouncement should have clinched the deal. "After that, I checked the earliest available census records for this area."

"I don't follow you." Melissa took another piece of coffee cake and passed the plate to her right. Dave took two of the generously sized squares. Pat took one, leaving the last piece for Carol.

Carol held the plate for a moment, staring at it. "Where did this come from?"

"I made it this morning."

"No, I mean the platter."

Melissa tilted her head to one side. "Way back when. I'm not exactly sure. I inherited it when grandma died."

"So it's a family heirloom?"

Melissa laughed. "Not hardly. It's just an old wooden plate. I like the pattern, so I use it a lot. Every few years I re-varnish it to fill the grooves and keep it sanitary. I guess that means it has no value as an antique. All my mother ever told me about it was that it came from one of the elderly spinsters in the family."

Pat peered at the plate Carol held. "You mean the Tarkingtons?"

"Lord, no," Melissa said. "I don't think there were ever *any* spinsters in the Tarkington family—except maybe me—in all the time since Brand Tarkington married Parley Breeton way back in 1762. I think it must have been one of Parley's aunts."

Carol set the plate on the table. "Parley?"

"She was one of the first babies born in Martinsville that first year here in 1745. When she grew up, she married Brand Tarkington, my great-great-who-knows-how-many grandfather."

Carol rolled her shoulders back and straightened her back. "As far as I know there were never any Tarkingtons in Brandtburg, Vermont, at least not in the 1700s."

"So? There probably weren't any Pontiacs there either." Dave Pontiac chuckled at his own little joke, but Carol responded only with a twitch of her brows.

"Why would it matter," Pat asked, "that there weren't any Tarkingtons in Vermont?"

Carol brushed the extra crumbs from the platter onto her own plate and turned the platter upside down. The bottom was blank. "It's interesting that this plate came through a family called Tarkington. It started out in the Brandt family. That pattern, the vines and interlocking initials, is one that was designed by Silas Martin in 1740, when he was eighteen years old."

"How on earth would you know that?"

"Good question, Melissa. I found documentation in a small museum in the heart of the Northeast Kingdom."

"Northeast Kingdom?" Pat's cake-laden fork stopped halfway to her mouth. "What's that?"

"It's an area of Vermont that has traditionally been rather, shall we say, standoffish with regard to the rest of the state. I've found the people there to be delightful on an individual basis, but I'd hate to move into one of those communities and try to run for any office other than maybe dog catcher."

Pat leaned to her left and nudged her husband with her shoulder. "Sound familiar, Davey?"

He turned a wry smile on his wife. "You wouldn't be suggesting my home town, now would you?"

"You're from here in Martinsville?"

"Born and bred and happy about it."

"Well, I doubt Martinsville can hold a candle to some of the longstanding feuds from northeastern Vermont."

"Sounds like those Appalachian families," Dave said.

"The Hatfields and the McCoys?" Carol thought about it a moment. "Very similar in some ways, but not quite that bloody for the most part."

"Back to the plate design," Melissa said. "You say it came from … from where?"

"Silas Martin, Homer Martin's younger brother. That museum I mentioned has a journal written by Sophrona Blanchard."

Pat almost choked on her coffee. "What kind of name is that?"

"Not too common, I'll admit," Carol said, "but it shows up every once in a while in the old census records."

Melissa mulled it over. "It sounds like a good name for a lazy cat."

"Sophrona was one of the unmarried nieces of Ira Brandt."

"With a name like that, no wonder she didn't marry."

Dave looked doubtfully at his wife. "Didn't marry? What does that have to do with the price of eggs in China?"

"Would you marry a woman named Sophrona?"

"Don't have to." He leaned closer to Pat and wrapped an arm around her shoulder. "I already got me a wife."

"Well, it's a ridiculous name."

"There are a lot of doozies like that in the old records," Carol said.

Melissa raised her hand, for all the world like a fourth-grader ready to ask a question. "What about that journal of—what did you say her name was?"

"Sophrona." Carol smiled her thanks at Melissa for getting them back on track. "She wrote in the diary only until she married"—she nodded at Dave and Pat—"and then gave up writing, but she did keep the diary, so it must have been important to her."

She paused for a sip of coffee. "The Brandts have lived in the northeast kingdom almost from when it was first settled by Europeans, long before the Martins moved into that area. Sophrona copied the design into her journal and wrote that Silas had drawn it for her and had made her a plate with the design carved into it." She held up the platter in question. "If you look at this design carefully, it appears to be her initials intertwined with his."

"It doesn't look like initials to me," Pat said.

Melissa traced the elaborate design with her forefinger. She couldn't see any initials in it, either, except maybe a capital B. "Were they sweethearts?"

"From the tone of the journal entry, it sounds like she was sweet on him, but I'm not sure he returned the feeling. After all, he left the area when Homer did, and to the best of my knowledge, never contacted Sophrona again as long as she lived. At least, there aren't any surviving letters from him, and I imagine she would have saved them if she'd received any."

"That's kind of sad," Pat said. "But maybe he wrote her and the letters just got thrown away. After all, if he jilted her ..."

"I doubt it. If you'd read her journal, you'd be as convinced as I am that she would have kept every single letter pressed between those pages. She had a lock of his hair in there. If she kept his hair even after she was married to somebody else, I should think she'd keep a letter, too."

"So they were sweethearts," Pat insisted. "Maybe their families kept them apart."

Dave made a gagging sound. "You're bound and determined to turn this into a love story, aren't you?"

Melissa set another pot of coffee to percolating, then held the now empty plate up to the light and inspected it closely. "So, if Sophrona Blanchard stayed behind in Vermont with her precious plate, how did *this* plate get made, who made it, and why has the design persisted?" She furrowed her brows. "You don't think this is actually Sophrona's original plate, do you?"

Carol shrugged. "It could very well be. There's no mention in Sophrona's diary—her journal—about a second plate like that, but there is an entry in which Sophrona complains that her platter was stolen. She accused her next-door neighbors, the Breetons, but by the time Sophrona discovered the theft, the Breetons were well on their way. She was quite peeved with her father because he refused to chase after the Martins to retrieve it. I'm afraid this is one of those mysteries that may never be solved."

"Wouldn't it be fun to find the answer, though?"

"Absolutely." Carol's eyes lit up with excitement. "That's what's so fascinating about the work I do. A lot of it feels like drudgery, going through old lists and such, but there are those ah-ha moments that make all the busywork more than worthwhile."

"You never really explained why you came *here*," Pat said. "Was it one of those ah-ha things?"

"Sure was. That news story, as I already told you, about Hubbard Martin and the cat."

"That would be Marmalade," Melissa said.

"Yes. That was the name."

"Once this storm is over, I'll introduce you to her."

Carol's eyes brightened.

"She belongs to my good friend Biscuit McKee and her husband Bob Sheffield. Or I should say, Biscuit and Bob belong to Marmalade."

"That's certainly the way cats seem to operate," Carol said.

"I still don't see," Pat said, "what this has to do with your coming here."

"As soon as I heard that the firefighter he interviewed was from Garner Creek, I looked up Martinsville on a map."

"You must have had a good one." Melissa refilled the coffee carafe. "Most maps don't show anything of Keagan County."

"KAY-guhn?" Carol stressed the sound of the first syllable. "I thought it was KEY-guhn."

"Common mistake," Melissa said. "Most people mispronounce it. It's the smallest county in Georgia, and a lot of folks don't even know we're here."

"That can be a very good thing," Carol said. "It's a peaceful area usually, isn't it?"

Melissa guffawed. "If you discount the various murders over the years."

Carol shrugged again. "At any rate, as soon as I saw the names of the other towns in the valley, I knew there was a connection, knew I'd found what I was looking for—or part of it at least."

"Which part?" Dave reached down the long table and snagged the coffee. "And what do the town names have to do with anything?"

"I found where the Martins and the other families ended up—"

"Yeah? How'd you do that?"

"Let her finish her sentence, Dave."

"Yes, ma'am." He saluted his wife with a mock grimace and then winked at Carol. "She keeps me in line." He took in a slow slug of coffee, and Carol took a moment to down the rest of her mug as well.

Setting it on the placemat, she pulled a well wrinkled, hand-drawn map from her back pocket and spread it out in the middle of the table. The others leaned forward. "Here's what I found." She pointed to Martinsville at the lower end of the dead-end valley, where the Metoochie River exited through a narrow mile-long gorge. "Homer Martin was the leader of the band that left Vermont in 1741. And here we have Martinsville." She tapped the name and then pointed to a town farther up the valley. "Garner Creek. Calvin Garner headed up a family that left with Homer Martin."

She ran her finger northward. In the middle of the valley was the town of Hastings. "Robert Hastings was an innkeeper in Brandtburg."

She looked around at her small audience. "Are you with me so far?"

When everyone nodded, she continued, pointing at Russell Gap, the only town that connected directly with the rest of the state via a county road that ran through a gap in the high cliffs that bounded the Metoochie River Valley on the west. The unbroken line of cliffs across the river to the east were so high, someone wanting to go to North Carolina had to head west from Russell Gap first, leave Keagan county altogether, and circle around well below Enders, the town just south of the river gorge, before they could find a way to turn back toward the east.

"The Reverend Anders Russell," Carol said, "was the oldest of the family heads in the exodus. Apparently his wife, Sarah Endicott Russell, insisted that their daughter Myra Sue, who was pledged to Homer Martin, be married before they left. I got that piece of information from a newspaper article."

"But, Homer's wife wasn't Myra Sue. Her name was Mary," Melissa said. "Mary Frances, in fact."

"Was she? That's interesting. I'll tell you how that might have happened in a little while."

"You're just trying to build the suspense," Pat complained.

"Doing a pretty good job of it, too," Dave said. "What about the other towns?"

"Well, that's where it gets a little iffy," Carol admitted, "but I think the similarity of names is too close to be sheer coincidence." Her finger lingered over the name of Braetonburg, the town just north of Martinsville. "The fifth family head was Willem Breeton, that's B-r-e-e-t-o-n. He was a widower."

"B-r-a-e-t-o-n is pretty close," Dave conceded. "Didn't people misspell a lot of things back then?"

"I wouldn't call them misspellings," Carol said. "They frequently just wrote words out the way they sounded."

"You forgot one," Melissa said. "Surreytown." She indicated the town at the top end of the valley, where the Metoochie River poured in through another long cliff-lined gorge.

"I didn't forget it. I'm just saving the biggest stretch of the imagination till the last. Another family in the group was led by Call Surratt. As I said, it's a stretch, but Surreytown could have been founded by the Surratts."

"Wait a minute," Pat said. "How many people are we talking about here?"

"I'm not sure of exactly how many people went with Homer Martin. There were a number of other families—the Everests, the Fountains, the Stickneys, and the Endicotts. Each of these men had numerous family members, but none of those names show up in the Georgia census records I had access to, except for the Endicotts, but they weren't in Keagan County. There were at least seventy in the group to start with, and most likely a lot more that we just don't have names for."

Dave let out a low whistle. "Seventy? That's some wagon train."

"These were the years before the Conestoga wagon was invented," Carol said, "so don't think of it as a grand procession like you see in movies about the old West. These would have been farm wagons and carts for the most part."

"Still, seventy is a lot of people to keep track of."

"True. Their wagons probably strung out a good quarter-mile or so. Maybe more. Of course, many of the people would have walked the whole way."

"Walked?" Pat spluttered her coffee, grabbed a napkin, and gave an apologetic glance at Melissa. "Walked all the way from Vermont to Georgia?"

"Well, it took them several years to do it, I would imagine."

Melissa nodded. "Martinsville was founded in 1745."

"So, four years," Carol said. "And I'm sure there were more than seventy when they started out, maybe even eighty or ninety. The official records don't always list the children, for instance, or at least not by name, and with that many families, it stands to reason that some of the women must have been pregnant, so more children would have been added along the way—if they survived. The Endicotts, for instance, had three small children when they left—I know that from a note in Sophrona's diary."

"Endicott?" Melissa leaned back in her chair.

"Yes. Worthy Endicott and his wife, Eunice Surratt Endicott."

"I wonder if they're the ones who founded Enders."

Carol looked at her map. "Enders?"

Melissa leaned forward and drew her finger along the line that suggested the Metoochie River, through the straight parallel lines designating the gorge at the bottom end of the valley. "Enders is a town a mile south of here, at the bottom end of this long chasm where the river widens out into a large lake. It's not in Keagan County, and didn't you say you found some Endicotts in the census?"

"Hmm," Carol said. "Yeah. Could be." She pulled the pencil from the top of her braid and jotted in the name where Melissa indicated.

"You can't get there from here," Dave said. "At least not by car."

"And the foot path is more than a mile long," Pat said. "Over the top of the cliffs."

"Well," Carol said, "they didn't have cars back then, and everybody was used to doing a lot of walking, and a mile wouldn't have been considered very far at all."

"You said they left Vermont in 1741?"

"That's right, Dave. April of 1741."

"And Martinsville was founded in 1745. How come it took them so long to get here?"

Pat slapped playfully at Dave. "Haven't you been listening?"

"Of course I have. But four years? I could walk all the way across the country in half that time."

"I doubt they had a specific destination in mind," Carol said, "so they may have wandered a bit. The wagons would have been burdened down with household goods, people who were ill, or those too elderly or too young to keep up. Roads existed, certainly, but they were primitive in many areas—not much more than deer trails." She turned to look out the window. "They were probably stalled periodically by heavy winter storms or spring rains. Then again, they may have tried out a number of other possible sites as they traveled southwards. There's no telling exactly what they were looking for, but they obviously wanted to be a long way from the Green Mountains of Vermont."

"And they settled here," Dave said, "in a dead-end valley that almost nobody can find, even nowadays with road maps." He snickered. "Sounds like they were running away from something."

Carol's mouth split into a wry grin. "You're right about that. The old records aren't a hundred percent complete, but there was a lot of ill feeling, especially after Homer's brand new wife was murdered on the steps of the church the day before they left."

"Oh, no," Pat breathed.

"Oh, yes. Shot clean through the heart, which was something of a miracle, considering the inaccuracy of the old rifles at that time."

"Maybe the shooter was aiming at something else," Dave said.

"Or someone else." Melissa's voice was grim. She set down her coffee mug. "The murdered woman was the Myra Sue you mentioned?" When Carol nodded, Melissa went on. "So Mary Frances was Homer's second wife. I never knew that. I wonder if she knew Myra Sue."

"Of course she did," Carol said. "Those families were all in a tight-knit community. From what I can tell, it was mostly the men who did the arguing. I wouldn't be surprised if Myra Sue's murder ripped apart women who had been friends since childhood."

Melissa examined the plate again. "When Diane Marie was killed a few years ago …" She looked up at Carol. "Diane Marie was Ida Peterson's sister—Ida and her husband own the Martinsville IGA. Her murder didn't split anybody apart. We all drew together the best way we knew to help Ida cope."

Carol thought for a moment. "I'd be willing to bet Diane's murderer—"

"Diane Marie. This is the South, remember, where doubled-up names are almost required."

"Gotcha. I bet Diane Marie's murderer wasn't somebody from here in Martinsville, though. Am I right?"

Melissa nodded. "He didn't live here. He came from up the valley originally."

"So there wasn't much reason for families here to take sides against each other. Back in 1741, though, the bad feelings between the Brandts and the Martins had been brewing for a long time. Nobody knows what the two families had against each other originally, but everyone in the surrounding communities eventually sided with either the Martins or the Brandts."

Pat frowned. "So, who killed Myra Sue?"

"I'm sorry to admit this," Carol said, "but it was my great-great-et cetera several times grandfather, Ira Brandt. According to everything I've read, he was mean even when he was sober, but he was downright nasty when he was drunk, and apparently he was drunk most of the time."

"That's no reason to kill someone."

"You're right, Pat, but I suppose we'll never know why he did it, although it was probably related to the long-standing feud."

"What happened to Ira after the Martins left?"

"Nothing."

"Nothing?" Pat sounded outraged.

"That's right. Nobody was left to bring any charges against him."

"I hope he died a miserable death."

"Pat!" Melissa said. "He might have had a change of heart. Maybe he spent the rest of his life trying to make up for what he'd done."

"And maybe he spent the whole time gloating."

Carol raised a hand. "Ira and Hubbard, his brother—"

Melissa held up her hand in unconscious imitation of Carol. "Hubbard?"

Carol's eyes twinkled. "Coincidence? That was another one of the reasons I looked into this valley, after the news report said the cat Marmalade saved the life of *Hubbard* Martin. It's not that usual a name."

"There've been a lot of boys named Hubbard in the Martin family," Melissa said. "They're usually the second son, and it happens every other generation or so." She paused and thought for a moment. "But the chairmanship of the town council always goes to the oldest son. Our current Hubbard is—or was—the town chair. I wonder why his mother didn't wait for a second son to give that name to?"

Dave planted his elbows on the table and took a deep breath. "She did. Hubbard had an older brother, name of Cornelius, who died years ago."

"How sad," Melissa said. "I didn't know that."

"Yeah. He fell out of a tree"—he let the silence hang for a few seconds—"that he and Hubbard were climbing at the time. Broke his neck."

Pat shifted in her seat to face her husband. "Are you saying Hubbard pushed Cornelius out of the tree?"

"Not saying he did; not saying he didn't. But you know Hubbard as well as I do. What do *you* think?"

## 1952

**HUBBARD MARTIN HAD** known without a doubt, the way younger brothers always knew, that Clara Black favored Cornelius. Didn't her eyes follow him everywhere? Didn't she try to tag along whenever the two boys wanted to go somewhere? And hadn't Corndog always wanted to include Clara? At least, for the last couple of years.

It had taken all Hubbard's powers of persuasion to convince his brother to leave Clara behind that day, to sneak out the back of the house. They had to go that way since Clara could see their front door from her house across the street.

"You don't want anybody to see you climbing a tree," Hubbard reasoned. He knew his sixteen-year-old brother had a reputation to maintain, and boys that age—almost men—had to uphold their dignity, even when their younger brother challenged them to a tree-climbing competition. Corndog wouldn't want Clara to think less of him. And Hubbard certainly didn't want her anywhere nearby.

When Corndog got his hand stepped on and he lost his grip and fell, after Hubbard swore he'd never let anybody know what had really happened—it was an accident, wasn't it?—after he ran to call for help and came back to find Corndog dead and all alone, Hubbard tried to forget about it. But he could never really forget, could he?

Later, after the funeral, Clara pretty much ignored Hubbard. She was always dabbing at her eyes and walking with her head down, like she was some sort of tragic character from a myth or something. But Hubbard noticed that she only acted that way when she knew somebody was watching her. He'd seen her at night—he had a cool pair of binoculars—dancing in her bedroom, her arms flung up over her head. He could almost hear the music on that brand new phonograph she'd bragged about. He could almost see through that nightgown she wore.

## 2000
## Azalea House

**"POOR LITTLE KID,"** Pat said. "Cornelius, I mean."

Dave snorted. "He wasn't little. He was well into his teens at the time."

Pat curled her lip. "What kind of teenager still climbs trees?"

"Corndog—that's what everybody called him—he wasn't the brightest light bulb in the bucket."

Melissa rubbed a hand across her forehead. Carol thought maybe she was cringing at Dave's mixed metaphor. "You were about to say something when I interrupted you," Melissa said. "Something about Ira and Hubbard Brandt?"

"Yes, well, the two of them left Brandtburg six or seven months after the exodus and were never heard from again."

All three of Carol's audience spoke at the same time. "Where'd they go?"

"Another one of those mysteries."

"Ira was probably drunk," Pat guessed. "Maybe he fell off his horse and broke his neck." She gave an emphatic nod. "Serves him right."

Melissa laughed. "Dave, is your wife always this bloodthirsty?"

"Only when she's trying to defend a poor unprotected bride who's already been dead for more than two hundred years."

Pat swatted at his arm.

"The point," Carol said, "is that we simply don't know what happened to the two men. They could have ended up anywhere. Ira had a wife and, by the time he was twenty-six, he had seven small children—four boys and three girls—one of whom became my great et cetera grandmother."

"Wait," Melissa said. "He abandoned his wife?"

"No. She died in childbirth the year before Myra Sue was shot."

"So, that means he abandoned his children."

"Not exactly. He farmed them out to live with other families since he wasn't in any position to take care of them, young as they were."

"Hmph," Melissa snorted.

"What about Hubbard?"

"I'm not sure, Pat, but as far as I know, he wasn't married."

The lights flickered, and everyone turned to look outside. The thick coat of ice over the accumulation of snow glimmered under the heavy clouds. "Yep," Melissa said, "ice storm of the century."

Dave stroked his chin. "Do you have a generator, Melissa?"

She groaned. "I've thought about getting one. I even stopped by the hardware store last week, but they were all sold out. He said he'd be getting in a shipment of them next week."

Dave raised an eyebrow.

"I know, I know," Melissa said. "It isn't going to happen. But if the power goes out, we have an open invitation to go to Biscuit's house."

"Why there?"

"That's right. You wouldn't know about it, unless Norm told you." She turned to Carol. "Norm is Dave and Pat's son."

"Norm didn't tell us anything," Dave said.

"Biscuit and Bob bought a wood burning stove last summer," Melissa said. "They talked a bunch of other families, including Norm and Maggie, into buying them, too. Biscuit offered to put us up if necessary, although you two could always go stay with Norm and Maggie if we lose power."

"No thanks," Pat and Dave said simultaneously.

Carol's forehead creased. "Would your guests be invited, though?"

"Of course. Biscuit and Bob have a huge old house—and no small children."

"In that case," Dave said, "we can relax. Any more coffee cake available?"

"Hog," Pat said as she batted her husband's elbow.

"No," Melissa said, "but it'll be time for lunch," she looked at her watch, "in about three hours. Think you can wait that long?"

Dave stretched his arms over his head. "I sure do hate to go outside in this mess. Now I wish we'd paid extra up front for three meals a day instead of just breakfast."

"Me, too," Carol said.

"We thought we'd be eating most of our meals with Maggie and Norm and Willie," Pat told Carol.

"I didn't really think about it," Carol said. "I guess I assumed there'd be restaurants."

"Oh, we have plenty of places to eat in this town, but ..." Melissa indicated the storm outside, "you probably couldn't get to any of them without major effort."

"I bet they'll all be closed anyway," Pat said.

The wind chose that moment to batter the house, and Melissa agonized internally over the fate of her prize Japanese maple that she could see bending under the weight of the freezing rain. She was going to have to go outside and knock off the ice. Otherwise she wouldn't have many branches left. She loved the way plants could regenerate, but the arching shape of that tree was perfect, and she didn't want to see what might happen if half the branches snapped off.

"Yeah," Dave said. "Not sure we'd get very far out there."

"I'd be willing to bet the restaurants are all closed today anyway," Melissa said, "like Pat just pointed out. But don't worry. I won't let the three of you go hungry."

Pat stood and headed for the stairs. "We'll settle up at the end, Melissa. You shouldn't have to foot the bill for all these extra mouths."

"I'm not worried about that. I know where to find you."

Carol re-folded her hand-drawn map and stuck it back into her pocket. "Thanks, Melissa, but for right now, I'd like to get some more reading done and look over my notes."

"I'll call you when it's time to eat, around twelve-thirty."

Dave came back and grabbed his mug. "I don't know about the rest of you, but I could use some more coffee in the meantime."

Melissa picked up the empty carafe. "That I can handle. Give me just a few minutes and I'll have some ready." She gathered up the plates as well. The lights flickered, came on, flickered, came on again, sputtered out. And stayed out.

They waited in a pregnant silence. Around them, the house was devoid of any of the normal electrical sounds—refrigerator, clocks, furnace. The only sound, other than the quiet breathing of the four people, was the faint tick of Melissa's grandfather clock. "Sure is quiet," Pat observed.

Melissa sighed and looked at each of her three guests. "Looks like you're going to have to wait for your coffee, Dave. We'll give it ten or twenty minutes to see if the power comes back on. But if it doesn't, I think we may all be eating at Biscuit and Bob's place."

Carol's eyes brightened. "Does that mean I'll get to meet Marmalade?"

Melissa nodded. "Pack up a couple of days worth of clothing. Dave, do you have anything warmer than those cashmere sweaters of yours?"

"Very funny. They're plenty warm."

"Carol, I'll get out some sweatpants, turtlenecks, and sweaters for you. And I have an extra pair of long johns that you'd better put on before we go outside. These storms usually last two or three days—maybe four." Melissa was already thinking ahead, planning what they could take. They'd have to take as much perishable food as they could carry. She hated to think what shape her fridge would be in when they got back.

She detoured into the basement to turn off the water, then came back upstairs and turned on the kitchen faucet to let the pipes drain as much as possible. After that, she went out to knock the ice off her Japanese maple.

**IT WASN'T EVEN** half an hour after the power finally went off and stayed off, that the phone calls began. Not that I was surprised. Those of us who had lived in Georgia all our lives—or even for a few years—knew that power outages in an ice storm as severe as this one were liable to last a long time. It was just one of the facts of life. That power station halfway up the valley really needed to be refurbished, and Bob had complained frequently to the county commissioners about the antiquated sub-stations.

"Biscuit," Ida said, "I hate to impose, but you know how you tried to talk Ralph and me into getting that wood stove and we said our generator would be good enough?"

"Yeah?" I knew where this was headed and automatically started planning where to put the two of them.

"We can't get it working. Ralph's been swearing at it—as if that would help—but something's stuck or frozen or just plain stubborn."

"Machines don't get stubborn, Ida."

"This one does, at least according to Ralph. We thought about going down to stay in the store—the generators there work just fine. At least I hope they're working. Ralph just took off to check on them. But I didn't particularly want to sleep on a hard floor between the frozen food and the dairy section."

"I totally understand," I said. "Come on over here once Ralph gets back, but be careful on that ice. Bring your pillows." I knew how much better I always slept when I had my own pillow. "And some paper plates," I added. "Just in case." I wasn't sure I quite trusted Bob's belief in the availability of our inside water.

"We'll bring sheets, too." Dear Ida. She obviously remembered the evening at Melissa's after our tap dance class when I'd bemoaned the fact that I had all those extra bedrooms in the house and not enough sheets to go around. Not that I'd ever had lots of guests at once.

I did occasionally wonder at the size of some of the families who had lived in this house, to have needed so many rooms. Oh, I kept two rooms ready in case of unexpected guests, but I left the others closed up all the time. At least I hadn't piled them full of junk, the way some people tended to do with any available space—my daughter Sally's husband, for instance, not that I was going to dwell on that fact. He could mess up a room just by walking into it. Thank goodness they hadn't needed to seek shelter here.

"We'll bring food," Ida added, bringing me back to the present moment. "I don't want everything in my fridge to go bad."

"Okay, but I wouldn't worry about it. How long can this last? Two, three days? And I have plenty of soup."

When I hung up, I heard Bob chuckling behind me. "How long

can it last?" He stretched out his legs, leaned back in the kitchen chair, and reached for his coffee mug. "I'd say from the look of the ice out there, we're not talking two or three days. I'd say a week, at least. Maybe longer."

"Surely not that long." Ida and Ralph were dear friends, but I'd never actually lived with them underfoot. I inspected the soup pot that had been simmering merrily on the stove until the power went out. "Would you move that onto the wood stove before it cools down too much? I'm going to fill the carafe with coffee and get the percolator going on the wood stove."

Bob rose, grabbed some oven mitts, and hefted the pot. "You've made enough for an army, it feels like."

"With Ralph and Ida coming—and probably Melissa and her guests, too—it's a good idea, wouldn't you say? And don't worry. I can always freeze what we don't eat." I'd wondered about it when Bob insisted we install a generator soon after we bought the house, and so far we'd never needed to use it, but as so frequently happened, Bob had been right. The problem with Georgia winters wasn't cold weather, but the danger of ice—thick ice that coated trees and power lines, ice that made driving either treacherous or impossible, ice that flattened shrubbery, froze water pipes, and blocked storm sewers. People who lived farther north, where they dealt with heavy snowstorms on a regular basis, simply couldn't understand why so many Georgians panicked when the weather forecasters predicted snow, which was almost always accompanied by freezing rain.

What usually happened was that people rushed to the grocery stores and cleared the shelves of milk, bread, and toilet paper. Crazy, but that was the way it was.

I pulled the heavy curtains closed over all the windows in the kitchen to conserve the heat, walked through our home office to close those curtains, and eventually ended up in the living room. Bob stood at one of the side windows. He held out his hand to me and I joined him. We had a clear view of the side of Matthew Olsen's house. Matthew lived just uphill from us on the corner of Beechnut Lane and Third Street. A merry trickle of smoke emerged from his chimney. "At least Matthew will be warm," I said. "And Mr. Fogarty." Matthew's parakeet was a chatty little creature, of whom Matthew was inordinately fond.

*I like him, too. Sometimes he sits on my head when I go to visit. He preens my whiskers.*

"Nick and—"

*You did not fill the bird feeders.*

Marmy interrupted Bob with several rather loud gurgles.

*Gurgles?*

She was almost as loud as Mr. Fogarty. "Ohmigosh," I said. "I just remembered. I forgot to refill the feeders." In this weather, food could be a real problem for the birds. I headed for the kitchen.

"I'll help. I need to go out there and check the outside faucets anyway."

*I will stay inside where it is warm.*

"I thought you already drained them."

"I did, but it never hurts to double-check."

*I will watch you through the window.*

He lugged the large birdseed bags outside, and the squeaky back door hinge seemed to call the birds. They didn't even wait for us to knock the icicles off the feeders and fill them all. Birds were every-where, perching on the ice-encrusted trees. The morning was alive with not only the calls of the birds, but a sound almost like castanets as a breeze clicked the icy pine needles together. Bob and I looked like a couple of steam engines making funny little puffs with each breath.

I made sure there was plenty of suet available. From what I'd read, birds needed the fat from suet to keep their energy stores up, espe-cially during cold spells. I scattered extra seed across the frozen snow while Bob fiddled with the outside faucets. I could see Marmy sitting on the wide sill of the bay window. She'd have lots of birds to entertain her.

*It is fun to watch the birds, but this windowsill is cold. I prefer a lap or my nest beside the warm stove in the wintertime.*

We scooted back inside just as the phone rang. Bob grabbed it. There's something about the configuration of the Metoochie River Val-ley that prevents cell phones from working. So, while the rest of the world chats on the go, everyone in Martinsville has to have landlines. At least we never have to worry about cell phone batteries giving out. A good thing when the power is out. Downed phone lines weren't some-thing to worry about, either. The phone lines in Martinsville are all bur-ied underground, part of a town improvement project that Sadie Masters had instigated and Margaret Casperson, the richest woman in the state of Georgia, had funded a number of years ago. That was when they buried the electric lines as well.

Marmalade jumped down from the sill, so I pulled the curtain back into place.

*Thank you. The draft was very cold.*

"Sure, Garner," I heard Bob say. "Don't worry about it."

Reebok Garner was Bob's assistant police chief, although he insisted on being referred to as a deputy. He practically lived at the station, but the station didn't have a wood stove. The town was too cheap to buy one, Bob's police budget wouldn't stretch that far, and neither Bob nor I had thought to ask the Martinsville Foundation for the money. I was pretty sure—absolutely sure—that Glaze would have okayed the request. On the other hand, if there had been a stove there, Bob might have felt obligated to stay at the station.

I mentally assigned Reebok one of the small single bedrooms upstairs. He wouldn't bring any food, but we had plenty. And I knew I could fit a small pan of milk to heat on the wood stove next to the soup, behind the percolator. Reebok wasn't much of a coffee drinker, but he sure did like hot chocolate.

"I wonder who else is going to show up," I mused after Bob hung up the phone. "Maybe I should call around and be sure everybody else is okay?"

Bob rubbed his scratchy jaw. I love it when he doesn't shave for a day or two. His mustache was luxuriant, but I really thought men should grow beards in the winter. It must be so much warmer. They had beards. We had long hair—at least some of us did. My hair kept my neck warm at night.

*Sometimes I keep your neck warm.*

Last night it had seemed particularly cold, and I'd woken around two in the morning to find Marmalade draped across my shoulder, with her warm breath tickling my neck.

She can be so comforting at times like that.

*You are welcome.*

I bent down and gathered her into my arms for a nice snuggle, and she meowed at me. I kissed her on top of her soft head. I love the way she smells.

*I like the way you smell, too.*

"You won't have to worry about calling quite everybody," Bob said. "Reebok told me the fire station's generator is working just fine, and Melody is at her parents' house in Russell Gap."

Hmm. Over the past few months I'd seen several meaningful looks between Reebok and Melody, the clerk at the town hall. That would be wonderful, I thought, if those two young people got together. I liked both of them immensely. Maybe I could invite the two of them down here for dinner. After the storm was over.

"I hope they don't get any calls," I said. "Even with a vehicle as heavy as the fire engine, the traction on ice this thick couldn't possibly be dependable."

"The engine and med unit have chains, but on this ice…" Bob let the thought trail off.

I hated to think what might happen if the ambulance slid off into a ditch.

*It is a good idea to stay inside where it is warm and safe.*

"As I tried to tell you earlier before Marmalade interrupted me"—Bob used his free hand, the one that wasn't around my shoulders, to scratch her under the chin.

*Thank you.*

"I saw Nick and Anita trailing into Matthew's house."

"Anita Foley?"

*She kicked me once.*

"Hush, Marms," Bob said. "I don't know why you ask. She's the only Anita in town."

"I have to admit, I'm glad she's not coming here."

"You don't like her?"

"Well, it's nothing I can put my finger on, but I think I'm going to have trouble with her on the library board."

"Ah," Bob said. "The ubiquitous, all-powerful library board."

"Quit laughing at me. You're not the one who has to deal with them."

I stepped away from Bob and held my hands out to the wood stove. There was another reason I was glad Anita and her husband hadn't tried to shelter in our house. Nick gave me the creeps. I guess he was a good enough dentist, but he had a way of looking at me that I didn't like. Nothing overt, nothing offensive. Nothing I'd ever mention to Bob, because there wasn't really anything to it. Not really.

The wind gave a vicious rattle. "I wonder who else is going to show up on our doorstep."

"I already talked to my mom," Bob said. "She and Dee would like to come, but they wanted some time to pack their things. I told her I'd be up to get her in half an hour, and she told me to wait longer than that. She wasn't dressed yet."

"Rebecca Jo? She always gets dressed first thing in the morning."

"I know, but apparently she slept in today."

"Maybe she just kept on her pajamas because they were warmer." I set Marmalade down and headed toward the phone, sure I would think of somebody to call before I reached it. Glaze. I needed to call my sister.

Before I could call anyone, though, Ida and Ralph showed up dragging a garden cart piled high with food—fresh, canned, and frozen, as well as a case—a whole case—of toilet paper. "What did you do? Clear off your grocery store shelves?"

"Help us get this stuff inside. And don't worry about the toilet paper—it's single ply so it'll work fine in your composting toilet."

"Thanks for thinking of that, Ida." Unlike the rest of the town, I hadn't run to the store to stock up on TP. "I hope the composting toilet will work with four of us. Five, actually, because Reebok is on the way. And I was just about to call Glaze."

"Don't worry," Ida said. "She'll show up."

Bob turned to Ralph. "Is your store going to be okay?"

Ralph shook his head. "Don't worry about it. It'll be fine. I went down there and made sure the generators were on."

They hadn't been here ten minutes when we gave up trying to fit all their food into the fridge. We just put it on the back porch. "I hope the raccoons are curled up tight in a den somewhere and won't come investigating," I told Ida. "Why on earth did you bring so many gallons of milk?"

"It'll freeze okay out here," she said. "And there's no telling how long this storm is going to last. Ralph does love his cereal in the morning."

He'd have to eat it five times a day for three weeks, I thought, to go through all this.

We scooted back inside, just in time to hear Reebok come in the front door.

*The raccoons would rather eat the birdseed.*

"I forwarded the police line to here, Chief," he was saying over Marmalade's loud meow. "I hope you don't mind."

"Good thinking," Bob said. "I doubt there'll be a crime wave during an ice storm, but there may be some calls for help. It's best we have the phone covered."

Eventually, of course, we all ended up with coffee or tea, except for Reebok, who had a gigantic mug—a soup bowl with handles, actually—filled with hot chocolate. Yesterday, while the bread was rising, I'd made a quadruple batch of my famous Molasses Chewy cookies—well, famous in Martinsville and in Braetonburg, where I'd grown up—so I hauled those out as well. I'd been planning to take them to the grandkids, Mom and Dad, Auntie Blue and Uncle Mark, and anybody else who seemed like they needed them, but—oh, shucks—we'd just have to eat them here. We migrated to the living room and sat absorbing the heat from the big stove. The fan on top of it, powered by the heat of the stove itself, spread the warmth around and still left room for the enormous soup pot and the coffee percolator. The fan spread the smells as well. Soup and coffee. Wonderful.

I sure was glad we'd bought the wood stove, but even more than that, I was glad we'd bought this big old house.

## Saturday, 18 April 1741
## Brandtburg

**"THE BRANDTS WILL** take over our house," Susan Breeton said to her older sister, MaryAnne, almost as soon as the morning sun brightened their small bedroom. "Once we are gone, someone will move in here and we will have no say in who it is."

"By the time we are gone," MaryAnne argued in her *reasonable* voice, "it will not matter."

"Perhaps we could burn the house behind us."

"Susan! How can you say such a thing? That would be such a waste."

Susan could feel her face turning sullen, but she could not hide how she felt. "I do not want to leave."

"Do you wish to stay here by yourself? You would find it lonely indeed. You are only twelve. How would you feed yourself?"

Susan might have agreed to stay behind if Silas Martin were also so inclined, but she knew he would go where his older brother led. "Why do we have to go?"

MaryAnne turned away, as if the subject pained her. "The men have decided."

Susan thought that a ridiculous idea. "None of *us* wishes to travel that far away. They did not even ask for our opinion."

MaryAnne looked somewhat scandalized. "You and I are but girls, Susan. We should not question them. I am sure the men have their reasons."

Susan was not so sure about that. From what little she knew of men—Silas Martin and Father excepted, of course—they seldom had good reasons for anything they did, at least as far as Susan could discern. "MaryAnne?"

"Yes?"

"Do you really believe that?"

"Believe what?"

"That we should not question the men."

MaryAnne stared at her for a very long time. "I … you are but twelve, Susan. How can you ask such a thing?"

"Have I not a mind, sister? Have you not a mind? Think of some of those men. Mister Homer Martin, Mister Worthy Endicott?" MaryAnne tried to interrupt her, but Susan raised her voice and filled it with all the scorn she felt. "Do you truly believe they know what is best for us? Even"—Susan faltered a bit before speaking this apostasy—"even Father seems to be going along with what those men say without thinking about it."

"He is still deeply saddened by our mother's death."

"Yes, but you know the care of the house and of our brothers has fallen on you and on me now that she is gone. We have had the responsibility of packing our household goods, of deciding what to take, what to leave, while"—this time she hoped she was not going too far—"while he has spent his evenings at the public house, probably listening to all the other men congratulating themselves on their good decision to leave."

MaryAnne's normally wide eyes narrowed and she repeated herself. "How can you say such a thing?" The heat had gone from her voice, though, and Susan thought her sister looked … thoughtful … rather than indignant.

Susan turned her back on MaryAnne and looked out the window toward the largest of the willow trees that grew between this house and Sophrona Blanchard's house next door, but her thoughts were not on the tree. They were on Silas Martin. Perhaps as they travelled, he would begin to notice her.


**"THEY WILL TAKE** over all our houses," Constance Garner remarked to her older brother Nehemiah, "once we are gone from here."

"Yes," he said. "They will. They have long envied the fertile land on this side of the valley."

She watched a small flurry of dust motes spinning in an early morning sunbeam. "I think I shall leave behind a posy on each bed frame."

"Be sure your posies do not resemble a witch's charm, else the Brandts may follow us to hunt you down as they did our grandsire."

Constance shivered when she thought about the frightening tale of Albion and Lucelia Martin, whose bodies had been found in a roadside ditch all those years ago. She was not supposed to have heard the story, for the women of the town were usually protected from hearing such gruesome details, but Constance reveled in listening from places where she was not expected to be. Nehemiah had caught her at it several times, but he had not given her away. As a matter of fact, at times he had joined in the listening.

She did not believe the Brandts would follow their wagons on this journey, but she could remember a dozen years ago, one of her earliest memories when she was but a child of four or five, how frightened she had been when the town put old Granny Surratt in the stocks for a day.

"I will not bind the posies," she said. "I will scatter petals on the floor instead."

"I would not waste the effort if I were you."

"You are not I. I do not want to leave, but I am determined to leave something of beauty behind me here."

She looked out the door to her garden in the front yard. Although she and her sister and mother had gathered all the early pickings of the garden to take with them on their journey, Constance knew the garden would continue to flourish for years to come, as long as whoever took it over had even half a care to nurture it as it deserved. The garden was of great utility and necessity, and the flowers in it had all been planted to ward off the insects and worms that would otherwise devour their food-stuffs, but the garden was a thing of beauty as well. Constance affirmed that she would scatter flower petals throughout the house before she left, no matter what her brother said.

**"THE BRANDTS WILL** take over every one of our houses," Bridgett Hastings told her younger brother, but since Lucius was but nine years old, he hardly listened to her, intent as he was on spinning his top across the wide-planked floor.

Bridgett walked from room to room, trying to imagine how they would look once they were empty. But of course, they would not be truly empty. The wagons would not hold much of this upstairs furniture. Most of the tables, most of the chairs, and all of the bedframes would be left behind, for, according to Father, they could be easily replaced whenever they arrived at the end of their journey. All of the tables and benches in the public house on the ground floor would remain for the new owner, of course. She wondered what it would feel like to sleep in a wagon for the months ahead as they journeyed southwards. She was sure it would be quieter than living two stories above the public house. She had been kept long awake the previous night by the shouts of Brandts and Martins having yet another row.

She looked out the back window at the remains of last year's garden far below. Bridgett had a feeling the journey might be quiet-er, but the work along the trail they were undertaking would be harder even than tending the inn, cooking meals for an undetermined number of guests every night, and the back-bending toil of raising a garden. She fingered one of the three tall candlesticks on the table beside the window, and the smell of the tallow felt comforting somehow. Those candles would not be packed until Monday morn, for they would need the light this evening and tomorrow night. Already the hundreds of extra candles and enough candlesticks for safety were packed in boxes that were neatly labeled with the contents. Bridgett tried to think of those candles lighting a new house somewhere—where?—but her imagination failed her. She did not want to leave.

**"THEY WILL TAKE** over this house," Edna Russell complained.

Anne shook her head impatiently at her younger sister. "Why do you fret so?" Anne knew that Edna deeply regretted having to pack up her broidery work for the trip ahead. Edna was never happier than when she had a needle in her hands. "We will be gone," Anne continued. "How will it matter?"

Edna tugged on a stray lock of her blond hair. "I do not like to think of a Brandt using our bed."

"Your feelings are unnecessary. We will take the mattress with us in the bottom of our wagon to sleep on as we travel. You know that. When we find a new home, Father and Thomas will build us new bed frames."

"I do not want to leave." Tears welled up in Edna's eyes. She was sixteen years old, but she still cried as readily as a baby. "I do not want to leave."

Anne found it hard to comfort her sister, for she, too, would rather have stayed here in the only home she had ever known.

**"THE BRANDTS WILL** take possession of this house when we leave." Nell Surratt thought this out loud, even though she knew her seven-year-old brother Edward would not care, and probably would not even listen.

He surprised her, though. "Do you think they will find my secret hiding place?"

Nell tightened her lips so she would not laugh at him. He had been so proud of himself for loosening a floorboard last summer so he could hide what he called his treasures. He had not been able to resist bragging to Nell about it, although he had sworn her to secrecy. Of course, she had known about it well before he boasted. She had eyes, did she not? She had kept his confidence for a day, until Mother noticed the uneven board and asked Father to nail it down. Luckily Edward had been outside tending to the goats at the time, as Nell explained that it was her brother's secret.

"It may be secret," Father said, "but someone is going to trip on it and break a leg."

"Can you not simply adjust it, Father? So it does not stick up quite so much?"

Mother studied the plank for several seconds. "I think I would like to move that table from the corner over to here. Would you do that for me, my husband?"

"You wish to keep it easy for him to open?" Father chuckled in appreciation. "You are a good woman, Geonette Black Surratt." He turned to his daughter. "And you, Nell, are so like your mother."

Nell had swelled with pride at hearing his praise.

"I do not think they will find it," she told Edward now, "for it is so well hidden."

Once again, her little brother surprised her. "I may leave it partly open. It would be a shame if nobody knew how hard I worked to prepare it."

"But then, if you make it easy to find, it will not be a secret anymore." She ran her hand along the edge of one of the packed boxes. "Everyone who tramps through this house will know its location."

"Oh."

"Think of what fun you will have imagining who might find it."

Edward's voice brightened. "He will have to be very smart to do so."

Nell turned back toward her brother. She wanted to see his face when she said what was in her heart. "Perhaps a girl will find it."

"A girl?"

She almost laughed at the outrage in his voice. No, on second thought, it was not outrage. It was complete disbelief. Her little brother had a great deal to learn.


**CHARLOTTE ELLIS LOOKED** around the room she had shared

with her two daughters ever since she had been widowed. There was little enough here in this parsonage to hold her. Most of what she treasured was already packed away, ready for the journey ahead of them. She wondered idly what would happen to this house. No doubt some of those grasping Brandts would claim it before the last wagon was out of sight.

The graveyard next door to it might give some people pause, though, and Charlotte felt something akin to real pleasure at the thought that the parsonage might remain empty for just that reason.

Her late unlamented husband had lain in the nearby graveyard these past fourteen years, and she was just as happy to be shut of his memory at last. Her sister expected her to take flowers to his grave every Sunday after services and she had done so, only during the summer, of course, for there were no ready flowers available during the cold springs, the frigid winters, and the bleak autumns. That was fine with Charlotte. Now she would have her summer Sundays free from the onerous chore.

## August 1983

**CHARLIE ELLIS LOOKED** around her room. It didn't even feel new anymore, now that she'd lived here with Daddy and Mommy for such a long time. Six whole weeks. She arranged her three favorite teddy bears just the way she knew they liked to be.

Mommy stuck her head in the door. "Are you almost ready? Can't be late the first day of third grade."

Charlie patted orange-haired Punkin and bright yellow Tink and fluffy black Wooly Bear. "You be good while I'm at school, and don't make too much noise."

On the way to school, Charlie asked, "Mommy? What happened to our old house?"

"The one in Martinsville? I've sold it to a real nice young couple who just moved to town. The Johnsons. They have a little boy named Roger."

"Are we ever going back there?"

"Probably not, honey." Mommy turned left onto the school's

front sidewalk and squeezed Charlie's hand. "You know though, some-day you may want to go back to Martinsville."

"But we can't. You sold our house."

"That house money is going to help pay for your college, Char-lie. And anyway, there are other houses in town."

"But how will—"

"Let's cross that bridge when we come to it."

# 2000

**WE CHATTED DESULTORILY** for a while, and I explained the rules about when to flush and when not to. "If it's yellow, let it mellow," I told them. "If it's brown, flush it down. As you know, there's a com-posting toilet in the powder room"—I gestured behind me to the room tucked underneath the stairs—"and it doesn't need water. Just a scoop of the sawdust from the bucket beside it. If you use one of the bathrooms upstairs, you'll need to use a bucket of water from the bathtub to do the flushing."

"Only if the water fails," Bob said. "For now it should be okay."

Ralph cracked a toilet joke, and Bob added one of his own.

*I do not understand.*

Men, I thought, as Marmalade jumped into my lap. But then I re-membered all the many, many reasons I loved having good men around. That didn't mean I needed to listen to this sophomoric humor. I turned to Ida. "Do you want to head up to the attic with me?"

She patted her husband's knee. "Sure. Why?"

"You know how I've been meaning to clear it out—"

"Yeah. Since the first day you moved in."

I ignored her sarcasm and gathered Marmalade into my arms as I stood. "Well, wouldn't this be a perfect time to check it out and see what's there? We could at least get an idea of where to start."

"Count us out." Ralph nodded at Bob.

"Don't worry," Ida told him. "You two are not invited in the first place."

Ralph didn't even bother to look insulted. "Fine with me."

I went back into the kitchen, set Marmy down next to her food dish, and picked up two of the lanterns we'd parked on the long kitchen table, handing one to Ida. "There should be plenty of light from the eyebrow windows up there, but let's take these just in case."

*I will go with you. I am not hungry now.*

"Sounds good to me."

Before we reached the first landing, though, the front door opened. "We're here," my sister called out.

Ida looked at me and raised her eyebrows. "Didn't I tell you?"

I knew darn well the compost toilet wouldn't handle nine people, and I didn't quite have Bob's faith in the dependability of our generator to run the water pump. Thank goodness we'd filled the tubs for flushing.

"Can we borrow some of your warmth?" Glaze stumbled in along with Madeleine Ames and Sadie Masters, all of them knocking snow and ice crystals from their gloves and hats. They dumped backpacks, canvas totes, carryon bags—Sadie's was neon yellow—and one big suitcase into a haphazard pile. Behind them, Tom Parkman, my sister's fiancé, waved a gloved hand. Glaze pulled off her knitted hat and shook out her prematurely silver hair. I caught a whiff of Glaze's signature scent. She always dabbed vanilla behind her ears.

*Smellsweet always smells good.*

"We brought sandwiches for every—oh! Hey there, Ida. Ralph. Guess we'll have to divide the sandwiches."

"Don't worry about food," I said. "There's plenty of soup."

Glaze muttered something that sounded like *why am I not surprised.* She knew the only things I liked to cook were bread and soup. And my molasses cookies.

"I love your soup," Tom said. Quite a compliment coming as it did from one of the finest chefs I knew. "I called Glaze to see if she was all right, and she said to meet her here. I hope there's enough room." He set down his duffle bag and held up a big tote. "Food," he said unnecessarily.

*I know you brought me some fish.*

Tom bent to scratch Marmalade's head. "Hello, Furball. How's it going?"

*I am well, thank you. WideLap gave me some chicken, but I will be happy to accept the fish I can smell.*

"I brought some salmon and a few other things as well," Tom

said, straightening up. "Hope that's okay."

*Of course it is okay.*

We all laughed when Marmy's loud meow seemed to answer him. He tended to bring her leftovers from his restaurant, and she obviously knew what to expect.

*Of course I do.*

It was going to be wonderful having Tom as an official member of the family.

*He is already a member of my family. I like Fishgiver. He is kind to SmellSweet. And he brings me special treats.*

Although to be honest, Tom felt like family already. I looked beyond him at the ice coating everything in sight. I sure hoped Glaze and Tom's wedding on Friday wouldn't have to be postponed. But if nobody could get to the church because of the weather… Maybe I'd still have a chance to get the dress I really wanted, instead of the second-best one I'd had to buy at Mabel's because somebody—I wish I knew who—had snatched up the beautiful indigo dress I'd had my eye on for months. The only trouble was, whoever had bought it would have to return it first.

"Ralph and I brought a green bean casserole," Ida said.

I pulled myself back from my dress musings. "And a whole wagonload of other food," I added.

Maddy took off her fogged-up glasses and pushed her hair back out of her eyes. "A wagon? How'd you get it through the snow?"

Out of the corner of my eye, I saw Ralph preen a bit, throwing back his shoulders. "Fastened some runners under the wheels," he said. "It worked just fine."

"I love good old ingenuity," Maddy said.

"The trouble was," Ida added, "the runners kept slipping on the ice, and threatened to bowl us over. Finally we just let it slide ahead of us and the darn thing barreled downhill and almost pulled us off our feet."

Ralph spread his hands in a *what can you do* gesture.

"We picked up Sadie on the way here," Maddy said. "We didn't want her hefting logs into that potbellied stove of hers."

"I could have managed," Sadie said. "But this"—she surveyed the faces around her—"seems like much more fun."

I pointed out the box of slipper socks. "Pick a pair, and you can leave your boots on those towels I spread out."

Sadie bent to rummage in her yellow carryall. "If you don't mind, I brought my tennis shoes. I don't want to risk slipping." She brandished one of the shoes. "I haven't worn them outside, so they won't track anything around."

"That's fine, Sadie," I said. The last thing we needed was a fall and a broken hip.

"We turned off Sadie's water," Glaze said, "so her pipes wouldn't burst."

"Good for you," Bob said. "Did you turn off your own water, too?" Of course he'd ask. Glaze and Maddy rented Bob's former house, the one he lived in before he and I got married.

"Does a bear—" Maddy began, but Glaze cut her off.

"Yes. We did."

Bob looked around the room. "What about the rest of you?"

Heads nodded and I breathed a sigh of relief. I'd hate to think of our friends going home to find busted water pipes.

"We still have water here," Bob said, "thanks to our generator and the heat produced by the stove."

"Come on up to the attic with us," I said, happy to change the subject matter away from water and toilets. "Ida and I were just headed that way."

"Sure." Maddy helped Sadie out of her electric yellow coat and slung it over the coatrack. "You're going to put us to work on cleaning up all that mess, right?"

"It's not really a mess," I said. "It's just ... well ... kind of full."

Sadie pulled her yellow cardigan more closely around her ample middle. "I've never been up there, but I'd be willing to bet *full* is an understatement, knowing some of the people who lived in this house before you."

Sadie and her yellow clothes, yellow house, yellow car, yellow accessories, yellow everything. There had to be a story behind it, but I hadn't a clue what it might be. I had thought periodically about asking her, but for some reason I couldn't. When I first met Sadie, I'd thought of her as a slightly ditzy old lady, but as I got to know her over the years, I realized there were hidden depths there. She'd turned into something of a role model for the women of Martinsville, and I had the feeling her reasons for wearing yellow must be incredibly deep.

Sadie was well into her eighties, and she'd lived in Martinsville all her life. "Well," I said, "maybe you can fill us in on who those people were. There's no telling what we'll find."

Maddy wiped her glasses again. "I'm ready."

My sister shivered and spread her wet mittens on one of the towels I'd placed beside the door. "I'd say it's a good thing heat rises."

I studied Glaze for a moment. She didn't look the same without a dog—without Gracie—beside her.

Gracie had wandered into my sister's life one day—obviously lost but in relatively good health, other than being very tired, paw-sore, and hungry—and simply refused to wander out of it. Until the day just three months ago, in September, when her first family found her.

## Saturday, September 23, 2000

**GLAZE AND I** had been taking our usual early Saturday morning walk—the library doesn't open until ten—with Gracie trotting along happily beside Glaze, and Marmalade weaving in and out of the foliage. I've never known a cat who likes to take walks the way Marmalade does.

*You are my person. I need to keep you in my sight.*

Gracie certainly didn't need a leash—she stuck to Glaze like powdered sugar on a doughnut—but Glaze had bought Gracie a whole rainbow array of bright-colored collars and matching leashes. That particular day, Gracie sported bright purple, probably to match Glaze's sweatpants.

Martinsville is a perfect town for walking around in any time of year, but I especially loved the autumn days for a long stroll. As a general rule, fall waits to come to Martinsville until late October, but so far September had been cloudy, with the temperatures well below normal. In fact, the entire summer had been unusually cool. I wore comfortable shoes, a skirt that reached to my mid calf, and a white blouse. I'd thrown a sweater about my shoulders just in case. Glaze had on her usual vibrant colors. That day she'd chosen bright purple sweatpants and a neon yellow blouse. With her prematurely silver hair, she looked like a Johnny Jump-up, although violas had their purple on the top and yellow on the bottom. The air was crisp without being cold, and the trees that lined the street—all the streets—had already begun to turn color, a month earlier than they usually did.

Martinsville lies at the bottom of a dead-end valley alongside the Metoochie River, and the streets running away from the river—all of them named for trees, some of which are varieties that aren't native to Georgia—rise to meet the cliffs that surround the town, except to the north, where the valley is considerably wider. Some of the original inhabitants of the town must have gradually spread out and started farms there. A couple of years ago, that farmland was bought up by developers, and Martinsville could now boast (or complain of, depending on how you looked at it) a suburb of its own—the atrociously named Happy Acres. I'd met only a few of the residents, mostly the ones who had come in to get library cards.

"He had a good library joke," Glaze was saying when I finally tuned back in.

"Library joke?"

She didn't get exasperated with me—at least not usually—when I missed a sentence or two. This time, she just laughed. The joke, whatever it was, must have put her in a good frame of mind. "What was the last thing you remember that I said?"

"Uh ..."

"Right. I was telling you about Radio Ralph's latest kick."

"You never listen to him. I thought you hated him."

Radio Ralph was something of a joke up and down the valley, although there were a lot of people who listened to WRRT. And if they listened to WRRT, Keagan County's very own radio station, then they listened to Radio Ralph Towers, who seemed to be almost the only broadcaster. His so-called news reports tended to be a mishmash of commentary and gossip. His weather reports were a disaster. In fact, when we heard one, we always planned for the opposite. If he said sunny—we took our umbrellas. If he predicted rain, well, then it was time for a picnic.

"Maddy had it on yesterday afternoon and I happened to hear his latest joke."

"What do you mean *latest*?"

"Maddy said he's doing a series of what he calls the Radio Ralph Laugh Lines. Each week he has a different theme. And this week it was libraries."

I groaned.

"That's what I thought, too."

"So what was the library joke?"

"The one from yesterday was," she pitched her voice up an octave or so, "how many librarians does it take to change a light bulb?"

"I don't know. Am I going to regret asking for the answer?"

"Probably."

"Okay. How many?"

"Are you ready for this? It takes six hundred forty-five point five." When I looked blank, she added, "That's the Dewey Decimal classification for light fixtures."

*What does that mean?*

I groaned again as Marmalade let out a squawk.

*That was not a squawk. I asked SmellSweet a question.*

"Glaze?"

"Yeah?"

"Did you ever wonder why Radio Ralph's initials are the same as WRRT's call letters?"

Glaze shook her head, and her hair swung forward from behind her ear. She pushed it back. "His real name's probably Horace James Podunkle, or something equally ridiculous. I'd be willing to bet he made up a name with RRT as the initials."

"Like a pen name?"

"Like an alias. A name like Radio Ralph Towers is absolutely criminal."

I chuckled. It wasn't that funny, but I'd found over the years that conversation between good friends—and I considered my sister a very good friend—was often laced with unexplainable laughter.

"Thursday's laugh line was pretty good as well."

"You mean pretty awful, don't you?"

She ignored my question. "Why did the librarian slip and fall in the library?"

"I have a feeling this one's going to be worse than the last one."

"Right."

"Okay, why did she slip?"

"She was in the non-friction section."

I elbowed Glaze in the ribs. "I hope there aren't any more of them."

*I did not understand it.*

"See," I said, "even Marmy agrees with me."

*I do?*

"I told Maddy to let me know what today's was. I'll be sure to pass it on to you."

We turned left at the bottom of the hill.

Glaze and I—and Gracie …

*And I, too.*

… had just passed Miss Mary's Dance Studio down on Main Street when I heard a shout. "Snookums! Look mom, it's Snookums!"

Gracie's head whipped up from where she'd stopped to investigate something—probably a bug. Gracie liked bugs almost as much as Marmalade did—and she bounded forward so fast she yanked the purple leash from Glaze's hand.

A couple of children piled out of a car that had stopped right in the middle of the street—not such a big deal as you might think, since Martinsville isn't exactly a busy metropolis. In fact, the only other cars in sight were parked along the curb. The two boys ran toward us, arms waving, shouting with joy, and everyone met in a flurry of arms and legs and paws and kisses and big wet dog licks. If we'd had any doubts whatsoever about where Gracie had come from, there couldn't be any question at this point.

The woman driving the car made sure her boys were well out of the way before she pulled into an empty parking space. She walked toward the happy melee, arms outstretched. Gracie—Snookums—broke away from the children long enough to jump up, placing her front paws against the woman's waist. She nuzzled while the woman stroked her tawny head. By this time, the two boys had surrounded her again.

Glaze didn't want to admit, I knew, that she hadn't put up many *Is This Your Dog* posters. In fact, to the best of my knowledge, she hadn't put up any. When Gracie—Snookums—moved into her life, Glaze hadn't wanted to search too diligently for the previous owners, even though she'd spent the first few days saying, "This isn't really my dog." I knew she'd felt a little bit guilty at the time for not even having put an ad in the *Keagan County Record*, our weekly newspaper, but as she and Gracie settled into a comfortable routine, she'd found less and less reason to advertise the dog that had found her. Gracie would have looked so cute on a lost dog poster, with her soft eyes and the brown spots freckling her pink nose.

"I take it you're the ones who found Snookums?" The woman—she looked familiar, and I was pretty sure she had a library card—extended her arm for a warm handshake. "I can't thank you enough. The boys were devastated when they found out Snookums was gone."

Glaze just stood there without saying a word, so I filled in. "Gracie—that's what we call her—showed up one day, hungry and with sore paws." I didn't want to accuse the woman of not taking good enough care of her dog, but I think some of my attitude must have echoed in my voice.

The children were oblivious. They ran up and down the sidewalk, shouting with glee as Gracie romped beside them.

"My husband died of a heart attack seventeen months ago," the mother said, "while the four of us were on vacation at the Grand Canyon. That was traumatic enough for the boys, but then when we finally returned home—we have a house in Happy Acres; we'd only been in it a couple of months—their uncle told us that Snookums had run away."

I'd read *The Incredible Journey*. I knew of dogs that had found their way home against incredible odds. "Do you know why she ran away?"

The mother's face tightened somehow. "My husband insisted that we leave the dog with his brother while we were on vacation. We didn't really have many other options. Our new neighbor at Happy Acres had offered to take care of Snookums, but she had some sort of family emergency the day before we were scheduled to leave. Grant, my brother-in-law, didn't want to drive down the valley from Surreytown twice a day to let Snookums out, so he suggested we let Snookums stay at his house. His backyard is fenced in, so we thought it would be perfectly safe."

*FreckleNose did not like him.*

The woman looked back over her shoulder, and I had the feeling she wanted to be sure the children, who now sat on the curb with the dog between them, weren't close enough to hear. "I've never believed Snookums ran away. I think that once Grant learned his brother—my husband—was dead, he drove her out of town, farther up the valley, and left her beside the road, especially now that you've said her paws were sore when you found her."

Glaze finally said something. "I didn't find her. She found me."

The woman looked at Glaze with sympathy. "Yes. Dogs do that, don't they? We got her from a shelter when she was about two months old. All the puppies were tumbling around playing, but Snookums left the rest of her litter and walked right up to us, as if she knew we were there to take her to her forever home." Her eyes teared up. "We put signs up all over Russell Gap and Surreytown," she said, referring to the two northernmost towns in the valley. "It never occurred to us to put signs way down here. I'm so happy we found her again." She extended her hand, this time toward Glaze. "I'm Linda Dalton, by the way. The boys are Eddie and Seth."

Glaze had gone quiet again, so I gave Linda our names, and then we stood there, looking at the boys and the dog—their dog Snookums. Glaze's dog Gracie. After the first round of enthusiasm was over, the children had settled into quiet stroking. One of the boys had his head nestled against Gracie's shoulder and one arm around her furry chest. The other boy, the younger one, had encircled her middle and sat there on the curb with a lop-sided smile of contentment across his face. Even Gracie—Snookums—looked contented, with her long tongue hanging out the side of her mouth. As I watched, she twisted her head and licked Seth's ear. His giggle was infectious, and I couldn't help but smile. He reached up and rubbed the funny lopsided freckle spot on her nose, as if to reassure himself that she was real.

After a few moments, Linda stirred. "I know you've cared for Snookums—Gracie—all this time. I understand she's ..." she gulped, "she's your dog now."

With howls of outrage, both boys shot to their feet.

"Ma, she's ours!"

"Mommy, no!"

Gracie barked and whirled around, her protective nature ready, but obviously unable to sense where the threat originated. I was reminded of the time not too long ago, shortly after she appeared, when she'd saved Glaze's life.

"Boys, you know better than to act like that." Plowing on despite her sons' objections, she said, "I just hope you might consider letting us visit once in a—" She broke off and laid her hand on Gracie's trembling head. "No. That wouldn't be fair. Snookums wouldn't understand."

"But Snookums wants to go home with us."

"Eddie," his mother said, "Snookums has a new home now."

Seth flung his arms around his mother's waist and raised his face. "Mommy, ple-e-e-ease don't give her away. Not again."

Gracie sat between her two families, looking back and forth, her tongue once more lolling out the side of her mouth.

*FreckleNose has a very long tongue.*

Marmalade let out a loud meow from the hood of Linda's car. She had probably jumped up there to avoid the tramping feet.

*That is right. It is safe here. And warm as well.*

Glaze stepped forward, picked up the dangling end of Gracie's purple leash, and handed it to Eddie. I had the feeling she would have given it to Seth, but the younger boy had buried his face against his mom's tummy. "Snookums is yours," Glaze said. "I understand." But I could tell her heart didn't agree with what her words were saying.

"Really?"

"Yay!" Seth abandoned his mom and threw his arms around the dog once more.

Eddie straightened and turned to my tall silver-haired sister. "Thank you, ma'am. We'll take very good care of her. And we're not going to let Uncle Grant watch her for us any more. Not ever." The determination on his young face was so at odds with his joyful behavior seconds before, it hardly seemed like the same boy.

Linda studied Eddie; I could see the pride oozing out of her. She laid a hand on his shoulder and turned her attention to Glaze. "Are you sure?"

Unable to speak, Glaze nodded.

"Thank you. Thank you so very much." She took a deep breath. "In the car, boys. Let's take Snookums home. We can do our shopping later."

Everyone piled inside, and Marmalade jumped down onto the

sidewalk.

*I want to stay with you.*

Glaze waited to speak—or even to move for that matter—until the car turned around. They made a left onto Pine Street, obviously headed toward Happy Acres with their beloved dog. "If the boy hadn't said *again* ... " She didn't finish her sentence. I caught a whiff of her favorite vanilla perfume as an errant breeze lifted her silver hair from her neck.

Gracie obviously hadn't been mistreated by Linda or her sons; if she had, I couldn't imagine the dog would have been so overjoyed to be reunited with the children. But now didn't seem like the right time to mention that to Glaze, especially since the dog hadn't even said good-bye.

*It is not the fault of FreckleNose. She did not know they would take her away from SmellSweet.*

We finished our walk without any talking ...

*That is not right. You and SmellSweet were silent. I spent some time mentioning that I would miss FreckleNose. She was warm to lie on top of.*

... with Marmalade purring noisily beside us.

*Noisy? You think I am noisy?*

Most Saturdays Glaze and I separate once we circle back to Second Street. She turns right to head to her house on Upper Sweetgum and I turn left to walk to the library. But that day I turned to the right along with Glaze, and she didn't even seem to notice.

As I walked with her all the way to the house she shared with Maddy Ames, I was sure she was stewing about losing Gracie, but I couldn't seem to focus on her loss. I had problems of my own.

*I would help you with them if I could.*

For one thing, I was thoroughly ticked off with Clara Martin. I'd already scheduled all three of my Petunias to work that day so I'd be free to prepare a report for the first meeting of the new library board the following Tuesday evening. Usually only two of my Petunias worked at a time.

*And me. I am always at work, making sure there are no intruders.*

Marmalade was particularly noisy with her loud purr. I suppose I should mention that she's been the not-so-official exterminator at the library ever since she wandered in off the street one day just a few weeks before I was hired, and began to eliminate the mice that had overrun the old mansion.

*It is my job.*

But I had no time to think about mouse patrol. I had no idea what the board would be asking me, so I had to have all the information available and well organized just in case. Clara had already requested a list of all the major donations. That was okay. It wouldn't take long to list everything. I just hoped I didn't forget anybody.

The town council, in their ineffable wisdom, had decided the previous month that there needed to be an official Board to oversee the library. I was fairly certain the idea hadn't come from any of the council members. It was Clara Martin, wife of Hubbard Martin, the chair of the town council, who wanted to run something else in town besides the dozen or so committees she already headed. There had always been a Martin—a direct descendent of Homer Martin who founded the town back in 1745—serving as council chair for as long as there'd been a town council. It wasn't written down as any sort of rule, as far as I knew, but it always happened like that, always with the oldest son taking over upon the death of the father.

For years, Clara Martin had been the one really running the town, despite how Hubbard had thought he was in charge. I remember wondering that day at the Town Council meeting, just what would happen if Hubbard had a fatal heart attack. Would the town name Clara as interim chair? Their son, in his early teens, was too young to take over the leadership, and anyway, he was a real loser, sullen, barely able to express himself in complete sentences and with a built-in slouch so bad he looked like a capital S when viewed from the side. His mouth generally hung open. Not that I was biased against him.

*Yes you are.*

If anything happened to Hubbard, I thought, Clara wouldn't even wait for official sanction. She'd just step right in and then it would take a special election to pry her out of the job. There wasn't anyone on the council who had the guts to stand up to her determination.

At any rate, once Clara had gotten the go-ahead to form the library board—a paid position, no less—she'd appointed two of what I assumed were her cronies. I didn't know Charlotte Ellis well, but to the best of my knowledge she'd never done anything objectionable. Not that I had anything against her, but I couldn't for the life of me understand anybody who didn't get a library card the second they moved into a new community. As far as I knew, Charlotte had lived here for two or three years already, but she hadn't come to the library until just a month ago. Now, I ask you, was somebody like that going to be a good addition to the board? Okay, so maybe I did hold that against her.

From what I'd heard, she was born in Martinsville and left when she was a kid. I'd gotten the impression that she had a mind of her own—and I hoped Clara wouldn't be able to dominate her. Charlotte was still fairly young. Around thirty, I guessed, but I had no way to know for sure unless I asked her. And I wasn't about to do that. I wondered, though, if she would be simply assertive or downright obnoxious. Only time would tell. I told myself to quit complaining. She might be a perfectly nice person. I needed to give her the benefit of the doubt.

Like most of the Ellis women down through the years, she'd never married. Bob had told me once that the "Ellis Girls," as they were known, had, over the years, been something of a town embarrassment. They kept churning out children—always daughters, never sons—always without what used to be called benefit of clergy, and always without any indication of who the fathers might be. But Charlotte was the last "Ellis Girl" left, and she didn't have any children, as far as I knew.

The other Board member appointed by Clara was Anita Foley, wife of the town dentist. I knew nothing about her either, other than the fact that she seemed pleasant enough when I ran into her in the grocery store or on the street. And she did have a library card, so that was in her favor.

*She kicked me once when you were not here.*

Marmalade let out a little yowl just then, but I was too wrapped up in my own thoughts to pay much attention to her. I hoped Anita wasn't anything like her brother, Radio Ralph Towers, our completely inept weatherman. There was a little voice inside me, though, that said if Clara had appointed Anita, then Clara probably thought she could count on Anita to rubber-stamp everything Clara wanted to do.

*Why would she rub or stamp?*

I had to admit that some of what Clara did, like overseeing the garden plantings around the gazebo in the town park, wasn't harmful—although the rest of the garden club members could have handled the plant choices perfectly well—but I couldn't see what good a library board would do. I already had my three elderly but incredibly efficient volunteers who were involved in every part of the library's business.

I called them my Petunias, because the first time I met them, when they volunteered to help me organize the new town library, they'd all three been wearing floral print dresses.

The three of them had all lived here their entire lives, and they knew everything there was to know about the town. They'd served as a sort of unofficial board from the very beginning, advising me about what people liked and didn't like, what they expected or not, and even what colors to paint the various rooms.

Green was for the gardening and nature books, dark blue for astronomy and science, red for self-help, beige for the biographies. The old mansion was broken up into a kazillion small rooms, and we'd just divided the Dewey decimal system accordingly. For fiction, we had three different areas. A lavender room was set aside for mysteries and the spacious pink room for romances. We had a ton of those. The elderly Mrs. Millicent swore the steaminess kept her old bones warm. Then there was the large central area on the second floor for general fiction. At the end of the day, we always had to check each room carefully to be sure nobody had fallen asleep in one of the comfortable chairs or had hidden out in any of the alcoves.

*I always help you. I am very good at finding children hiding behind the chairs and tables.*

All the paint and all the books, so far, had been donated, on top of the houseful—mansion-full—that came with the Millicent family's original bequest of the mansion and all its contents to the town "to be used as a fine town library." If truth be told, there wasn't much of a budget at all. My minuscule part-time salary and the monthly expenses of the mansion for water and electricity were paid through the town treasury. Office supplies and toilet paper used up what little monthly allotment the library had been granted. Margaret Casperson, the wealthiest woman in town—the wealthiest person in all of Georgia for that matter—had donated the new computers, which formed absolutely the most up-to-date checkout system available, now that we were headed into the twenty-first century, and she had earmarked a generous monthly donation for buying new books. So what on earth was a board going to accomplish that wasn't already being done?

To top it all off, Clara had decided the board meetings would be held on Tuesday nights, the last Tuesday of each month. Tuesday was my tap dance class. I was already one of the slowest ones in the class—Sadie at age eighty-something could dance circles around me, and here I was going to have to miss one class a month. I was fairly sure Clara had scheduled the meetings on Tuesdays just to spite me.

And how on earth had Clara managed to wrangle an agreement from our town council—tightwads that they usually were—to pay the board members? At least the town wrote the checks, so the money didn't have to come from my budget.

"Thanks for walking with me."

*You are welcome.*

I had to shake myself. When I get on autopilot like that, I flat forget what's going on around me. I took a moment to focus on my sister, who had stopped at the end of the short path that led to her front door. She didn't look happy about walking inside by herself.

*I will stay with SmellSweet. She can give me some catnip. She laughs when I roll in it.*

Marmalade let out a squawk …

*Squawk?*

… and preceded Glaze up the path and onto the steps to the small front porch. My sister turned to me, and I could see the tears beginning to well in those luminous green eyes of hers. "I'll be okay," she said. "I just need some time to get used to the idea."

I thought about telling her that when Linda came into the library next time, I'd be sure to ask how Gracie was doing, but instead I just said, "I'm sure Gracie—Snookums—will be okay."

"I know that," she snapped. She turned on her heels, stomped up the rest of the steps, and opened the door for Marmalade, who let out one of her long meows before she disappeared inside.

*Smellsweet is unhappy for now, but she will be happy soon. She walked FreckleNose because she had to, but she likes cats better than dogs. We do not have to be walked.*

I couldn't be upset with my sister. Not when her heart was breaking.

Of course, now that she and Tom were officially engaged, maybe her broken heart would mend faster.


## December 2000


**"BISCUIT?" I TURNED** to find Ida looking at me with a question in her eyes. Over her shoulder I could see the ice storm raging outside the living room windows. "Are you here with us or did you go somewhere else?"

"La-la land," my sister said, but I could hear the affection in her voice. She'd definitely done a lot of healing since losing Gracie. Of course, Tom helped her attitude a lot.

"Come on, ladies," I said. "We're going to explore!" I bent to retie Sadie's yellow shoelaces—they always seemed to be coming undone.

*That is why I call her LooseLaces.*

It was a wonder she hadn't tripped on them countless times. I sure didn't want the first time to be while she was climbing my stairs. Marmalade ran up the stairs in front of us. Thank goodness she was smart enough to stay out from underfoot.

*Of course I am. I would never trip anyone.*

As I climbed that first flight of stairs ahead of my friends, I thought about how much I enjoyed having Marmalade around.

*I enjoy being here with you, too.*

It had taken me a long time to get used to seeing Glaze without Gracie at her side. I know I'd hate to face a day without Marmalade.

*I will not leave you.*

I couldn't imagine life without her, the way she always purrs as if she's talking to me, the way she warms my lap during the day and my neck at night.

*I like to snuggle with you and SoftFoot.*

I wondered for a moment just how many other pets had lived here in this old house.

*Pets? You think I am a pet?*

She let out a yowl just then, and I realized I don't really think of her as a pet. More like a comforting companion.

*Thank you.*

A rather chatty companion.

*But you do not listen.*

Still, I wondered how many other dogs and cats had called this home. Barley, of course. He was the elderly dog that belonged to Elizabeth Hoskins, the woman I'd bought the house from.

*His body is buried in the back yard near the fence. I watched her bury him.*

But before Barley, I had no idea. Surely there must have been dozens of animals that ran up and down these stairs.

How sad that there was no way ever to know about them.

I took a detour when I reached the second floor. "I'm going to draw all the curtains closed to conserve heat. I should have done it early this morning."

"Or last night," Glaze said. She and Maddy headed for the guest rooms at the end of the long hallway. Ida went with Sadie over to the big windows in the sewing room. I love the way friends just jump in when something needs to be accomplished. I ducked into my puzzle room—I used it for other things of course …

*My favorite toys are on top of the bookcase.*

… but I'd spent so much time in there working on crossword puzzles after Diane Marie died, I always thought of it as my puzzle room.

*You could spin my feather toy around for me if you want to.*

I thought briefly about having a short playtime with Marmalade. She loves the feather toy Bob made for her. In fact, we have to keep it tucked high on the top of the bookcase so she won't rip it to shreds.

*I would not tear it apart. I like it too much.*

Once everything was snug on the second floor—and once I'd explained the toilet procedure to the newcomers—I propped open the door to the flight of stairs that headed up into the attic. "The stairs are creaky," I said, "but they're safe. Just watch your footing."

It wasn't as dark up there as you'd think it would be. Eyebrow windows set into the roof along the front and back of the house flooded the space with winter light. Surely they weren't part of the original architecture. I doubted eyebrow windows had been invented back whenever this house was built. The roof must have been replaced a time or two, and that was probably when they'd been installed. Still, we'd need the lanterns if the clouds thickened much more.

A couple of card tables, their spindly legs folded in as if they'd been relegated to "time out," leaned against the wall off to the right of the stairs, and I saw another three farther down the way. Why would anyone need five card tables? Maybe a bridge club? "Feel free to poke around," I said as the women spread out, weaving among the old trunks and dressers and stacks of miscellaneous items.

Glaze crossed her arms. "There doesn't seem to be much organization here."

"Humph!" Ida drew her fingers across the top of an old trunk, leaving a trail in the dust. "There isn't *any* organization here."

The sight of all that … that stuff was a bit daunting, I had to admit. Not only were there numerous trunks and boxes, but a lot of items weren't packed up in any way. The tops of several rickety-looking dressers were piled high with unidentifiable jumbles. I walked over to one of them and brushed aside a hodgepodge of costume jewelry. An old penny whistle caught my eye, so I picked it up and blew into it. Of course, it let out a piercing shriek, which brought all conversation behind me to a stop.

"Sorry," I said. "Couldn't resist it."

Maddy stepped closer to me. "Could I see it?"

"Sure."

She lifted it to her lips and played a merry little tune.

Naturally, we all applauded.

# November 1866

**JOSH HAWLEY'S MARE** was not quite lame, but she had slowed down so much, Josh thought perhaps the nag was on her last legs. He wished he could have stolen a better animal, but there were so few available in the aftermath of the war. He felt bad for the man who now would have to walk, but his own need had been far greater. Or so he had reasoned.

He spotted a wavering light between the heavy branches of the trees ahead of him. Perhaps the farmhouse he was looking for. Alpheus had told him it was the first he would come to after the wide bend in the river below Braetonburg. The thought of warm food and a more welcoming bed than the rough dirt he had been sleeping on for the past months was enough to spur him onward, and his horse may have sensed the smell of sweet hay ahead, for she picked up her pace a tiny bit, her feet squelching through the mud that had formed on the trail as soon as a light rain began falling an hour before.

Josh shifted the pack he carried on his back. It was lighter even than the threadbare rolled blanket that spanned the horse's narrow shanks, but still it had rubbed a raw spot on one of his bony shoulders, and he longed to be shut of it.

He pulled the horse to a stop as soon as they broke from under the dubious shelter of the overhanging trees. It would not do to approach too closely without warning of some sort, and in the ever-decreasing light of dusk, whoever was in the cabin would want to see him clearly.

"Halloo, the house!" His voice came out as little more than a croak. That was what came of chilly autumn nights and a soggy seat on a near-useless horse. He cleared his throat and tried again. "Halloo!"

A curtain twitched, and Josh had to steel himself not to duck. They had no reason to trust him, but Alpheus had sworn they were peaceful, so Josh sat there unmoving, although he studied the window opening for any sign of a rifle. The horse snorted and swayed her head from side to side as if she wanted to toss it but was just too weary. He knew exactly how she felt.

A young woman peered from the door and studied him. "What be you wanting, stranger?"

He lifted his hands slowly to show they were empty. "I come with a message from your brother, Alpheus Hoskins, for you and your mother, and your brother Lemuel."

She looked confused, and he added, "That is, if you be Miss Henrietta Hoskins." Alpheus had drilled him on the names repeatedly, and Josh had repeated them to himself most of the way from Illinois, over the four months it had taken him to travel this far.

He could still almost hear his cellmate's voice. One of fifty-four men crammed into that rat-infested room. "Lemuel wanted to come with me to sign on as a drummer boy," Alpheus had told him, "but I convinced him he would be the man of the house and was needed to care for his sister and our mother."

Josh watched as a skinny boy—he had to be Lemuel—stepped in front of Miss Henrietta. "Where is Alpheus?" He sounded suspicious. Good for him, thought Josh. It did not do to trust a stranger in these times. Josh could see that the boy held something, probably a knife, hidden behind his thin legs.

"If it be okay with you, might I bring my horse a bit closer so I need not shout?"

The brother and sister looked at each other—a swift glance, but Josh could sense an entire conversation in it.

*Do you think it will be safe, sister?*

*He looks not like a brigand.*

*How would we know?*

*He knows our brother's name and our names as well.*

"Aye," the boy said, "but keep your hands in sight and come slow."

Josh chuckled a bit. "I doubt this old bag of bones could go any faster even if I spurred her, and"—he spread one foot in its stirrup away from the horse's side—"as you can see, I have no spurs left. They were stolen from me by the soldiers that took your brother and me prisoner."

Miss Henrietta put her hand over her mouth and took a step forward.

By this time Josh had reached the mounting block near the front door. Keeping his empty hands plainly in view, he eased himself from the saddle, just as the rain, which had been a mere drizzle, began to fall in earnest.

"You may put your horse in the barn." She indicated the sturdy structure behind the house. "There is fresh hay and clean straw."

"I thank you."

"We have no oats."

"This nag has been eating naught but roadside grass. She will no doubt be delighted with hay, and even more so with a roof over her miserable head."

By the time Josh stepped inside the snug cabin, he was thoroughly drenched, and he paused politely just inside the door to give his clothes a chance to drip off some of the excess moisture. He pulled his limp hat from his narrow head and shrugged off the pack, dropping it onto the floor beside a sturdy chest.

"There is food," Henrietta said. "There is not a great deal of it, but you are welcome to share what we do have, and you are welcome to sleep in the barn." She gestured across the small room. "Come, sit yourself down near the fire, and eat." She said nothing about her brother.

Josh thought perhaps she was afraid to hear the news he carried—as well she might be.

He dropped gratefully onto the bench beside the table, glad to have found shelter, glad to have located this hidden valley in the first place. If Alpheus had not given him such explicit directions, he doubted he ever could have found it. He had hardly dared enter that narrow gap in the cliffs north of here. It was wide enough for two wagons to pass side by side, but forbidding enough to daunt anyone. He inhaled the scent of pottage rising from the bowl Miss Henrietta had placed before him. Real food. Food without vermin crawling through it. He could barely restrain himself to wait for the blessing to be said.

The elderly mother—she must have been at least forty—never spoke a word during the meal, but sat like one turned to a clod of earth. Lemuel was the one who finally asked the question. "What can you tell us about Alpheus?"

"Is he living?" Miss Henrietta had little hope in her voice, but Josh could hear that she still held just a hint of possibility. "Or have you come with bad news?"

Josh dropped his eyes. "He promised me that if he made it out and I didn't, he would tell my family. And I, uh"—he spread his hands in a helpless gesture—"I promised him the same." He averted his eyes even further so he would not have to watch the tears filling Miss Henrietta's eyes.

He reached into his shirt pocket and pulled out a lump of something wrapped in a stained kerchief and handed it to the boy. "They … the ones who captured us … stole everything else, but they did not seem to want this. Alpheus said he wanted you to have it."

Lemuel unfolded the cloth carefully and wiped the back of his hand across his eyes. "His tin whistle." He held it out for his mother to see, and she reached a tentative hand to touch it briefly before she subsided back into a shrunken silence.

Miss Henrietta placed her fingertips on her lips. "Was he … did he die peacefully?"

Josh did not have the heart to tell her what it had really been like at Alton prison. The smallpox, the bloody flux, the starving and freezing men in the winter, the starving men and the ravenous insects in the summer, the persistent rats all year long. His brow furrowed and he took a deep breath. "His last words were of the three of you, and his last breath was peaceful." That first part was true, but he hoped he would be forgiven for the second part. That was about the biggest lie he had ever told.

## 2000

**NEXT TO WHERE** the penny whistle had been was a dilapidated old straw hat with a green ribbon tied around the crown. It looked like it had definitely seen better days. I passed it by and inspected the pile of necklaces. I tried to unravel them, but got the chains more tangled up than before. I'd be willing to bet a bevy of little girls played dress-up with all these things over the years. Under the necklaces was a weighty pocket watch attached to a chain.

Marmalade levitated onto the dresser and poked her nose at the cloudy reflection in the mirror.

*There is another cat in there, but it does not smell like a cat.*

That poor mirror, I thought. It looked like countless generations had mistreated it. I could see nicks and scratches all up and down the mirror edge. Marmalade turned away from the mirror, bent her head, and nuzzled one particular pendant that, when I inspected it more carefully, looked like old tarnished silver.

*It smells of sadness.*

I loosed it carefully from the rest, picked it up, and turned it over. There were initials of some sort on the back, but I couldn't make them out, other than what I thought was an S, and maybe an H.

## December 1811

**ROSE HASTINGS NEVER** imagined she would be willing someday to give up the silver pendant that was a treasured remembrance of her mother. Rose had been only thirteen when her mother died giving birth to a stillborn child. Now, on the eve before Rose's wedding, she sat quietly in the room she shared with one of her three surviving sisters and unclasped the hook. She studied the engraving on the back. ASH woven together with RSH.

Astaline Shipleigh Hastings had, as far as Rose knew, loved Reuben Sewell Hastings for her entire life. Rose could recall so clearly the times she had spied on her parents as they held hands in the garden at the end of a long day, her mother leaning her head gracefully against Papa's broad shoulders. The pendant was a constant reminder of that love, and Rose had worn it every day since her mother's death. She could not bear to part with it now, but Baxter Hoskins, the man she would marry in just a few hours, held a deep belief that jewelry was not only an extravagance, but an offense against God.

She did wonder sometimes why she had agreed to marry him. Several of her friends had told her it was bad luck to marry a man with the same last initial as one's own. Rose thought that was naught but a fanciful idea, but Baxter's strait-laced approach to life had given her pause at times. Still, he had a broad smile and was like to be a good provider and a kind father to whatever children they had.

North House, the home he shared with his mother, two sisters, and three brothers was small, dark, and inconveniently placed, being far up the valley from the town, almost closer to Braetonburg. Rose would miss her family, although she knew they would visit frequently. She would miss this house she had grown up in. The house she had been born in, in fact. It was roomy enough for a dozen or more children—Rose had always loved children. She and her three younger sisters and two brothers had not filled the house, although they had done their best to keep it lively! She took a deep breath. The death of Mary Etta and Electa so long ago still caused her heart to feel pain. Mary Etta in particular had been a favorite of hers—such a bright, happy child.

She often wished she could have seen the house when her great-great grandfather Robert Hastings, the innkeeper, had first built it, soon after the founding of Martinsville. So few travelers came this way, of course, the house had been used more as a pub than an inn, but Robert must have been ever hopeful, for he had furnished the place with beds aplenty.

She opened the hinged lid on the pendant and gazed at the miniatures of her parents, painted with what must have been a brush with only two or three hairs, the lines were so delicate. She counted backwards and found that she was a year older now than her mother had been when these portraits were made just after her marriage to Papa.

It should have been Mary Etta or Electa who received this, Rose thought, remembering her older sisters, the ones who died of the Fever within a few days of each other, leaving Rose as the eldest.

Rose studied the portrait of her father with his fine cheekbones, strangely at odds with the rounded nose he sported. Everyone called it the Hastings nose, for his father and grandfather had been encumbered with the same shaped appendage. When she looked at her own reflection in the white wood-framed mirror atop her dresser, she breathed a thankful sigh that her own nose was like that of her mother. The nose passed through the generations from father to son, apparently. Both her brothers had that same nose. Tomorrow, she would become a Hoskins. She hoped that any sons she bore would favor her own nose or that of Baxter.

The house was singularly quiet. Her brothers had both hared off to the Wild West the previous year, intent upon becoming cowboys. Nobody in the family had heard a word of them since that first letter saying they had arrived in the town of New Madrid near the Mississippi River and were staying at the boarding house of the Widow Parsons. They had not bothered to answer any of her letters to them.

She turned and gazed at the bed where she had slept with Lilian, her youngest sister, ever since Mary Etta and Electa died. How strange to think that tomorrow morning she would wake a married woman next to Baxter. She hoped Lilian would not miss her too much. She closed the pendant reluctantly and considered which of her sisters she must give it to.

None of them, she finally decided. They would argue over the right. She of course had been entitled to the pendant upon the death of their mother, for Rose had been the eldest surviving child. But the next in line were the twins. Emma and Caroline could never agree on anything, not even on which one of them had been born first. The midwife attending their birth had said Emma was first, while Aunt Julietta insisted it had been Caroline.

Rose remembered how the two girls had fought over the set of hair combs their mother had left when she died. One of the combs had a broken tooth, and the twins quarreled constantly over which of them deserved the unblemished ornament and which would have to make do with the damaged one, until finally the remaining intact hair comb had been broken during one of the girls' numerous quarrels.

She wondered what to do with the two other items she treasured, but to which she knew Baxter would take exception. The intricate basket fashioned from bundles of long pine needles that was given her by her father and the rabbit fur muff from her Aunt Lydia. She still remembered the day Aunt Lydia gave her the muff. She had tucked a note inside it. Rose could not recall just where the note had gone. Surely she would have kept it? If she closed her eyes, she could almost see her Aunt Lydia's rounded writing.

*October 3*
*My dearest Niece,*

*Although I love my sons with all my heart, they are not liable to appreciate my passing on their grandmother's muff to them. My mother was your grandmother, of course, so you, as the eldest living granddaughter, should be the one to use your grandmother's muff. It was quite precious to her. I believe it was a gift to her on her 16th birthday from her grandmother, although I may very well have the story mixed up.*

*If you look closely, deep inside, you will find her initials MD for Margaret DeWitt, sewn there by her grandmother. Mama added the H for Hastings soon after she married your grandfather.*

Giving up any hope of finding the note, Rose picked up the basket and the muff and closed her fist around the silver pendant, then headed for the attic. She would place the necklace there, perhaps beneath one of the many hatboxes that littered the place, and then she would not have to make a decision. The muff and basket could go into one of the many drawers.

At the base of the attic stairs, though, she paused. The tremors that had shaken the house last night and had even caused the church bell to ring, waking everyone in the house, would surely not occur again. Not while she was on those stairs. She knew they were as sturdy as the rest of Beechnut house, but the thought of being shaken off her feet as she ascended or descended made her think twice about her errand.

Telling herself not to be a silly goose, she started firmly upward. The muff, the basket, and her mother's lovely necklace needed to be placed where they would be safe from prying eyes.

**OVER THE NEXT** few years, her sisters came of age and went to husbands of their own, and, of course, her brothers were gone.

So when Papa began to fail, he deeded the house to Baxter. Baxter was not averse to moving into such a fine house. Apparently fine houses, unlike fine jewelry, did not offend the sensibility of Baxter's Heavenly Father.

Rose nursed her father until his death seven years later, but, except for just one time, she never again set foot in the attic, lest the lure of her mother's lovely pendant and the soft warmth of the rabbit fur muff should cause her to disobey her husband's edict against jewelry and any sort of what he called frippery.

On that one and only time, she crept from bed one night after Baxter was snoring loudly, and took his pocket watch, the one he had inherited from his father. He treasured it as much as Rose had treasured her mother's silver pendant. She hid it in the drawer under her spare apron. The next morning, she busied herself with preparing his breakfast and did not say much when he questioned her except, "I should think you would be more careful with something you value so highly."

When he finally left the house in a sour mood, she carried the watch to the attic and placed it on the floor behind an old trunk. Let her grandchildren or great-grandchildren find it someday and wonder where it had come from.

## 2000

**I CARRIED THE** pendant over to the light of one of the windows where I made out an A, an S, an H, and what I thought was probably an R. Lovely thing. All it needs, I thought, is a bit of polish to look like new.

"What do you have there?"

I handed it to my sister. "Pretty, isn't it?"

She nodded and ran her finger around the oval rim. "Did you open it?"

"Open it? What do you mean?"

"There's some sort of catch here." She fiddled with it for a moment and I heard a tiny *snick* as the cover sprang open. Two miniature portraits nestled side by side—a dark-haired woman and a large-nosed sandy-haired man. "I wonder who they are."

"The necklace was just sitting in a jumbled-up pile." I nodded toward the dresser. "I thought at first it was all just costume jewelry."

*I showed this to you.*

I thought about it. "I might not have noticed it if it hadn't been for Marmalade."

"I'd keep this safe, if I were you." She handed it to me, closed my fingers around it, and turned away. "Let's see if we can find any more treasures up here."

*I can help!*

I went back and rummaged through the hodgepodge of necklaces, but nothing else seemed to be of any particular interest. I slipped the pendant into my pocket, but then on impulse took it back out and fastened it around my neck, wondering as I did so why nobody had treasured it enough to keep it in a jewelry box. And why consign it to the attic?

When I bent to take another look at the old pocket watch, the pendant swung forward and clanked against the dresser, so I tucked it inside my sweater to keep it safe and out of the way. I slipped the watch into the deep side pocket of my fleece vest. Bob would be interested in it, I was sure.

Next to this dresser was a rather lovely white one. Too bad I hadn't known it was up here. I could have used it in one of the guest rooms—the one where Ida and Ralph would be sleeping, perhaps, although I'd need to replace the clouded-over mirror. I slid open the top drawer, wondering if I might find a treasure of some sort in there, but it was empty.

I glanced around at the rest of the room. I saw a hula-hoop propped in the gloom of the back corner at the far end of the cavernous space. Nearby, there were a number of lamps, an old desk, and several bed frames with no mattresses. I lifted the top of a desiccated shoebox and found it full of rocks. Rocks? A twisted coat hanger lay beside the box, too bent out of shape ever to be of much value. A deep cast iron skillet sat next to a pair of ice skates on the floor near my feet. Ice skates? In Georgia? The dark brown leather was in terrible shape, all dry and cracked, and the finish on the runners was dull and pitted. I shoved them—and the skillet, and the box of rocks—in back of a lovely old cheval mirror, so nobody would trip on them. I'd noticed the mirror the very first time I ever peeked up here, but the glass surface was dim with age, although not as bad as the mirror on that first dresser. I probably should have taken it up to Garner Creek or Russell Gap and replaced the mirror. Surely you could get mirrors cut to fit a tall oval shape like that? Or maybe Frank Snelling at the Frame Shop could point me in the right direction. After the ice storm was over.

"At least there don't seem to be any cobwebs," Glaze said.

*That is because I eat the spider webs. They are very tasty.*

Marmalade let out one of her long, complicated, loud meows. She so often sounded like she was commenting on a conversation. I secretly thought she could understand some of what we said …

*That is because I do understand.*

… and I knew Bob felt the same way. But I suppose anyone who's ever been owned by a cat thinks the same thing.

*They do if they are smart.*

"I think it looks wonderful," Maddy said. "I can almost imagine a murder up here. This would be a perfect place."

Glaze hummed that eerie theme from *Jaws.* "What do you mean *almost*? You've probably got it halfway plotted already."

"Is my attic going to show up in your next thriller, Maddy?"

She grimaced. "Ever since Glaze hired Dee and me, I've been too busy to do much writing." She gazed around the enormous space. "Still, this just might spawn some new ideas."

"While you're spawning," Ida drawled with an exaggerated southern accent, "let's get some work done." She picked a hatbox from off the top of a stack of round boxes and opened it. I could see the bedraggled end of a white feather poking through some tissue paper. She pulled out the limp hat and placed it on her head. "What do you think? Fashion statement of the year?"

*I will play with the feather if you will give it to me.*

Marmalade commented in her catly way, and Glaze shook her head, but not without some compassion. "That hat is really pathetic, Ida. I wonder why anyone ever saved it?" She shook her head again and bent over a near-by trunk.


# 1882


**CANDACE SURRATT'S FRAIL** fingers hovered over the quilt drawn up to her chin. "I want ..." she said, but her voice was barely more than a whisper.

Her younger sister, Frances Surratt Endicott, whom everyone called Fan, bent closer to hear Candace. Two pins fell from her elaborate hairdo. Fan was a logical nickname for two reasons—Fan was short for Frances, but even more, for all her long life Fan had always seemed to flutter everywhere she went, usually dropping hairpins along the way. "What did you want, dear?"

"My hat. I want..."—Candace's voice cracked with the effort—"... to be buried in my hat."

But Fan didn't hear that last part. She had risen to lift the hatbox down from the top shelf of an elaborate armoire that had, as their sister Emily often said, seen better days. "Here you are dear. Here is your hat." She moved back to her chair and balanced the hatbox on her lap. "I remember when you bought this hat, that time you spent in Atlanta helping Aunt Florence after cousin Walter was born." She lifted the lid and fluffed at the bedraggled plume, no longer nearly as white as it had been when Candace bought the hat so many years ago. "Poor little hat. It has lost some of its bounce, has it not?"

Across the room, the youngest of the three sisters let out a strangled wheeze. "Of course it has lost its bounce. She has worn it every time she walked out of this house for the past thirty years."

"Forty-two," Candace croaked.

Candace and Fan and Emily were something of an anomaly in

Martinsville. At a time when most women were dead before their fiftieth birthdays, these three had lived into their seventies.

Fan smiled at Candace. Emily continued her tirade. "It's embarrassing, having a sister who won't even consider a new hat. Everybody talks about it."

"Only when you point it out to them, Emily." Fan's voice for once was firm.

Candace paid no attention to them. For a moment, she was back in the sun-washed streets of Atlanta, preening in her new hat. She would have paid for it herself, although it would have emptied her reticule, but Aunt Florence had tisked at her. "Put your money away, child. Let me buy the hat. You have been such a help to me these last three months. I will be right sorry to see you go tomorrow."

Candace was always amazed that Aunt Florence called her *child*. After all, Candace was almost thirty at the time, and Aunt Florence was barely forty-two.

"Thank you," Candace said. "I will be sorry to leave, Aunt." Candace was not sure how much help she had been. The governess did everything that needed to be done for the new baby and the other seven children as well. Mostly, she had just kept Aunt Florence company. Aunt Florence did love to gad about, showing Candace "her" city. Candace had loved Atlanta. They had ridden almost every day in Aunt's open carriage along the wide streets, although Candace did wish there had been more trees lining them, the way there were in Martinsville. Still, Atlanta was a young town.

Aunt knew everyone in the city it seemed and was constantly waving to this person and nodding at that carriage and smiling right and left, like a queen. The weather, Candace remembered, had been perfect. There was no rain to make the streets muddy, and a gentle breeze every day kept the weather fairly mild. Aunt had even taken her to see an opera, performed on a raised platform in the front room of the White Hall Inn and Tavern.

Candace had worn an almost-new gown, the color of ripe raspberries, that Aunt Florence had had made over so it fit her like … like a queen's dress.

Candace was not particularly musical—Fan and Emily were the ones with lovely singing voices—but even so, she had enjoyed the experience, although she could have done without that soprano who had a voice that would have shattered an iron skillet if there had been one available.

As they left after the performance, Candace had seen the most glorious young man, about her own age, with a sweep of blond hair under his dashing top hat. He carried a gold-tipped walking stick with a golden lion's-head handle. At least, Candace assumed it was gold. Real gold.

He walked past, almost brushing against her wide skirt, but did not even give her a second glance.

Candace's wrinkled body began to quiver, but she was not aware of it. Instead, she remembered that last day, at the train station, when the young golden-haired god—for so she thought of him—came up to her as she waited for her aunt who had turned aside to greet someone, took her hand, and said, "I simply must kiss the hand of a lovely young woman wearing so fetching a hat."

"My, my hat?" Candace practically stuttered at such a stunning turn of events. She had never had her hand kissed. And she had never been this close to such a thoroughly handsome man. Nor had she ever known a man to be so bold. Before she could say anything more, ask his name, introduce herself, her aunt had appeared and whisked her away.

"I know who that is," Aunt Florence said, "and I know of his family." She sniffed derisively. "You will not be well-served by speaking to him. It was most improper of him to have approached you without having first been introduced."

Despite all the wheedling and coaxing Candace could contrive, Aunt would not say another word. As Candace boarded the train, she looked back over the crowd. He stood next to an elderly couple—probably his parents. He must have met them arriving from somewhere. He lifted his hand to his head, pointing as if to a hat, and then blew her a kiss. Just then, the fluffy white plume caught a stray breeze and swayed until its end tickled her nose. It felt almost like the kiss had jostled her new hat as it winged its way to her cheek. Or her lips. She turned onto the train car's platform, blushing, and dove into the darkness of the coach. As soon as she reached her compartment, she looked out her window, and he bowed to her. When the train began to roll, Aunt Florence was there on the platform, but Candace failed to see her. All she saw was the young man's ethereal smile.

When he was out of sight, she swore she would never wear another hat as long as she lived.

Candace moaned, interrupting her sisters' argument. "Bury me in my …" she said, but her voice trailed away.

Fan, stricken, looked at Emily.

"It is bound to happen sooner or later." Emily studied her first-born sister. "It looks as if it is going to be sooner."

**IT *WAS* SOONER**. Just three days later. Fan barely had a chance to say goodbye before Candace slipped away.

It did not take them long, after the funeral, to clean out their sister's room on the top floor of the house on Fifth Street where Fan and her husband had lived for more than forty years.

Emily poked through the contents of the small jewelry box that Candace had received on her sixteenth birthday. "I think I will keep this brooch," she said. "It is the only thing of any value in all this mess."

Fan looked over her shoulder. "That was our mother's, wasn't it? I wonder why Candace never wore it?"

"She was too busy wearing that silly hat of hers."

When Fan opened the armoire, she found a long scarf tucked between two dresses. "I would love to have this scarf," she said. "Is that acceptable to you?"

Emily glanced up from the shoes she was sorting. "Is that the one Father brought back from over the ocean? Remember the hideous one he brought for me?"

Fan *did* remember. Each of the three scarves had been hand-painted in a floral pattern. The one Fan held now was the one Candace had chosen—as the oldest, she had first choice, of course. It was truly lovely, unlike the other two. "What did you ever do with yours?"

"I threw it out, of course."

"But it was a gift!"

"It was ugly," the ever-practical Emily said. "The most unlikely collection of reds and yellows and greens."

Fan laughed, her memory softened by the passage of so many years. "I was left with the one painted in garish oranges and blues."

Emily shuddered. "Yours was almost as horrible as mine. How

could Father ever have had such bad taste? I hope you got rid of yours as well."

"I did not have the heart to throw it out." She looked up toward the ceiling, as if she could see through into the attic. "I consigned it to the bottom of a trunk."

Emily followed her sister's gaze. "I hope I die before you then. The last thing I want to do is clear out all your mess."

"You know you will not get your wish, sister. You are younger than I."

"Come help me with these shoes. There is no need for you to sort through those awful dresses. We know neither one of us wants to keep any of them." Emily moved Fan out of the way and closed the door to the armoire with a thump. When she did so, a hatbox fell off its perch. Emily opened it, took one look at the contents, and tossed the box onto the growing pile they had set aside to give to the church—most of what they'd sorted through, in fact—but Fan retrieved it.

"What do you want that old thing for?" Emily's indignant question was even louder than usual.

"I do not really know. I guess it just reminds me of her. She loved it so much."

"Surely you are not planning to wear it." Emily tilted her head to one side as she studied her sister. "Are you?"

"No." Fan ignored Emily's exaggerated sigh of relief. "Although I suppose I could replace the feather with something a bit fresher."

"Replacing the feather will hardly help," Emily said. "The hat is in wretched condition, and you know it."

"We probably should have buried her in it," Fan said.

"What? And have everyone laugh at us? Nonsense!"

"Oh, Emily, can you not have a little charity toward our sister?"

"I paid for her burial, did I not? And you looked after her for years. I would say that was charity enough from both of us." Emily turned aside and ran her hand along the chipped front edge of the old armoire. "I cannot imagine that anyone would want this monstrous thing. What shall we do with it?"

Fan would have liked to move it to her own bedroom, but now that Emily had pointed out the chipped edges—really, Fan had never before noticed them—she wasn't sure it would be a good idea. She waved her hands around ineffectually. Before she could dither any more, Emily settled the matter. "We'll give away all the contents and leave the armoire here. It is far too heavy to move."

**WHEN FAN DIED** six years later—three years after the death of Emily—she willed the contents of the house—hatboxes and trunks and even the old armoire—to her cousin Eliza, for Fan had no surviving children of her own, other than her second daughter Priscilla, who had said she wanted nothing to do with any of the contents. At the last moment, though, Prissy, who had married Cletus Martelson, claimed the oldest hatbox, and gave it to her youngest daughter to play with. Eliza moved most of the contents to the attic of her and her husband's house on Beechnut Lane. It was a huge attic. It could hold the remains of many households.

# 2000

**"YOU KNOW," I SAID**, as I studied Ida's ridiculous hat, "when we came up those stairs this morning, I figured we'd find just a whole lot of junk with maybe a few treasures here and there."

"You can say that again," Ida said.

I ignored her. "But then I revised my guess to a whole lot of treasures and a little bit of junk."

"I'll vote for that," Maddy said, still obviously pleased with the penny whistle.

"But both of those ideas are wrong, I think." I saw a few blank looks, so I went on, gesturing to the lamps and dressers. "So much of this is just, well, ordinary. It only seems extra wonderful because it's old, and maybe because there's such a mystery about where it came from."

"What sort of story," Glaze said in her quiet voice, "can you come up with about this?" She held up a wrinkled silky scarf, all covered with ghastly orange and blue flowers. "I just dug down to the bottom of this trunk, and it was sort of crumpled in the bottom."

Pat stepped closer to her. "How absolutely hideous," she said with what sounded almost like awe. "I can see why it was crumpled.

Are those flowers hand-painted?" She ran her finger across the design. "I think they are. You can tell from the texture. It's uneven on the edges of the petals."

"Why would anyone spend so much time," Glaze said, "painting something so ghastly?"

"Feel free to keep it," I said, and delighted in the hoots of my friends.

"I don't think so." She started to stuff it back into the trunk. "It's been here all this time. It can stay a little while longer."

"No," Sadie said. "Give it to me. It looks like just the sort of thing Easton would wear. I'll give it to her the next time I see her, if you don't mind, Biscuit."

"Be my guest." As much as I disliked Easton Hastings, I could see that it was the sort of dramatic accessory she might enjoy. And she could carry it off with that hair of hers. Looked like lava flowing down a mountainside.

"It'll look better once she's ironed it." Sadie sounded so certain.

Glaze had wandered away by this time. "Everything's so … so peaceful up here," she said.

Ida perched a fist on her hip. "Where'd you get a silly idea like that?"

"It is." Glaze pointed to a wide-brimmed straw hat sitting on one of the trunks. "Imagine this woman out placidly weeding her garden, protecting her face from the burning rays of the sun."

"I can imagine her all right," Ida said. "Arguing with her sister about who bakes the better biscuits or complaining to her husband that he spends too much money on corn liquor."

Maddy jumped right into the fray. "Maybe she spent her time planning revenge for … well, for an insult of some sort."

I thought about Clara. "A definite possibility," I said.

"There's a very high probability," Ida said with a distinct chuckle, "that all of us are wrong."

"Spoilsport," Maddy said. "I wanted at least one murder up here," and we all laughed.

*There are no dead bodies here.*

Marmalade let out one of her catly comments. I did wonder what she was meowing about.

"If somebody wanted revenge"—Glaze's voice sounded from the far side of the attic—"she could use this." She held up an old flat-iron. "There are three of them here, along with a cast iron griddle."

"I think they were called girdles back in the seventeen hundreds," I informed my sister.

"Doesn't matter what they called them," Maddy said with melodramatic flair, "any one of those would make a great murder weapon."

"Get over it," Ida told her. "You're not going to find a single murder, even though you want one so desperately."

## Tuesday, 15 April 1873

**ELIZA RUSSELL HOSKINS** had not so much as looked at Gideon, much less spoken to him, for more than a month, not since the day he had hurt her so badly that she had not been able to walk well enough to attend church. He had never hit her that hard before.

She had no one to turn to. The first and only time she had ever complained to her mother about how rough Gideon was, Mother had said, "You are the one who wanted to marry him. You are the one who made your bed. Now you must lie in it." She had gone on to preach to Eliza about how "a woman's duty is to stand by her husband without complaint," but after Eliza's first dumbfounded reaction, she had for the most part quit listening.

After Mother's caustic instruction, Eliza determined that she would do her duty to Gideon as expected, for she saw no other choice open to her. She would cook his meals and maintain the house, she would cooperate with his children, the ones he had from Leonora, his first wife, the wife who had so tragically drowned in her bath the year before Gideon married Eliza, although with those seven children already almost grown, there was precious little she had to do with the raising of them. Gideon's eldest son was, after all, only three years younger than Eliza herself.

In the thirteen years since then, Eliza had tried in so many ways to keep Gideon happy, to prevent his anger. But nothing had ever worked. He would be his jovial self for weeks at a time. He was well liked in the town, respected by the men, admired by most of the women.

But then something would set him off, something would go against his grain, someone would say something he took exception to, and Eliza was always the one who paid the price, although it had never before been quite so bad as it had been that horrible day a month ago.

He had even seemed to blame the severe winters of the last six years on Eliza, as if it had been her fault a mountaintop on the other side of the world had blown to pieces and sent clouds around the earth blocking the sun. She had read about Krakatoa in a newspaper once, and had even shown Gideon, but he had simply backhanded her and told her to mind her housework and leave the thinking to the men.

Eliza longed to tell someone, to confide in a friend. Suella Russell had stopped by to visit a number of times, but when Suella asked if there might be a problem, all Eliza could imagine was what would most definitely happen to her and Young Gideon if Suella's husband Luther, the swarthy village blacksmith, confronted Gideon. She had no doubt Gideon would vent his anger on her and her beloved stepson.

"Mother," Young Gideon said, and shoveled in another mouthful of oatcakes. When he swallowed, Eliza smiled to herself to see his prominent Adam's apple bounce up and down. He had become such a fine young man. "I, uh, have need of that shirt." He indicated with a nod a sleeve hanging out from the pile waiting for her services. Ironing was a hot and tiring business, and Eliza preferred to get it done early each Tuesday before the heat of the day built up too much.

"That is your Sunday shirt." Eliza lifted the heavy flatiron in her hand and placed it back on the Oberlin iron stove to reheat. "What need have you of it this early in the week?" She picked up the second of her three flatirons and applied it to the dampened apron spread before her on the padded board she used for ironing. Steam rose and momentarily fogged her spectacles.

She swiped a finger across the lenses and watched with mounting speculation as Young Gideon blushed a vivid red beneath his normally ruddy complexion.

"I, uh, that is, um, it is—"

"You might want to hurry yourself." His father's voice was deceptively calm. "There is work to be done."

Young Gideon, like everyone else in the family, was better trained than to cross his father, but Eliza knew from experience that the boy's speech would only get worse the more his father prodded him. Could the man not be patient with his own son?

Young Gideon held a special place in Eliza's heart. He was the only one of Gideon's children who had ever called her Mother. She saw in him a mild reflection of her own fears, her own way of not being quite sure just how to act, lest she bring about the quick explosive anger of her husband. Of all Gideon's children, Young Gideon was the only one who had seemed to need her. He had been an awkward ten years of age when his mother died so suddenly and so unexpectedly. Now, at almost twenty-four, he had grown into the gangly length of his legs and had filled out the bony width of his shoulders, but he still had something of the air of a child about him, particularly when his father taunted him for his slow uncertain speech.

"Well?" Gideon stood, shoving his chair back away from the table with such force it fell over. "Speak up."

"C-c-courting," Young Gideon finally managed to say. "I ... I need it to g-go ... uh ... courting."

"Courting? You?" His father practically cackled, so great was his incredulity.

"That is a fine idea," Eliza said to the boy. "You are a man now, and it is high time you thought of having a wife." She wondered mightily just who his intended might be, but she would not ask in front of Gideon. She noticed a loose thread on the bottom hem of the apron, set the iron back on the stove, and took her stork scissors out of her pocket to trim the thread. She would need to take a stitch in the hem later so it would not ravel more.

"How were you planning to provide for her, assuming she accepts your suit?" Gideon sounded even more venomous than usual. "Or had you even thought that far ahead?"

"The town has grown large enough to need two veterinarians. Dr. Shaw has ... asked m-m-me to j-j-join his practice."

Eliza was quietly astounded that Young Gideon had managed to say one complete sentence without messing his words, but of course his assurance could not have lasted through that second sentence in the face of his father's contempt. The whole family knew of Gideon's scorn for the elderly horse doctor.

"I h-h-had hoped that, if sh-sh-she will, uh, c-c-consent to be," he gulped, "to be my w-w-ife, that, uh, that she and I c-could…" He looked around the kitchen with the attitude of a mouse cornered by a particularly vicious cat.

"You wish to bring your wife here to live," Eliza said in the gentlest voice she could manage. How lovely it would be to have another woman's presence here in the house. She put her scissors back in her apron pocket—she always kept them handy—and picked up the second flatiron.

"You will expect me to provide for her, then," Gideon said. "Why should I be willing to do that?"

"I am sure, son,"—Eliza marveled at her courage in speaking up, although she knew she would be sorry later—"that she will be of great help to me in the house." She cringed when Gideon rounded on her, slamming his fist against the table.

"Are you unable to keep house without a helper? And not even any children for you to care for."

She tightened her grip on the flatiron, remembering to lift it off the apron before she left a scorch mark. Her barrenness had pained her at first, until she discovered how little she wished to provide yet another child to her violent husband. She did not answer Gideon, nor did she even look at him, but kept her eyes on the boy. "I am certain there will be children soon enough once you are married."

How ironic that she and Gideon could not even agree about something as joyful as the marriage of their son. Of Gideon's son, she corrected herself. But then she remembered these last thirteen years of caring for the boy, of being so proud of him as he followed his heart's desire to become a veterinarian. *My son indeed,* she thought. She smiled at Young Gideon and found his face was becoming even redder than before. He could help bring foals and calves into the world without hesitation, but no doubt the thought of his own future children was more than he could handle quite yet.

With a muttered curse, Gideon kicked the fallen chair and left the room. Eliza set the apron aside and lifted Young Gideon's good shirt from the basket. "I will have this ready for you well before this evening."

Young Gideon stood and kissed Eliza's cheek. "Thank you, Mother." He righted his father's chair, squared his shoulders, and smiled at her.

**BY THE TIME** Young Gideon married Amelia Stockwell in June of the following year, Eliza had ironed many shirts and aprons and had cooked many meals, still without ever talking to her husband. It was a small victory, but one she took pride in. Sometimes, though, she wondered whether he even noticed her silence.

She welcomed Amelia into her house, not only for the help the younger woman would be with all the chores, but because Eliza had been so desperately lonely for the past six years, ever since Gideon's mother died in 1878. The beatings had not begun until after her death. Mayhap the presence of the elderly woman had provided a curb of some sort on his anger, but even with his mother present, Gideon had ranted and shouted a good deal at both the women.

Eliza had loved Mother Grace—which was what she called her mother-in-law—from the depth of her being, and had found comfort from Gideon's coldness in Mother Grace's warm companionship.

It constantly amazed Eliza that two people as loving as Grace and Arthur Hoskins had produced a son as hard-hearted as Gideon, although she did have to admit that he had gotten much worse ever since their deaths.

She spent large swaths of time helping the other women in town when they birthed their babies. She had always had what the women of the town call *the touch.* But she had no sisters, no mother now, no beloved mother-in-law, no daughters of her own for daily interaction.

It took no time at all for Eliza and Amelia to develop a rhythm, to discern each other's strengths, and to learn to delight in the ways in which each could bolster the other. Amelia was a master at making jams and preserves, while Eliza's jellies always seemed to be either rock-hard or far too runny. On the other hand, Eliza could iron all morning long without flagging, while Amelia's wrists seemed to give out after less than an hour spent lifting the heavy irons from the stove.

Eliza knew how Amelia's wrists must feel. Gideon was careful never to hit Eliza's face, but sometimes her legs and arms throbbed so much, and her own wrists were so weak she could barely lift the flatirons, could barely stand at the padded board. But stand she did. She would not have him accuse her of neglecting her work.

Gideon timed his beatings carefully, it seemed to Eliza. Never when Young Gideon was present. Never when Amelia was in the house. Eliza had come to dread those times when Amelia left to run an errand. Amelia would so often return to find Eliza quivering, but Eliza would not show her shame to her daughter-in-law. She continued to do her work despite her aches. The only time Amelia had to take over the ironing was when Eliza had been called to a birthing.

Amelia did not say anything when Eliza's sleeve fell back one day and revealed the dark blue bruises of fingerprints on her forearm, but Eliza was sure she had noticed them. There was something in the tension of the young woman's back as she turned away.

When Eliza discovered how much Amelia enjoyed mending, she gave her the stork scissors. "You will use them much more than I, I am certain. My mother-in-law, Mother Grace Hoskins, gave them to me. She was a dear woman, and now I am delighted to pass them on to you, my dear. Be sure to keep them close to you at all times. I have always kept them in my apron pocket."

Amelia hugged her mother-in-law briefly but warmly. "I will do the same, then."

Less than a week after that, Eliza came home one Tuesday morning from a birthing that had gone far more quickly than she had expected. She looked forward to some quiet time with Amelia. Perhaps they could knit together after the ironing was done. Gideon had gone to Garner Creek the previous day and was not due back until suppertime. Young Gideon was probably up by the cliffs helping Amos Garner with that mare of his, the one that always had trouble foaling. Or he might be out at one of the local farms assisting the cows. *This is the month for births,* she thought. *We both help to bring new life into the world, Young Gideon and I.*

As she entered through the front door, she smelled the unmistakable stench of scorched cloth. Then she heard a scuffling and scrabbling from the kitchen. "No! Get off me!" Amelia's voice was twisted with anger and pain.

"You do what I say, or I'll upend you in the bath the way I did Leonora."

Eliza froze at the shock of it. She crept into the kitchen in time to see Amelia's hand, closed around the stork scissors, rake the point across Gideon's back. He roared in anger and raised his fist to strike Amelia. Eliza stepped to the padded ironing board, lifted the flatiron, noting as she did the scorched imprint of the hot iron on Gideon's best shirt, and brought the iron down with all her might onto the head of her husband as he straddled Eliza's beloved daughter-in-law.

If it had been either of the other sons of Gideon Hoskins who had walked in at that moment, Eliza would undoubtedly have ended up first in jail and then at the wrong end of a rope. As it was, Young Gideon, once he understood what had happened, comforted his wife and thanked his mother. He dug a grave in the Old Forest behind the house after night fell. Between the three of them, they carried Gideon out there, dumped him without ceremony into the hole, and covered up his despicable body. They hid the grave under a pile of brush and stones and fallen leaves.

Eliza went back inside, cleaned up the blood that had spilled onto the floor from Gideon's head and back, washed the dried blood from the now cold flatiron and used it the next morning to iron the pile of laundry neither she nor Amelia had completed the previous day. The scorched shirt went into the ragbag. She cleaned the stork scissors and tried to return them to her daughter-in-law, but Amelia cried out in horror. "I could never use them again, never."

Eliza decided that she, too, would be unable to use them, but she was far too thrifty to throw them away. Instead, she wrapped them in a square of gingham cloth and took them to the attic, where she placed them in a trunk. Someday, someone would find them, someone who did not know their history, and the lovely scissors would be used again. But not now.

Eliza would buy a new pair of scissors for Amelia. One that was free from such a harrowing past.

Meanwhile, Young Gideon let it be known around town that he had come home on Tuesday to find his father's horse in the yard, which was completely true. The horse *had* been there. Young Gideon preferred not to lie. If the men wanted to assume that the horse had come home without its master, then so be it. Tobe Martin, who had finally regained enough use of his leg to be useful, and his son Morgan, who managed quite well even with his jaw that had been so badly scarred during the War Between the States, organized a search party. The men of the town traced the road between Martinsville and Garner Creek, checked the riverbank, and inspected the ditches beside the road, but no sign of Gideon was ever found.

Betsy Clough was indignant at church the following Sunday. "He ran off and abandoned you?"

"No, no," Eliza replied. She, too, hated to lie. "I am sure he would never leave me willingly." He certainly had not been willing to leave in the way he had, she thought with grim satisfaction. "After all," she said, "his horse was here. He could not have gone far without his horse. I think perhaps something …" She paused and took a deep breath. "I think something happened to him."

It certainly had.

Beside her, Amelia reached out and took Eliza's hand.

Betsy heaved a deep sigh. "How good it is that you have Amelia to comfort you in your grief."

Eliza nodded. "Yes, indeed. I treasure this girl like my own daughter and would do anything to protect her. Anything at all."

**IN 1930, WHEN** Young Gideon and Amelia's only son Perry, the fifth of their seven children, married Elizabeth Endicott and brought her to live with him and his aging parents in the house on Beechnut Lane, Elizabeth used the flatirons because she had no other choice.

But when Martinsville—and the entire Metoochie River Valley—had electric lines installed, a project completed under the new WPA, Elizabeth insisted on having one of those modern electric Hotpoint irons. She had no need for the old flatirons, so she took them up to the attic one day, stashed them off to one side, and promptly forgot about them. Not a week later, when Perry and a friend stopped by, she had the two of them take the ugly desk from the front room and put it up in the attic as well.

While they were at it, she directed them to get rid of the hideous cheval mirror. She could barely see herself in it. She had no need for old-fashioned furniture, particularly pieces that were scratched or stained or clouded over. She intended to purge this house of everything useless, like that sickle, or whatever it was called. She'd found it in the broom closet. As long as she had them working like this, she told them to take down the ugly sampler that hung above the front door and put it upstairs as well. She hated preachy sayings that always seemed intended to tell her she wasn't as good as she needed to be—something about being swayed by reason. Whatever that was supposed to mean.

These hard times would not last forever, and Elizabeth planned to be ready for the good times that President Roosevelt said were coming.

# 2000

**"THOSE FLATIRONS DEFINITELY** need to be displayed somewhere," Maddy said. "Do you have a big display shelf of some sort, Biscuit?"

"Not hardly. I've never been one to hang onto things that ultimately just need to be dusted."

Maddy looked at me like she thought I was crazy. "You wouldn't need to put out all three of them."

"Ha! I don't need to put out even one of them."

"Why would there be three in the first place?" asked Ida. "You only need one iron."

"Two of them heated on the stove so they were ready when the first one cooled off." Glaze spoke over her shoulder as she wandered away from our cluster again.

"There's your answer," Maddy said. "Let's take this downstairs and put it on the wood stove. It won't take up hardly any room."

"I'd rather have the room for coffee and soup," Ida said.

"And hot chocolate," Glaze added. Her voice reverberated from the inside of the trunk she was inspecting.

"Maybe there's a note in the hatbox, or at least a label of some sort." Ida seemed determined to find out more about that white-feathered hat of hers. She removed the tissue paper that had been wrapped around it and began to inspect the lining while Glaze abandoned her trunk and studied the hatbox lid carefully.

"Nope," Ida said. "Nothing." She handed the box to Sadie who had reached out for it.

"That's not fair," I said. "Don't you think they would've known we'd be curious someday?"

"Wait." Sadie peered at the bottom of the box. "Somebody wrote something here." We all trooped after her as she walked close to one of the windows. "The lettering is rather childish. It looks like a little girl wrote it."

"Maybe it was a little boy," Maddy said.

"No," said Sadie. She read, carefully enunciating each word. *"My mother, Prissy Endicott Martelson, gave me this hat for my eleventh birthday. It belonged to my grandmother Fan Surratt Endicott. Now it belongs to me Sarah Priscilla Martelson."* Sadie looked around at each of us. "At least she spelled all the names right."

"Martelson?" Glaze looked at me.

"Our mother was born a Martelson," I told the group of women, "and we had a great-aunt Sarah who was our grandfather's sister."

"But we didn't really know her," Glaze said. "She died shortly after I was born, but apparently she was a real corker. There're some good stories about the shenanigans she pulled."

"I seem to think I met her once," I said, "when I was very young. It's one of my earliest memories, in fact. All I remember is how ancient she looked. I was fascinated by the veins on the back of her brown-spotted wrinkled hands." I rubbed my own blue-veined hands, recalling how one of my daughters had asked me once long ago, "Mommy, why do you have grandma hands?"

"What on earth," Glaze asked, "is a Martelson hat doing here?"

"I think Sarah's daughter married a Hastings and ended up in this house," Sadie suggested. "I don't recall her name for sure, but it's a possibility. She could have lived here, stuck the hatbox in the attic once the feather began to look like—"

"Watch what you say about my favorite hat," Ida warned with a lilt in her voice.

"Once it outlived its usefulness," Sadie amended.

"Well, useful or not, you can't have it back," Ida said to me. "I've claimed it and I'm going to keep it on." She pushed the white feather back so it didn't droop against her cheek. "At least until it gets a bit warmer up here. Everybody knows you lose most of your body heat through the top of your head." She rummaged around on the top of another dresser.

"I didn't know that," Glaze said.

*I think it is warm enough here, except for the floor, which is cold.*

"Look what I found," Ida said, and I turned to see her holding up an elaborate filigreed hair comb.

Glaze reached out for it. "Oh, how lovely. The pattern is so intricate. It looks like butterfly wings."

"You're more than welcome to it," Ida said. "That is, if Biscuit won't mind."

"Of course I don't mind," I said, knowing that Ida's thin hair would never hold even a simple barrette. "Is it tortoiseshell?" I hoped it wasn't. The use of tortoiseshell had been banned for years, but this was probably old enough to have been made before the ban went into effect. I was on the side of the turtles.

*There are turtles who live beside the stream in the woods.*

"I have no idea." She handed it to Sadie, who took a good look.

"It's not tortoiseshell, and it's certainly not ivory. I'd say it was some sort of bone or horn."

"I never saw a cow with a horn that broad."

Sadie nodded as if she agreed with Maddy. "Buffalo maybe? I can't think of any other animal that would have a horn big enough." She handed it to Maddy. "Too bad it has a broken prong."

"How on earth did they get such intricate carving done without lasers?" Maddy turned it over and examined the back of it. "It's a little rougher on this side, but still pretty darn smooth for something that had to have been carved out so slowly."

She handed it back to Sadie, who ran her fingers over the edges. "You're right. They must have drilled a narrow hole to start with and then enlarged it from there—maybe with tiny rasps?"

Once it returned to Glaze, she pulled her hair back over one ear and inserted the comb. Its dark beauty shone against the silvery whiteness of her hair, and the broken prong didn't even show.

"It looks like it was made for you," I said.

# 1806

**"IT'S MINE." EMMA HASTINGS** gritted her teeth and wrenched the elaborate hair comb away from her twin sister.

"No, it is not! You broke yours and now you want mine."

"I did not." By this point Emma was yelling, and she knew their sister Rose would soon step in to separate them, but she was truly angered. She was sure Caroline had been the one to break one of the prongs, back when Mother was still alive. Unless it was one of their young brothers who had broken it. But he had surely broken Caroline's, not Emma's. She ran out the front door with the hair ornament in her hand and in her hurry did not notice the collection of lead soldiers her brothers had lined up on the front steps—not until she tripped over them and tumbled to land painfully, stretched full-length on the paving stone path.

By the time Rose arrived to assess the damage—some scratches, a little blood, a torn pinafore, and one broken soldier—the twins had joined forces to deny that they had been fighting and to berate their brothers for leaving toys on the step to trip up unsuspecting sisters.

At least now there was one less thing for the twins to argue about. The second comb, the whole one, was whole no longer. The tip of one of its prongs now matched the broken tip of the other twin's comb, and it no longer mattered which comb belonged to which girl.

When Caroline married a number of years later, she took her broken hair comb with her as a memory of her mother. When Emma married a few months after that, she left hers behind in the attic. Who, after all, would want a broken hair ornament?

## 2000

**IDA BROKE THE** temporary silence. "How long do you think this ice will last?" Without waiting for an answer—which was just as well, because none of us could have had any way of knowing the answer—she went on. "Not that I don't truly appreciate your hospitality, Biscuit," and she gave an elaborate bow which I mirrored, "but I sure am going to miss my showers while we're here."

"It doesn't mean we can't keep clean," Sadie said.

*I keep myself very clean.*

Sadie patted Marmalade's head. "My mother taught me how to take a bath in a cup of hot water."

"A cup?" Glaze made a little boat out of her cupped hands. "What do you mean, *a cup*?"

"Don't sound so incredulous, dear. It's simple really. If you pour some hot water from the teakettle into a cup, you can dribble enough onto a clean washcloth to get it wet. Then you start at your face and work your way down, wringing out the cloth and pouring a bit more clean water onto it as needed. It's a simple process."

"Did you have to do that often," I asked, "or was it a once-in-a-while sort of thing?"

"Way back when," she said, "before we had running water in the house, it was a real chore to fill a bathtub."

I could well imagine, especially when I found what could only be an old-fashioned bathtub leaning up against one of the walls at the far side of the attic. I tried lifting it, and it was surprisingly light. "It can't have taken that much water to fill this thing," I said to the group as they gathered around. Glaze helped me carry it to a more open area.

"You'd be awfully cramped trying to bathe in there," Glaze said.

"We would," Maddy said, "but people were smaller back then."

"Even so," cautioned Sadie, "it was even more trouble to empty it after the bathing was done, carting tepid, dirty water out back and dumping it far enough away from the house so you didn't end up with a mud puddle at your back stoop."

I eyeballed the dimensions and tried to imagine the whole process. "I can see what you mean."

Ida looked dubious. "I'll still miss my showers."

## June 1741

**SIXTEEN-YEAR-OLD** Constance Garner twitched the reins just a bit to correct the tendency of Plover to veer to the left. Pigeon, Plover's singularly placid teammate, followed whatever lead Plover took. The big bay tried as often as he could to reach the tender grasses that grew beside the trail, and Constance spent a good deal of time suggesting otherwise to the two horses. Other than watching Plover, she had little to do as she drove the Garner wagon, for the unusually dry countryside they moved through was singularly lacking in interest, even for someone as naturally inquisitive as Constance.

She missed the water that had been so freely available back in Brandtburg. The big rain barrel outside their back door was a constant source of pleasure to her, to say nothing about the creek that ran close by their house.

She had been used to walking in the creek often. Her excuse was to gather watercress, which grew abundantly along the slow-moving edges of the creek, but one benefit was that, barefoot with her skirts hiked up above her knees, she could stay long enough in the water for her feet to be scrubbed by the sandy creek bottom and washed clean.

Constance liked clean feet. She liked clean hair, too, and had been known to remove her cap if no one was watching, bend over and dunk her head in the water, although once she had overbalanced and ended up completely drenched, almost losing her gathering basket— and her cap—in the process.

On days when she already had an abundance of cress, she could scoop a bucket of rainwater from the barrel and splash it on her face and arms, much to the dismay of her mother. Augusta Hastings Garner, like most of the women in Brandtburg, had always distrusted water, except for the yearly bath.

But there had been no bath this year so far. Instead, they plodded down the trail, leaving all that was familiar behind them. Homer Martin seemed bent upon getting as far from Brandtburg as possible, as quickly as possible. Unfortunately, the entire company was limited by the speed—or lack thereof—of the slowest wagon, which so far had been the Russell's.

Constance could not blame the Reverend, though. His daughter's death—murder—on the church steps had seemed to deflate Reverend and Mistress Russell. The death had hit Constance's sister Mary Frances even harder. Of course, Mary Frances had been Myra Sue Russell's very dearest friend. No wonder Mary Frances still cried near constantly.

Enough tears to bathe in.

When we reach our destination, Constance thought, I will beg Father to request a rain barrel from Mister Fiske.

Poor Cyrus Fiske had been kept more than busy preparing for the journey. His services as a cooper had been much in need, for the barrels and casks and kegs he produced were masterpieces that would keep the rain from anything inside them, and Constance felt fairly sure that every family now traveling would require more from him once they reached their journey's end. Pray God it would be soon.

Constance continued planning as Plover and Pigeon plodded along. The house we build at our journey's end must be shaped like an L, she thought, so the roof will funnel the rain properly into the barrel.

She wrinkled her nose as the unwelcome thought of Mistress Black popped into her mind. A widow now, since her husband had died in the fighting that last day in Brandtburg. The Widow Black scorned the thought of a yearly bath and reeked accordingly, although some, Constance had noted, particularly some of the men, seemed to enjoy the scent of the woman. Constance could not imagine why.

# 2000

**MELISSA'S VOICE RANG** up through the attic stairwell. "Anybody up there?"

*I am here, GoodCook. So is WideLap and Smellsweet and Loose-Laces and the others.*

"Sure," we all chorused, along with Marmalade who meowed what sounded like a greeting.

"Come on up and join the fun," I added.

Melissa's curly head poked into sight over the top step. "I brought reinforcements. And food."

Ida snorted. "We'll certainly be well-fed as long as we don't freeze to death."

"Not a chance," I said. "Heat rises, and we have enough wood to power that stove for weeks."

Maddy shivered. "Let's hope the storm doesn't last that long."

"It'll take us that long to clean up this place," Ida said.

Three other women had crowded up the stairs behind Melissa. I knew Pat Pontiac, of course. She and her husband Dave had visited Maggie and Norm a number of times over the past few years, especially after Maggie and Norm adopted Willie, and they always stayed at Melissa's B&B. From what I'd heard, they were looking for a house now that Dave had retired. It sure was taking them long enough.

The second woman in the line was a stranger. In back of the stranger, I could see the top of a head and knew it was Charlotte Ellis. Her distinctive black hair was a dead giveaway. I'd always suspected that she dyed it at home. It was too perfectly uniform in color. If she'd had Sharon do it at the Beauty Shop, Sharon would have given her just enough highlights—Sharon could work magic on hair—to make it look natural.

"I hope it's okay if I horn in on you," Charlotte said. "I saw Melissa trooping by and asked if I could join them." She made a face. "My house was already getting really cold."

"Not a problem," I said. And I really did mean it. Charlotte had been a little bit of a pain in the butt with the library committee, but I could let bygones be—well—bygones. In weather like this, we all had to help each other out. "There's plenty of room," I said. "Ida, you and Ralph can take the first bedroom on the left. Charlotte, would you mind the small room next to that? I doubt we'll spend much time in the bedrooms except to sleep." I thought for a moment. "There's a larger room on the other side of you, Charlotte. Melissa, if you don't mind sharing with your guest?" They both nodded. "Then there's another single. I'll put Reebok in there."

"Let's not worry about all that now," Sadie said. "We'll sort ourselves out this evening."

"Right," Melissa said. "For now, I want you to meet Dr. Carol Mellinger. She's here to do some research on Homer Martin and the first families that came to Martinsville."

Carol fielded the multiple questions gracefully, and within minutes we all had a general outline of why she was here, why she was interested in Homer Martin, where she'd come from, and how long she planned to stay.

"Bob just told us to come up here." Pat twirled her ankle and inspected the heavy slipper sock she wore. I was glad Bob had handed them out. "He didn't enlighten us as to what was going on."

"I've been threatening to clean out this attic—or at least organize it—ever since Bob and I moved in, but I just never got around to it."

Carol glanced around appreciatively. "This looks like a wonderful project. And right up my alley." Before I could comment, she went on, "But first, I'd like to be introduced to the famous Marmalade." She bent and held out a hand.

*What does famous mean?*

We all laughed when Marmy meowed a hello right back at her.

Carol let Marmalade sniff her fingers, then stroked her for a moment, complimenting her on being so well known—so famous—after having foiled a murder attempt, and explaining that it was a radio story about Marmalade that had introduced her to our valley.

Finally, she gave Marmalade one last pat and straightened up. "Do you mind if I join in the treasure hunt?"

*You are very welcome here.*

I smiled my consent, and she reached for the old hobbyhorse that Bob had been so sure was broken. She rocked it back and forth a couple of times. "What a lovely piece."

Melissa bent down to study it. "It looks hand carved, wouldn't you say?"

"I'd say it was well used, too," Sadie said. "I wonder whose it was." She took the folding chair I offered her. I pulled up another one for myself to keep her company for a few minutes. She was surprisingly sprightly for her age, but I thought having a chair handy for her might be a good idea.

"Whoever it was," Maddy said, "I'll bet he was a little terror. Look at that chunk he gouged out of the hoof."

"And that mane." Carol shook her head at the tangled, faded brown yarn. "It sure has seen better days."

"Straggly, is what I'd call it." Ida pulled another chair away from a lineup of them next to the wall and sank onto it. Why on earth were there so many folding chairs up here? Maybe for some long ago, long forgotten party?

"I wouldn't talk if I were you," Maddy said. "It's not as straggly as that feather on your old hat."

Ida pinned her with a gaze. "My hat was well-loved."

"How would you know?"

"I have a feeling about such things." She rose and took one end of the hobbyhorse. "Here, Glaze, help me turn this thing over."

"Okay, but why?"

"Sometimes people hollowed out the bellies of the horses and hid jewelry or money in them. You never know until you look."

They lifted it and inspected the bottom. "No secret door," Glaze said, and I could hear the disappointment in her voice. "It's held together with pegs, not screws."

"That could mean it's pretty old," Carol said.

"Of course it's old," Ida said. "Just look at it."

Maddy grinned. "It's about as pathetic as your hat."

"Can it," Ida said, sounding a little sharper than I thought was necessary in the face of Maddy's teasing.

"Look!" Glaze ran her finger along the underside of the rocker platform. "There's a signature or something."

"Take it over there to the light," Sadie instructed.

Ida bent closer once the horse was under a window. "*Ephraim Alonzo*, it says." She looked around the circle. By now most of us had grabbed chairs and hauled them to the large, relatively clear central area. "Anybody know who he was?"

## November 1796

**"THE BABE WILL** not be born until the late winter," Naomi Russell Hastings said, her face softening in the chill November twilight. "And then 'twill be a mighty long time after that before he can ride a hobbity horse."

Ethan paused in carving the face of the little wooden horse and smiled at his wife. "You think I know that not?" He had chosen the best block of hickory he could find. It would last through many children. He turned his head down as if to hide his face from his wife so she would not see the blood rising to his face as he thought of this, but Naomi was well aware of what her husband thought, for she thought it herself. Life with Ethan had been much more pleasant than she had feared before her marriage. She looked forward to the making of many more children. "The horse can stand guard over his basket," Ethan said, "when he is just a wean."

Naomi's sister-in-law, Astaline Shipleigh Hastings, picked up Rose, her two-year-old daughter, while Mary Etta and Electa, the two older girls, played at her feet. "No doubt Mary Etta will try to claim it for her own."

Naomi was aware of the small furrow that appeared on Ethan's forehead, but she did not think Astaline noticed it. Ethan was ever a most generous man, but despite the fact that he had lived with his older brother Reuben in this house for all his life, she could tell he wanted this hobbity horse for his own child alone. Naomi could imagine the house would soon be filled with children, for Astaline was expecting her fourth any day now. And Naomi knew without a doubt that she and Ethan would have many children of their own. The children, she decided, would have to learn to take turns on the hobbity horse.

Mother Margaret DeWitt Hastings craned from her rocking chair to peer at the horse head. "A fine stallion, that is."

Naomi smiled a secret smile, rubbing the increasingly active bump beneath her skirts. She could almost hear the child three years from hence rocking to and fro on the horse and squealing with delight. He would be born upstairs in the same room where his father had slept as a child. Eventually he would have brothers that he could lead—she had no doubt he would be a strong leader—and he would have sisters, too, sisters that he would bedevil no doubt, but be quick to defend, as her own brothers had both teased and protected her.

"I thought to name him Ephraim Alonzo," her husband said, "after your father and my own."

The baby inside her turned a somersault, or so it felt. "You are a good man, my husband, and I think that will be a fine name for our son."

Mother Hastings placed a hand over her heart, obviously remembering her deceased husband. "My Alonzo would have been pleased, God rest his soul." She turned to her daughter-in-law. "And your father, Ephraim Josiah. What a shame that he did not live long enough to greet his namesake."

Naomi rubbed her stomach again. She had missed her father every day for the past six years.

Ethan patted the little horse's rump. "All I have yet to do is mount the legs on the rockers I have prepared." He glanced across the room and Naomi followed his gaze. She couldn't imagine how long it would take their son—Ephraim—to grow legs long enough to reach from the step up to the cunning saddle.

"Have you some yarn for the mane?" Ethan smoothed his hand

along the side of the little horse and leaned over to address a rough spot on one of the front hooves.

"Yes! And for the tail as well." She rummaged in the basket beside her on the table and held up a ball of dark brown yarn she had dyed using oak bark. "I put some aside when you began the carving." Playfully she tossed the ball at him.

He grabbed at it, but as he twisted to catch it, his knife gouged deeper into the hoof, sending a small chunk of wood tumbling off to the side.

"Oh, Ethan, I am that sorry."

"It is no matter, Wife. I can wedge the missing piece back in place." He picked up the fragment and fitted it as best he could. "It might not show too much."

"Ephraim will ride the horse hard," Naomi said, rising to place her hand on her husband's shoulder. "And children do not notice such things."

"Our son will notice," Ethan asserted. "He will have as keen an eye as his father. Come. I have something to show you." He took her hand and guided her across the room to where the rocking platform sat near the wall. "Close your eyes."

When she had done so, he lifted the platform and turned it over. "Feel here," he said, placing her hand on the bottom side, beneath the sturdy step.

She felt the carved letters and began to sound them out. "E-p-h-r—Ethan! What if I had not wanted Ephraim Alonzo as a name?"

He set down the wooden base and touched her gently on the shoulder. "The names of your father and mine for our first child? How could you not agree?"

She laughed up at him. She did agree indeed. She wondered, though, what her husband would do if the child turned out to be a girl.

**IN THE END** though, it was a boy, but Ephraim Alonzo died two days after his birth, despite the guarding presence of the little horse, and when the next child died before he was five, swept away in the raging storm waters of the 1802 flood, Ethan, in despair, threw the hobbyhorse out behind the privy, much to the desolation of seven-year-old Rose, his one remaining niece, for Mary Etta and Electa had died of a fever just the year before.

After Naomi recovered—although one never really recovers from the death of one child, much less the deaths of two—she retrieved the small horse, which by this time was badly weather-stained. The wedge, she noticed, had come loose, and the little chunk from the hoof was gone. She searched for it, but could not find it. Undaunted, she brought the horse back inside. Ethan's mother grumbled when she saw it. "My son does not want it in the house," she said.

Naomi straightened her back. "We will need it for the next child." But not wanting to see the pain in Ethan's face when he came home that evening, she took the horse up to the roomy attic. There would be time to bring it down when it was needed. And there was plenty of room on the base of it to carve the names of many more children.

When Rose discovered the rocking horse in the attic two weeks later, she made sure to ride it only when her aunt and uncle were busy with other concerns, for she knew, even at that young age, that they would not wish to hear the rhythmic creaking of the attic floor.

# 2000

**"I HAD A** great-grandfather named Ephraim," Pat said, "but I'm pretty sure he was Ephraim Robert, not Ephraim Alonzo."

Sadie pursed her lips. "My great-grandfather was Ephraim Josiah Russell. He had a daughter, too, my grandfather's sister Naomi. She married a Hastings, but she never had any children that I know of."

I loved the way some people were so aware of their family trees. I only had a vague recollection of names, and precious little information about dates. Of course, I wasn't as interested in genealogy as a lot of the women here in our little circle.

We all turned when Bob called from the stairs. "Biscuit?"

His voice was audible, but muffled somewhat by the sound of ice pellets hitting the roof. I walked to the doorway. "Yes?"

"I called mom to see if she and Dee were packed yet. They'll be freezing soon if we don't get them down here. I told her I'd walk up there and help them get through the ice."

"Good idea. Tell them to bring their pee-jays and their own pillows. Looks like they'll be staying a day or two." They could take the largest guest room at the end of the hallway.

Pat stepped up beside me. "Take Dave with you, Bob. That way you two can each carry a suitcase and hang onto an arm."

"Will do."

"Be careful," I called after him, "and send them up here to the attic when you get back."

"Will do," he said again. "Are you warm enough up there?"

"Absolutely! Heat rises."

*I am very warm and comfortable, although the floor is somewhat cold. Please sit down so I can get on your lap.*

Ida harrumphed a bit. "Hasn't risen quite fast enough for my taste."

Pat ignored Ida and turned to me. "I remember Rebecca Jo, of course, but who's Dee?"

I tended to forget that Pat didn't necessarily know the new people in town anymore since she and Dave had moved away. "Dee was Bob's sister-in-law, but she divorced his brother." His cheating, lying, embezzling, sniveling brother, I thought, but I didn't say it. "She moved up here to stay with Rebecca Jo. That's Bob's mother," I added in an aside to Carol Mellinger. Was she feeling swamped with all these names? "Dee is really a big help to Rebecca Jo."

"Unless Rebecca Jo has changed drastically," Pat said, "she's about as much in need of help as an oak tree in a gentle breeze."

I laughed. "You're right, but Dee's good company for her, and Rebecca Jo loves her like a daughter."

The wind moaned under the eaves just then, and Pat shivered. "I wonder who else they'll collect along the way?"

"It won't matter." Glaze pointed at the stack of hatboxes. "We'll have enough hats for everyone."

"Let's try all of them on." Maddy picked up one of the boxes, a rather faded blue with a white ribbon around it, and handed it to Carol. "Here, this one's for you."

Carol looked delighted. "I always wanted an antique hat."

But it turned out to be a man's hat made of white straw. She inspected the red and blue striped ribbon that wound around the crown. "Didn't they call these boaters?"

"They sure did," Sadie said. "Wallace had one. It had belonged to his older brother." I could see her thinking back over her eighty-some-odd years, most of which she'd shared with Wallace her husband. "Of course," she added, "all the men had them back then. I was only five, but I vividly remember—one of my first memories—the park was a sea of boater hats the day most of the men left to become soldiers in the Great War."

I could hear the capital letters in her voice. The Great War, the one that was meant to end all wars. Fat chance of that. But wouldn't it have been lovely if it had happened that way? Instead, it had wiped out almost an entire generation of young men in Europe and a large percentage of the young men in this country.

"Wallace's oldest brother Ruel left that day. It was the last we ever saw him. He's buried in Flanders Field."

"I'm so sorry," Carol said.

Sadie shrugged. "Wallace adored his brother, but we lost so many. It seemed like the telegrams never ceased."

Carol ran her hand around the fabric pad that lined the inside rim of the hat and broke the silence that had followed Sadie's comment. "There's a name written here," she said, "but it might not be much help. All it says is *Loren.*"

We turned as one toward Sadie, but again she lifted her shoulders. "I seem to recall the name, but I don't know which family he belonged to."

"Another mystery." Pat lifted a second blue box from the stack and handed it to Carol. "Try this one instead. The box matches, so it's probably related to Loren's boater."

We all agreed. A duplicate white ribbon tied this second blue box. Carol set the boater back in the first box and opened the other. "I hope it's not another man's hat," she said as she lifted the lid. It wasn't. A perky red bow adorned a trim navy blue felt cloche.

I stepped over to the side of the attic and pulled out one of the card tables. If we were going to be opening all these boxes, we'd need plenty of horizontal surfaces. Of course, as soon as I set it up, Marmalade jumped up onto it.

*Thank you. It is not a lap, but it is better than the floor.*

# Friday, April 20, 1917

**ELLA FREEMAN WAS** determined not to cry. She never could cry prettily, the way Doris, her next younger sister, managed to do. Instead, Ella's eyes got red and puffy, and her nose dripped horribly. She certainly didn't want Loren's last view of her to be an ugly reminder while he was away fighting the war in Europe. *Winning the war in Europe*, she thought.

She steeled her spine, straightened her tight-fitting cloche—the navy blue was very good for her delicate coloring—and left her bedroom. She was halfway down the stairs when the smart side of her brain told her to go back and get a handkerchief. Just in case. She was not going to cry, not at all, but her feet turned her around. She could at least choose a pretty lace-edged one. Maybe then he'd see how daintily she dabbed at her eyes.

But she was not going to cry.

"I want to go, too," her youngest sister whined as Ella reached the front door.

"No, Harriett, you'll just get in my way."

"I promise to be good. Everybody else is going."

That was almost true. Ella would be late if she lingered much longer. Each of her sisters had a beau, and all of them were going off to war. Ella wondered if any men would be left at home at all. Only the very old and the very young. Her three brothers, thankfully, were far too young for war service, even if the war lasted a whole year. Of course, it couldn't last that long.

"Is it all right, Mama, if I take Harriett with me?"

"Keep her close to you," Mama called. She'd refused to go herself, saying she wanted no part of this war.

Ella took Harriett's hand. "Stay close by me. There will be motor cars everywhere."

They joined the trickle of people headed downhill past their house on Sweetgum. Everyone turned right at the corner onto Second Street and went directly to the town park. Morgan Martin, the chairman of the town council would, she knew, give a long-winded speech to see the young soldiers on their way. Well, they weren't soldiers yet. Loren had explained to Ella that they would all need training first. "I hope the war isn't over before they finish giving us our uniforms and teaching us how to march," he'd complained only last week.

With all the hordes of people, it was a wonder she found Loren, but there was a special link between the two of them. He waved his boater as soon as she stepped into the park—he must have been watching for her—and in her hurry to join him, she dropped her sister's hand. She brushed past Eustace Russell, who was still too young for a uniform but was wide-eyed with excitement. Next to him was his sister Sadie, standing with young Wallace Masters. Beside Wallace was the elder Masters boy, Ruel. He raised his hand in a greeting.

Ella wondered why she noticed everyone so intently. Maybe that was what happened when people went off to war and you never knew if they would come back. Of course—she chided herself abruptly—that did not apply to Loren. A little farther on, Doris held hands with Aaron Hastings. Ella and Loren stopped under a spreading poplar tree, facing each other, not even a foot apart.

"Well," he said.

"I suppose so," she said.

He took her hand. And then there wasn't that much more to say.

They turned to face the bandstand when a group of town musicians began to play rousing songs. Many of the people sang along, especially when the national anthem was played.

Eventually, Morgan Martin stood, cleared his throat, and spoke in a rich, deep voice—surprising in a man of such advanced years. Ella knew he was at least sixty, far too old to go to war himself. His voice was surprising, too, in that it came from a face so badly disfigured. He was still a handsome man, if you discounted the livid scar that covered a great deal of his left jaw.

"When I served as a drummer boy in the War Between the States," he boomed out, "I found out firsthand, at the Battle of Chickamauga, what our young men will be facing." He reached up and touched his scar, and the crowd quieted, although whether it was respect or awe, Ella was not sure. "What they will face," he repeated, "as they go to stop the Kaiser's spread of aggression in Europe. I trust that they will return to us, to you, carrying the banner of victory."

He went on in that vein for quite a while, but Ella didn't really listen. She'd heard his drummer boy speech countless times over the past number of years. He spouted it every Independence Day, and worked it somehow into every other holiday oration. She knew he and his father had both returned horribly injured from the fighting. It was a miracle either one of them had survived, but she didn't like hearing about that aspect of war. Instead, she focused all her attention on Loren's hand and the way her own hand felt while he held it.

When Mr. Martin finally wound down, wishing them "good luck and Godspeed," she turned her face up, hoping that Loren might give her a kiss. Everyone else seemed to be doing that—wasn't it her turn to receive her first kiss? But instead, Loren swept his boater off his head and handed it to her.

"I'll be wearing a uniform," he said, "so I won't need this. Keep it safe for me, would you?"

She reached for it numbly. "Of course I will." Part of her wanted to rip off her own hat and press it into his hands. *Keep this tucked in your uniform shirt,* she wanted to say. But of course, she said no such thing.

"I'll be back to reclaim it soon. As soon as this war is over."

She nodded, not trusting herself to speak. The tears were too close to the surface. And she would *not* let him see her eyes puff up.

He raised a finger to touch the tip of her nose. And then he was gone, squeezing between Ruel Masters and another young man into a Model T driven by Ruel's father. She wasn't even sure where they would head from here. She hadn't paid much attention to such details. She only knew he was leaving her behind. With his hat. Beside Ella, little Wallace Masters held a hat just like Loren's.

When the car was lost to sight behind the trees that lined Juniper Street, she sank onto one of the wooden benches, placed the boater on her lap, and pulled her ridiculously tiny handkerchief from her pocket. She knew there would be a lot of tears now that Loren was not here to see her.

Before she could begin to cry, though, her little sister popped out of nowhere. "Have you seen Colin?"

Ella shook her head. She did not care where her ten-year-old brother had gone. He certainly could not get lost. Not in Martinsville.

"Maybe he did it, then," Harriett said.

"Did what?"

"He said he was going to hide out in one of the automobiles."

It took Ella a moment to register the sense of this. "He what?"

"He wants to be a drummer boy, just like Mr. Martin."

Ella scoffed. "There's not much room to hide in a Model T. In fact, there isn't anywhere to hide."

"Yes there is. Mr. Masters has a trunk on the back of his."

"Colin wouldn't fit in that. It's much too small."

"Yes, he would," Harriett said stoutly. "He told me he tried it out last week. He can curl up in a really tight ball."

Of course, Mr. Masters brought the truant home after he delivered the soldiers to the Tallulah Falls Railway depot in Cornelia. "Found him hiding away in the trunk," Mr. Masters said. "My son saw the latch was loose before we left, and he strapped it back down without looking inside." He looked sternly at the young stowaway, but Ella could swear he had a glint of laughter in his eyes. "It's a good thing Ruel noticed that strap. You might have bounced out of it at thirty miles per hour, and we'd have left you in our dust." He turned back to Ella and her mother. "As it was, the only reason I knew he was there is that I heard him hollering after the train pulled out of the station."

"I couldn't get out once the thing was buckled shut," Colin complained. "Now I'll never get to be a drummer boy."

"And a good thing, too," his mother told him. "I won't give my boys to be cannon fodder."

Mr. Masters looked aghast.

Ella burst into tears and ran upstairs.

She received a letter from Loren the very next day. He'd posted it before he even left Martinsville. Three days later she received another letter.

*Dear Ella,*

*I hope you found your brother before he starved to death in the trunk. Ruel and I had a great laugh in the train after he told us that he had seen Colin curled up, hiding, before we even left Martinsville. He debated with himself—but only for a second or two—about whether or not to expose the little scamp, but decided it would be much more fun for the boy to almost get away with it, so he latched the clasp as if he was unaware of the live baggage within. He did suggest to his father just before we jumped on the train that he check the trunk before returning home.*

*Home. I love that word. But I am off on a great adventure and I know that once we send the Kaiser running, all of us will have years worth of stories to entertain our children with.*

*I will write to you as often as I can, but we have been told by a most intimidating sergeant that there will be many times when letters will not be possible. Keep my hat ready and waiting. This war will be over soon and I will return for it.*

*Most sincerely,*
*Loren*

*Most sincerely*? Could he not have signed it with *love*? But perhaps she was expecting too much. He had referred to children, though. It could be he was thinking of the children he and Ella would have after they were married. She spent many sweet hours planning the wedding and decided that it would be about six months after he returned from the war. They would have to wait that long because he had to propose first.

After that, the letters came regularly at first and then with more and more time between them.

**IT HAD BEEN** almost a year since Loren left. It was a warm day, and Ella delighted in the freedom she felt at not having on a corset. The War Industries Board had decreed that women must give up their metal-framed corsets so the United States could use the metal to build battle-ships. Although many of the older women said they felt bereft without their foundation garments, Ella thought it was one of the best decisions she had ever heard of. That day, she strode farther up Sweetgum Street to visit Loren's mother and to take her a gift. She had not bothered to try to wrap it, since it would have made such an unwieldy bundle, and also because everyone had been enjoined to save paper whenever possible.

"Come in, dear," Mrs. Garner called when Ella knocked on the screen door. "Let's go into the parlor." She pointed Ella in that direction and then brought two tall glasses of tea from the icebox. "I know we never sit in here, but I've been doing some mending and the afternoon light here is better for my eyes."

Ella detested the scratchy horsehair sofa, but she sat and crossed her legs at the ankle. She wanted to ask if there had been a letter from Loren, but was fairly sure his mother would have said so right away if there had been.

"What are those contraptions you have in your hands?"

"They are coat hangers."

"Coat hangers? Whatever are they for?"

"Well, I suppose to hang coats on, but they work well for dresses and other articles of clothing, too. By using these, you don't have to fold your clothes or hang them on pegs." She handed over one of the two wire devices. "Your dark blue dress would wrinkle less if you hung it on one of these."

"Coat hangers? Hmm." Loren's mother studied them intently. "Well, I never saw such a thing. They certainly are ugly, aren't they?"

"Yes, but they're very efficient. My sister and I have begun using them, and my father hung a rod from the ceiling of our bedroom so we can hang our dresses side by side." Ella stood and lifted a newly mended dress from the back of the nearby wingback chair. "Here, I'll show you how they work."

"Does your mother use them as well?"

Ella blushed, not wanting to admit that these two coat hangers were ones her mother had refused even to try. "You know Mother. It may be a while before she condescends to use them." She smoothed Mrs. Garner's dress and held it up. "Mister Breeton has begun selling them. He said he would keep them in stock as long as he could, but until the … the war is over, he may not be able to order any more. Because of the metal, you know."

"I must say that dress certainly hangs well." Mrs. Garner turned when there was a knock on the front door.

"I'll get it for you." Ella still held the dress when she opened the door.

Mrs. Garner was right behind her.

Sydney Russell, the delivery boy, held out a yellow telegram envelope.

Ella twisted the coat hanger in her hands so hard, it was a wonder Mrs. Garner's dress didn't get a tear in it. Mrs. Garner collapsed, screaming, on the hall floor.

When Ella finally returned home, she took the ruined hanger with her. Colin said he'd repair it for her, but it was bright and sunny the next day, and he wanted to play outside. When he gave up on the project, he left the hanger stuffed under his bed.

Ella wore her navy blue cloche only one more time, the day her sister Doris married Aaron Hastings, just three weeks after Aaron returned from the fighting.

**SEVEN YEARS LATER**, the day before Ella agreed to marry William Jay Breeton, she bought two matching hatboxes at Breeton's Dry Goods store, blue with white ribbons to tie them shut. Loren's boater and her cloche wouldn't fit together in the same hatbox. She gave the boxes to her friend Elizabeth Endicott Hoskins, who consigned them to the attic on Beechnut Lane when her husband Perry refused to wear a boater. Elizabeth favored wide-brimmed hats anyway, so the loss of the cloche was not a problem to her way of thinking, and after all, the attic was large.

# 2000

**"TRY IT ON,** Carol," Melissa said, indicating the navy blue cloche.

Carol looked at me. "Is that all right?"

"Of course it is. It's not like I have any claim to"—I waved my hand around the attic—"to all this."

"Other than the fact that this is your house," Ida commented drily.

"I suppose so," I said, "but up here it feels more like a museum than part of my house. Anyway, I think it's safe to say the hatboxes and their contents are completely up for grabs." I didn't say so, but I hoped nobody would claim that boater. Perhaps Bob would want it. Or better yet, I might take it for myself. It had a jaunty look to it that I liked.

I couldn't help it. "I'm going to claim my hat right now." I opened the other blue box with its white ribbon. When I pulled out the boater, I was halfway expecting objections, but everyone seemed to think it fit me perfectly. Yes! I tilted it to a jaunty angle and rejoined the group.

"Hand me the next one in the pile, if you don't mind," Maddy said. "I'm not tall enough to reach that high."

Carol lifted off the next box, gave it to Maddy, and then pulled on the cloche. Her long braid stuck out the bottom.

Ida cocked her head to one side. "Nope. It looks like you just sprouted a tail. Take it off and give it to Dee. You try on the next one."

"Fine with me." Dee reached for the cloche. "I like dark navy, and that perky red bow is perfect."

"It looks great on you," Melissa said a moment later. "It's a keeper."

Maddy opened the large flat hatbox and gasped.

The hat was a deep indigo blue, and a gorgeous matching silky scarf flowed around it and trailed away in back as Maddy lifted it from the hatbox. "This is absolutely beautiful! I've never worn this color, but I've always loved it. Can't you imagine it with exactly the perfect dress?"

"It wouldn't matter if you wore it with jeans," Dee said. "It would still look stunning."

"I know it must be old," Maddy said, "but it looks good enough to wear to a wedding." She grinned at Glaze. "Maybe to yours. It'll go perfectly with that dress I bought a couple of weeks ago."

"Dress," Pat said. "What dress?"

But I had a sinking feeling I knew what dress. A feeling that was reinforced as Maddy described it.


**HOW LONG HAD** I had my eye on that perfect matron of honor dress in such a lovely shade of deep indigo? And wouldn't you know it, exactly one day before I drove up the valley to Mabel's Dress Shop in Garner Creek, somebody had come into Mabel's and bought it. Well, I could have spit, only librarians don't act like that. Not usually.

*Cats do not spit, either. Unless we are provoked.*

"Don't worry about it, Biscuit," Sarah Watkins had told me. She's worked there for a couple of years now and she's going to school part time to become a counselor. I have to admit, she can usually figure me out. She was diplomatic enough not to remind me that she'd suggested several times over the past few months that I could put a deposit on it.

"I wasn't working yesterday," she informed me when I asked who'd had the nerve to buy my dress, "so I don't know who bought it, but maybe whoever it was will return it with the tags still on. You never can tell."

"Nobody returns a dress as wonderful as that one."

"You'd be surprised."

So I kept hoping and called a couple of times to see if the dress was available—or if they'd been able to order a replacement. Sarah finally informed me, very gently of course, that they would call me if and when the dress became available, but in the meantime, since that particular style had been discontinued—*not having sold well enough* she said with particular emphasis—would I like to try on some other styles or colors?

No, I wouldn't *like* to. But, as I said, Sarah was so nice about it, I just had to drive up there and give it a try. I found a dress that was a good second choice. On the rack it looked like a rather faded straw color, but Sarah talked me into trying it on, and then raved about how it made my eyes look absolutely stunning. I could go with straw-colored stunning, although I would have much rather had indigo spectacular. Rather than wait and get absolutely desperate the week before my sister's wedding, I decided to go ahead and buy it, fully expecting that my purchase would propitiate some sort of shopping god, thereby ensuring that the dress I wanted would be returned the next day.

It didn't work, and I was stuck with a second choice dress.

And now Maddy would be wearing my dream dress. I suppose I should have been grateful that *my* dress would fit a slim young woman like Maddy.

I came back to the conversation when I heard Maddy say, "Yeah. I had to take in the seams a lot, but it finally fits." Maybe I should have spit after all.

*I will spit for you. When? Now?*

Although I'd told our entire tap dance class of how I had my heart set on buying a gorgeous dark purple-blue dress at Mabel's, I'd never really described the dress in detail. But Madeleine Ames should have known this was the dress I wanted. She should have looked at it and said, "I bet this is the dress Biscuit's been talking about."

Now here we were, just two and a half days before the wedding, and not only was Maddy going to be wearing *my* dress, now she'd have that stunning hat to wear with it.

It wasn't fair.

*What are you talking about? And I still do not know who to spit at.*

Just as Marmalade let out one of her conversational meows, the wind gave a particularly vicious moan. If this storm kept up, there wouldn't be a wedding—at least not on time—because nobody, including the bride and groom, would be able to get to the church.

## October 1934

**ELIZABETH ENDICOTT HOSKINS** felt slightly insulted that her husband Perry didn't even look at her as she walked down the stairs carrying Lyle. He just kept on honing that hunting knife of his.

"Perry." She modulated her voice so she would sound patient rather than irritated, which is what she truly was. "We absolutely have to leave for church in just a few minutes. If you don't put on your tie right now, we'll be late."

"Fine with me," Perry grunted.

"Now, how would it look to all our friends and neighbors if you're not there on time for your own son's baptism?" She laid the baby on the sofa and chucked him under his pudgy chin.

Perry grunted again. "I don't give a hoot what they think."

"Yes, you do. You know Myrtle would write about us being late in that column of hers, and then how would that sound? Everybody up and down the valley will read about it."

"Nobody reads that silly gossip column of hers."

Elizabeth knew quite well that Perry read his little sister's column every single Wednesday when the *Keagan County Record* was delivered. She'd seen him trying to make it look like he was reading the sports page. She had never pointed out to him that all she had to do was look at which direction his eyes were pointing. It didn't pay to have a husband too aware of a wife's little tricks, but really, it was so obvious. If the sports column was on the right-hand page, his eyes would be headed toward 'Myrtle's Musings' on the left-hand page.

She put a heavy pillow between Lyle and the front edge of the sofa before she stepped away and picked up the hatbox she'd left sitting on the hall table. She knew Perry was watching her as she lifted the deep blue hat and set it in place atop her head, so the curls she had arranged so elaborately on the sides of her head showed to perfection. She planned to tie the long scarf at the nape of her neck rather than in front. Even as young as the baby was, Elizabeth knew Lyle would reach for the fluffy bow, and she didn't want her new hat getting pulled awry in the middle of the baptism.

"Perry," she said, "hurry up and get your tie on." She hated having to keep reminding him, but it had to be done, or he'd spend half the morning sitting there with that confounded knife. "I laid the nice dark blue one out for you. I probably should have brought it downstairs with me." She opened the drawer of the hall table. Now, where had she put her scissors? It wouldn't do to leave the price tag hanging off the edge of that elegant brim! But first, she had to look at herself one more time. She'd paid an outrageous price for the hat—almost three whole dollars, but it was worth every penny. She looked at Perry's reflection behind her. "What are you doing, Perry, acting like you've got all day? Would you hurry up?"

**PERRY HAD ALREADY** placed the whetstone back into its box. It wouldn't take him but a second to run upstairs and find a tie. If he knew Elizabeth, she'd already laid one out for him on the bed. He bunched his leg muscles, getting ready to stand, but at just that moment, Elizabeth told him to hurry up and get his tie on.

Perry did stand up. But gosh darn it, he took his time about it. Why did she always have to boss him around like that?

As he stood, she told him she'd laid out a blue tie. He had to admit she made dressing easier because he never had to make up his mind about hardly anything.

He ambled toward the stairs, watching her reflection in the mirror as she tilted her head from one side to the other. She might be bossy, but she sure looked pretty in that dark blue hat. He had a feeling she'd picked his tie to match it.

Just before she told him a second time to hurry up, he'd been about ready to say, *I'm just admiring how pretty you look.* The words were on the tip of his tongue. But what came out was, *Leave it be, Eliza-*

*beth. I've got plenty of time while you're fussing with that silly hat of
yours.*

They were halfway to the church before Perry noticed that Elizabeth had left off wearing the hat. He would have asked about it, but there was something about the set of her lips that told him maybe that wouldn't be such a good idea.

## 2000

**MADDY FINGERED THE** indigo hat. "It's never even been worn. Look, here's the tag still on it." She grinned. "Two dollars and ninety-five cents." She placed it on her head with all the elegance of a beauty queen, but the tag dangled in front of her left ear.

"You look like Minnie Pearl," Sadie said.

"Who's Minnie Pearl?" Maddy asked.

"Grand Ole Opry." Sadie obviously didn't want to explain further, but that was okay. Maddy eventually seemed to recognize the reference. "Why would anybody buy such a gorgeous hat and then never wear it?"

"Probably hoping she and her husband would go someplace fancy," Ida said with what sounded like resignation. "Only they probably didn't."

Poor Ida. I doubted Ralph ever wanted to go anywhere he'd have to dress up for. Bob and I didn't dress up often. Our regular Friday evening dinners at Tom's restaurant were casual affairs, and my work didn't require special clothes. He wore a uniform to work, of course, but my job at the library always saw me in a long skirt or comfortable slacks. Sandals in the summer and comfy low-heeled shoes or boots in the winter. Of course, there were always weddings and funerals to attend. "Maybe she bought it for a wedding that ended up not happening," I suggested.

"Oh," Maddy said, "that's a sad thought."

Ida cleared her throat. "Not every wedding needs to happen."

Although she didn't mention any names, I was pretty sure where that comment had come from. We all—with the exception of Carol—knew something of the history of Ida's sister's disastrous marriage.

"Enough with the hats," Pat said. "I want to know what's in these trunks."

There was quite a collection of them—old steamer trunks, military footlockers, and some contraptions that were no more than glorified crates. They were stacked haphazardly around the perimeter of the attic, some of them highlighted by the mid morning light from the eyebrow windows, some in pockets of gloom in the far corners of the enormous room. "Okay," I said. "Go ahead and pick one."

"This one," Pat said, pointing to one of the dome-topped steamer trunks. "I wonder why these trunks have rounded lids. You couldn't stack anything on top of them."

"That's exactly why," Carol said. "The people who bought these generally had plenty of money, and they didn't want their possessions piled with other people's luggage on trains or steamships. Hence the domed lids."

"Makes sense, I suppose," Pat said, "although it sounds very unfriendly."

Glaze looked up from an old gramophone she'd been toying with. "Are you sure you have the right to open these? Don't you think whoever put them here might want to keep them private?"

"If they'd wanted that," Ida said wryly, "they would have taken the trunks with them when they moved or died."

"Silly," Maddy said, "you can't take trunks with you when you die."

"Then their family members should have cleaned it all out."

"I don't know who all has owned this house. Not before Elizabeth Hoskins." I turned to Carol. "Elizabeth was the elderly widow woman we bought the house from. She waited until after her dog died, and then she moved into an assisted living place in Hastings."

*She buried her dog in the back yard, but not close to the other bodies.*

Carol looked at Marmalade quizzically. She *was* meowing a lot. "Is any of her stuff up here?"

"I don't know," I said. "I never thought about it." Recalling some of the other things Elizabeth had left behind, I wasn't so sure I wanted to open any of the trunks. Glaze must have caught the reservation behind my tone because she gave me a wicked grin. If it hadn't been for Glaze and her dowsing rods, we might never have discovered all those bodies buried in the yard.

Glaze shuddered slightly, but I don't think anybody noticed except me.

I heard sort of a grunt from across the attic. Charlotte Ellis had picked up the bent coat hanger I'd seen earlier.

"That's definitely a garbage item," I called to her.

She had sort of a funny expression on her face. "It reminds me of a conversation from a while ago."

"You had conversations about coat hangers?" Ida sounded incredulous, and I could see why.

"Not really," Charlotte said. "Just something my college roommate and I talked about." She didn't elucidate, and I didn't ask. Really, what could possibly be interesting about a coat hanger?

## September 1993

**CHARLIE ELLIS UNPACKED** her small footlocker with a great deal of care. It had belonged to her daddy when he was in the service. It wasn't every day somebody went to university for the first time. Especially somebody in her family. Her mother had kept telling her she was blazing a brand new trail. That was the term she'd used. "You'll be the first Ellis Girl who's ever graduated from college," Mom had told her, "just as I was the first one ever to graduate from high school." Even with mom facing a huge health challenge, both her parents had been adamant that she "go and don't worry about us. We'll be fine."

She'd received a ton of advance letters. The college had sent her a list of what to bring, although they hadn't mentioned anything about teddy bears. She'd brought hers anyway. Now, looking around the small room, she wondered where she was going to put everything.

The dorm room door opened and a tall blonde woman walked in. She sure didn't look like a college girl.

"Hi." She smoothed back her short hair with an impatient hand, even though Charlie could see that not a strand was out of place. "I guess I'm your roommate."

"Are you sure you're in the right place?"

The stranger double-checked the number on the door. "Room 401. Yeah." She spread her hand in what might have been a half-hearted wave. "Name's Tricia. Tricia Moody."

"Charlie. Well, really it's Charlotte, but only my mother calls me that, and only if I'm in trouble. Charlie Ellis."

"I know what you mean." Tricia stepped back out into the hall and brought in a suitcase, then closed the door behind her. "My mother always called me Pat. Or Patricia if she was mad at me. I used to ask her to call me Tricia, but she never would."

Charlie wondered about the past tense, but didn't want to ask. Somehow it didn't seem polite to ask a brand new roommate if her mother was dead.

"I sort of picked this bed." Charlie waved her hand at it. "I hope that's okay."

Tricia raised a negligent shoulder. "Fine by me." She hauled her suitcase onto the other twin bed, sat down next to it, and rubbed her tummy. "I'm about ready for lunch. Want to go down together?"

Charlie really did want to get unpacked first. She'd just started hanging her blouses and didn't want them to get too wrinkled.

Tricia held out her hand. "What kind of hanger is that?"

Charlie passed it to her. "My mom and I made them. Well, we didn't make them exactly, but we took regular old wire hangers and covered them with yarn. It makes the clothes hang better. They don't slip off."

Tricia didn't look convinced.

"My mom's been sick a lot lately. I'm pretty worried about her."

"Will you have to quit school if she dies? I wouldn't want to have to find a different roommate."

Charlie gaped at Tricia. What kind of question was that? Charlie didn't know what to say. She took back the coat hanger when Tricia handed it to her. "I guess I'm ready for lunch if you are."

**"WOULD YOU QUIT** bouncing around on that chair?" Tricia said over lunch. "You're getting on my nerves."

"It's just that, well, I sort of have a question." Charlie paused for a second, but Tricia just looked at her. "What I mean is, you don't look anything like a college student."

"Why not?" Tricia had her mouth around a thick sandwich, so the words came out sort of garbled.

"You look older, or something."

"Guess that's because I am." She put the sandwich down, half-eaten already. "I worked for a while after high school. That was when my mom died."

"Oh, I'm sorry. I ..." She pushed her bright red bangs out of the way. "I can't imagine life without my mother."

Tricia raised an eyebrow. "That's okay. My father and I managed without her, but I finally just wanted to get out of the house, and my father said he'd foot the bill, so I applied here."

Charlie stared at her. "You make it sound like it was no big deal. I know how hard I had to work to get admitted." Charlie took a bite of her own sandwich. "Are you really smart?"

Tricia made a noncommittal sound.

"So, what are you?" Charlie asked. "About twenty-four, twenty-five?"

Tricia picked up her Reuben and took another big bite. "Twenty-eight," she said around a mouthful.

Charlie made a face. "How can you stand those?"

"Stand what?"

"Your sandwich. I can never chew through all those layers of beef."

Tricia took a minute to work her way through all those layers. "Tastes good, though," she said, and pulled one more recalcitrant layer up past her lips. After a few more bites, she pointed at Charlie's right arm. "What happened to it?"

"My arm?"

"Yeah. Why's it so crooked?"

Charlie looked around the Commons. "I hardly even think about it anymore. It happened when I was a little kid. Six or seven, I think. My mom and I went camping one summer, and I broke my arm. We'd already spent a couple of days hiking way back into the Appalachian Mountains, so it took forever to get me out of there."

"Why didn't she call for help?"

"Even if we'd had cell phones back then, which we didn't—nobody had them—they wouldn't have worked out where we were. She splinted my arm right after it happened, but by the time she got me to a doctor, I was in pretty bad shape. The arm's just never worked quite right, but Mom couldn't afford to pay for the extra operations they wanted me to have. Doesn't matter—I don't use it to write with."

Tricia pushed back her chair and stood. "I'm ready for some dessert."

## late March 1741

**BRIDGET HASTINGS HAD** seldom been so frightened as she was this very moment. Her mother had insisted that she take her nine-year-old brother Lucius with her into the woods. They needed more moss before they left on their long trip, and they needed time to wash it thoroughly, dry it, and pound it into usable powder.

Moss was not a favorite food of anyone in Brandtburg, but if the corn stores began to give out or were consumed by mice, the moss could be used to stretch the remaining corn. It could be added to soups and stews, or mixed with water to make a jellylike gruel. As long as it had been soaked and rinsed enough times, most of the bitter taste would be gone.

She knew of a woodland glade on the slopes of the mountain to the east of Brandtburg, but it was a far piece to walk, and she had been glad of her brother's company at first. She easily found the glade, and the two of them harvested the compact cushions of moss, packing them into the rough sacking they had brought with them.

The return trip, slower because of their heavy mossy burden, was none the less pleasant, for Lucius had a light-hearted approach to life and seemed to make a game of every obstacle they came across, whether it was a tree fallen across the path or a stream they had to ford in the still-chilly March weather.

It was one of those streams that turned out to be his downfall. Instead of stepping carefully from flat stone to large boulder to protruding rock, he tried to go faster, and his slight body could not keep up with his feet. Bridget heard the loud crack, even over the rushing sound of the water, when he fell and struck his arm the wrong way.

Now he not only had to be dried off with a hastily-built fire lest he catch his death on the way home, but Bridget had to bind his arm to his side, even though he screamed as she did it, and then carry his moss pack as well as her own.

She tried not to let her irritation show. He was just a small boy and had always been adventuresome. But in this case, with all the extra work it caused her, she could not stop herself from raising her voice. "Could you not take better care? What help will you be to us on the trail to the south if you have to be tended all along the way?"

"I'll mend fast, Sister," he assured her, but Bridget, angry though she was, could hear the fear in his piping voice.

She reached out and ruffled his hair, something he normally hated for her to do. The fact that he did not object now let her know just how very hurt he must be, and she was more afraid than ever.

# 2000

**PAT WENT BACK** to her steamer trunk and stared at it suspiciously. "It's probably locked."

"Only one way to find out." Ida motioned with her hands.

So Pat lifted the lid. "Oooh, look!" She pulled out a thick bundle of fabric, covered in rainbow-hued colors. "It's embroidered."

Sadie reached toward it. "What fine needlework. The stitches are so small and close together, I can barely see them."

"Why would anybody put it"—Glaze swept her hand toward the steamer trunk—"in there?"

"It feels like there's something inside it."

"No telling what it's wrapped around," Carol said, "but a lot of times old worn-out—or badly stained—pieces of linen were used to protect other items."

"Even if it is stained," Pat said, "it's gorgeous. All those roses must have taken somebody forever to embroider."

Ida pointed. "It's stained alright. Such a dark brownish red, it looks like somebody spilled a whole glass of wine."

"You're right," I said, "but I wonder why they didn't clean it? If they'd soaked it right away, they could have gotten the stain out, don't you think?"

"Maybe they couldn't," Maddy said. "If they were having dinner and the table was laden down, it wouldn't make sense to disrupt the meal."

"Still, I should think that back then—whenever this was—a tablecloth this pretty would have been worth moving people and platters and such."

"Or at least," Pat said, "they could have poured a glass of water on it to dilute the wine and keep the spill from drying out."

Melissa touched Pat's arm. "I guess they needed you there to set them straight."

Melissa lifted the bundle and studied it. "Do you think they had products that would clean something like this back then?"

Carol, of course, was the one to nod and answer her. "Boiling water and plenty of salt."

"It's not just stained." Ida pointed to a ragged rent next to a whorl of light green leaves and vines. "It's torn. No wonder they dumped it up here."

Pat shifted from one foot to another. "Can we find out what it's wrapped around?"

We crowded around her.

"Maybe it's a body," Maddy said, and Glaze elbowed her in the ribs.

## Late Autumn 1792

**"THIS WILL MAKE** a lovely wedding present for my brother." Lydia Hastings Sheffield smiled at her grandmother across the expanse of cloth that draped loosely between their matching oversized embroidery hoops. "Surely both Reuben and Astaline will find it exquisite."

Edna Russell Hastings set down her needle and rubbed her gnarled fingers. She could not remember a time when she had not had a needle either in her hands or close by awaiting her expertise, except for the four long years of the trek from Brandtburg, when her fine needlework had been packed away in the bottom of a sturdy box. "If Astaline does not treasure it, I just may ask for it back."

Lydia set aside her own needle. "Are your hands bothering you overmuch, Grandmother?" She reached across the short distance between them and held her grandmother's hands, warming them between her palms. "You could rest them awhile and I will make you some tea as soon as I finish this daisy."

"No, my dear. They just feel a bit stiff, but I do not want to stop, for we have only a few more hours until your brother Reuben will return."

"That is no reason for you to force your hands to do work that hurts you. He knows we are making him the finest wedding tablecloth in the world."

"Knowing something is one thing, but seeing it is quite another. I would have this covered over before he returns from the schoolhouse."

"I know. I know. *He must not see it until the day he is wed.* You have said that often enough."

"Did you ask about tea because you yourself need a rest?" Grandmother grinned with that wicked glint in her eye that Lydia loved. "Or perhaps a trip to the privy. I know the babe must be pressing in a very inconvenient place." She giggled, more like a girl of ten than an ancient woman of sixty-seven.

"I need not hurry away quite yet, Grandmother. There is time for one or two more flowers. And then for tea-brewing."

Lydia ran her hand lovingly across the design that she and her grandmother had worked so long to perfect. Dandelion blooms and daisies predominated, their bright yellow and white blossoms set off by a field of green leaves and vines that meandered all the way around the edge, with just enough dark blue sprays of iris and bright red roses to emphasize the exquisite design. An enormous central oval of flowers and leaves in multiple shades of green was placed so that one could set a large platter in the center of it without covering any of the design, except for the nine multicolored butterflies that spread their wings in a ring in the middle of the oval.

Reuben Hastings was the best brother in the world, Lydia thought. Had he not made these two new-fashioned circular embroidery frames so that she and her grandmother could work together, their toes almost touching as they sat facing one another close enough to the fire to be warmed by it, but not so close as to risk a stray spark singeing the fine linen?

The two of them, she and her grandmother, had quite a reputation in Martinsville for their meticulous embroidery, and no wedding was considered complete until the bride and groom had received a broidered cloth of theirs. Lydia did wonder, though, how much longer her grandmother would be able to wield her needle. The larger-than-usual frames they each held had helped a great deal, for Grandmother no longer had to hold the fabric taut nor change the position of the cloth so often, but Lydia could not help but notice that Grandmother paused ever more frequently, and Lydia had to help her reposition the fabric in the frame each time Grandmother completed one section.

She lifted the one yet-unfinished edge of the cloth to calculate how long it might take them to complete it. There was still plenty of time. Reuben would not wed Astaline Shipleigh until midsummer. Lydia wished with all her heart that their father, Alonzo Hastings, had lived long enough to see his well-loved son married. But Father was dead and Reuben had taken Father's place as the village schoolmaster. Life went on.

She shook herself slightly. She must not dawdle in daylight dreams like this. There was broidery to be finished before the wedding.

The real limit, though, to how soon the cloth must be completed, would be how soon Lydia's baby would come. Early spring, most likely. The tablecloth would be finished well before then. Lydia dropped the edge back onto the large expanse of plain linen that she had spread beneath their chairs so the part of the long tablecloth that drooped to the floor would not risk being soiled should someone have been thoughtless enough to track dirt onto the foot-smoothed floorboards of Beechnut House.

## 1806

**FOURTEEN YEARS LATER**, Lydia's back ached from the strain of sitting across the bed from her brother Reuben all night long. She could not even stand up, much less leave the room, for her hands were twined around the fingers of her beloved sister-in-law, Astaline Shipleigh Hastings, whose latest babe had been born dead the previous evening. They had not taken the time to bury the child, not while the mother's life was still in question. She doubted that Astaline was even aware of her presence, but Lydia was unwilling to let go for fear that her dear friend's tenuous hold on life was dependent on Lydia's handclasp.

*Forgive me my arrogance*, Lydia thought, *for I know I cannot rule when death will come nor stop it if it is time for my friend to go.* Still, she hung onto Astaline's hand with all her might, trying to will the color back into Astaline's cheeks.

Reuben was bent forward over the other side of the bed with his forehead pressed against Astaline's cheek, one of his hands gripping her shoulder and the other her arm, as if he too thought he might be able to hold back his wife from dying. His light brown hair brushed her chin, and Lydia feared it might tickle, but there had been no response from Astaline. No response at all.

In point of fact, Astaline had not made a movement or a sound since late the evening before, after all her living children had retired for the night, when she had opened her eyes briefly and looked, first at Lydia and then at Reuben. Her lips had moved slightly, but—as if the effort of speech was too great for her—she had sighed heavily, closed her eyes, and remained thus all through the night.

Dawn had just begun to break when Astaline gasped in the death rattle Lydia well remembered from her darling grandmother's passing. Reuben cried out and gathered his wife's lifeless body into his arms. When Lydia finally managed to convince Reuben to let go, she straightened the silver pendant her sister-in-law wore, smoothed the bedclothes, and went to call Rose, the twins, Lilian, and the two boys.

Lydia's own anguish was severe, but she could not give in to it. There were arrangements to be made for the burial of Astaline with the body of her stillborn child—arrangements that Reuben was in no shape to deal with. Astaline's body still needed washing, the bedding with all the blood from the birth needed to be soaked and cleansed, the food the neighbors had already begun to bring needed to be set out, although she supposed she could depend on the other women to take care of that. She would ask them, though, to spread the wedding cloth on the long table. Astaline had loved it so, despite the large wine-stain that dated from the time of her wedding. Fortunately food platters could always be arranged to hide the stain.

Astaline had been well loved, so likely everyone in Martinsville would choose to attend the funeral—and the gathering thereafter. It would be fitting to use the bright, beautiful wedding tablecloth for Astaline's farewell. Lydia hoped the food would last.

The next day, Reuben managed to make it through the funeral service, although he could not be convinced to toss a handful of dirt onto his wife's coffin. Lydia asked her husband Curtis and one of the other men to walk with Reuben back to the house, for she feared her brother might run away or do something else equally drastic. He had been like a crazy man since Astaline's death. Lydia doubted her own husband would react that way when it was time for Lydia to die. No, Curtis Sheffield was more levelheaded than Reuben.

Once she reached the house, she drew her husband aside. "Will you stay close to my brother? I fear he is not in his right mind."

Curtis laid a comforting hand on her shoulder. "Reuben is sad, my dear, but I cannot see that we need be too concerned. He has his children, after all, and tomorrow he will return to his job as schoolmaster."

Lydia was not convinced, but she deferred to Curtis' opinion for now. She would keep an eye on her brother herself. She studied the table one last time to be sure all was in place and groaned inwardly when she saw that Catherine Martin Tolland had brought one of her unfortunately solid loaves of bread—that woman could not bake a decent loaf to save her soul. Catherine must have teeth made of iron, Lydia thought, for she seems not to know that her bread is inedible. Either that or she soaked her bread for an hour in milk before trying to eat it.

Lydia stepped to the side counter and chose the sharpest kitchen knife. She doubted many people would try the bread, for everyone knew Catherine's reputation, but she pulled the loaf on its sturdy cutting board closer to the edge of the table, so people could cut the rock-hard loaf without having to lean over. She truly hoped nobody would let the knife slip. The last thing they needed was for someone to cut off a finger at the funeral feast. Quietly, she admonished herself for such levity.

Perhaps, she thought, I should simply slice the bread myself, but Reverend Jonas Russell spoke then, asking everyone to draw close around the long table for a prayer. Curtis had apparently taken Lydia's request to heart, for he steered Reuben up next to Lydia. Between the two of them, they should be able to support him should he choose to collapse. His face looked dangerously pale.

Reuben waited until the amen before he snatched up the long bread knife and plunged it into the table, right through the lovely cloth. "I will not say amen to a God who has taken my beloved!" With that he ran, cursing, from the house while Lydia, Curtis, and everyone else in the room stood in shocked silence.

By the time Curtis convinced Reuben to return home several hours later, very few of the women had eaten anything at all, yet the funeral feast had been consumed—the men of Martinsville were sanguine enough not to waste good food simply because of a man's overwhelming grief. He would, they knew, recover from it, although Lydia had her doubts. Her brother's anguish was far too deep.

The women cleared off the remainders—including the entire uneaten loaf of Catherine's bread—and said their goodbyes to Lydia, as well as to Rose, Emma, Caroline, Lilian, and the boys.

Lydia waited for the last of the guests to leave before she asked Rose to help her remove the tablecloth and fold it.

"I do not know what to do with it," thirteen-year-old Rose said as she ran her fingers over and over the leaf design, carefully avoiding the hole where the knife had torn through the fabric.

"Your father may not want to be reminded too much," Lydia said carefully, watching the girl's tear-streaked face to be sure her words were understood. "The cloth can certainly be repaired, but perhaps now is not the time to do it. Why do you not set it aside for now? Later I will help you stitch it up." She inspected the tear. "It is a clean cut. We should be able to restore it so no one will notice." She knew she would be the one responsible for the sewing, for young Rose was not known for her dexterity with needle and thread.

Rose nodded. "I will put it in the bottom drawer of my armoire. Father will never find it there."

Lydia stayed for three weeks to help the children ease into their new life without a mother. She felt sure Reuben would not remarry, but Rose and the twins were old enough now to take on the responsibility of managing the household, and Reuben's labor in the schoolhouse would be enough to keep his mind occupied so he need not brood for too much longer.

**THE DAY LYDIA** left to return to her own home, she promised Rose,

"I will visit often, but if you ever need me, let me know. I want to be a help to you."

"Thank you, Aunt Lydia," Rose said, fingering the silver pendant she had taken from around her dead mother's throat. Beneath her restless fingers she could feel the engraved letters. ASH and RSH. As the oldest surviving daughter, she was entitled to wear it now. Her twin sisters had each gotten one of Mother's special hair ornaments made of the horn of a buffalo, and the youngest sister, Lilian, had a particularly delicate fan as a remembrance. Rose was sure the girl would break it the first time she used it.

As soon as Aunt Lydia's cart disappeared around the corner, Rose went to her room, unearthed the torn tablecloth that she could not look at without remembering her mother's death and her father's fury, and stuffed it into the rag box in the attic.

## 2000

**SADIE PICKED UP** the three hatboxes that were strewn across the card table, stacked them, and moved them to one side.

Maddy retrieved the one that held the indigo hat and placed it near the stairs. "I might as well take it down with me and keep it with my suitcase, since I'm certainly not leaving it here."

Sadie nodded absent-mindedly, her thoughts obviously elsewhere. She indicated the linen-wrapped bundle. "Lay it out here, why don't you?"

"It looks like it's gift-wrapped," Melissa said. "These folds are so intricate."

"The dress—I'm assuming it must be a dress in there," Carol said, "probably has a full skirt, so this linen would be placed in such a way as to keep one fold of the dress from resting directly on another fold."

"Somebody take a picture before we mess it up."

I hurried down to my bedroom for my camera. It wouldn't hurt to have a full record of what we were unearthing, not just this linen-enclosed parcel, but everything else as well.

The beautifully embroidered tablecloth enfolded a real treasure.

The dress was quite simply gorgeous, with elaborate panels of chocolate brown velvet that were overhung with a lace so intricate it almost hurt my head to think of the work that had gone into making it.

"And look at this hat," Pat said. She lifted an elaborate confection of laces and ribbons and frills from the box that had been wedged into a corner of the trunk. "Isn't it marvelous?"

"Try it on," Maddy said.

"And if it fits, feel free to keep it," I said, thinking how much I wanted to get the attic cleared out. Anyway, I didn't think the style suited me at all.

On Pat, though, it was lovely.

"It's yours," I said, and I went back to inspecting the dress. I wiped my hands on my pants, afraid to sully such a beautiful creation, but I had to investigate the corner of an envelope I saw peeking out from between two of the folds.

"Pay dirt!" I exclaimed as I opened the heavy, parchment-like paper.

Melissa peered over my shoulder. "What is it?"

"A wedding invitation. Melanie Surratt and the Right Reverend Zenus Hastings Hoskins," I read aloud. "Hoskins," I said thoughtfully. "Eighteen-thirty-two. He must have been grandfather or great-grandfather to Perry Hoskins." I nodded in Carol Mellinger's direction. "Perry married Elizabeth."

"The one you bought this house from?"

*She had a very old dog.*

I nodded.

*He liked to sit in the sun.*

Carol shook her head back and forth. "It's amazing what a web of relationships we find when we look hard enough, isn't it?" She touched the dress with the tip of her index finger. "Of course, the dress could have come to Perry and Elizabeth through an aunt or uncle as well. Not all old items are handed down directly from mother to daughter or father to son."

We all nodded, but she wasn't finished. "Speaking of relationships and the web they form, wait until you hear the story I have to tell." No matter how much we plagued her, though, she wouldn't say anything more about it. "First, let's take a really good look at this dress."

# 1832

**MELANIE SURRATT HOSKINS** surveyed the chaos in the attic and turned to her sister. "I never suspected I was marrying into such a mess."

"There's no way you could have known." Elspeth flicked her finger over a trunk and lifted a line of dust. "Zenus probably doesn't have a clue what's up here."

Melanie spread the wide expanse of plain linen and helped Elspeth position the dress on it. "I wonder if Mother Hoskins was responsible for any of this jumble."

"Probably not." Elspeth laughed, entirely without humor, and studied a shabby-looking rocking horse. "If it was not completely utilitarian, your father-in-law would not have had it anywhere in the house."

Melanie nodded grimly. Everyone in Martinsville knew about the late, the legendary, the unlamented Baxter Hoskins and his parsimonious approach to life.

"I am surprised your Zenus turned out as well as he did," Elspeth said.

"I believe Zenus got tired of living like a monk all those years when he was growing up." Melanie fingered the gold pendant Zenus had given her on their wedding day. It held a miniature portrait of him, and Melanie was inordinately proud of it. "It is a shame that Mother Rose Hoskins is so set against jewelry. Did I tell you, though, that she complimented me when she first saw my pendant?"

"She did?"

"Yes. She particularly liked the tiny portrait of Zenus. She almost seemed to want to tell me something about it, but then she tightened her lips and said nothing." She looked around the attic in some confusion. "How will we ever find a safe place to store my dress?"

Elspeth spread her arms wide. "This is about as safe as you can get. You can pick any one of those trunks while I pull out the ragbag."

"Just any trunk?"

"Sure. Imagine you and Zenus are heading out of New York harbor for an around-the-world tour."

"Taking my wedding gown with me?"

"Why not? Maybe you two will sail for twenty years and then you and he can have an anniversary celebration, with him in his top hat and morning coat and you in your wedding hat and this gorgeous dress." Elspeth turned to inspect the dress in question, lying on its wide linen sheet, then piled a number of other linen pieces beside it as she took them from a box of clean rags. She paused over a small, tightly-compressed bundle wrapped in a swath of dark gray fabric.

"What is that, Sister?"

Elspeth set the bundle aside and waved an airy hand. "Nothing we need be concerned with.

Melanie insisted, though. Opened, the package revealed a bonnet such as had not been worn for decades. Shirred around the outer edge, it looked limp and, somehow sad.

Elspeth scoffed. "Let me throw that away."

Melanie pulled it away from her sister's grasping hands. "It must have meant something to someone. See how it has been cleaned and folded tidily?" She looked around for a better place to stow it, and her eyes rested on a short stack of hatboxes. Unsure whether they were empty or full, she lifted several lids until she found one that had nothing in it. "There," she said. "It will be safe like this."

"And your dress will be even more safe, once we find the proper trunk to stow it in until your first daughter has need of it for her wedding day." Elspeth pushed the hat box with its pathetic contents to one side. "So which trunk will you pack your extensive wardrobe in?"

"This one." Melanie indicated a dome-topped steamer trunk. She pulled it open and uttered a little exclamation of dismay. "There is no room." The trunk was filled almost to the top with papers—old cards and letters from the look of them. She opened one of the flat pasteboard boxes stacked in each of the corners of the trunk and found more letters, tied into bundles with various-colored ribbons.

"Of course there is room," Elspeth said. "Or there soon will be." She opened another trunk at random—one that was flat on the top and not nearly as romantic looking. It was still three-quarters empty. Scooping handfuls of letters and several layers of the boxes from one trunk to the other, she worked quickly. When one of the letters caught on a splinter in the rough edge of the trunk, she ripped it loose and tossed it into the second trunk. Eventually, there was a space roomy enough so they wouldn't have to compress the wedding dress. "That domed lid makes this trunk a perfect choice, because it is less likely to press down on the dress." She pulled off the splinter, discarded the torn piece of envelope, and made sure the resulting edge was smooth enough not to catch on the dress.

Melanie appreciated her sister's care over the dress, but she gave a rueful look at the second trunk. "What if somebody wants to read those letters? They are all out of order now."

"Read them?" Elspeth sounded aghast. "Nobody reads those things."

"Then why keep them?"

For a moment, Elspeth's face went blank. "Just in case, I suppose."

"In case of what?"

"Do you think there's enough room for the hatbox as well as the dress?"

Melanie sighed. She had lived with Elspeth long enough to know when not to press an issue. Elspeth had always been like that. If she did not know an answer or did not want to have to think about something, she just ignored it, changed the subject, and went on with her life.

Melanie removed several ribbon-tied stacks of letters from one corner of the steamer trunk. A single folded paper sat beneath two of the stacks, along with a sealed envelope, but Melanie didn't even glance at the inscriptions except to note that the handwriting on both was rather spidery. She set the bundles and the single sheet aside and pulled out two pasteboard boxes, which left an open space almost all the way to the bottom of the steamer trunk. The hatbox was not that big around, but it *was* fairly tall. "I cannot just toss these in that other trunk," Melanie said. She put one of the tied bundles carefully in the flat-topped trunk, placed the single letter and the envelope on top of it, noting the stain of dark red sealing wax on both, and added another of the beribboned stacks on top of the sealing wax letter. Then she put the two pasteboard boxes on top of that.

"What are you doing that for?" Elspeth was far too impatient.

"It looks like an old letter of some sort," Melanie said. "It is less likely to get crumpled this way." Maybe someday, when she had time, she would come back up here, retrieve the letter, and read it.

"Get your hands out of the way." Elspeth closed the flat lid with a decided thud. "Now," she dusted her hands off, "help me spread this out." She lifted one of the larger pieces of linen she'd taken from the rag box, an old embroidered tablecloth that had a rip along one side of it. "I wonder why someone did not repair this rip." Together they unfolded it to its entire length.

"It really is a lovely tablecloth. Look at the intricacy of the design." Melanie was tempted for a moment to take the cloth, repair it, and use it on the big table downstairs.

"Nonsense," Elspeth said. "It is far too busy-looking with all those butterflies and flowers. You need a cloth that is much more elegant. Anyway, this is badly stained. It looks like wine. They really should have cleaned it right away." She clucked her tongue at such sloppy housekeeping.

Melanie wanted to object. The tablecloth was truly lovely, and she was sure she could simply place platters of food to cover the stain, but it was very difficult for her to countermand her sister once Elspeth had her mind made up. And she did have to admit the tablecloth was large enough to protect every single fold of her wedding dress.

Once it was spread across the opened trunk, they placed the dress on it, gathering up the linen and tucking it carefully between each fold of material. "You look so good in this light brown," Elspeth said, fingering the high lace neckline. "You need another dress precisely this color, but with a little less lace and velvet."

Melanie laughed. "I have plenty of dresses already, and I will certainly never need another one, especially not one with any lace or velvet at all. You know quite well that neither lace nor velvet would befit the wife of a minister."

"Oh pshaw," Elspeth said. "Admit it. This color is perfect for you. It makes your eyes glow—you looked like a fawn when you walked down the aisle." She reached for another piece of linen, probably a dishtowel, and used it to protect the first sleeve. "I can't wait to see my niece wearing this."

"Are you not being a bit premature? I have to have a baby first. And what if it is a boy? Zenus said he wants a boy to follow in his footsteps."

"Oh, that is not a problem." Elspeth waved her hand airily

through the early afternoon sunshine that pierced the gloom of the attic through the windows on the front of the house. "Let him have his boy first time around. You will have plenty of girls later."

Melanie could feel Elspeth's eyes on her waist. Elspeth probably thought she was being surreptitious about the examination, but really, Melanie knew everyone was just waiting for her to announce impending motherhood. She and Zenus had married three months ago. And then, just two weeks later Grace, their other sister, had married Arthur Hoskins, the brother of Zenus. Already Grace had confided that she felt certain—well, almost certain—that she was with child, so surely, Melanie thought, it will not take me long to conceive. Delilah, the fourth sister, whom they all called Dolly, was not married yet, but she was the youngest, so there was time.

"Did you hear what our sister Grace said about the child she is expecting?"

Melanie pulled her thoughts back, "No. What did she say?"

"She is so sure the child will be a boy, she and Arthur have already chosen a name. Gideon Zenus Hoskins."

Melanie supposed she should feel flattered that Arthur wanted to name his first son after Zenus. The two men were so close, they might as well have been twins, but she really did not care. All she wanted was to conceive herself and to give birth to a healthy child.

It took the two sisters almost an hour to arrange the dress and the associated undergarments to their satisfaction. Before closing the trunk, Elspeth reached into one of the capacious pockets on her apron and withdrew Zenus and Melanie's wedding invitation. She opened it to show her sister. "I am including the newspaper announcement of your wedding as well. It will be safe here." She tucked the invitation into yet another fold of the linen, making sure it did not touch the dress itself.

"Do you not want to keep it?" Melanie knew she sounded reproachful, but her sister reassured her.

"I want to see your daughter's face when she opens this trunk for the first time and reads such an elegant invitation."

**MELANIE'S FIRST CHILD** was a girl, but she died within a day. The second was a boy who lived. The third was yet another boy. By then, Elspeth had married David Russell and moved to Russell Gap. Then

Zenus was offered a pulpit in Russell Gap, so he and Melanie took over the parsonage there. Grace and Arthur and little Gideon moved into the house on Beechnut Lane and assumed the care of Mother Rose Hoskins.

Soon thereafter, Melanie gave birth to twin boys. Over the years of bearing one son after another, Melanie ceased to think about her beautiful brown lace and velvet wedding dress, and when Elspeth caught the scarlet fever and died at age thirty-two, Melanie had no one to remind her that a wedding dress was tucked away in the attic of her sister Grace's house, awaiting a loving hand and another young bride, a bride who was never born.

## 2000

**"HELLO! ANYBODY HOME** up there?"

"Come on up, Rebecca Jo," I called out. "Is Dee with you?"

"She certainly is. And so is Amanda. And Easton."

Oh dear. Easton.

*She does not like cats.*

Where on earth was I going to put all these people? Rebecca Jo and Dee could stay together, of course. I'd give them the largest of the guest rooms. Since Rebecca Jo was my mother-in-law, as well as one of my Petunias, I wanted her to have the best room. It was one of the few guest rooms that had a double bed. Surely Rebecca Jo wouldn't mind sharing a bed with Dee. I made a mental note to ask first. I might have assigned Sadie to that room—she was just as much a favorite as Rebecca Jo, but I'd have to put Easton in with Sadie, and I didn't want to coddle Easton in any way whatsoever. I hoped Sadie wouldn't mind having Easton in a room with her. Sadie was about the only woman in Martinsville who actually liked Easton Hastings.

That left Amanda Stanton. What was I going to do with her? I doubted she knew Charlotte well enough to room with her. Anyway, Charlotte was in the tiny room. I hoped the bed would be long enough for her. And Amanda? Maybe the room with the green wallpaper.

By the time they made it to the attic—my mother-in-law was still pretty spry, but she took her time whenever she had to climb stairs— we'd cleared a place and set up four more chairs in our impromptu ring.

"Did Bob assign you to rooms?" I hoped he hadn't.

"Nope," Dee said. "He just told us to head up here and have fun."

"That'll be easy," Rebecca Jo said, glancing around her. "I love attics. No telling what you'll find."

"Before we start on a scavenger hunt," I said, "I need to think about where everybody's going to sleep." I quickly re-counted the number of beds. "Half of them aren't even made up," I said, "and I don't know how many sets of sheets I have."

"You know me," Maddy said. "I'm happy sleeping in my sweatpants with a blanket wrapped around me."

Easton made a face.

"Let's not worry about it," Rebecca Jo said. "Dee and I can share a room." I was glad she agreed with what I'd already decided. "We brought our own sheets," she added, "but they're full-sized."

"If you don't mind sharing, there's that room at the end of the hall with the full-sized bed."

"Fine with me." Rebecca Jo looked at Dee. "What about you?"

"Not a problem."

Good. That was solved.

"Ralph and I brought sheets, too," Ida said, "but ours are twin. I've seen those guest rooms of yours."

"Let's just sort everything out when it gets closer to bedtime," Rebecca Jo suggested, echoing what Sadie had said earlier.

"That sounds fine to me." Sadie took a seat and waved Easton over to sit next to her. "Would you like to share a room with me, dear?"

Easton actually looked enthusiastic about it. She and Sadie both loved to feed the birds. Maybe that was the bond that held them together. And they both loved music. Easton had a gorgeous voice. I had to admit Easton had improved quite a lot since she'd moved to Martinsville. It had been touch and go there for a while, with many of the married women in town—myself included—ready to throttle her gleefully. As soon as I had that thought, though, I remembered the strangled body that had been tangled in the wreckage of the town dock on Halloween several years ago, and felt a pang of remorse. Losing her sibling like that can't have been easy for Easton.

I let Melissa do the introductions. Most of us knew each other, of course. But Carol Mellinger was brand new to everybody, and Amanda Stanton was the massage therapist who'd moved here from the Atlanta area a couple of years ago and set up a practice just north of town, so Pat might not have met her yet. Amanda was really good at what she did. My shoulders and back (and neck and feet) could attest to that fact.

"We've got a great crowd here," Melissa said, "but can you think of anybody who might not have gotten shelter from the storm?"

We all looked around at each other. I certainly couldn't think of anyone else.

Sadie raised her head suddenly, as if she'd just remembered someone. "What about Melody?"

"She's fine," I said. "Reebok told Bob she was visiting with her parents when the storm hit and decided to stay there. Melody's the clerk at town hall," I told Carol.

"Maybe we should go through your address book, Biscuit." Melissa had an undercurrent to her voice that Pat picked up on.

"Why?"

"Well," Melissa said, "there's no telling who it might remind us to call. Of course, if Melody's at her parents' house, we won't have to look under T for Melody."

"T?" Pat sounded indignant. "Whaddya mean T?"

Melissa spread her hands and looked at me. "Or maybe she's not under T for Town Clerk. Did you put her under C for just plain old Clerk, since that's easier?"

"You can laugh at my system if you want to, Melissa, but I know exactly how to find anyone I want on that list."

Maddy swatted me playfully on the shoulder. "I still remember the day Glaze told me about your system, Biscuit. It's crazy, but it does have a certain logic to it." She twirled her finger next to the side of her head. "Nick Foley is listed under D. For dentist." Predictably, everybody laughed. Everybody except Easton. I noticed that Charlotte didn't laugh either, but she nodded. Maybe she had a methodical mind like mine. Was I methodical or just plain nuts?

Maddy had more to say. "I asked Biscuit where she'd put my brother's name, and she said he wasn't under J for John or A for Ames. He was under P for heaven's sake."

Melissa broke in. "Not to worry, anyone. Once you catch onto

Biscuit's way of looking at the world, you'll understand. The P is for priest," she explained for Carol's benefit. "St. Theresa's is the Catholic church in town."

"Then I assume I'm under Y for yellow," Sadie said, "but I'd rather be under Q."

That one stumped even me. "Q?"

"For Queen Bee."

Dee made a loud raspberry. "I suppose you can put me under the fourth letter of the alphabet—not for Dee, but for divorced."

"Oh for heaven's sake, Dee, that's not who you are."

"You could put her under C for creative," Rebecca Jo said.

"Or L for lucky lady." Glaze was as glad as I was that Dee had gotten away from that awful husband of hers.

Pat stepped back and looked Dee up and down. "How about P for perky person?"

"I keep her under S." Dee looked a question at me. "For Sister," I said. She hugged me for a long time.

"All right," Rebecca Jo said. "You might as well tell us where the rest of us are."

"That's easy," I said. "You're listed under O for Other Mother."

"Wait a minute," Glaze said. "If Dee is S for sister, where'd you put me? Not that you couldn't have two people listed under S."

"You're L." When she gave me a blank stare, I said, "Little Sister."

"You know," Ida said, "this is the most self-centered address book I've ever heard of. It's all about their relationship to *you*."

"But isn't that how we always see other people? You can put Sharon under N in your address book because she's *your* neighbor, but I'll leave her under B for Beauty Shop."

"Was Annie McGill under R for Redhead?" Melissa turned to Carol and explained. "Annie … uh … before she died … used to own the Heal Thyself store, the one I mentioned this morning, only Pumpkin renamed it to Healthy Self. Annie had long, long red hair."

"No," I said, after a moment of silence. "She was under H." There was another moment of quiet.

Melissa broke the suspense. "For head, comma, red?"

"Herb store," I said. It made perfect sense to me.

Before we got too sidetracked, I took a few moments to reiterate the bathroom instructions. "Sorry you'll have to go downstairs if you need the facilities," I said, "but nobody ever put in a bathroom up here."

Glaze gave an exaggerated shiver. "Why doesn't that surprise me?"

"We could use that chamber pot," Sadie said, pointing to an old red-rimmed white enamel pot that stood between a dowdy dresser and a crooked floor lamp.

Good grief. The things we were liable to find. I lifted the lid with some trepidation and peered into it. Clean and empty, thank goodness, but there was a huge rusted area on the outside near the bottom where it was badly dented.

## Summer, 1837

**TIMOTHY HOSKINS HATED** doing his chores each morning, especially now that he was seven years old. Before this, for the past three years, his brother Euston had been the one to empty the thunder mugs each morning. And before Euston it had been Zenus, and then their sister Kathryn, from the time she was seven, and Arthur had taken his turn as well. But now Zenus was fourteen, Kathryn was thirteen, Arthur was twelve, Euston was nine, and Timothy was seven. "Seven is the magic number," his father had said only yesterday on Timothy's birthday. "More age means more responsibility." Father had definite ideas about responsibility. He was a minister, so he thought about things like that a lot.

Timothy was not sure he liked the idea of taking on more responsibility. He had liked egg-gathering much better. *More smelliness* is what he thought this new job of his entailed, but naturally he couldn't say that to Father. If this had anything to do with age, then Grandmother ought to be the one emptying the chamber pots because she was one of the oldest people Timothy had ever seen. Kathryn had told him once that Grandmother was almost fifty years old. He wanted to know how many chamber pots she had emptied, but he did not dare ask.

Instead, he dutifully went into the room where his mother and father had their bed, raised the edge of the quilt, and pulled the pot from underneath the wooden frame, careful not to disturb the lid. Euston had always made four separate trips, from the various sleeping rooms to the privy. Then he would carry all four empty pots together down to the river to rinse them.

Timothy saw no reason why he should have to make four trips to the privy when, by carrying two pots at once, he could make do with only two trips. He was tall for seven. He was strong. He could lift that much. He lined two of the four pots up at the bottom of the back porch steps, hoisted the other two by their handles, and carted them to the outhouse.

He had just finished emptying the second one into the privy when he heard a loud clatter, followed almost immediately by the sound of his father's shouts. "Who did a blame fool thing like this?"

Timothy dropped the second pot, not even caring that the side of it caved in when it hit the corner of the flat rock step of the privy, and quickly considered his options. Maybe he could hide out on the cliffs above town. Maybe he could go to live with his cousin Nathaniel. Maybe he could run all the way to Braetonburg and never come home again. Maybe he could—

"Timothy!"

When Father used that tone of voice, Timothy knew his options had decreased drastically.

"Coming, Father."

He was pretty sure he would be emptying chamber pots for the rest of his life, until he was as old as Grandmother.


## 2000


**"SO," I TOLD** the newcomers, "there's no telling what you're liable to find. We've just been poking around and seeing what comes up."

Easton screwed up her face. "Have you found anything interesting up here?" She sounded as if she didn't think it was possible. Was I going to have to put up with two days of her negativity? I hoped the storm wouldn't last that long.

Maddy began telling her about the wedding dress, but Rebecca Jo cut through Maddy's monologue. "Let's explore some more! This is just what we need for a snowy, icy day. Looks like we could spend hours up here."

"And never get through half of it," Easton said, but I managed to ignore her. Sort of. I hoped she wasn't going to grump about everything. I noticed Charlotte Ellis tightening her lips. My opinion of Charlotte went up another notch.

*What is a notch?*

"I have something I saved for you," Sadie said, handing Easton the ugly orange and blue scarf.

Easton's eyes lit up.

It takes all kinds.

*All kinds of what?*

"Too bad it's so ugly," Pat said, and several of us nodded in agreement.

"I don't know why you're all so negative about it. I think it's positively striking." She draped the scarf around her neck and pulled her waist-length hair free of it.

Except for the wrinkles, the scarf did look striking. Of course, with that volcanic hair of hers, Easton would look striking wearing a feed sack.

I studied the scarf for another few seconds before deciding that even if it looked striking on Easton, it wasn't worth keeping. She was welcome to it.

"I'd iron it if I were you," Ida drawled.

"She can't," Maddy pointed out. "There's no electricity. Unless you want to use one of those flatirons." She pointed. "Before you get started, though, you have to see what we've already found." She led the way to the hobbyhorse, and then made Glaze show them her hair comb. Next, of course, we had to re-open the hatboxes to show off our discoveries, the ones we weren't wearing. I really liked my straw boater.

Ida twirled around so everyone could see her white-feathered hat from all angles, and I made a big deal of exhibiting the silver pendant. "I thought I'd wear it to Glaze's wedding," I announced. As soon as I said it, it sounded like a very good idea.

"Speaking of weddings," Glaze said, "we found this just before you all got here." She lifted a corner of the brown wedding dress. "There was even an invitation tucked inside it. From 1832."

Even Easton oohed and aahed over that one.

Eventually, after we'd recapped what all we'd found, Sadie motioned to Easton to join her, and the rest of us fanned out to investigate on our own. Dee stuck fairly close to Rebecca Jo, and Amanda joined Carol and Melissa at one of the trunks.

After a couple of minutes, Rebecca Jo called from the other side of the attic, "Hey, Maddy! Come look at this. I bet you could use it in one of your horror novels." From behind a tall dresser, she pulled out a lampshade that was straight out of the Victorian era.

"It's a convolvulus shade," Carol said.

"A what?" Rebecca Jo paused before setting the thing on one of the flat-topped trunks. "I never heard that term."

"It's supposed to look like a trumpet-shaped flower, a convolvulus. Shades like that were prevalent under Queen Victoria."

I'd been right about the timing. "I think it's fairly hideous." I ran my finger around the inside top rim of it and came up with a smudge of soot. "Candles?"

"Not every town had electricity back then," Carol said, "although there's no way to know for sure just when this was manufactured. The soot seems to indicate candlelight, though."

"Maybe it would look better in candlelight." Maddy sounded dubious.

Carol made a sound that might have been agreement, or possibly not. "If you'd seen your house back during those years, Biscuit, you probably wouldn't recognize it. The Victorians liked their rooms completely jammed with furniture, doodads, lamps, tables, what-not shelves." She readjusted a pencil in her braid. "Fluted lampshades like this were particularly popular."

I couldn't imagine messing up my living room like that. "I'm more into the wide-open-spaces look."

"And it's wonderful," Carol said, "but if you'd had a living room like your current one back then, it would have been judged to be extremely sparse."

"Yeah," Maddy said. "People probably would have felt sorry for you to have so little furniture."

I made a face. "I'm glad times change."

# 1859

**LEONORA MARTIN HOSKINS** relished those times—short and, unfortunately, far between—when her husband Gideon rode up to Garner Creek on business. Sometimes, not often, he had to travel to Russell Gap, and then was likely to stay the night in the hotel there, but she knew today he would return sometime after nightfall.

On this day, while her two older children were at work—they were both apprentices—and her three younger children were in school, Leonora ran through her chores as quickly as she could. Then she heated pans of water on the enormous wood stove in the kitchen, closed all the curtains tight, dragged her tub from the large pantry closet where she stored it, and dumped in the pails of steaming water. Her parents had given her the tub when she married Gideon Zenus Hoskins eighteen years ago. They must have known Gideon better than she had, for Mother referred to it as a washtub. It was certainly big enough to handle all the washing as their young family grew. But Mother had taken Leonora aside after the wedding ceremony and told her the true intended use of the oval shaped tub.

"You'll have to bend your knees a bit, my dear, but once it is filled with warm water, you'll find it provides the most delicious way to relax after the children have gone to sleep."

The tub was the most wonderful wedding gift Leonora had received, certainly more useful than the numerous tatted doilies from her cousin, and more attractive to her way of thinking than the matching candlestick holders with trumpet-shaped lamp shades her older sister had given her. To Leonora's way of thinking, even the most graceful tapers could not make those garish shades attractive.

Just that morning, before Gideon left at dawn to ride northward, he had slammed the front door so hard, one of those candle stands fell from the hall table, breaking the hideous shade. Fortunately, the candles had not been lit; otherwise he might have set fire to the table skirt. She doubted he even heard the crash, for he had charged out to the stable and left without a backward glance. While their youngest son, Young Gideon, cleaned up the broken glass and went outside to dump it down the privy hole, Leonora took the second lamp up to the attic. She had never liked it, so it was just as well to get rid of it. Perhaps one of her children would want it some day. With practical thrift, she removed the candle from it for re-use elsewhere.

She hoped Gideon would expend all his pent up anger during the ride. Hopefully his business dealings would go well and he would return this evening in a better mood than he had been in when he left.

Leonora never knew what would set him off. Some days he was equable. Others he was like a bear, cranky after a winter's hibernation.

She tested the water, eased out of her clothing, and sank into the tub with a sigh of relief. She had almost two hours before the children would return from school, more than enough time to have a long soak and then get the kitchen returned to rights in time to begin preparations for the evening meal.

Ah. She loved this tub. Gideon did not like it, of course. She had mentioned the possibility of bathing in it only once, soon after they were married, but he had ridiculed that idea saying it was a wasteful use of time and effort. He found fault with almost everything she did, had, said, or wanted, but as long as she was able to complete her bathing and empty the tub—one bucket at a time—onto the vegetable garden out back before he returned home, he could not complain. With Gideon, it was better simply not to mention some of her activities during the day, such as the visits she made to friends in the town, the knitted gifts she created for various widows, and, of course, her luscious baths.

Once her muscles began to relax in the deliciously hot water, she spent part of the time wondering how Young Gideon, her twelve-year-old, was faring with his examinations. He was a studier, was Young Gideon. He always had been, and Leonora was exceedingly proud of him. The other children cared not for schooling, but Young Gideon, like his mother, had always loved books and animals.

It wasn't long, though, before she fell asleep, resting her head on the thick cloth she had placed along the rim of the tub. The water had hardly begun to cool, and she slept so deeply, she did not hear the front door open. She did not hear Gideon walk in. She did, however, hear his roar of disapproval. She did feel the clout of his hand as he bellowed his fury. She did feel the strength of his fingers as he grabbed her ankles and lifted them high out of the water.

Within just a few moments, she felt nothing more.

## 2000

**I STUDIED THE** soot-blackened lampshade. "Maybe I could clean it up a bit."

"For heaven's sake, Biscuit," Ida said. "There's a lot of good stuff up here. Why would you want to waste time on something that's not only useless, but ugly as well? Just dump it."

I had to admit, she had a point. "Does anybody want it?" Silence. "Going once, going twice, rubbish stack it is."

That felt good. Ida and Maddy had their hats, and I'd gotten rid of one candle-lampshade. That left only about half a million or so items to be dealt with. Well, maybe a couple of thousand. Or five hundred. Anyway, with three down, there weren't quite as many decisions yet to be made.

*I do not understand you. What are you thinking about?*

What on earth was I thinking? At this rate, it would take us till next winter to complete the job. "Let's go, ladies," I said in my best cheer-the-team voice. "There's still a lot of ground to cover."

*What ground? All I see is the floor.*

Carol laughed. "You're right, Biscuit. We can't spend all day on every item. On the other hand, we don't want to go through things so fast that we miss something."

"Spoken like a true historian." Charlotte picked up a cardboard box from a miscellaneous stack. "What do you want to bet there's a treasure in here?"

I was glad to see that she'd finally started getting involved. Before this, she'd just been sort of hanging around the edges.

"Is it heavy?" Amanda sidled closer to Charlotte.

"No. It's fairly light."

"Maybe it's a key to a safe deposit box," Amanda said. "That would be exciting."

Together they lifted the lid.

Together they peered into the box.

Together, they lifted a layer of tissue paper.

"What is it?" several of us asked at the same time.

Together, they sighed.

"Tissue paper." Charlotte's lips thinned. "It's all yellowish around the edges."

"That's it?"

"What do you expect, Maddy? Something priceless in every box?"

"You're the one who was betting there'd be a treasure there."

Charlotte screwed up her face. "I bet there *was* a treasure in there to begin with. Too bad it's empty now."

Marmalade jumped up onto the trunk and poked her head into the box.

*It is not empty.*

She let out an indignant yowl and pushed the box onto the floor, where it landed upside down.

"It might not be empty," Carol said.

Dee bent to pick it up, and more tissue paper fluttered out, along with a grainy black and white photograph, which she passed around the circle.

*It still is not empty.*

"You'd better check that box more carefully," Carol cautioned. "No telling what else could be stuck in the bottom of it."

Beneath one more layer of tissue paper, Charlotte found a yellowed newspaper clipping.

She'd barely read the date when the photograph reached Sadie, who tapped it with her fingernail. "This is a picture of my father"—she turned to the back of the picture—"in 1902."

I ran downstairs to get my magnifying glass so we could make out the details. Dee leaned over my shoulder as I studied it. The photo was surprisingly clear considering its age. A set of weathered blocks of stone steps protruded from the steep terrain. A man stood halfway up the stairs, his hand raised in apparent greeting, and off to the side of the picture was the most amazing bridge I'd ever seen, which was the main reason I'd gone for the magnifying glass.

The bridge looked like it could have grown in Narnia or Tolkien's Lothlorien because the trees seemed to be reaching across the chasm toward each other. There weren't any leaves on the branches, though. When I mentioned that, Maddy said, "Those aren't branches.

They're roots."

Dee looked up. "Says who?"

"Says the book I read about India." She gave an apologetic shrug toward Carol. "Researching one of my novels. The story never went anywhere, but I enjoyed learning about these living root bridges. They're marvels of engineering."

Dee pulled us back to the topic. "You kind of look like your dad, Sadie. I've never seen a photo of him before."

"We didn't have any. Up until his dying day he had an aversion to being photographed. I asked him about it once, and he told me the last time he had his picture taken, it darn near killed him. He never would give us any details, though."

"We may have the answer here." Charlotte waved the clipping. "Let me read it to you."

*Metoochie River Valley News*
*April 30, 1902*

# Trip of a Lifetime
# Ends in Near Tragedy

EDITOR'S NOTE: We rejoice that Andrew Russell is alive and well. The exigencies of modern travel caused a delay in this, our seventh installment in an ongoing series of articles from India as reported via telegraph by our friend and neighbor, Andrew Russell. Mister Russell has, as you will know if you have been a faithful reader of these weekly reports, been on an extended visit to the country of India. The last report we received arrived in our offices more than two months ago, and the News had been unable to verify the whereabouts of Mr Russell until we received this report from him on Monday of this week.

Mr Russell sustained extensive injuries, which prevented him from traveling to the nearest telegraph office.

"I had a brush with death," Mister Russell writes, "during my visit to the Meghalaya area of India when I tumbled down twenty-seven precipitous stone stairs near a Living Roots Bridge said to be between 500 and 1,000 years old."

His report continues:

"It takes 15 years to grow a bridge, for the people here weave together the aerial roots of a local rubber tree. In the mountainous village of Mawlynnong, I observed two such bridges, and was informed there are others farther upstream. My visit to the rest of the bridges was curtailed when I tumbled down those stone stairs leading up to the second bridge I visited.

The kind people of Mawlynnong carried me down the mountain on an improvised stretcher seven miles to the next village, where a most efficient doctor saw to the repair of my broken arm and shin. It has taken me almost five weeks to recover sufficiently to travel another fifteen miles to a telegraph office.

I have a photograph that was taken as I ascended those near-fa-

```
tal stairs, which I trust the News
will print, along with my other
photographs, after I return home."
```

"Well," Sadie said, "that sure answers my question. But why—how—did it end up here in Biscuit's attic?"

"There's another clipping," Charlotte said. "Or rather, part of a clipping. Attached to the back of this one. It's torn, though."

```
     Trip of a Lifetime
     Filled with Wonder
EDITOR'S NOTE: This is the
fourth in our series of weekly
reports from India by our friend
and neighbor, Andrew Russell.
     JHARKHAND, INDIA. The Neem
Tree is grown for its medici-
nal properties in the Jharkhand
area of India. The word Jharkhand
means 'the land of forests,' and
the forests here are exceedingly
```

"That's all," she said. "No date. The paper's ripped." She turned the paper over and inspected the back. "It looks like part of an obituary on this side. I wonder what kind of sadist would keep a fragment like this to drive us nuts with wondering?"

*What is a saydissed?*

Carol waited for Marmalade to stop meowing. "I doubt the person was trying to be intentionally unkind, which is what sadists do. There's no telling how the paper got torn. I'm just glad he or she saved even this little bit."

*Oh.*

I studied Carol. Maybe it was just because she was a historian, but sometimes she said things that seemed to me to be totally unnecessary.

*It was not unnecessary. She answered my question.*

Charlotte fingered the box. "I sure do wonder what was packed in this tissue paper to begin with."

"Yeah," Melissa said. "And what happened to it, whatever it was?"

# 1911

**AMELIA STOCKWELL HOSKINS** fingered the letter from her cousin Mary, deciding she'd better read it before she opened the rest of the package. Mary had a penchant for sending the most ridiculous gifts, but still Amelia looked forward to hearing the news. Mary and her husband led a truly exciting life. In her last letter she'd enthused about their upcoming trip to Europe. Amelia wondered if February through April was a good time to travel, but she supposed Paris and London would be marvelous regardless of the time of year.

Three of Amelia's daughters ran through the kitchen, and she took a moment to grab the youngest and wipe her face. "Playing in the dirt again, I see?" She patted the girl's round behind and sent her on her way, then sat at the small table where the light of the early morning sun would make it easier for her to read.

She glanced at the clock. Young Gideon, her husband, would return soon for his noon meal, if the calving had gone smoothly.

She skimmed the letter quickly. There would be time later to read it more carefully after she found out what the package contained.

Individual phrases caught her eye. She laughed when she saw one particular phrase. *I know you might not have much need for opera glasses in Martinsville.*

"No, Mary," she said aloud. "I haven't much call for opera glasses." With her smile still in place, she fished around through the box, which was lined with old newspapers, and found the glasses nestled snugly into a bed of tissue paper. Exquisite things they were, all inlaid with mother-of-pearl. Useless, of course, but still lovely.

She heard a shout from outside and peered through the back window to locate the source. Taking up the glasses, she used them to focus in on her daughters as they traipsed toward the house. She knew that look on their faces. *Look what we found.* The little one must have been the lucky finder. Amelia scanned her daughter top to bottom with the opera glasses and saw something wiggling frantically inside the girl's apron. Hopefully it wasn't a snake again. No. As she watched, an enormous and highly indignant bullfrog jumped from the apron and bounded back toward the creek that ran through the trees behind the house. All her children were inveterate explorers, encouraged by their veterinarian father to investigate everything with fur, feathers, or scales.

The oldest of the three motioned toward the grape vines growing beyond the garden, and Amelia grinned as they changed direction as smoothly as if they had been a school of fish. She'd be washing purple muscadine stains out of their aprons tomorrow.

She lowered the opera glasses. Mary's gift wasn't so useless after all.

# 2000

**MELISSA TOOK THE** box from Carol and inspected it. "Wondering about what was packed in this box is going to keep me awake all night long."

"You can't let it get to you," Carol said. "The best thing to do—if there's no way to find an answer—is to get interested in something else."

"Like this," Pat said, lifting a mortarboard from a drawer. "What do you think? High school or college?"

"That's high school," Melissa said. "I had one just like it, but I threw it in the air and never did find it." She took it from Pat and inspected the lining. "I inked my initials inside mine. Somebody else with M T initials probably found it and kept it."

*What are empty nishals?*

She handed it to me and I passed it on to Amanda.

*Mouse droppings!*

"When I graduated from high school," I said, "I got my diploma and then headed the wrong way to get back to my seat, which meant I had to practically climb over people's laps."

"Embarrassed, were you?" Ida didn't sound as wry as she usually did.

"What do you think?"

"What do I think? I'm happy to find somebody else who did something dumb at graduation." She paused for two beats. "I fell off the stage."

A chorus of commiseration erupted from all of us.

"It's not a very tall stage," Ida said. "I didn't get hurt. Not physically. But I was pretty sure at that moment that I wanted to die."

"I imagine we all have a story like that," Rebecca Jo said. "The funny thing is, we're probably the only ones who remember such moments."

I looked around the group. Everybody had turned thoughtful. Charlie barely glanced at the mortarboard, but she didn't pass it on, either.

## Wednesday, June 2, 1993

**CHARLIE TRIED ON** the mortarboard one more time, tilting it this way and that. Maybe she should put her hair in a twist of some sort at the nape of her neck? Or leave it long like this? Thank goodness the black and gold didn't clash with her red hair.

Over the reflection of her shoulder in the mirror she saw her dad walk up behind her. He wasn't wearing his usual smile. Or rather, he was, but it looked forced somehow.

"I'm so proud of you, Charlie. You're going to do well."

She started to grin, but felt it freeze on her face. "What's wrong, Dad?"

He wrapped his arms around her, careful not to dislodge the mortarboard. "I guess I'm just feeling a bit nostalgic, honey. Your mother and I were talking last night about how empty the house is going to feel when you go off to college in a few months."

"Dad, I—"

He made a funny face at her. "None of that, now. We'll be fine. It'll take some getting used to, but once I retire next year, your mom and I are going to do some of that traveling we never got around to." He stepped back and held her shoulders at arm's length. "You did a great job on getting those scholarships. I know it was a lot of hard work for you, but Mom and I are darn proud of our girl."

"Daddy!" She sniffed rather inelegantly. "It's a good thing I haven't put on my eye makeup yet."

"Don't know why you wear that stuff when you'd be the prettiest person on the stage anyway."

She stood on her tiptoes and planted a kiss on his cheek. She loved the way he smelled. All comfort and Old Spice. "Dad? I've been thinking."

He didn't rush her. He just waited. She loved how patient he was. How patient he had always been.

"Thanks for all the years you've loved me. I know I was a brat when Mom and I first came to live with you, but—"

He put a finger on her nose. "You've always been the light of my life, honey. Did I ever show you the album with all the pictures your mom sent me before you and she came here?"

Charlie laughed. "Only about five hundred times."

"All the way from when you were born."

There was something niggling at Charlie that she had simply never understood. She wasn't sure why she'd never thought to ask before. "Dad? Why didn't we live with you right from the start?"

He put his hands in his pockets. "Your mom could probably answer that better than I can, but she felt like she had to stay in Martinsville to take care of your grandma." He rubbed his smooth-shaven jaw. "Your grandma got sick right after she found out you were on the way into the world."

"Why didn't you move to Martinsville, then?"

"My business," he said simply. "It was here, and I couldn't uproot without losing everything. The important thing was that your mom and I never lost touch."

"Why …" Charlie wasn't sure she even wanted to ask this. "Why didn't you two get married until … until when you did?"

"That's a hard one to answer, honey. There's always been something about the Ellis Girls"—Charlie could almost hear the capital letters in his voice—"that's kept them from marrying. All but one of them, from what I understand, and that was a hundred or so years ago."

"One? Who was she?"

He lifted his shoulders. "You mom mentioned her name. What was it? Clovis? Or something like that."

Mom stuck her head around the door. "Am I interrupting anything deep and important?"

"Course not, Mom. Come on in."

Naturally, Mom had to adjust the mortarboard a little, but Charlie could tell it was just an excuse. She knew they'd miss each other once college time came around. Still, Charlie was ready to spread her wings a little.

"Mom?"

"Yes, honey?"

"What was the name of the Ellis Girl who got married?"

Mom looked a bit startled. "Other than me, you mean?" She looked at Dad and raised an eyebrow. "Is this a good topic for such an important day?"

He spread his hands. "She asked."

Mom gave one last tweak to Charlie's cap. "There were two of them. Clovilla Ellis was a great-aunt of yours, five or six generations back. She married George Moon. They had one daughter, Eliza, who became, uh …" Her words petered out, and Charlie saw a funny look pass between Mom and Dad.

"Eliza Moon ended up owning a fancy furniture store," Dad said.

"So I might have some cousins?"

"I'm not sure," Mom said. "Eliza had one daughter. Lorinda, who married a Hastings, but I don't remember his first name." She stepped back a few paces. "Hastings is an old name in Martinsville."

Another one of those looks passed between her parents. Charlie was ready to ask more about it, but Mom shooed them out. "Time to go. We don't want to be late for the big day."

Charlie gasped. "My makeup! I don't have my face on yet!"

Dad laughed. "I told you, you don't need any."

Mom understood though. "Just hurry, sweetie. We'll be waiting downstairs."

**MOM AND DAD HAD** a family graduation party for her, of course, just the three of them. They went out to dinner at her favorite Italian restaurant. The day after graduation, so it wouldn't interfere with the sleepover she had with her girlfriends the night before. Charlie laughed at her dad because he kept yawning throughout the meal.

"I can yawn if I want to. You girls had the place rocking last night."

"All night," Mom added.

Charlie grinned around a mouthful of spaghetti. "We had to dance! It kept us awake—"

"Us, too," Dad said.

"So we wouldn't miss breakfast. Those cheese grits were fabulous. And the initial pancakes."

Mom laughed. "It's a good thing all your friends are named either Heather or Jennifer. All I had to do was make a lot of J's and H's." She reached out to touch Charlie's arm. "And one great big beautiful C."

Charlie didn't tell them she'd spent part of the night sitting next to Jennifer—one of the Jennifers—who had her arms curled around her knees and was rocking back and forth. "How did you get so lucky, Charlie," Jen had asked her. "I mean your parents love you and like each other and there's no drinking here and no fighting and no …"

All that was true. For Charlie at least. Poor Jen. She'd gone on and on for a long time, and Charlie hadn't known quite what to say.

**HER FOLKS WAITED** to bring up the subject until just a couple of days before they drove Charlie to college. "We need to talk with you, Charlie."

After Charlie pulled herself together, after she asked all the questions—how long will the chemo last? How much is it going to hurt you, Mom? What's going to happen? Should I stay here?—and after they'd all cried together, her parents tried their best to reassure her.

"Even if something happens to one of us, you'll be safe," Dad said. "We've saved for years. The house is paid for, there's more than enough money set aside for college, and it should last, especially since you got those scholarships."

The funny thing was, Charlie had been wanting to change her last name so it would match her dad's, but now, with mom sick, she put that idea out of her mind. She'd be an Ellis Girl. Always. The first one ever to get a college education.

# June 1952

**PERRY HOSKINS CAME** close to throwing a fit when the mortarboard hat he'd ordered six months ago for Lyle's high school graduation arrived in the mail. Just three months ago, Lyle had quit school and left home, for no apparent reason at all. He'd said something about digging holes and stormed out of the house, suitcase in hand.

Perry hadn't remembered the order until this arrived. He should have remembered. He should have cancelled it. He did remember that the order form had said NO RETURNS in big red letters. He was out three dollars and fifteen cents, and he didn't like it.

He felt Elizabeth, his wife, walk up beside him. "Oh, dear," she said.

"What are we supposed to do with this?"

"Don't huff, Perry. It's bad for your blood pressure."

"I'll huff if I want to." He hurled the offending hat across the hall.

Elizabeth hurried to pick it up. "You've bent it."

Perry didn't like the tone of accusation in her voice, and told her so.

"But he might come back. He knows I need him."

Perry stiffened his back and walked into the living room where he picked up his favorite hunting knife and passed it from one hand to the other. He didn't bother to say anything when Elizabeth took the hat and headed for the attic.

# 2000

**EVENTUALLY CHARLIE LET** go of the mortarboard. When she handed it on, Pat almost curled a lip. "It's bent." She skimmed it, like a Frisbee, across the group and onto the reject pile. "We have enough good stuff to hang onto here without wasting space on junk like this."

Thank goodness for Pat. Without her I might have ended up keeping practically everything up here. "You're going to get a gold cleanup star," I told her.

She grinned almost maniacally. "And brother have I earned it."
*Widelap is not your brother.*


## September 1994


**CHARLIE ELLIS LOOKED** at Tricia with a gloriously happy expression. Tricia stared back at her, but Charlie wasn't put off by it. Tricia had her own way of reacting to the world. Charlie wasn't going to let that get her down.

"I missed you this summer," Charlie said. "It's good to be back, don't you think?"

"I guess."

"You don't sound too sure." Charlie opened her suitcase and began transferring clothes into the dresser. "What—aside from ignoring my letters—did you do this summer?"

"All I did was work and sleep and eat. I'm not too big on writing letters."

"I noticed. But you must have read mine." She paused, a yarn-wrapped coat hanger in her hand. "Don't tell me you didn't read them."

"I read them. I just didn't have much to say."

Charlie laughed. "You never do." She loved having a roommate. There was a girl down the hall who'd been assigned to a single room. Charlie couldn't imagine being all by herself like that. "I'm glad we're roommates. It means I get to do as much talking as I want to, and you have to listen."

"I don't *have* to."

"That's what makes it all the nicer. You don't have to, but you're always all eyes and ears."

Charlie went on prattling about her parents and their latest shenanigans. "I swear, they really like each other, even after all these years together. They just had their eleventh anniversary in July."

Mom had responded so well to the chemo. The doctors were hopeful. Everything was looking good. But Charlie didn't want to tell Tricia about it. As much as she liked Tricia, there were some things Tricia just didn't seem to get. She was a lot like Charlie's friend—former friend—Jennifer, who had hardly had a thing to say to her since high school graduation.

Tricia stopped her own unpacking. "Eleven? Does that mean he's your step-dad? You didn't tell me that."

Charlie sat on the edge of her bed. "No, he's my real dad. Mom and I moved to Atlanta so they could get married when I was eight. It's just that …" She screwed up her face. "It's kind of a long story."

Tricia waved her arm around the room. "Classes don't start till tomorrow."

So Charlie explained about how the Ellis women had, for the past two hundred years, never married. "And the Ellis Girls—that's what they were always called—always had daughters. Not a single one of them ever had a son. And we were all redheads." Charlie's face took on a look of wonder as she fingered her shoulder-length hair. "Red hair must have been in our genes."

"So your mom was the first Ellis Girl to marry?"

"Not quite. There were two others way back when. Clovilla El-lis married a George Moon, and their daughter Eliza had a girl named Lorinda. I love that name. Lorinda married a Hastings."

"How do you keep all those people straight?"

"It's genealogy. It's important."

Tricia raised a pointed eyebrow. "Why?"

Charlie didn't have an answer to that.

"So, how come your last name is still Ellis?"

Charlie didn't seem daunted by the question. "When I was old enough to understand such things, I asked Mom about it. She said she'd been willing to break with tradition, but only so far. She kept the Ellis name, and Dad didn't seem to mind."

"Ellis," Tricia mused. "She must have been pretty proud of the name."

"You betcha she was. I'm named for Charlotte Ellis. She was one of the founding mothers of Martinsville, the town where I was born. Mom said I had every right to be proud to be descended from one of the founders." Her face clouded a bit as she wondered how much longer her mother would be around to tell her such things.

"You know," Charlie went on, "since you don't have a teddy bear, I'd be happy to loan you one of mine."

Tricia looked at her like she thought Charlie had gone crazy.

"I guess maybe I'll grow out of it someday, but I think it's nice to have a bear to hug while college is going on. I felt kind of sorry for you last year without one."

"If you say so."

Charlie almost regretted having made the offer. "For now, though, I want to get unpacked and head to the bookstore. You wouldn't believe the list of textbooks I have to get."

"Of course I'd believe it," Tricia said. "I've got a list just as long."

## 2000

**THE TRUNK SADIE** and I had been going through, the one filled for the most part with letters, could have been any age. It was made of wood, fastened with a simple metal clasp, and heavy as the dickens, which we'd discovered when we dragged it away from the wall and closer to the middle of the room, just outside our informal chair circle. I lifted yet another bundle of ribbon-tied letters, slipped out the bottom one—assuming that it would be the oldest—and glanced through it, noting that the date was 23 August 1863. My hopes soared. This was written during the middle of the Civil War. Surely there would be information about how much Martinsville had been impacted by the fighting.

*My dearest sweetest most wonderful Darling,* it began, and went on with each sentence more cloying than the last, filled with such an abundance of protestations of everlasting love and so many declarations of anticipation of their upcoming nuptials, that I couldn't help but wonder just how quickly after the wedding the disappointment must have set in. Surely no marriage could endure this amount of expectation. There wasn't a word about the greater events that were swirling around her. Surely she couldn't have been ignorant that a war was going on? I untied the ribbon and flipped quickly through the rest of the letters. They weren't in any sort of chronological order, but I could see the content got progressively worse as the wedding day approached.

I wondered what Sadie would think of this ninny, and I had just opened my mouth, ready to interrupt her when I noticed the look on her face. She held a folded envelope of some sort, and I could see from across the card table that the blob of dark red sealing wax on the back of it seemed to be intact, I put my bunch of syrupy letters onto the reject pile. "What did you find, Sadie?"

"Something interesting, I hope," Maddy said from farther down the room where she was opening yet more hatboxes. "These are all so dull." She held up a rather squashed-looking tam in a pathetic muddy orange color. I couldn't imagine anyone looking good in a hat like that.

But Easton materialized from behind an empty bookcase—why hadn't I paid attention to that bookcase before? I could use it in the puzzle room—and snatched the hat from Maddy's hands. She settled it on her head, and it came alive on her fiery lava-colored locks. So much for preconceptions about colors, I thought. The mud-colored hat even seemed to go with the wrinkly orange and blue flowered scarf.

"Love this hat," Easton said and headed for the cheval mirror.

*The hats I like best are the ones with feathers or ribbons.*

"Be my guest for now," Maddy answered in what sounded to me like a rather dry tone of voice. "We might need that one back if we find a museum that wants all this stuff." But Easton ignored her. I was fairly sure Maddy wasn't serious.

"That museum can't have everything, though," Maddy said. "I plan to keep my penny whistle."

## 1868

**LEMUEL HOSKINS PULLED** out his penny whistle, the one he had inherited from his brother Alpheus. All this fuss and bother over a wedding. He did not see much sense in it. After all, Josh Hawley had been hanging around their house for the past two years, ever since he came that horrible rainy night, to tell them how Alpheus died in prison right near the end of the war.

Lemuel did not think he needed so much help. After all, he was the man of the house now, ever since Alpheus died. He had to admit, though, that Josh was right handy when it came to repairing the leak in the roof or chopping up enough firewood to last them through the winter.

His sister came out onto the porch wearing a crown of daisies on top of her head. It looked kind of dumb to Lemuel, but he had learned not to say everything that was on his mind. Henrietta had a heavy hand when she was not pleased with her younger brother.

Next to him, Josh let out a big sigh.

The daisies must have looked just fine to him.

Lemuel piped a merry little tune as Henrietta walked down the steps to where the Reverend Russell waited with Josh and Lemuel. The other people standing behind them hushed their murmurs, and Reverend Russell started talking.

It did not take too long. Even so, Lemuel's stomach was growling long before the final words were spoken.

**ALMOST TWO YEARS** later, when Henrietta had a baby, they named him Alpheus. Lemuel stood as the godfather to the boy. He wished the baby would grow faster, so he could teach him how to fish.

# 2000

**I TURNED BACK** to Sadie. She hadn't paid any attention at all to the byplay between Maddy and Easton. "What is it?" I asked again.

"It might not be anything," she said, raising her voice a little, "but I think you're all going to want to take a look at this."

Like metal filings to a magnet, everyone surged toward the card table, even Easton.

"You're the historian," Sadie said to Carol. "Take a look at this and tell me if you think it's ever been opened."

"I wish I'd thought to bring my white cotton gloves with me," Carol said.

"Gloves? Why?" Dee spread her arms. "It's actually fairly warm up here."

"It's better not to get the oils from our fingers on artifacts like this," Carol explained. "On the other hand, this doesn't look like it's been handled very much." She inspected the sealing wax carefully. "It's possible to open a sealed letter using a heated thin-bladed knife. The danger with doing that is that the wax imprint hardly ever matches up exactly when you reheat the knife and try to return the wax to its original position." She tilted the paper back and forth, scrutinizing it from every angle. "I'm no expert—"

"You're the closest thing to an expert up here," Ida said.

"—but this dark red wax looks intact. I'd have to guess that this is still in exactly the same condition as it was the day it was closed up."

"Wait till you read what's on the front," Sadie said.

Carol turned the envelope over.

*This Letter is Not to be Opened any Sooner*
*than One Hundred Years after my Death*
*Mary Frances nee Garner*

After we all gasped—and you may be sure every one of us did just that—Carol handed it to Ida on her left, obviously intending it to go around the circle that surrounded Sadie and me and our card table. Ida looked at it, read the inscription out loud again, as if to be sure that's what it really said, and handed it to her left, to Rebecca Jo.

We all knew Mary Frances Garner was the wife of Homer Martin, the founder of Martinsville. "She must have already been married when she wrote this," Rebecca Jo said. "Otherwise, she would have signed it Mary Frances Garner."

Dee took the letter next. "Why didn't she just sign it Mary Frances Martin?"

When it reached me, I marveled at the thick richness of the paper. "They sure don't make paper like this nowadays."

"Wait a minute," Ida said. "Mary Frances Martin died in 1818. So why didn't somebody open this letter in 1918? That would have been a hundred years later, like she instructed."

Sadie leaned over and gazed pointedly into the old wooden trunk. "If it was lost in here, probably nobody could find it in 1918."

"Either that," Melissa said, "or nobody knew about it to begin with."

Beside me, Carol shuddered.

"This is definitely a keeper," Maddy said.

"Shouldn't you wait," Pat asked, "to find out what it says?"

"Are you kidding? Something from Mary Frances Garner Martin? We'll need some sort of display box to keep it safe."

"Or just put it back between these two stacks," Pat said, indicating the letter bundles. "Looks like they protected it for all these years."

"Yeah," Ida said. "Protected it so well that nobody knew it was there."

"There's another letter with it," Sadie said. "No envelope for this one."

"It's so special," Amanda said. She touched the sealing wax on the envelope gently before handing the letter back to me.

I made to give it back to Sadie, but she waved it away. "You or Carol read it," she said. "My eyes aren't what they were sixty years ago."

I heard a distinct snort from Ida. "You just don't want to be the one to break a seal like that."

She had a point.

I gave the letter to Carol who handled it with what seemed to be reverence.

"The instructions clearly say to open it," Pat said.

"Not exactly," Carol said. "It says it's not to be opened before 1918. Nothing indicating that she expects it to be opened at all."

"Of course she expects it to be opened," Pat retorted. "Who could resist opening something like this?"

"I'm surprised she'd trust people to wait a hundred years," Ida said.

"Maybe that's why it was buried so far down in this trunk."

"But it wasn't," Sadie said. "It and this other letter were fairly close to the top, under a couple of boxes, and stuck between two bundles of ribbon-tied letters."

"That could give us a clue," Carol said. "What were the dates on those other letters?"

"The ones in the bundle right on top of this are from 1811," Sadie said.

"And underneath it?"

"I haven't looked." She pulled out the stack, took out one letter, and said, "1812. These two stacks have similar ribbons. And the handwriting looks the same. They were probably all written by the same person. Whoever received them must have just grouped them by years."

"But why was this piece in between those two bundles?" Glaze ran her hands through her silver hair. If I do that to my hair, I end up looking like a dandelion in full seed, but her hair settled back into its perfect configuration. Good thing she's my sister, I thought. Otherwise, I'd have to hate her.

*You do not hate SmellSweet.*

"Looks like we're piling up the mysteries," Pat said. "Go ahead, Carol. Open it and read it to us."

Carol read the date, 30 July 1814, and stopped. "When did you say Mary Frances Martin died?"

"Eighteen-eighteen," Ida and Sadie and I all said at the same time.

"So she wrote this four years before her death."


*Saturday, 30 July 1814*
*My dearest Husband,*

*It seems strange to be writing this Letter to you so long after your Death, but I must tell You, my Beloved, since there is no one else in whom I can confide, and my Heart is too heavy to carry this Load of Anguish alone. I have kept our Secret for all these Years, the Secret you learned only after you arrived here all those many Years ago, and I see no reason to divulge it now, for it would bring Shame on our Son and Dishonor on his Children and their Children. I wish you could have come to know him better.*

*Two of our Descendants are dead, my Dear, and it was my grievous Fault. They always called me great-grandmother, although to be correct, you and I were their great-great-Grandparents. That many "Greats" become unwieldy in Conversation, I am afraid. Jason and Henry were the first and second Sons born of Jerrod, whom I wish You could have known. You would have liked Jerrod a great Deal, as he has much your same Appreciation for Life. Jerrod was Son to our Son John, who named his first Son Jerrod Silas. The middle Name was in honor of Silas Martin, who was the One who truly led us to this Valley and whom John idolized.*

Ida interrupted. "Why is she telling him all this? Homer knew who his son was. In fact, John was twenty or thereabouts when Homer finally died. And Homer certainly knew the name of his own brother. "

"Shhh," Maddy said. "Let her keep going."

"And Silas wasn't the leader," Pat added with some asperity. "Homer was."

"Maybe Mary Frances had Alzheimer's," Ida said. "Only I think they didn't call it Alzheimer's back then. They just said people were senile."

Pat peered over Carol's shoulder. "Why does she have all those silly capital letters?"

"That's the way a lot of people wrote back then, " Carol said. "They capitalized most of the nouns." She cleared her throat, glanced around to be sure she had everyone's attention, and continued.

*The Old Church caught Fire two Fortnights ago. I was distraught, that is my only Excuse, and I could not foresee the Consequences. Otherwise I would never have called out as I did. "Save my Husband's Doors," I screamed as the Flames burst through the Windows.*

*Jason, who was but a mere seventeen Years of Age, was the first to respond. His older brother Henry followed his Lead, and together they tore the Doors—your Doors—from their Hinges and pulled them to Safety.*

*The Price they paid though, with their very Lives, was far more than I would have asked, even though it would have meant the Loss of the Doors You carved so lovingly for me. I insisted upon helping to care for the two Boys until the very End. Young Emeline Russell whom Jason told me some time ago he planned to marry as soon as he could support a wife, stayed with him until the very end, and her Pain was terrible to see. I knew how she felt, for she mirrored the Anguish I felt when you and I were torn asunder.*

"What?" Ida's indignation was almost palpable. "Since when were Mary Frances and Hubbard Martin 'torn asunder'?"

"Hush," Pat said. "I want to know what this is about."

*In less than a Fortnight they both were dead, and despite the fact that it is against all sacred Laws, I wished for their Death much sooner, for their Agony was painful to watch. If the Tears of those of us who surrounded them through those Days could have been transmuted into healing Waters, the two dear Boys could have been totally Immersed in them—and thereby made Well.*

"Whoa," I said. "I've heard that story before, about the two boys saving the doors and dying in the process. Bob told me soon after we started dating."

"He told me, too," Glaze said.

"I never quite realized what a tragedy it was, though. Well, their deaths, yes, of course. But this kind of pain? It never occurred to me how horrible it must have been for the ones who survived."

"An eye witness account," Carol said. "I must say Mary Frances did a good job of capturing the anguish."

Pat blew her nose. "Yeah. She did too good a job. Poor Emeline."

*I must admit that Jason was ever my favorite of the three Sons of Jerrod. As he lay dying, Emeline told him through her Tears that she knew he had taken one of her Gloves. 'You may keep it forever, if only you will live,' she told him time and again, and he will indeed keep it forever, for when we prepared the Body for the Burial, the Glove was found, only slightly fire-damaged, in Jason's Pocket. Emeline tucked it between his Hands before we wrapped the Shroud around him.*

*You may be pleased to know that Men have begun to wear long 'trowsers' rather than Breeches. The Legs of the Trowsers reach all the way to their Shoes and each contains a Pocket secreted in the side Seams. I do not mean to treat the Death of these Boys lightly, but there is so much I wish to share with you.*

*It was the Decision of the entire Town to bury the Boys in the Center of the Graveyard, within the Wall of Stone that covers your Grave.*

"It doesn't cover Homer's grave," Ida grumped. "It surrounds his grave."

"She was distraught." Pat pointed at the letter. "That's what she says."

"*The wall of stone that covers your grave,*" Carol repeated.

*I feared that the Gravediggers might thereby with Inadvertance disturb your Bones, and yet I could not divulge the Reasons for my Fear, so I merely kept Watch, sitting on the Wall above your Grave as they dug, much to the Chagrin of Ketchum, Jerrod's third Son, who said he feared that I would catch an Ague from the Rain that fell much of that Morning. Between the Two of Us, I do believe that Ketchum had more Concern about his own Health than about Mine, but he felt himself obliged by dint of Familial Ties to stand beside Me as I guarded your Bones.*

"Listen to that," Ida said. "She did it again. She says *the wall above your grave.*"

"Beside it, above it," Pat said, "what's the difference? I think it's sweet that she didn't want Homer disturbed even while he was dead."

I took a quick look at Glaze. We both knew what it felt like to dig up bones when all you were expecting was good rich dirt. She met my gaze and shrugged. Now was not the time to go into *that* story.

*Ketchum stood by throughout the entire Digging from the Moment the Ground was first broached, and I could tell the Moisture streaming down his Face was not caused entirely by the copious Rain.*

"Ketchum may have been crying, but he still sounds like a real loser," Dee said. "Imagine him worrying about catching a cold when he should have been holding an umbrella over his great-grannie's old head."

"I wouldn't be too hard on him," Pat said. "Those graves were being dug for his two brothers." She scratched at the back of her hand and a few flakes drifted up into the still air, but I was pretty sure her thoughts weren't on her winter-dry skin. "I can't imagine how horrible it must have been to lose two children like that."

Those of us who were mothers turned inward.

"I wonder if they even had umbrellas back then," Melissa—who had no children—said. "Does anybody know?"

"Of course they did," Maddy said. "There were umbrellas shown in paintings on the pyramids."

"Why would they need umbrellas in a desert?"

"They weren't for rain, Melissa. They were sunshades."

"You probably learned that in research for one of your books," Glaze said.

Maddy took off her glasses, and her eyes seemed to unfocus. "Never thought about that. Ancient Egypt would be a great setting for a murder."

"I'm going to have to pick up some of your books."

"Well," Maddy admitted to Carol, "I haven't had anything pub-lished."

"Yet," Glaze said, and Maddy favored her with a blazing smile.

Carol took a deep breath.

*I will direct that this Letter remain sealed until a Period of Time of at Least one hundred Years has passed from the Day of my Death. I do so want to proclaim my Love for You while I am still alive, but know that such a Proclamation could bring Dissension into our Community as well as the Shame I have already spoken of. I know that my Everlasting Soul is truly damned, but I long ago ceased to fear Death. That is perhaps one of the Advantages to such a long Life. Nothing that comes Hereafter can hold much Terror for me. Being separated from You for so much of my Life has been Punishment enough for Me to last through Eternity.*

    *Know that I remain always*
      *Your devoted Wife,*
        *Mary Frances*

Complete silence greeted Carol's last words. What was there to say in the face of such despair?

"I'd like to know,"—leave it to Ida to break the mood—"is what she meant by all that *secret* stuff."

Rebecca Jo nodded. "And why would saying she loved her husband shame her and her family?"

"Maybe people didn't talk about such things back then," Amanda suggested.

"Do you think she really believed her soul was endangered?"

Carol appeared to consider Maddy's question carefully. "If she believed she was in fact responsible for the deaths of those two boys, then I can see how she might have thought that."

"But it wasn't like she planned their deaths."

"True. But try to see it from her viewpoint. She was already an old woman, and those two boys were just beginning their adult lives. She probably thought she had literally stolen their lives from them." Carol paused as if choosing her words carefully. "Most people back then really did believe in the distinct possibility of eternal damnation, just as she said." She scanned the letter again. "When did Homer die?"

"Seventeen-sixty-eight," several of us said at the same time.

"And she died in 1818? It's sweet that she thought being separated from him"—she quoted directly from the page—"*for so much of my Life has been Punishment enough for me to last through Eternity.* It sounds like they shared quite a love."

"I still don't get the part about the wall covering his grave," Pat grumped.

"No matter whether we understand it or not," Maddy said, holding out her hand, "this is going in a special place until we can get a display box for it."

Carol handed her the letter.

"I'm commandeering the top drawer of this white dresser for the really special finds," Maddy said. "Any objections?" Nobody had any, of course, but Maddy explained her reasoning anyway. "If we just put these back in the boxes or trunks, we'll never find them again."

"You may need to use all three of those drawers," Melissa said, "not just the top one."

Maddy opened the second drawer. "Empty." The bottom drawer seemed to be sluggish. When she tugged on it, the dresser gave a distinct sideways tilt as one of the front legs collapsed. Some of the tangled jewelry on top fell off, and we all jumped up to set things to right.

Glaze bent to her hands and knees. "The leg's broken, but I think I can just wedge it back in place. We'll have to be careful opening and closing the drawers, though."

"Use some beeswax on that sticky bottom drawer," Sadie said.

I ran downstairs to grab a beeswax candle, and the drawer did open and close somewhat more smoothly afterwards.

"The bottom drawer is a lot deeper than the other two. Lots of room for saving things." Maddy held up the letter. "I sure wish we knew the story behind this one."

"Are you sure you want to use that dresser," Easton said, "since the leg is broken? Even if the drawers are opening okay now."

Pat harrumphed. "With a broken leg like that, I'm surprised they didn't just throw it out."

Sadie's eyes widened. "They could have just repaired the leg. People didn't used to throw things out so readily as they do nowadays."

Pat turned in a broad circle, surveying the attic. "I can see that."

"So," Dee said, "Why do you suppose they didn't fix it?"

Like so many of the questions we asked up here, there wasn't an answer.

## 1841

**GIDEON HASTINGS WAS** always careful not to mark his wife's face.

Once, when he hit her in the stomach, she reeled backward against the white dresser that stood beside their bed, causing it to tilt dangerously. His second blow caused Leonora to bruise her thigh against the edge of the dresser, but of course, Doctor Garner—the fourth generation of Garner doctors in Martinsville—never saw that particular injury.

When he came to set Leonora's broken arm, she told him she had tripped going downstairs. He lectured her—kindly enough, but with an odd intensity, for she had had numerous such falls over the past few years. "You must take better care of yourself," he said, alluding indirectly to the fact that she was expecting her third child.

It was a wonder she had not lost the babe, for she had fallen hard. "I will be more diligent, Doctor," Leonora said, careful not even to glance at Gideon who stood nearby puffing on one of his omnipresent cigars.

"Clumsy you are, my dear," Gideon said, a teasing lilt to his voice, that caused the doctor to chuckle appreciatively.

"I'm sure your wife will take more caution," Doctor Garner said, "particularly as she has the other little ones to care for."

## 2000

**NOW WE NEED** to find more treasures for your little collection," Dee said. Maddy refolded the Mary Frances letter carefully, put it back in its envelope, and placed it in the top drawer.

Maddy dusted off her hands. "What's that other letter about, Sadie?"

Sadie waved the single sheet. "Something about a book club and Mark Twain. Anyone want to read it out loud?" She handed it to me.

## 1781

**LOUISE MARTIN BREETON** raised the quill yet again, but still the words would not come. She looked across the room to where the body of her newly deceased mother-in-law lay, crumpled on the bed, not yet ready to receive visitors. This was most inconvenient. She dipped her quill and wrote, for the moment not even worried about how her words would sound. Betsey Surratt Martin was as plainspoken as Louise herself, and would not cavil at hearing the truth.

*Tuesday, 20 November 1781*
*Dear Betsey,*
*Please forgive the informality of this note, but I am sure you will understand the reasons for it once you have read it. I fear I must cancel our meeting of the Bluestocking Literary Society tomorrow evening. I had so looked forward to our discussion of the newest Mark Twain book,*

## 2000

**SADIE INTERRUPTED ME.** "They had a book club!"

I could see why she sounded so delighted. She and Rebecca Jo had started a book club here in town some years before I was hired as librarian. It was still going strong.

*but my mother-in-law died just moments ago, and the funeral will have to be held tomorrow due to the Thanksgiving feast on Thursday.*

## Thursday, 22 November 1781

**THIS THANKSGIVING FEAST**—Mary Frances calculated in her head—the thirty-sixth since the founding of Martinsville, was a merry assemblage indeed. The death of Bridget Hastings Breeton had not put a pall on the celebration as far as Mary Frances could tell. How sad, she thought, to have lived almost fifty years and then be forgotten within a day after her funeral.

What a different story it had been just nine months before, when Silas Martin died. That had been a bleak February indeed. Mary Frances still missed her brother-in-law. He had been such a fine man.

One of her favorite quotes by Mark Twain—such an entertaining writer, whom she might never have known about if it had not been for the Martinsville Bluestocking Literary Society—she always had to stifle a laugh at the pretentiousness of that name. For a moment she lost her train of thought. Oh yes. Mark Twain had written, *The two most important days in your life are the day you are born and the day you find out why.*

Silas Martin had certainly known why he had been born. In large part to curb the base stupidity of his older brother—Mary Frances still shivered to think of the man she had been forced to marry all those years ago—and more importantly to record the daily life of this company in his fine drawings. She knew that Louise had inherited the leather portfolio. Often she was tempted to ask Louise if she might see the collection, but Louise still grieved her father's loss. Perhaps some day.

From her vantage point on a bench under one of the spreading oaks, she studied the crowd gathered around the plank tables that had been erected on the village green. Silas would have relished sketching this scene. The harvest had been a good one, so unlike the devastating cold year they had gone through but six years before, and the table was piled with plenteous food.

Beside her, Louetta Tarkington Martin stirred. "Silas would have enjoyed drawing this."

"I was thinking precisely the same thing." Mary Frances smiled at her dear friend. Silas had been a fortunate man indeed to have found such a woman.

## 2000

**THIS TIME IT** was Melissa who interrupted. "Thanksgiving? In November, huh? I think I read somewhere that it wasn't always celebrated in November."

We all looked at Carol for confirmation.

"It did vary from colony to colony until it was formalized in 1863 by president Lincoln, to be held the last Thursday in November."

"But, it's not the last Thursday," Pat said.

Carol nodded. "Right. Roosevelt changed it to the next-to-last

Thursday in, uh …"

"Nineteen-thirty-nine," Maddy supplied.

Most of us spoke at once. "Why?"

"To boost the economy by adding an extra week to the Christmas shopping season."

"Yuck," Amanda said. "That is so useless."

"Cancel that thought." Pat parked her fists on her hips. "I love Christmas shopping."

"As Maddy said, it was to boost the economy," Carol said. "You know. After the depression."

*What is a depreshun?*

Marmalade jumped onto Carol's lap, and Carol bent to kiss her on top of her sleek head. She murmured to Marmalade exactly the same way I do.

*Not exactly.*

"Let's go around the circle," Melissa said. "What about you, Amanda? Do you have a good Thanksgiving story?"

I loved Amanda's shy smile. "Actually," she said, "I do. The first Thanksgiving I spent on my own after I graduated from massage therapy school, money was a little tight." She gave a wry smile, and I could imagine just how tight things had been until she built up a regular clientele. "So I went to one of the local churches and asked if I could help cook. Every year they gave a big dinner for homeless people and folks who didn't have anywhere else to go for the holiday."

"Sounds like fun," Melissa said.

Marmalade came back to my lap, and I wrapped my arms around her.

Amanda grinned. "I peeled and chopped potatoes for two solid hours and then spent another three in a steamy kitchen. And yes, it was loads of fun. Everybody got to telling knock-knock jokes."

*What are noknok chokes?*

"So," Pat said, "share some of them with us."

"I can't. I never remember punch-lines."

*What are punge lines?*

A woman after my own heart. "I never remember them either," I said, "but that means even if I've heard a joke before, I still think it's funny because it feels brand new."

*What are you talking about?*

Marmalade, after a number of querulous meows, jumped out of my arms and hopped onto a nearby dresser.

*Goat poop!*

"Rebecca Jo's next," Melissa said.

"I was just a kid during the depression," Rebecca Jo said. "The year I turned ten …"

## 1932

**YOUNG THOUGH SHE** was, Rebecca Jo knew her family was hard-pressed to celebrate Thanksgiving this year. She'd heard her parents talking about something called the great depression, but they didn't sound like they thought it was so great.

Daddy told her that they were safe because Martinsville had fared better than most. "Our town is largely self-sufficient," he'd said.

"That's a tendency," Mommy explained, "that extends back through the years to the founding of the town."

Rebecca Jo didn't care about any of that. She just wanted to know one thing. "Will we have a turkey?"

She didn't like the way her folks exchanged one of those glances.

"Your daddy and I have decided that a nice big fat chicken will be more than enough for us this year."

"Chicken?"

Mom smoothed her hair back off her forehead. "It makes better gravy."

"Will we have smashed potatoes?"

"As many as you want," Mom assured her.

## 2000

**"SO," SADIE ASKED,** "did you enjoy the chicken?"

"Sure did." She turned to look at me. "What about you, Biscuit?"

"I can't help but remember the first Thanksgiving Bob and I celebrated here."

"Here?" Pat swept her arms around to indicate the attic.

"No, silly. In this house."

*I was there, too.*

Marmalade jumped in my lap, again. I had to admit I was happy she always managed to come back to me.

*Of course I do, Widelap. You are my human.*

"We invited Rebecca Jo, of course." I nodded to my mother-in-law and she patted my arm. "We couldn't have our first Thanksgiving without her. And my parents drove down from Braetonburg."

"That was before I moved here," Glaze said. "Otherwise I would have loved to attend."

"It wasn't a large gathering, but it felt like we filled the whole house with laughter and love. The aromas from the kitchen helped, too. We spent hours sitting around that evening just talking."

If only we'd had the wood stove back then, I thought, it would have been complete.

*Complete?*

Marmalade whined just then, and I realized that we hadn't needed a wood stove or anything else. Just each other.

*And me.*

And Marmalade.

"Thanksgiving was never special when I was a kid," Ida said. "My mother hated cooking, and a turkey was beyond anything she ever wanted to tackle."

"What did you eat?"

Ida gave Pat a rueful glance. "Spaghetti."

I wasn't the only one who gasped. "Spaghetti?"

"With a jar of Chef Boyardee meatball sauce. At least the color went with the canned yams." Her gaze turned inward for a moment. "Maybe that's why Ralph and I started the IGA. A good grocery store selling good food to people. And if they don't know how to cook, I'm always happy to provide preprinted recipes."

Melissa looked at Charlie. "What about you? Any good Thanksgiving stories?"

Charlie got a blank look on her face. "Not really," she finally admitted.

## Early November 1994

**THE DINNER CHOICES** in the Commons looked particularly unappetizing. Charlie turned up her lip. "Everything is orange," she told her roommate Tricia. "Let's go for pizza."

"Pizza's orange, too." Tricia looked straight ahead.

"No it's not. It's red. Sort of."

Tricia shrugged and stepped out of the line. "Fine with me."

"I talked to my mom this morning," Charlie told her as they headed down the street. "She said to invite you for Thanksgiving."

Tricia shrugged again.

Charlie ignored it. She knew Tricia was just sort of shy about expressing any sort of emotion. "You'll get to meet our next-door neighbors, the Barkers on one side and the Palmers on the other. I've known them practically forever." She giggled. "Mrs. Barker gives the best hugs. She's—well, she's sort of built for comfort, if you know what I mean."

Tricia raised an eyebrow, but Charlie stepped ahead of her to push her way into the fragrant—and packed—pizza parlor.

"I guess nobody else wanted orange, either."


"**THIS IS A** really good idea," Charlie told her roommate two weeks later as Charlie's little car neared Atlanta. "Mom insists she wants as normal a Thanksgiving as possible."

"It's not normal to bring me home with you," Tricia said in her usual flat voice.

"She said nothing could be more normal than for me to bring my roommate home, especially since you don't have anywhere to go."

Tricia raised an eyebrow.

"I mean, I know you probably have all sorts of places you could go, but with your parents dead …" Charlie stopped suddenly, hearing her own words and knowing that her mom could very well go at any time. They'd almost lost her this past summer. But she was doing better now. She was. "I … uh … I wish I could have invited you home last year when we were freshmen, but she was having a lot of trouble with the chemo."

"I know. You told me."

Charlie fell silent. She couldn't figure out Tricia sometimes. They got along pretty well at college, but there they had classes and papers to keep them busy. She hoped this wasn't a mistake. A whole week was beginning to sound like a very long time.

**IT WASN'T QUITE** as bad as Charlie feared. Dad and Mom both seemed to like Tricia. The girls kept busy for the three days leading up to the holiday, and then the Parkers and the Palmers came, bringing most of the food with them. They'd watched Charlie grow up ever since third grade, and there was a lot of story telling and laughter around the table.

Charlie kept trying to bring Tricia into the conversation, but nothing seemed to interest her. Charlie was afraid this had been a mistake. Mom looked awfully gaunt. She just wasn't up to all this, and that must have been what made Tricia act so withdrawn.

When Mom told Charlie to invite Tricia back for Christmas, Charlie told her that Tricia already had other plans.

## 2000

**NO MEMORIES OF** Thanksgiving? How could that be? I studied Charlie. Maybe she just didn't have any happy memories. But that didn't figure—hadn't Sadie said that she really liked Charlie's mom? If Sadie liked her, she had to be the kind of mom who'd make the holidays special. Or maybe not. What did I know?

"Well then," Melissa said after a long pause, "How about you, Sadie?"

"We always had Thanksgiving by candlelight. Even after electricity came to the valley." She ran a palm over her soft wrinkled cheek. "Candlelight is very flattering. I didn't think anything about it back then, but I do remember thinking one year how pretty my grandma looked in the candlelight, even though she was so old. She looked softer somehow." Sadie's eighty-year-old face crinkled up into a huge smile. "She must have been, oh, in her sixties at the time."

"Funny how the age that's considered old keeps increasing," Rebecca Jo observed.

"I think sixty's pretty old," Charlie said.

Rebecca Jo gave her a pointed stare. "You'll change your mind about that when you're forty or fifty."

Ida raised her voice. "Before this discussion deteriorates any further, do you mind if Biscuit continues?" Without waiting for an answer, she said, "Go on, Biscuit," but Pat interrupted her.

"I forgot what we were talking about. I mean what the letter's about."

"Louise Breeton is cancelling the book club meeting," Maddy said, "because her mother-in-law died."

"Oh, yeah. Thanks." She nodded toward me to continue.

*If I seem less than distraught over her death, you must excuse me, for I have never believed in pretending to affection where none exists, and I never could feel warmth toward Bridget Hastings Breeton, but I suppose I must observe a proper period of mourning, and our occasionally riotous book discussions would, as you well know, not fit into that idea of proper behavior for the newly-bereaved.*

*As to the cancellation of the book society, I am sure Jerrod will be just as happy not to have you walking all the way across Martinsville to Frederick's and my house in your condition.*

*I read recently that Mister Twain said that: "The man who <u>does</u> <u>not</u> read good books has no advantage over the man who <u>cannot</u> read them." I would imagine the same could be said for women who do not read. Forgive me, dear, if I seem to be disparaging your brother's attitude—you know I refer to him—but we all know how he tries to discourage any reading by his wife. Could you please let your good-sister know that our meeting will have to be postponed? I am sure that a note coming from you will pass relatively unnoticed, whereas one from me would cause him to raise his eyebrows as far onto his low forehead as possible. Oh dear, I am being spiteful. Almost all of the Surratts, yourself excluded of course, bring out the most malicious side of me.*

*I will have Albert run this letter to your house as quickly as his legs can carry him. He is so proud to be nine years of age now.*

*Feel free to use him as your errand boy to inform others of the can-cellation, for I must attend to the body.*
*Affectionately,*
*Louise Martin Breeton*

## 20 November 1781

**ABSENTMINDEDLY, BETSEY TOOK** the note Albert Breeton handed her. She had so little patience with anything that interrupted her work. Her babe would be delivered soon, she felt, and she still had a multitude of chores that must be taken care of before she could spend time a-birthing.

She sighed as she looked at the note. Louise was as wordy as ever. She read the first two paragraphs and the last one and handed the note back to Albert. "Take this to Mistress Surratt."

"Which one, Ma'am?"

"The one who lives in the next street over." She pointed in the general direction. "Then take it on to ..." She combed her memory for the names of the other women who should be notified. "Ask Mistress Surratt to tell you who else should be told."

Albert spun on his spindly legs and took off up the hill. Only belatedly did Betsey recall that she had glimpsed the words "I am being spiteful" somewhere in the middle of that missive. Oh dear. She hoped she had not made a mistake.

## 2000

**"SHE SURE DIDN'T** like the Surratts much," Rebecca Jo said.

"Except"—I pointed at the note—"for Betsey here."

"I like that Mark Twain quote," Maddy said.

Dee agreed with her. "I wonder which book they were planning to read?"

"What's a bluestocking?"

I'd heard the term, but wasn't sure enough about it to answer Amanda. Instead, I looked at Maddy, as did most of the other women.

"It referred to intelligent women who liked to read, so it's a perfect name for a book club, which is what this sounds like."

**I GUESS WE** couldn't expect to find treasures—or enigmas—every time we turned around, but after at least ten minutes with nothing exciting, I'd begun to get rather bored with the ordinariness of most of what I looked through. "I wonder if Clara and Hubbard are okay," I said to the room at large. It was a little late to be thinking about them, considering how our house was already pretty full—and I certainly wouldn't have wanted Clara and Hubbard here. So soon after his near death—although, as heartless at it sounds, I for one wouldn't have missed Hubbard Martin one bit—Clara still managed to throw her weight around. She'd missed the October library board meeting, what with Hubbard still being in the hospital at the time. Rebecca Jo, Sadie, and Esther Anderson, my three invaluable library volunteers—my Petunias—must have been working tirelessly behind the scenes, because they'd somehow or other gotten all three of themselves appointed to the board during the time Clara was out of commission, which meant Clara didn't have a majority anymore.

The funniest thing was that, at that first horrible meeting, three months ago, September twenty-sixth—it was the day before Hubbard Martin fell off the cliff and just a few days after Gracie, I mean Snookums, was found by her forever family. Anyway, what was funny was that the Board had never gotten around to officially electing a chair. I guess Clara just assumed she'd be running it. But at the October meeting, Charlotte Ellis got herself elected as chair. Clara liked to have a fit when she found out about it at the third meeting. Guess she never read the minutes of meeting number two. She accused Charlotte of highhandedness, and I saw Charlotte's eyes go all steely, but there was nothing Clara could do about it except take it out on me.

Charlotte might turn out to be almost as hard as Clara to deal with, though. I looked over the trunk I was investigating and studied her for a moment. She was turned away from me. She'd acted pleasant enough since she arrived. I was probably worrying for nothing. At least she seemed to know how to deal with Clara, which was more than I could say for myself.

She hadn't been in that meeting two minutes before she'd just happened to mention that she was directly descended from the original

Charlotte Ellis. So there, Clara Martin. No need for you to be so proud of your husband's lineage when Charlotte could trace hers back just as far. According to this present-day Charlotte, her ancestor had been one of the most important founding mothers of Martinsville.

I'd never read anything to dispute that contention. But then again, I'd never read anything to uphold it either.

Anyway, the reason Clara had thrown a hissy fit at the first meeting was that I'd quite logically left her name off the list she'd asked me to compile—a list of who the biggest donors were. Turns out she considered a dozen boxes of ratty old paperbacks to be a major contribution. I'd been far more concerned about remembering to include Margaret Casperson's donation of a complete state of the art computer checkout system, Dave and Pat Pontiac's set of more than a hundred leather-bound classics Pat had inherited from her great-uncle, which they'd given the library when they sold their house, and Ida and Ralph Peterson's gift of the set of old diaries and five antique glass-fronted solid oak bookcases, which had belonged to Ida's grandparents.

Still, as picky as Clara could be, I was glad she'd found shelter from this storm. I was equally glad she hadn't come here. Surely she would have called if she needed help. Or maybe not, I thought, remembering our confrontation at the meeting. She couldn't fire me, not without a majority on the library board, but I was pretty sure she would have liked to. She certainly wouldn't have lowered herself to ask me for any help.

"She and Hubbard are at Matthew Olsen's house." Glaze sounded distracted as she leafed through a stack of what looked like more greeting cards, still in their envelopes, occasionally pulling out a card and reading the message within. "Sadie said she called Clara when the storm first set in, and Clara told her Matthew had invited them."

Matthew was a saint, as far as I was concerned.

But then, something changed inside me. I'd never thought that Clara and Hubbard were particularly happy together. I'd never seen Hubbard reach for her hand as they walked down the street. I'd never seen Clara tuck her arm into Hubbard's as they left the town council room after a meeting. I'd never seen either of them look at the other across a room the way Bob and I tend to reach out to each other no matter the physical distance between us. Even though Bob and I had been married for five years, we still felt connected.

Clara and Hubbard had been married a lot longer, of course, but even after Bob and I had a bunch of years together under our belts, I couldn't imagine that we wouldn't still respect—and like—each other.

With Hubbard so debilitated now, I wondered what sort of strength Clara was relying on to care for him, to continue to care for him even though, from everything I'd heard, the prognosis for any sort of recovery was practically nil.

Practically nil.

Maybe that was what kept her going. The hope that someday his brain would make those connections that had been disrupted. That maybe someday he'd be able to talk.

Maybe Clara was the saint after all.

# 1968

**CLARA BLACK CAME** that close to saying no when Hubbard Martin asked her to marry him. For one thing, Hubbard was three years younger than Clara. And for another thing, from the time Clara was just a little girl, she'd been pretty sure she was going to grow up to marry Cornelius, Hubbard's older brother. After all, Cornelius would someday be in charge of Martinsville. That was what the town council chairman did, right? And Clara had seen enough of Matilda Martin, Cornelius and Hubbard's mother, to know that all the women of the town kowtowed to just about anything Mrs. Martin wanted them to do.

So Clara had never paid much attention to Hubbard. She wasn't going to settle for second-best when she was pretty sure, if she played her cards right, she could have the first-best. Cornelius was better looking than Hubbard. Clara could imagine how handsome their children would be when she married him. The girls would have her curves. The boys would be tall and would take after Cornelius, with his high forehead and his perfectly straight nose.

But then, when Cornelius was only sixteen, he fell out of a tree and died. It took Clara almost a dozen years to get over the loss of

Cornelius. Really, the loss of her dreams. There wasn't anybody else in town she was interested in.

But then, Hubbard up and proposed to her. With Cornelius dead, Hubbard would be the next chairman. That was the way it always worked. The oldest son. The oldest surviving son. All Clara had to do was wait for Hubbard's father to die. And Clara would be the First Lady of Martinsville. Hubbard was beginning to look better and better, despite his lumpy nose and his less than perfect physique.

**HUBBARD MARTIN HAD** never really doubted that Clara would marry him. He was as good as Cornelius. He was the oldest son now. He was going great places.

Why wouldn't she want to be his wife?

When he asked her, though, she hesitated just a few seconds before she said yes. He thought she'd be swept off her feet. Instead it was like she was stepping onto the frozen Metoochie River, not knowing whether the ice was thick enough to hold her up. She'd looked down at him—he should have waited until she was sitting down so she'd have had to look up at him—from his face all the way down to his shoes.

Hubbard seldom felt unsure of himself.

Until Clara made him feel that way.

He'd still marry her. He'd get what Cornelius had always wanted. But somehow or other, the conquest didn't feel quite as good as he'd thought it would.

## 2000

**GLAZE SET ONE** envelope aside and picked up another.

"I knew Matthew bought one of the wood stoves," Sadie said, "and there was smoke coming from their chimney when we walked down here, so it must be working just fine."

"Good," I said. "Bob and I saw them walking into Matthew's house. Hubbard sure was moving slowly."

"Considering he fell off the top of a cliff fairly recently," Glaze said, "I'd say any kind of walking is a miracle."

I thought back to what I'd seen. "He was slow for sure, and he was leaning pretty heavily on Clara, but at least he was walking. Sort of."

Now that I thought about it, Clara had carried nothing but one small suitcase and nothing else. Of course, she was holding Hubbard up with her other arm, so she couldn't have managed a casserole dish or a second suitcase.

Ida and Melissa and Tom had brought so much food here with them, we were set for another week—although I hoped the storm would be well gone by then—but I wondered if Matthew would have enough food for everybody. Nick and Anita Foley. Clara and Hubbard. Plus Matthew.

*And the bird.*

And Mr. Fogarty, the parakeet. That made five people.

*And one bird.*

The storm just had to end soon. Matthew's house was large, but not *that* large. And he had a pantry, but it wasn't nearly as big as ours, although I imagined he'd have plenty of birdseed to keep Mr. Fogarty well fed.

*Humans do not eat birdseed.*

Amid the general hubbub, Amanda said, "I'd like to find a hat at some point, although I don't have a reason to wear a hat very often. Not ever, in fact. Except for my fuzzy winter one."

Sadie leaned forward in her chair. "I've been wondering something, Amanda. Why did you leave your massage practice in Atlanta? I know you can charge a lot more for your work there than you can in this area of the state. Has it been worth it for you to move here?"

Amanda ducked her head. It was nice of Sadie to try to draw her into the conversation. I'd never encountered her in a social situation before this. She had always been so soft-spoken each time I'd been to see her, and she was now, too. "I got tired of how people in the city expected to be pampered." I had to lean closer to hear her.

"But you pamper us all the time," Sadie said. "That's just what you do."

"I know, but you"—she looked around the ring. Most of us were her clients—"all of you *appreciate* being pampered. You don't *demand* it." She paused and licked her lips. "Not everybody was pushy like that, but the clients who were, they just made my life miserable."

Easton let out a quick breath through her nose. She sounded like a steam engine. What was her problem? She pushed back her masses of red gold hair. Why didn't she get hat hair like the rest of us in the winter?

*She does not wear a hat.*

I leaned down to stroke Marmalade. Maybe Easton's voluminous hair kept her head so warm she didn't need a hat.

Within minutes, Ida held up a shapeless length of dark blue fabric. "Look at this!" When she shook it out, it resolved into a bibbed, full-skirted apron.

"I never heard of a dark blue pinafore," Rebecca Jo said. "They were always white, weren't they, Sadie?"

"As far as I know," Sadie agreed. "At least mine always started out white, but they didn't stay clean for very long, as I'm sure I've already mentioned. I had a tendency toward blackberry stains." She grinned. "They sure were delicious."

"If I remember correctly," Rebecca Jo said, "you had a tendency toward dirt, too, always grubbing around in that garden of yours on your hands and knees. I can't believe you didn't do it when you were a girl, too."

Sadie was in her eighties, Rebecca Jo only in her seventies.

"Were the two of you friends when you were young?"

"We knew each other, of course," Sadie told me, "but there were too many years between us to call us real friends."

"Until we made it to our forties and fifties," Rebecca Jo said. "Then the difference didn't seem so very important after all. That was when Sadie and I, along with Esther Anderson—that's Tom's grandmother," she explained to Carol, "we three formed the Martinsville Women's Reading Club."

Which was still going strong after all these years. The members had been among the first to get cards when the town library opened, and of course those three stalwart women, Sadie, Rebecca Jo, and Esther, became my indispensable library volunteers.

Ida spread the pinafore across the unexplored trunk next to her. It was hard to believe after all we'd found, that there were still trunks we hadn't investigated. "This would be very practical," she said.

"I might have avoided a number of spankings," Sadie commented, "if my pinafores had been that color to start with."

Amanda looked aghast. "You got spanked for dirty clothes?"

Sadie sighed. "It was a whole nother time back then."

## August 1783

**DONDRA LEE HASTINGS** tapped her heels rhythmically against the stacked stones of the wall on which she sat and studied the newest stain on her apron. Her young brother Alfred had taken the full basket he had gathered and headed, not toward home, but toward Widow Surratt's house. Dondra Lee knew her brother always gave half of the berries he collected to the elderly woman, probably in hopes of receiving the benefit of the widow's berry-filled scones or pies. Not just the hope of it. Dondra Lee knew for a fact that the little scamp was usually successful. His berry-stained mouth was always a dead giveaway.

Dondra Lee never had enough berries to give away to other families, even when, like today, she gathered them from the abundant bushes on the edge of the old forest above the cemetery. Luckily her four sisters collected more than enough for the whole family. Dondra Lee ate quite a few of the ones she picked and then gave most of the rest to her father. She could not resist the flavor as each of the tiny bumps on every berry burst under the pressure of her tongue. And she enjoyed the smile her father always had for her when she held the basket so carefully for him to scoop out the berries with his one good hand. He enjoyed fresh sun-warmed berries as much as she did.

She wondered if angels up in heaven knew about blackberries. Probably so. After all, blackberries were heavenly indeed, an opinion she would never express aloud for fear it would get back to the ears of Reverend Jonas Russell. He was newly ordained and apt to interpret scriptures rather more strictly than his grandfather, the former minister, had done. She pulled a blackberry thorn from where it had embedded itself in her apron, leaving a small tear in the fabric, and wondered, too, if blackberries would stain an angel's white robes. Probably not.

Mother would be annoyed about another basket only half-filled, and angry indeed about another ruined apron. Dondra Lee would have to continue to wear it, much to her own shame, for Mother had claimed she would not sew another apron for a girl who was so irresponsible.

Dondra Lee thought it would have made more sense if her aprons had been a dark gray or blue—or even berry-colored!—rather than white, but all the girls in Martinsville wore white aprons, which some of the women had begun to call pinafores because of the way the top bib was pinned to the forefront of the dress.

The other girls already teased her about her name. Her grandfather, Donald Lee Garner, Mother's father, had been close to dying near the time of Dondra Lee's birth, and Mother had sworn to her father that she would name her son after him. But then, right after her grandfather died, Mother gave birth to a girl, so she named her daughter Dondra Lee.

With a name like that, Dondra Lee thought, I will have to endure a lifetime of teasing, so they might as well tease me about my stained aprons as well. She vowed to herself that when she was grown and married and had daughters of her own, their aprons would all be dark blue, no matter what anyone else thought.

She sighed, eased herself off the stone wall that surrounded the grave of Homer Martin, and headed home. There was milk to be churned for butter. And her father would be looking forward to the remaining berries.

## 2000

**"AT LEAST A BLUE** pinafore is interesting, even if we don't know where it came from." Glaze held up a stack of the greeting cards she'd been working on for quite a while. "I'm sure these meant something to somebody at some time. They're not really junk, but they're awfully boring."

"Why do you keep going through them, then?" Pat waved her hand like she was swatting at a flying insect. "Just toss them. We need a great big garbage can up here."

"No!" Carol's voice rang with authority. "At least wait until we've gone through everything. Then we—I mean you—can make informed decisions."

"We," Maddy said. "You'll need to come back when we start on everyone else's attics. After all, you're the closest thing we have to an expert."

"Well," Carol said, "when you put it that way…"

"You have to come back to see the daylilies in the town park," Melissa said. "They're spectacular."

*There are always a lot of bugs at the bottom of those flowers.*

Glaze pointed to a very short stack of cards. "I've put aside the ones I thought were at least interesting, the ones that have notes that seem to say something worthwhile."

"That's a good start," Maddy said. "It'll save us time later. Hand me the stack of good stuff and I'll put it in the dresser drawer."

But before she stashed the cards away, she lifted the top one and opened it. "No wonder you kept this one, Glaze."

"See how it's paper-clipped to the one right below it?"

## Wednesday, February 14, 1945

**LYLE HOSKINS HAD** searched for the perfect card. Everybody had to give a valentine to everybody else in the class. That was what Mrs. McChesney told them all last month—"So you'll have plenty of time to plan." He'd spent forty-five cents of the money he'd earned from his paper route to buy a big package of funny valentines so he could give one to everybody else. But not for Sheila. No. For her card, he spent a whole dollar and a half.

He signed his name carefully, imagining how much she'd love the card. It told her just how much he loved her, even though he'd been trying to work up the nerve to tell her for the last couple of months.

He'd spent so much time with her at recess, ignoring the calls of the other boys to play ball with them.

He'd walked her home a couple of times and tried to carry her books for her, but she wouldn't let him.

He daydreamed about her all the way to school. And all during school. The teacher had said they couldn't distribute their valentines until the very end of the day.

He watched her surreptitiously as he placed his other valentines in the little pockets Mrs. McChesney had set up along the back wall.

He waited for a moment until Sheila stepped away from the group. Taking a big breath for courage, he approached her and held out the card to her.

"Oh," she said. "I have one for you, too." She pulled a small envelope from her pocket, gave it to him, and walked back to her desk, where she gathered up her books and her sweater. She left the room with several girlfriends.

He was so delighted that she'd given him a special card, it took him a moment to notice that she hadn't taken his. Maybe she wanted him to deliver it to her at home after school.

He picked it up. Maybe he should wait and open hers at the same time she opened his.

He couldn't wait.

He opened it.

He made it home before he began to cry.


# 2000


**"WELL," PAT SAID,** "don't keep us waiting. What does it say?"

Maddy opened the card below it, the one it was paper clipped to. "This one is pretty flowery. Sort of standard Valentine fare. Love you forever, hearts and roses, that sort of thing. It's made out to *Sheila* and signed *Lyle*."

I looked at Glaze and she returned my gaze pointedly. No wonder she'd saved that card. "Lyle lived here," I said. "He was Elizabeth Hoskins's son—the son who got disowned." Carol looked a question at me, but I shook my head. I didn't want to go into the reasons right then.

"The writing looks kind of like a kid's," Maddy said, handing the card around the circle.

"And the other one," Melissa reminded her. "What about it?"

I could tell Maddy didn't want to read it.

"It's from Sheila. It's not really a card. Just a note."

It went around the circle after the first one.

> *I'll be your buddy*
> *I'll be your pal,*
> *But I don't want*
> *To be your gal.*
> *—Sheila*

No wonder Lyle turned out to be the kind of guy he was, I thought, and then could have kicked myself. I shouldn't blame Sheila. He'd been in his forties or thereabouts when I'd met him, but if he was anywhere near that sleazy when he was a kid, no wonder Sheila didn't want anything to do with him.

"Back to the search," Rebecca Jo said, and I heaved a big sigh. No sense wallowing in bad memories.

After only a few minutes, Carol let out a loud, "Oooh, I bet this will be good."

We all stopped our various chores and clustered around the stained wooden box she'd placed on one of the flat-topped trunks.

"Where did you find it?" I asked.

"It was on top of the armoire."

I looked toward the heavy one at the back of the attic, but she pointed at the ugly monstrosity standing beside her. I wondered why on earth there were two armoires up here.

"I thought the only thing up there was hat boxes," Dee said.

"I reached up and felt around," Carol said.

Maddy gave a theatrical shudder. "Good thing there weren't any spiders."

*I already told you I eat the spider webs.*

Carol screwed up her face, but didn't groan or anything. She must not have been too concerned.

Maddy gestured about the room. "There aren't many cobwebs up here."

*That is because I eat them!*

"I wonder what spider webs taste like," Carol said, and I couldn't help but grimace.

"I can't say I was ever tempted to try them," Ida said.

*They taste almost as good as mice.*

Maddy waited until Marmalade finished one of her imperious yowls. "Biscuit must dust the attic on a regular basis."

"Are you kidding? I've hardly set foot up here. Each time I get to the top of the stairs, I look around and say, 'I can't tackle this thing today.'"

Glaze guffawed. "It took the ice storm of the century to change your mind?"

"What it really took," I said, "was a bunch of willing friends."

"Not that we had any choice." Dee's grin took the sting out of her comment.

Carol cleared her throat and turned back to the little box. "Anyone care to guess what's in here before I open it?"

"Only if I can shake it first," Maddy said, as Dee asked, "How heavy is it?"

"No you can't," Carol told Maddy, "and it's fairly heavy for something that's only ten or twelve inches long. I'd hate for anyone to shake it just in case the contents might be fragile."

Maddy shrugged. "I guess that makes sense. But can you wiggle it around a bit and see if it rattles?"

Carol did. And it did. Rattle, that is.

"Tin soldiers," Sadie suggested.

"Jewelry." Glaze sounded definite, although why she thought it would be jewelry was more than I could guess. Why would anyone leave jewelry in an attic? Of course, there was the pendant I'd found.

"Jewelry," Dee scoffed. "Not in a crummy box like that. Maybe it holds a minor fortune in rare coins, though."

Ida harrumphed. "Not in a crummy box like that." She laughed at her echo of Dee's objection. "Although it might be a penny collection."

"If the pennies are as old as the box looks, they might be worth something."

*I think you should open it.*

"Why don't you open it?"

Carol nodded in response to my comment and then bent to pat Marmalade. "What? And spoil the anticipation?"

"Do you do this with all your history projects?" Melissa asked.

"Do what?"

"Try to figure out beforehand what they're going to reveal."

Carol rumpled her forehead. "No. That would never work. If you form too many advance opinions, there's a big temptation to try to make what's in front of you agree with your preconceptions. Either that or you'll be disappointed if you build up high expectations that don't work out." She rubbed the back of her neck before reaching for the box and unclasping a rawhide knot from the loop that held it in place. "Homemade, I'd guess, and probably by a youngster."

"Why do you say that?" Ida queried

"See how lopsided the knot is? If it had been a craftsman, he—or she—would most likely have followed one of the knot-tying conventions of the time. There were a number of intricate, fairly well known ways of forming a rawhide knob like this, all of which resulted in a regular pattern and a smooth surface where you could trace the individual strands of rawhide. It was a skill that most adults mastered, because these fastenings were used on so many implements."

"Who woulda known," Dee breathed.

"I've come across lots of sloppy adults in my time," Sadie remarked. "Why couldn't this have been put together by someone who was just in a hurry?"

"Or didn't set any store by the contents of the box," Ida said.

Carol gave a non-committal hum. "You're both right. Maybe I'm making an unwarranted assumption. Let's find out what we have here." She opened the lid to reveal a rough cloth bag, tied loosely closed with a piece of heavy twine. She lifted the bag carefully, and it rattled. "There's our sound," she said unnecessarily. "And look! A whirligig!"

*What is a whirly gig?*

"A what?" Dee sounded thoroughly confused.

"It's a toy."

*Oh. Thank you.*

"You're welcome." She set down the bag, still unopened, and lifted her discovery from the bottom of the box. It looked like it might be fragile, and she displayed it carefully.

I'd heard of them before, but had never seen a handmade one up close, other than the ones when I was a kid that we concocted from paper and straws—paper straws, since plastic ones hadn't been invented yet. We put them together with glue and straight pins back then.

"That's a far cry from the cheap plastic pinwheels you get at the county fair each summer," Maddy said, thereby revealing her age as somewhat less than mine, although of course I already knew she was in her thirties. I wondered what her reaction would be if I mentioned paper straws.

*What is a pin wheel?*

"Amen to that," Glaze agreed. "Does it spin like they do?"

"I think a whirligig is a better toy than a pinwheel," Carol said, "although they're fairly similar."

The little windmill arrangement was formed from a piece of what looked like it might be bamboo, with a thin nail poked into the end of it. On the head end of the nail was a short piece of wood, roughly carved to form a vane at each end.

"That won't work," Maddy said. She reached for the little contraption and held the bamboo handle upright in front of her face, blowing across it, the way you would a pinwheel. The vane, which now was parallel to the floor, hardly moved at all.

"There are usually two cross pieces that form an X," Carol said. "I wonder what happened to this one? Still, this might work with only one blade." She took it back and held the handle horizontally off to her side, so the vane looked like a single propeller on an airplane wing. "Imagine a small boy," she said, "running down the lane." She spun in a circle and the little arm that had been still for who knows how many decades turned around and around, creating a sound rather like the one I'd heard outside not long before—icy pine needles clicking against each other.

It was like a little bit of magic.

*I like magic.*

If I tried spinning like that, I'd fall over in nothing flat.

*Do not fall!*

"Don't worry," Carol said. "I used to take ballet, so I know how to spin without getting dizzy."

She must have read my mind.

## September 1783

**ALFRED HASTINGS FELT** like he was flying, as he ran down the long lane that began between the big trees at the bottom of the cliff and headed all the way toward the river. Wouldn't it be fun to fly? Really fly, like one of those hawks soaring above the town? But people could not fly, could not ever fly. Except, Alfred thought, when he dreamed. He dreamed a lot about flying, which is one reason he had made the whirligig. Not that he needed an excuse to run.

Alfred had been running almost from the moment he learned to walk. His ma always told everybody that his first steps had been on this very lane as they headed downhill toward Aunt Louisa's house. Ma had set him down for a moment, letting him hold onto her skirts, and he had leaned forward, and it was like his little legs—here his mother always fluttered her fingers when she told the story—had to run to catch up with the speed his head was going. He liked that story.

He deliberately did not look to his left as he passed his house. He knew that Ma was sitting there on the shadowed front porch in her favorite rocking chair shelling beans. He sensed her waving to him. "Come help Dondra Lee and me with the shelling, Alfred!"

He had already done his morning chores. He had emptied the chamber pots into the privy, rinsed them in the river, brought in wood for the stove, milked the goat, and tidied his bed. Now he had to shell beans?

"I will, Ma," he called back to her, and kept on running. "Be right there!" He ran right on past the garden and the pond and even past Beechnut House, and kept on going until he made it all the way down to the river, his little whirligig singing its whirly song all the while until he finally stopped and retraced his steps.

While he trudged back uphill, he fingered the bag of marbles in his pocket. They were his other treasure, besides the whirligig. Pa had made them. Alfred couldn't remember when exactly, only it was before Pa went off to war. Uncle Jonah had given him the string-tied bag he kept them in. Uncle Jonah lived with Alfred and Pa and Ma and Alfred's five big sisters now that Uncle Jonah's wife was dead.

Alfred rattled the marbles inside the bag. He liked that sound.

Ma always said that poor Uncle Jonah was unlucky, although Alfred did not know why, nor did he understand why Ma called him *poor*. Uncle Jonah was the best marksman in the whole valley. He brought down more deer than any other man alive, and his hunting kept three families in meat—the eight people in Alfred's family and the no-good Ellis sisters—that was what he had heard Ma call them when she thought he was not listening—and the unfortunate Widow Surratt and her five children. *The poor widow*—that was the way Ma always referred to her, but Alfred thought Widow Surratt could not be very unfortunate, not the way she made the best blackberry pies in the whole town. His mouth watered just thinking about how good her pies smelled. And tasted.

This summer had been a good one for berries. He had collected baskets and baskets of them. Alfred hated to be disloyal, but really, the Widow Surratt's pies were a whole lot juicier than the ones his mother baked. Every time Alfred went out with his sisters to collect berries, he always took a bowlful of them to the Surratt house. And she always had a piece of pie waiting for him the next day if he just happened to stop by, which he always managed to do.

Pa's lame arm, from the War for Independence, was never going to get any better, and he couldn't hold a rifle steady, so Uncle Jonah had to do all the hunting and a lot of the chores that Pa used to do. Ma told Alfred not to pay any mind when he heard some of the people in the town complaining about how Uncle Jonah had never gone with the other men to fight in the war between the Redcoats and the rebels. "He had his reasons," she said, and Alfred figured they had to be good ones.

He had a hard time remembering what Pa had been like before the war, but he imagined Pa had been a lot like Jonah was now. Jonah had two good arms. That made Jonah lucky, as far as Alfred was concerned. And Jonah had said he would teach Alfred to hunt once he was big enough to hold a rifle.

Alfred used his finger to twirl the vanes of his whirligig. Pa didn't like Jonah overmuch, Alfred could tell, but Alfred was not sure why. Maybe it was because of that war business. People were supposed to get along with each other. That was what Ma always said. And brothers should get along better than anybody else. Alfred wished he had a brother, but all he had were sisters. Big sisters. Sisters who spent a lot of time telling him what to do.

Uncle Jonah and Pa had left the house early that morning to go up on the cliffs above town to fell some trees. Alfred had not thought much about it, but he wondered idly how much good Pa would be at helping. Didn't you need two good arms to swing an ax? Maybe just one arm would work with the long two-handled saw.

A woodpecker rat-a-tat-tatted on one of the trees in the woods behind the house, and Alfred heard his mother calling him. "Alfred Finlay Hastings! Come here this minute!"

Uh-oh. When she got to yelling his middle name, he knew he had used up all his time and had better hurry. He stretched his arm out to the side so the whirligig could help him run faster.

Once he came abreast of the garden his steps slowed, but he knew better than to dawdle too much. Ma was slow to temper, but when she got it in her mind that Alfred was lacking in some way, she let him know it fast enough.

"Put your playthings aside, Alfred," she said as he climbed the steps. She huffed her voice out, so Alfred knew she was upset with him for not coming right away when she called, but the whirligig had made him keep running.

"You have work to do." Ma motioned toward an empty bowl sitting on the porch floor in front of her rocker.

"Yes, ma'am." His big sister, Dondra Lee, moved a bit to one side to make room for him. He laid the whirligig on the porch floor beside him, right next to Ma's feet. All his sisters were lined up on the porch by now. It took a lot of time to shell the buckets and buckets of beans from their big garden. It was not his favorite chore. He'd rather pick—and eat—the grapes that were ripening on the vines at the side of the garden. He lifted the basket of beans his mother indicated and began popping open the dried pods and spilling the contents into the wooden bowl.

After a while, his mind wandered, and his fingers kept forgetting to continue at the routine task. In his mind, he played at a game of marbles with Will Surratt, who had four other children in his family, all of them younger than Will. The trouble was, Will almost never could take the time to play now, because his mother kept him even busier than Alfred's mother kept *him*. Will was the man of the house now, ever since Will's father died. No wonder he had to work so hard.

Mother gasped suddenly, and her bowl of shelled beans fell from her lap onto Alfred's whirligig. He cried out in consternation as one of the blades broke under the weight of the bowl. Beans spilled across the porch, and the bowl rolled toward the edge. "Jonah," Mother said. Something in her voice made Alfred want to cry. He shifted his position so he could look up the lane the way she faced.

Uncle Jonah carried someone, a man, over his shoulder. Alfred noted the way the arms dangled limp, the way the hand on the end of an arm brushed the back of Uncle Jonah's legs, the way Jonah staggered down the lane. "Pa?"

"Frank?" Ma started to run, but she tripped on the discarded bean bowl and fell to her knees, knocking Alfred over as she did so. "Frank," she whispered, as Jonah hauled Pa up the steps.

"A tree fell on him, Minnie," Jonah said. "I …" he paused for a long time, just looking at Ma, and Alfred wondered why. "There was not anything I could do."

Ma looked at Jonah, and the look she gave him was one Alfred had never seen before. "Lay him in the parlor," she said, loudly enough to be heard over the wailing of Alfred's sisters. "I will get him … ready. Alfred, run to the Widow Surratt's and ask her to come help me."

Uncle Jonah stayed Alfred with a word. "No! Do it alone, Minnie."

Alfred saw his mother gulp, as if swallowing a mouthful of bitterness.

Once Pa was laid out so all the neighbors could come by the next morning to see him, he did not look like Pa anymore. Alfred reached in his pocket, on top of the bag of marbles, and pulled out what was left of a juicy blackberry he had been saving for himself. It was a little bit squashed, but Pa probably would not mind about that. Not now. He tried to slip it beneath his father's hand, just in case Pa might need it sometime. But when Alfred went to lift Pa's hand, it was as lifeless and as cold as one of Alfred's marbles and lay as still as the broken whirligig where Alfred had placed it in the bottom of the wooden box the night before. "You'll have to be the man of the house now," Ma had told him, but Alfred did not understand why. Would not Uncle Jonah be the man of the house, now that Pa was gone? Still, he put aside his beloved playthings and took on more of the chores.

Uncle Jonah moved out to lodge with the minister and his family. Alfred objected, but when he asked why, his mother just said it would not be seemly for Uncle Jonah to remain with them. "He has lived here for a long time," Alfred reasoned.

"Hush," Mother said, and Alfred wondered why her neck and face became rather pink.

By the following year, when Ma stopped wearing black and married Uncle Jonah, who came back to live with them then, Alfred had a hard time remembering the man who had fashioned the wooden box for him and who, with his one good arm and one lame arm, had painstakingly made the rawhide knob to fasten it.

# 2000

**CAROL UNTIED THE** string around the neck of the cloth bag and looked inside. "This has to date back at least seventy-five years, maybe more. Possibly even to the time of the Civil War." She cocked her head to one side. "It could be even older, I suppose."

"I wonder how anything that old can be in such good shape," Maddy mused. "The bag is stained, sure, but it looks like it just this minute came from being crumpled up in a little boy's pocket."

"Blackberries," Sadie said. "I told you I always had a dirty pinafore. I can remember stains of about that same shade on my pocket. I ate as many berries as I could when I was sent out to collect them, but I could never resist wrapping a few in my handkerchief and putting them in my pocket to save for later." She let out a surprisingly youthful giggle. "After all these years, I can almost taste the summertime in those berries sliding down my throat."

A cloud of grief seemed to cover her face for a moment, and I wondered if she'd just remembered the last thing her beloved Wallace had tasted—a blackberry from the batch Maggie had asked me to deliver to Sadie as Wallace lay dying on the hospital bed in Wallace and Sadie's front room.

*SlowWalker enjoyed tasting it.*

Sadie caught my eye and nodded. Yes.

Carol picked up the bag again and tipped it open. "How sweet. Handmade clay." Out spilled several dozen brownish spheres.

"Marbles?" Amanda reached for one and rolled it back and forth between her palms. "Did they have marbles back then?"

She handed the marble to Dee to look at as Marmalade jumped up onto the table and nosed the bag.

*What are marbles?*

"Of course they had marbles back then," Carol said. "Marbles are toys that have been around for centuries.

*Thank you. They smell very old.*

"Yes. They've been found in the pyramids of Egypt and in the ashes of Pompeii. Native Americans used them, and so did the Aztecs."

*Purr-mids? Ashes? Azz-ticks? I do not know what you are talking about.*

"I ought to give a lesson about ancient civilizations sometime."
*Oh.*

"Think of it, Biscuit," Ida said, glancing at Marmalade who was being exceptionally noisy, "you could have a fortune up here. Maybe you could sell these to a museum."

Carol shook her head. "Clay marbles like these don't have much monetary value, but can't you just imagine someone fashioning them for a favorite child?"

"Is there any way to tell how old these are for sure?" Dee held her marble up to the light from the window, although since it was solid clay, I'm not sure what she expected to see. "It's not anything like the glass marbles I used to play with when I was a kid. I could see light through them, and they had the most beautiful patterns and swirls in them, but these are just kind of dull-looking."

"Glass marbles weren't produced until 1915," Maddy said.

I looked sideways at her. "How on earth would you know that?"

"Research for one of my historical horror books. I had the homicidal maniac slip and fall as he ran across a schoolyard in the middle of the night where some kid had left a marble behind. I figured he might just shatter a clay marble, so it had to be glass. I know from personal experience how durable the glass ones are."

"Don't be too sure of that," Carol said. "These clay marbles were pretty tough, too."

"So, if you're so smart," Ida jabbed an elbow at Maddy who deflected it easily, "can you tell how old these marbles are?"

"They're obviously handmade." Maddy poked at one of the slightly misshapen lumps. "So they're at least from the Civil War era, but they could just as easily be from well before the Revolution. Clay marbles weren't mass produced until 1884."

"That doesn't mean these couldn't have been made *after* 1884," Rebecca Jo said.

"But they probably wouldn't have been," Maddy explained. "The factory that made clay marbles turned out more than a million a day. They were really cheap, so everybody played with mass-produced marbles back then." She screwed up her lips. "At least all the boys did."

"I vote for Maddy to be the caretaker of the new Martinsville Museum," Ida said.

Maddy looked inordinately pleased. "Unless Carol wants the job," she said, but it sounded like her heart wasn't in the offer.

"How about if I just sign up to be a visiting consultant instead?"

"We need somebody to keep minutes," Ida said.

"Minutes?"

"I think we just formed the Martinsville Museum Society."

At least Clara wouldn't be the president of it, I thought.

Carol wagged her finger in Ida's direction. "I'm worried about you."

"Why?"

"You've caught a whopping case of Feveritica Historiatica."

"Right," Ida said. "What the blinkin' beanie are you talking about?"

"Blinkin' beanie? That's a new one. Is that a Georgia phrase, or did you just make it up?"

"No," Ida said. "It's just something that's been around in my family for a long time. My mother always used to say it. And so did my grandma."

Pat piped up. "We need a name. We could call ourselves the Blinkin' Beanettes."

Carol groaned along with everyone else. "What about the Attic Historic Society?"

"Or the Attic Society of History," Melissa suggested. "Then we could call ourselves the ASHers."

"No," Sadie called from across the attic where she sat, still sorting letters. "What about the Women's Attic History Society? Then we'd be W-A-H, the WAHs."

"I can top that!" Dee called out. "The Women's Attic History Original Overlookers. The WAHOOs!"

Ida screwed up her face. "Very funny. But," she turned to Carol, "what was that disease you labeled me with?"

"Feveritica Historiatica. The name's made-up as of about a minute ago, but the disease is still real. It's the deadly Historian's Fever." Her gaze swept around all of us. "I'm afraid you've all caught a major case of it, my dears."

Glaze waved her arms around. She talks with her hands even more than I do. "You ought to call it *Historia hysteria.*"

"It is characterized," Carol went on, "by an inability to stop thinking about the people we meet in old letters."

"And old trunks," Dee added.

*There are no people in there.*

"And through old hats." Ida flipped back her feather with an insouciant air. "Anyway, why would I want to stop thinking about them? They're interesting."

"Yeah!" Pat looked up from the trunk she was investigating. "And there's no telling what we'll find next." She unrolled a dilapidated circus poster.

I couldn't help but think about the last time I'd been to a circus, when I took Annie McGill. Melissa met my eyes, and I could tell she was remembering the same thing. We'd had such fun that day.

## Summer 1898
## Russell Gap

**OBADIAH MARTIN WAS** not happy. All through his fifteen years he had wanted to see a circus, and now that there was one here in the valley, he thought it was a pretty poor excuse for what should have been spectacular. He had been practicing his spitting lately, so he tried it out, and the stream landed just beside one of the measly tents.

"Ugh!" The voice came from behind him, at about the level of his waist. He turned to see a round face between two braids that stuck out at an impossible angle on either side of the wide face. "You almost hit me with that horrible stuff. You spit right here in public. My momma says that is not polite."

"What does your momma know about anything?" Too late he thought to look around to see if anyone could overhear him.

A large callused hand descended onto his shoulder, and Obadiah looked up to see the hand was attached to William Fenton, a farmer who lived just north of Martinsville and who frequently had comments to make at town meetings. Obadiah's grandfather, Tobe Martin, was the chairman of the town council, and he had complained mightily about William Fenton and his frequent opinions.

Obadiah should know. His father made him attend the meetings, usually, so Obadiah had heard Mr. Fenton arguing about all sorts of things. Just last month Mr. Fenton had questioned the safety of our town's streets now that three people had what he called Auto Mobiles. Mister Breeton had an Olds Experimental Wagon, Mister Garner had one of Long's Steam Tricycles, the first one in the state of Georgia, and Mister Surratt had somehow gotten one of the Callihan kerosene fueled vehicles. They spooked all the horses. They were very noisy. They were very exciting.

Not that Obadiah was interested in anything else the council discussed, except for the automobiles, but Father and Grandfather both always quizzed him after the meetings. "You are going to be the town chairman after I am no longer with you," Father was always telling him. "You need to start training for the position early. It is a real honor being directly descended from the great Homer Martin, the man who founded Martinsville." Of course, by that time, Obadiah had usually stopped listening. He'd heard that lecture so many times, he could repeat it word for word.

Obadiah couldn't quite meet Mister Fenton's eyes. "Hullo, sir," he said, grudgingly.

Mister Fenton didn't let go of Obadiah's shoulder, but he used his free hand to pat the little girl on the head. "Thank you, Isabella honey. I'll take care of this from here. I bet you are really enjoying this circus, are you not?"

"Oh yes, sir. This is wonderful! I saw the goats dancing on their hind legs and got to pat one of the baby goats!" Isabella jumped up and down on her sturdy little legs, setting her braids to bobbing as if they had a life of their own. The shiny roller skate key she wore on a string around her neck caught the light. "The people in the shows all wear such beautiful bright clothes!"

"Now, that sounds good. You run on now and have a good time, all right?"

She nodded her agreement, threw another disgusted glance at Obadiah, and ran off to grab onto her mother's skirt.

Fenton raised his hat. "How d'ye do, Missus Hoskins?"

Nancy Geonette Hoskins inclined her head. "Quite well, Mister Fenton. Thank you for asking." She took her daughter's hand. "Do enjoy your day."

"Oh, I intend to." Fenton tightened his grip slightly before letting go of Obadiah's shoulder. "Now, young man, have you been trying out your father's chewing tobacco," he asked, "or were you merely expressing a private opinion about something?"

Obadiah didn't want to rub his shoulder, but he just had to. That man's grip had been worse than a vise. "I didn't mean nothing by it."

Fenton took off his straw hat, rubbed a hand over his brow, and replaced the hat. "Now, you and I both know spitting is something we men do. In a place like this, though, where there are liable to be women's skirts—or little girls—in the way, it is not a good idea, but I should not have to remind you about such a thing, should I?"

"I guess not, sir."

"Do you think I am going to expect you to remember that?"

"Yes, sir."

"Now, do you want to tell me what you were so upset about?"

"You can't do anything about it."

"I did not say I could." Mister Fenton turned and walked toward one of the booths nearby. "But I also did not say that I could not, now did I?"

"It's just," Obadiah let out a long breath and kicked at a stray rock so it bounced a few feet ahead, "I've heard about circuses ever since I was knee-high to a grasshopper, and I read about them, too. All about the trains they come in on and the elephants and the tigers and the jugglers and the clowns."

"Seen any train tracks in this valley lately, have you?"

"No sir, but I hear that's what circuses always use."

Mister Fenton chewed on his bottom lip for a few steps. "Sounds like you are a mite disappointed, huh?" He stopped walking as a meandering juggler crossed their path, with three balls up in the air. When one of the balls dropped to the ground, Mister Fenton bent, scooped it up, and tossed it back in one swift smooth motion.

"Like that," Obadiah said. "Their jugglers can't even keep the balls up in the air."

"Did you ever try juggling while you're standing still?"

Obadiah hunched his shoulders.

"Did you ever try it while you're walking?"

Again, Obadiah shrugged.

"Well? Speak up."

"No," he admitted. "But jugglers are supposed to be able to."

"That so?" They walked a bit farther in silence. "How do you think this circus could manage to transport a tiger or an elephant without a train?"

"I dunno. Walk, maybe?"

"How fast you figure an elephant can walk?"

"I dunno."

"Would you want a man-eating tiger walking through your town?"

"Guess not. Why are you asking me all these questions?"

They came to a stop in front of a small pen that held a dozen or so goats who immediately joined them, poking their noses through the wooden slats, which Obadiah could see they'd gnawed chunks out of here and there. Several of the goats placed their front feet on the top rail and said *meh-eh-eh-eh*, almost as if they were speaking to him. Obadiah reached out to pat the long ears. He was surprised at how soft they were, almost as soft as the ears of his momma's milk cow.

From behind the goats came a voice. "Next show is in another twenty minutes."

"Show?" Obadiah was interested despite himself.

"World Famous Dancing Goats. Ain't you heard of 'em?"

Obadiah shook his head.

"Worth seeing." The fellow turned to leave, and three of the goats followed him to the other side of the pen. He called back over his shoulder, "The tickets are only a nickel." He made it sound like a bargain, even though a nickel was half what Obadiah had paid to get through the main gate.

Mister Fenton bent down, tugged off a handful from a nearby tuft of soft weeds, and offered it to the nearest goat. "You need to chew the hay and spit the sticks," he said.

"What does that mean?"

Mister Fenton smiled. "Now who is asking the questions?"

Obadiah grinned—just a little—in spite of himself. "I do not understand what you mean."

"Now, you just think about it. Here you are all upset because there is no train, no elephant, no tiger." He turned to lean his back against the fence, and one of the goats nuzzled at his shoulder.

Obadiah turned his back to the fence as well and was rewarded with a gentle tug on his shirt.

"Sounds to me like you have been chewin' on the sticks and spittin' out the good hay. Look around you, my boy. Where else are you going to get a wonderful time like this, something you can remember for the rest of your life?" He pushed himself away from the fence and headed toward a small booth with enticing smells coming from it. "How about if we go try out a wonderful new invention called a doughnut?"

"A what?"

"There is another question from you." Mister Fenton elbowed Obadiah's arm in a friendly fashion. "I hear the dough cooks all the way through, since there is no middle to get in the way. Downright tasty, or so I hear. It will be my treat."

Obadiah raised an eyebrow, a habit he knew he had gotten from his father, whose face had been so badly scarred during the War Between the States, that for a while he hadn't been able to move much more than one eyebrow. Or so his grandmother Irraiah Martin had told him.

"If you say so, sir." He was relieved he would not be expected to pay for the doughnut, since he had no more money now that he had spent his ten cents buying a ticket to get inside.

When Mister Fenton handed him his very first doughnut on their way to the goat show, Obadiah decided that maybe this circus was not so bad after all. And neither was Mister Fenton. By the time they saw the marvelous performing horse and the dancing goats, he had forgotten all his previous disappointment. And little Isabella Hoskins had been right. The costumes were pretty wonderful.

## 2000

**"JUST A FEW** years ago, the Big Apple Circus came to Vermont," Carol said. "They set up in a field in Shelburne." She gestured with her chin at the poster. "The Big Apple Circus is a lot classier-looking than that one, and they had the most amazing show horses and acrobats and clowns—same as that one, I would imagine. I guess it's all in the tradition of the traveling circus."

Pat took a good look at her poster. "This only mentions one horse—*Diamond, the Wonder Horse*," she read.

Melissa's face took on an impish air. "Does it say Diamond performed for the crowned heads of Europe?"

"What?"

"That's what the ringmaster kept saying about every single act the last time a circus came here to the Metoochie Valley."

"No," Pat said, "but it does say their acrobat is world-renowned."

"Only one acrobat?" Ida sounded dubious, and I couldn't blame her. "What good is a circus with only one acrobat?"

"You don't have a railroad here in the valley, do you?" Carol must have already known we didn't because she went on without waiting for an answer. "Circuses traveled by train. All the wagons and animals and roustabouts, the tents and the performers, to say nothing about the elephants and tigers."

"I wonder why they didn't mention the elephants on my poster," Pat said.

"I doubt that circus had any," Carol said. "You couldn't just walk an elephant from town to town."

"Must have been a third-rate outfit," Maddy said.

"Then how did they get our circus here?" Melissa asked. "We still don't have trains in the valley."

"Eighteen-wheelers?"

I nodded. "I seem to remember seeing some parked off on the far side of the lot, but I didn't pay a lot of attention to them at the time."

"You were too busy looking for the cotton candy," Melissa said, and I laughed in spite of myself.

Pat spread the poster out on Rebecca Jo and Dee's card table. "I wonder where they performed?"

"Probably not here in Martinsville," Dee said. "Not if they had to walk the horse," she emphasized the singular, "and all the performers the length of the valley."

"They must have used wagons," Maddy said.

"Still," Amanda said, "wouldn't it make more sense for them to perform in Russell Gap? That way people from both ends of the valley could travel to see them."

"I hope everybody enjoyed seeing the horse." Pat sounded discouraged.

"I think it's a great poster, Pat." I smiled at her. "Would you like to keep it?"

"Absolutely!"

"But remember the museum," Maddy reminded her. "You may have to give it up—but by then you might have gotten tired of your one-horse circus."

"Not a chance," Pat said. "This poster is pretty much priceless. I can't wait to show it to Dave."

"I have a couple of friends in Vermont," Carol said, "who really got a lot of value when the circus came to Shelburne."

This sounded like it was going to be good. She had that undercurrent to her voice that presaged a story.

"They'd just moved into a new house. Chris, the husband, was big into gardening, and he kept complaining about how his brand new compost pile was still so small. 'I need something to jump-start it,' he told Jean—Jean is his wife."

"Jump-start? I can understand that," I said. "A new compost pile takes a while to cook down into something usable. I was pretty lucky when we moved in here, because Elizabeth already had a big working compost pile."

"Yeah," Glaze said drily. "She liked to plant things."

Things like bodies, I thought, but I didn't say it.

"Well," Carol went on, "Jean went to the circus management office and cooked up a deal. She arranged for Chris to get a truckload of elephant poop for his compost pile. It was his birthday present. The only trouble was, the circus wouldn't deliver. Chris had to take his practically new pickup truck to the circus grounds, shovel the poop himself, and then unload it once he got it home. Do you have any idea how messy fresh elephant poop is?"

"Bet his compost pile was really happy, though." I should have thought of elephant poop myself. Maybe next time around. If the circus ever came back to the Metoochie Valley.

"I don't know about the rest of you," Maddy said, "but Glaze and I had kind of a small breakfast, and my tummy's rumbling. Any chance we could quit for now?" She turned an apologetic grimace on Rebecca Jo. "After you've just climbed the stairs, now here I am wanting to make you go back down again."

Rebecca Jo waved a hand through the air, rather like the queen. "Keeps me flexible," she said. "If I don't use it, I lose it."

*What did you lose, BookLady? I can help you find it.*

Marmalade left my side and started poking her nose into corners.

"What are you doing Marmy?" I looked at the rest of the group who had stopped their journey toward the exit to watch Marmalade's antics. "I sure hope there aren't any mice up here," I said.

"Don't worry about mice," Dee said. "I don't see any droppings."

*There are no intruders here. But BookLady said she has lost something.*

I finally just picked her up and bundled her downstairs with me. We found the men playing poker around the big kitchen table. The table was way too long for a poker game, so they were gathered at one end of it. Reebok stood with his back against the pantry door, still nursing the big mug of hot chocolate I'd given him several hours ago. Or maybe he'd gotten a refill. There had been a few more additions while we women were upstairs. Father John Ames, Maddy's brother, sat holding what I recognized as a very good hand as I passed behind him. Across from him sat our town doctor, Nathan Young, who smiled widely. "Thanks for letting us invade. I hope Marmalade won't mind having Korsi here."

*You are welcome here, GoodHands. GrayGuy will be good.*

"You are both more than welcome." Korsi was Nathan's office cat. Marmalade jumped out of my arms and sniffed Korsi's tail where it hung off Doc's lap. "I see you've made yourself at home."

"We all did," Father John said, leaning down to pat Marmalade.

*Thank you, SoftVoice.*

"Fine with me. The more, the merrier."

*What does that mean, Widelap?*

Henry Pursey, the minister at the Old Church, had just gotten up to get himself some coffee—I saw where he'd left his cards facedown on the table. I'd have to be sure the carafe was kept full. We were going to work that campfire percolator overtime for sure, but that was okay with me. The coffee grounds would be a great addition to my compost pile.

"Hello, Marmalade," Henry said, and she meowed at him.

*Hello, EarlyWalker.*

Henry was such a self-effacing man. He was a darn good minister, too. It was an open secret around town that he'd signed up for the two to four a.m. prayer slot in the perpetual adoration chapel at St. Theresa's Catholic Church—Father John Ames was a particular friend of Henry's, and apparently he'd had trouble filling that time slot, so Henry had volunteered. The couple that prayed there from four to six had told Ida about it, in complete confidence, and of course she told our entire tap dance class, with instructions not to tell anyone else. So naturally, almost everybody in town was in on the story.

Dear Henry thought he was still completely anonymous. Marmalade and I took late night walks occasionally, not very often, thank goodness, since I didn't usually have a hard time getting to sleep, and we'd seen Henry heading down the hill from the parsonage and slipping into the little prayer chapel several times.

*I always greet him but he does not always hear me.*

I did wonder how they were going to keep the twenty-four hour prayer schedule going during this storm. "Henry," I said, "where's Irene?"

"She left last Monday to visit her sister in Ohio." One side of his mouth turned up in a funny quirk. "I called her near lunchtime yesterday and she said they were eating outside on the patio because it was so balmy."

I had to raise my voice over the groans from around the table. "She deserves a little balminess."

"Maybe she can send some of it our way," Tom said from his regular seat at the end of the table. He slapped his cards down on the table. "I'm out."

"A good thing," I said. "It's time for lunch."

Ralph made a big show of consulting his watch. "It's past time for lunch, I'd say."

Ida stepped behind his chair and patted his thinning gray hair. "Pore little growing boy." Her southern accent was wildly exaggerated. "He has to be fed real regular-like or he's jus' gonna shrivel up and blow a-way."

I did a quick head count. "Okay," I said, "we have twenty-one people here."

*And one cat. Do not forget me!*

"I think that's enough," Dave Pontiac said.

Glaze chewed on her bottom lip. "Is there anybody else we should check on?"

Nobody could think of anyone they hadn't either called already or seen going into one of the houses that had a wood stove.

Doc made an impressive bow—impressive because he managed to keep his enormous coffee mug level enough not to spill a drop—and said, "I'd like to acknowledge the salesmanship of Bob and Biscuit, who managed to get enough people to buy those wood burning stoves so that everybody in town has a safe place to gather."

Amid the cheers, Bob raised his voice. "That's not why we did it. We got our stove installed for free."

"Now we find out," Ralph said.

"All they had to do for free installation was talk five other families into getting them." Glaze turned to me. "So why did you keep going and sell, what, a dozen of the things?"

I looked at Bob. He looked at me. "It was fun," we both said.

"I heard that Matthew talked another dozen or so families into buying the things," Doc said, "which means he probably got his installation for free, too."

"I didn't know that."

Doc smiled. "You and Bob aren't the only sales force in town."

"I have to admit," I said, "that I got caught up in the challenge, but more than that, I just love the thought of a wood stove."

*I like how warm it is.*

"We know," Maddy drawled. "But the real reason is that you wanted a place where you could keep a soup pot bubbling all winter long."

*I like it when Widelap makes soup because she shares some of the chicken with me.*

"And what's wrong with that?"

She spread her hands and batted her eyelids behind her thick glasses. "Did I say anything was wrong with it?"

"Enough of this," I said. "There's enough food for all twenty of us, but you men have to get out of the way for now, and clear your cards off, so we can lay it all out on the table." There was some good-natured grumbling to the tune of *I finally got a good hand and you're telling me I have to forget it,* but their stomachs took over and the exodus to the living room was smooth enough. As they walked out, I noticed somebody was missing. "Where's Tom?"

"Outside somewhere," Bob said, "communing with nature."

"In this kind of weather?" Easton sounded aghast.

"Good idea," Carol said. "I've been sitting for way too long." She headed for the hall coat rack and donned all those layers that are a necessity with such intense weather. "A walk sounds like just the thing to get my appetite working. Would I have time before we eat?"

With all these women to do the work, we certainly didn't need one more person. "Plenty of time," I said.

"Anyone want to join me?"

"Walking on ice like this is liable to be dangerous," Sadie warned. "I'll stay inside, thank you."

*I will stay with you, LooseLaces, where it is warm.*

"Me, too," Rebecca Jo said, patting her stomach. "Lunch is calling me."

Carol looked for a moment like she might change her mind, but then straightened her shoulders. "Nope. Too little exercise leaves me feeling logy. What I really need is my cross-country skis. I don't suppose you have a pair?"

She didn't quite cringe when we all looked at her like we thought she'd lost her mind.

"Okay. So I'll just take a quick turn around the yard." She looked outside at the big outdoor thermometer we had on the front porch. "A very quick turn," she added.

"May I go with you?" Reebok waited for her to nod before he reached for his parka.

"I'll have some hot chocolate brewed for you by the time you get back in," Glaze said.

That was funny. I was surprised that Glaze hadn't offered to go outside too, to be with Tom. I raised a quizzical eyebrow at her, but she turned around and headed for the pantry.

*She wants to stay away from the cold.*

"Make that two." Carol called after her. "Hot chocolate is perfect in this weather."

"You got it."

"Be careful on those stairs," Ida warned.


**CAROL TOOK A DEEP** breath as Reebok quickly closed the front door behind them. Immediately, she could feel the hairs in her nose freeze. "Must be ten degrees or lower," she said.

Reebok stepped sideways to study the outdoor thermometer. "You're right. But then, you looked at the thermometer, didn't you?"

"Yes, but I didn't have to. Are your nose hairs freezing?"

Reebok looked at her quizzically, but took a breath and got that funny look on his face that told Carol he had turned his attention inward. She almost laughed at the way he wiggled his nose, rather like a rabbit.

"Maximum of ten degrees," Carol said. "Any warmer than that, the hairs won't freeze."

"That must be something you learned in Vermont." Reebok looked around the yard beyond the deep covered porch. "I've never seen it as cold as ten degrees here in the valley. I doubt it's ever been that cold here."

"Really? I can't imagine a winter that isn't this cold at least part of the time. But we never get ice like this, even during sugar time."

"Sugar time?"

She rubbed her mittened hands together briskly. "Late winter, early spring, when the sap starts running in the sugar maples. The weather has to be warm during the day—at least above freezing—and cold at night. When that happens, people get the sugar shacks fired up, collect the sap, and cook it down into the best syrup in the world."

"I've had real maple syrup," Reebok said. "But only a couple of times. It's really expensive."

Carol smiled. "I buy it by the gallon from a farmer up the road from me."

Reebok looked incredulous. Carol laughed and said, "Let's go try some ice walking." She headed for the ramp, but Reebok forestalled her. "I think the steps might be safer. We can hold onto the bannister."

Carol laughed again. "Did you ever go ice skating?"

"No. Well, once, when I was a kid, but I wasn't very good at it."

"The trick is to relax completely and trust your body's inborn sense of balance. Before I do this, though, I have to ask. Why is there a ramp?"

"The Chief's sister. She gets around really well with her wheelchair, but she can't manage stairs."

Carol wondered if he was trying to make a joke of some sort—it would have been in really bad taste—but she took one look at his earnest young face and decided that Reebok was just exactly what he seemed to be. "Where did she hole up during this storm?"

"She lives down in Athens. Teaches at UGA."

"Gotcha. Thanks for the info. Now let's see what we can do about this great slide." She took a few quick steps across the ice-free porch, raising her arms out to each side, and slid down the icy ramp like an Olympic skater, one foot behind and slightly off to the side from the other. At least she felt like an Olympian, even though she did wobble a couple of times. "Wheee!" The ice at the bottom of the ramp was thick enough to hold her weight, and her momentum carried her a good ten feet across the yard before one foot broke through and she was dumped rather unceremoniously onto her side. She whooped and hollered and extracted her leg from the ice hole, but when she tried to stand up, the ice was so slippery she couldn't keep her feet underneath her.

Reebok looked like he didn't believe his eyes, but Carol could tell the moment he made up his mind to try it. "Don't hunch your shoulders like that," she cautioned. "Stay as relaxed as you can, and try not to run into me."

He advanced toward the ramp like French royalty stepping onto a tumbril, about to be escorted to the guillotine. "Don't be afraid of it," Carol said. "If you don't get up some steam it won't work."

He backed up a few steps, until he was against the front door, took a deep breath, and hit the flat area at the top of the ramp, not quite as fast as Carol had been going, but pretty close. As the ramp tilted downward, his hands went out and his eyes opened wide enough that Carol could see the white all the way around them.

"Yee-haw!" He landed in a heap about six inches from Carol.

"Great planning," she said, and they collapsed onto the ice, laughing their heads off.

"Want some company?"

"Tom," Carol said. "Where've you been? Everybody was look-ing for you."

"Just sitting out on the side porch in the swing."

"You missed all the fun."

"No I didn't. I could see both your performances." He took a running start and sailed down the ramp as if he'd been born to it.

Not only that, he ended up on his feet.

"Show-off," Carol said.


## January 1979


**CLARA MARTIN FELT** like she'd been born to head up the town. She'd been as patient as she could be for as long as she could be, wait-ing for her chance, but enough was enough. She'd been married for eleven interminable years, and her husband wasn't getting any younger. The trouble was, her father-in-law showed signs of staying as hale and hearty as old Tobe Martin had done way back when. And Clara was tired of playing second-fiddle to Matilda Martin.

Most of the Martinsville Town Chairmen died when they were in their sixties, except for Tobe, who hadn't croaked until he was ninety. Since the war between the states hadn't killed him off, or so the story went, there wasn't much that could carry him away. It had been his wife's death that took the heart out of him. Irraiah Martin hadn't been any spring chicken herself when she died.

Clara had taken pains to learn as much as she could about the wives of the previous chairmen, but most of those women were just footnotes in Martinsville history. Clara certainly couldn't see any reason why she should settle for a footnote, when she could just as easily be a force to reckon with.

As it was now, Clara's mother-in-law, Matilda, was the head of the town garden club. She led every fund drive and every fete that came around. She always organized the food at funerals.

Clara couldn't wait to get her hands on those jobs. And why should she stop there? She didn't like the music the band played at the

Independence Day celebration. It was always the same old dreary pieces. She didn't like the schedule for putting up the town's Christmas decorations and taking them down. Why not put them up sooner and take them down later? She thought the council meetings ought to begin at 7:30 rather than seven, so she'd have time to get her dishes washed and dried and put away, but she'd have to be the First Lady before she could suggest any of those changes. She wouldn't be First Lady until Hubbard was the Chairman.

And he wasn't the chairman yet. Clara thought long and hard about it before she decided to invite her in-laws over for Sunday dinner. It could become a regular tradition. After a month, maybe two, she could slip a little rat poison or—she'd have to do some research on this—some other easily obtainable substance into his portion of meatloaf. Not enough to kill him, of course. Clara wasn't a murderer. She'd give him just enough to make him sick. Sick enough to resign the chairmanship. Hmm. Yes. That would work.

## February 1979

**HUBBARD MARTIN FELT** like nothing was going right. He had a lousy cold, but that was February for you. He caught colds easier than other people because his nose was bigger. More room for germs to get in. At least one thing was going right. Clara had finally begun to warm up to his parents. He'd had worries about his wife for so long. He just couldn't seem to make her happy, no matter what he did.

His business was good enough, but somehow there just never seemed to be enough money to keep Clara's mood up. He'd done everything he could think of to bring in more income, but nothing seemed to work. The only time she was happy was when she was shopping, and he couldn't increase her monthly allowance. He just couldn't.

To top it all off, he'd read in the *Record* just yesterday that Dave Pontiac's concerns were thriving—the jerk. Businessman of the year, the *Record* predicted. Rich as the dickens it sounded like. Some people had all the luck.

Hubbard thought a great deal about Dave Pontiac over the next two months. Why should Dave have all the luck, all the money? It took him a while to make up his mind, but Clara wasn't happy, so he called Dave.

They had a right satisfactory discussion. Hubbard was sure Dave didn't think so, but Hubbard ended the call happy as could be.

## June 1979

**EVERYBODY IN TOWN** attended the funeral. Hubbard was distraught over his father's death, of course. So was Clara. She really had not thought there was any danger. All she'd wanted was for him to resign. That was all. He'd been sick for months, and everybody said he ought to step down. After all, who could keep going with such pain?

Ulcers, some people suggested.

Stomach cancer?

Indigestion?

Maybe some nice antacids would help?

Clara had been careful not to make any suggestions, but she'd wrung her hands a lot when Mother Martin complained about how poorly her husband was doing. And Clara had taken her father-in-law plenty of bowls of soup when he felt too bad to come over for Sunday night dinner. That soup had been perfectly safe. She hadn't wanted her mother-in-law to eat any leftovers and get sick herself. It would have looked suspicious.

Once the coffin was in the ground, Mrs. Martin took Clara's warm hand between her two cold ones. "You were so good to him in these last months. How can I ever thank you enough?"

Clara wiped at her eyes, even though they were perfectly dry. "I'm so sorry for your loss."

The next town council meeting was in two days. Maybe she'd buy Hubbard a new tie. Understated. Suitable for a mourning son. But a good quality, of course. Suitable for the new Council Chairman.

And maybe a new dress for herself as well. Hubbard had increased her clothing allowance by a substantial amount three months ago, and she definitely felt like a new dress would be a good idea. After all, the First Lady of Martinsville needed to set a good example for the lowlier women of the town.

# 2000

**THANK GOODNESS FOR** my big kitchen, although even with the size it was, it was straining a bit with thirteen women in there. Luckily, there was enough to do that we could divvy up the jobs. I looked around. Not thirteen. Twelve. Carol was outside playing. Not twelve. Eleven. Easton had chosen to go into the living room with the men.

"We may have to eat in shifts," I told the women who were left, "or at least balance plates on our laps in the living room. This table may be big, but we've never managed twenty-one chairs around it at once."

"You don't even have twenty-one chairs," Glaze reminded me.

I thought about all the ones up in the attic. Maybe that's what they were there for. Might as well use them. I did a quick calculation and then called out to the men in the living room. "Would some of you go up to the attic and bring down a dozen and a half folding chairs?"

"Get the ones from along the wall," Pat hollered. "Don't mess up our circle."

Dave poked his head around the doorway and grinned at his wife. "We wouldn't dream of messing up your circle."

"While they're doing that," I suggested, "let's open the table up and put the leaves in it."

"It has leaves?" Glaze look bewildered. "You never told me that."

*I thought leaves were outside on trees.*

"You never asked."

Once they brought the chairs down and began placing them around the now-extra-lengthy table, we had to tell them about some of our more exciting discoveries. Unfortunately, but not surprisingly, they were not especially impressed with hats and wedding dresses.

"Better you than me," Dave said to Pat.

"You go right ahead and enjoy it all by yourselves," Ralph told Ida.

Bob pulled me to one side for a quick hug. "It sounds like you're having a great time," he whispered in my ear.

"You want to join us?"

"Uh … no. I think I'll pass."

"You're missing all the fun," I warned him. "It can only get better from here on as we dig deeper."

"You can tell me all about it later."

*I will tell you about it, too, after you give me some chicken.*

I was privately amused that Tom kept his seat at the foot of the table. That was where he always sat when he ate with us. Bob was in his usual seat at the other end. Glaze, of course, sat to Tom's right, so her left elbow wouldn't gouge anyone while she was eating. People always seemed to gravitate to the same seats—whether it was a school lunchroom or a board room. Sit there once, and the seat was yours. Or so the thought seemed to be. I wondered how long it would take for our other houseguests to claim a regular seat.

We took our time over the meal. Naturally, there was a lot of discussion about the weather and how long we thought this storm could last.

*I have tried to tell you that this will be a long storm, but you do not pay attention to me.*

Finally, I licked the tip of my finger and used it to rescue the last few sesame seeds that lay scattered around my plate. Then I stood. "Attic time," I pronounced, and most of the women pushed their chairs back.

"You know," Henry said in the kind of voice that made us all sit down again—I felt like I was on a pogo stick—"it looks like the storm is here to stay for at least a few more days. That means we won't be able to have Glaze and Tom's wedding on Friday. At least not at the church."

Bob picked up on what he was saying right away. "You could get married here instead." He looked at me with raised eyebrows.

"But we were going to decorate the church," I said. "All those candles and the red bows."

"We could place them around the living room," Pat said. "I'd help … that is, if I'm invited."

Within seconds everybody was spouting suggestions like crazy. The only ones who hadn't said anything were Reebok of course—he hardly ever had a comment, Amanda of course—she was almost as self-effacing as Reebok, and the bride and groom.

"No." Tom's voice finally cut through all the chatter. "Not without my grandmother and parents here."

"I'm sure we could manage to make our way up the hill and usher them down here," Bob said, and several of the men agreed to help.

"No!" Glaze's voice was even firmer than Tom's had been. I noticed that Charlotte, sitting directly across from her, looked startled at the outburst. "No," Glaze repeated, a little less loudly, but no less firmly. "Not without Mom and Dad."

Oh. They were five miles away in Braetonburg, and there was no chance in the world of their making it through on the impassable road.

Tom put his arm around my sister's shoulder. "We'll just have to wait."

But then I saw Bob cock his head to one side and raise his eyebrows. I wondered what that was about.

*He is thinking very hard.*

A loud meow from Marmalade broke the rather awkward silence that followed Glaze and Tom's pronouncements. Melissa called down the table to Carol. "You need to come back in the summer. It's beautiful around here."

"I think it's beautiful now," Carol said, and we all groaned.

*I think it is beautiful, too, as long as I am on the inside looking out.*

"No, really. We have heavy storms so often in Vermont they don't slow us down. I just whip out my cross-country skis and take off across the fields. I love snow."

"Snow's one thing," Dave said. "But I bet you never have ice like this."

"That's true," she said. "I couldn't believe how hard it was to walk just—what?—three or four blocks to get here. I imagine spring comes early, though. Maybe in March?"

Ida guffawed. "More like early February. That's when the crocuses bloom."

Carol's eyes widened. "We get blizzards in February on a regular basis."

I'm always faintly surprised that northerners have such a hard time envisioning the difference in the seasons this far south, but I suppose when you're up to your ears in snow, you maybe don't want to think about those of us who are welcoming the daffodils. Of course, when I'm up to my ears in spring greenery, it's hard to imagine four feet of snow somewhere else.

*I have four feet!*

"Come back in July," Melissa said, speaking over Marmalade's somewhat querulous meow. "Like I told you, the daylilies in the park are glorious during the summer."

I could certainly understand Melissa's invitation to Carol, but I was ambivalent about those plants. I'd never seen bumblebees or honeybees or hummingbirds visiting them, even though their vibrant colors did perk up the green of the grass in the town park.

"I like daylilies," Carol said. "Orange tiger lilies grow wild in the roadside ditches in Vermont."

"But our daylilies are historical," I said, "so you have to see them."

At her look of inquiry, I explained. "Some of the oldest books in the Martinsville library are a set of diaries that were started in 1797 by Faith Breeton Hastings, Ida Peterson's great-great-great-great-grandmother's younger sister, who was born here in Martinsville in 1787, the year before Georgia became the first southern state to ratify the constitution." I figured a historian would be interested in such details. I nodded toward Ida. "Why don't you tell the story?"

"It's been quite a while since I read through those things," she said, "so I may be a little shaky on some of the finer points. Correct me if I get something wrong."

"You expect *me* to remember the details?"

"Of course," Ida said. "You're the librarian."

*And I am the library cat.*

"And you obviously remember details after that explanation you just gave. Was it really all one sentence?"

There didn't seem to be a response to that, especially since I had no idea whether my description of the diaries had been so succinct, so I just leaned back in my chair and folded my hands in my lap, not knowing what else to do with them.

*You could scratch my ears.*

Marmalade placed her front feet on my knees and nuzzled my

hands out of her way, so I scratched her ears while I listened to Ida's story.

*Thank you, WideLap.*

"Faith and Chastity were the only surviving children of Louise and Frederick Breeton. Louise had been one of the original barn babies, and she—"

"Barn babies," Carol interrupted. "What are barn babies?"

"When the Martins and the others arrived here, the first structure they built was a barn to shelter all the livestock," Ida explained. "Apparently the people slept in there or in their wagons until they could get cabins built. Three of the pregnant women couldn't wait long enough, though, and their babies were born in the barn. There were two girls, Parley Breeton and Louise Martin."

Beside me, Melissa muttered something.

"What?" I didn't want to interrupt Ida's explanation, but I was curious.

"Louise must have been Homer and Mary Frances' daughter," Melissa said, with a question in her voice.

Ida didn't seem to have heard her. She was busy counting off on her fingers. "Louise married Frederick Breeton when she grew up. They were my"—she ticked off all the fingers of her left hand—"great-great-great-great-great-grandparents. The third barn baby was a boy whose parents named him Barnard Surratt." She put the emphasis on the first syllable of the boy's name.

"You're kidding," Carol said. "Barnard?"

Bob spoke up. "His folks must have had a sense of humor."

*Why?*

"Or a lack of imagination," Ida said.

*Why?*

"At least they didn't call him Barnyard," Dave said, and Pat poked him in the ribs again.

"I bet the other boys called him that," Henry said.

*Why?*

"I'm glad he wasn't a girl." Maddy giggled. "Just think. She would have been Barnetta, or Barneeva, or Barnestasia …"

*I do not understand what any of you are saying, CurlUp.*

"Just a bunch of jokes," Carol said, for no apparent reason, at least none that I could see.

*Oh. I do not understand jokes.*

"To get back to the story," Ida said loudly, after the hilarity, and Marmalade's yowls, died down. "According to the diary, the two girls, Faith who was twelve by that time and Chastity who was fourteen, talked their father—that was Frederick Breeton—into ordering some daylily bulbs from Savannah. They were delivered by cart in 1799 to the general store, which was owned by Frederick. He'd inherited it from his father, Pioneer Breeton."

"Pioneer?" Carol's voice held enough excitement to boil water. "He was one of the young sons of Willem Breeton, who owned the dry goods store in Brandtburg. Their whole family left with Homer Martin in 1741."

"Looks like storekeeping ran in the family, " Ida said, "because Frederick was still at it fifty years later. That October—in 1799—the two sisters planted several dozen daylilies at the edge of the town green, and they bloomed the following summer, the first summer of the new century."

"And they're still blooming?" Carol sounded skeptical.

"Well, not those original ones exactly." Ida gestured at me. "Will you explain it, Biscuit? You're more of a gardener than I am."

Bob touched my arm briefly. "I need to check on something. Back soon."

He gave a jerk of his head toward Tom, and Tom followed him from the room, but I was more concerned with answering Ida's request than with wondering what those men were up to. "Daylilies expand so quickly they can crowd themselves out," I told the group. "It's just about impossible to kill the things, but they bloom better when they're not jammed too close together, so every four or five years, you need to dig them up, divide the roots, and replant them farther apart." I waited for nods of understanding. "After the initial planting, as long as Chastity and Faith lived, they divided the plants and replanted the flourishing roots every four years or so, until eventually the whole central area of Martinsville was surrounded by daylilies. It started out as the town green," I told Carol, "but now we call it The Park. There's a gazebo in the middle where we have community band concerts on summer evenings. Melissa's right. You should come back in the summer to see them blooming. It's a riot of colors."

"Those diaries are pretty interesting," Glaze commented. "I found lots of good stories in there."

I stared at my sister. I had no idea she'd read them.

*You could have asked me. I slept in her lap sometimes while she read them. The books smell very old.*

Carol shifted her weight in her chair—those things tended to put everyone's butt to sleep—and leaned forward. "What's your favorite one?"

"I'd have a hard time picking a favorite," Glaze admitted, "but there was one that touched my heart in particular. Biscuit and Bob told me about it the first time I visited Martinsville, before I moved here." She smiled across the table at me. "After that I wanted to read more. The story started on the day before the fire that destroyed most of the church in 1814."

"That would be the fire Mary Frances wrote about?" Carol had a question in her voice.

"What are you talking about?" Doc wasn't the only one who asked.

Maddy pushed her chair back. "I'll be right back. You need to hear the whole story, and it's better if you hear it from the horse's mouth."

*There is a horse? Where?*

Naturally, a re-reading of the hundred-year letter raised as many questions with the men as it had with us. None of which were answerable.

"Something screwy's going on," Reebok said.

My sentiments exactly.

"The boys became local heroes," Glaze said, since Reebok obviously hadn't heard this story. "As Mary Frances wrote, they wrenched the doors from their hinges. The fire apparently started when an oil lamp fell over, although nobody knows for sure. The story goes that their great-great-grandfather, Homer Martin, had been responsible for carving the doors, and their eighty-nine-year-old widowed great-great-grandmother was calling out, 'Save the doors, won't somebody save my husband's doors!' The boys did manage to save them, but they were both so badly burned in the process that they died"—she indicated the letter again—"within a few days of each other."

Carol cringed. "Burns are awful at any time, but back then, with no regard to antiseptic treatment, a horrible burn was almost automatically a death sentence."

"Back to the diary," Glaze finally said. "Faith, the diary writer, wrote that her fourth baby was starting to come. She was twenty-seven years old at the time and already had three sons. The next entry, written by Chastity, the older sister—"

"My great-great-great-great-great-grandmother," Ida said, again holding up one finger after another.

"Right. Chastity wrote that the church had burned down but that she and Faith missed seeing the fire because Faith had been trying to get her baby birthed for more than twenty-four hours. After the church was gone, she finally delivered a baby girl. The last sentence Chastity wrote for that day said—I think I have the words right—'Faith held her child, kissed her forehead, named her Hope, and went home to the angels.' They buried Faith beside the burned-out building, and then they rebuilt the church."

Although many of us already knew the story, we all heaved a sigh of regret.

"What happened to the baby?" Carol's eyes had a suspicious shine to them. She passed a hand across them and said, "You'd think I'd get used to hearing about tragedies like that, but they always get to me."

"Me too," Ida said, taking up the story. "Chastity raised Faith's three sons and little Hope along with her own four children. Hope was the first baby to be baptized in the rebuilt church."

"It's a shame the diary had to end on such a sad note."

"It didn't," Ida said. "Chastity continued to write in her sister's diary every evening until she ran out of pages. Then she started her own diaries. We have the whole set. They cover more than seventy years—"

"Seventy-six," Glaze said.

"Until Chastity died in …" Ida looked inquiringly at Glaze.

"Eighteen-seventy-three," my sister told her. "She was eighty-eight years old, which was amazing, considering the normal life span for women at that time was less than fifty years."

Bob and Tom walked back in and seated themselves. Bob touched my shoulder briefly.

*He is happy about something.*

"Did I miss anything?"

"Yes, but I'll clue you in later. Where've you been?"

He looked—not sheepish, but almost secretive. "Just clearing up some loose ends."

I knew I wouldn't get more of an answer than that. "We just told Carol about Faith and Chastity's diaries." I turned back to Carol. "They're all buried at the cemetery on Third Street," I said, "beside the Old Church."

"The dates carved below the boy's epitaph are badly worn," Bob said.

"Some of those old tombstones are great," Ida said, "although as Bob says, a lot of them are almost unreadable now."

"That doesn't apply to the tombstones of the Town Council Chairmen," Bob said. "Those were maintained quite well."

Ida made a derogatory sound.

"They read like a *Who's Who*. Homer, John, Jerrod, Ketchum—"

Carol interrupted his list. "Ketchum?"

"Martinsville history is just full of great names," Glaze said.

"Like Jonas," Pat offered.

"Don't forget Tobe," Bob said. "That's always been a favorite of mine. Ketchum's son," he explained to Carol.

"I lean toward the name Pioneer," Ida said.

"Pioneer was the son of Willem Breeton," Carol said. "He was thirteen when they left Brandtburg to come here."

"Right," Ida said. "You mentioned that. He married Bridgett Hastings when he grew up, and their son Frederick married Louise Martin—one of the barn babies—and their daughters were Chastity and Faith."

I could almost see the wheels working away in Carol's head as she tried to keep all these names straight. I was having a pretty hard time of it myself. "Faith," Carol said. She pulled her pencil from her braid and extracted a little notebook from her pants pocket. "Faith was the one who kept the diaries. The one who died in childbirth." She started writing.

Ida nodded and held up five fingers. "The sister of my great, great et cetera."

"If you're collecting unusual names, don't forget Zenus," Pat said. "The one on the wedding invitation we found."

"Like I told you," Glaze said, "the town is full of them."

"What I don't get," I said, "is why Hubbard Martin threatened not to hire me when I first applied to be librarian, just because I had such a strange name." I turned to Carol. "My birth name was Bisque, which is where the nickname Biscuit came from, even before I was old enough for school."

"Bisque?"

"Our mother is a potter," Glaze explained, pausing as if to give Carol a chance to roll her eyes, but the expected reaction wasn't forthcoming. "It's a good thing there weren't any more of us kids. We might have had a brother named Kiln, or Clay, and probably a sister named Slurry or Wheel."

"Or Teapot," I said. It was a longstanding joke between us, and everybody around the table had heard it before, except for Carol.

We watched in disbelief as Carol dissolved in laughter.

"It wasn't that funny," Ida said.

"No, no," Carol gasped. "It's just that you had no way of knowing." She pulled out a handkerchief, a large flowered one, and wiped her eyes. "My mother is—was—the church organist, and her favorite time of the year was Christmas."

I heard the indrawn breaths. I think we all knew where this was headed.

"My older brother is Kris, with a K, and the younger one is Santa—but everybody calls him Sandy because he gleefully pummeled anyone who called him by his birth name as soon as he got old enough to do it." She took a deep breath. "Luckily I have only one sister. We call her Misty."

"Misty? That doesn't fit," Maddy said.

"Her real name …"—here Carol gasped again—"is Mistletoe."

"I should think you'd have at least one Noel," Dee said.

"Or you and she could have been Holly and Ivy," Amanda suggested.

"Don't worry," Carol said. "We've thought of them all. Carol is actually my middle name."

Melissa squinted at her. "Your card says *C. C. Mellinger.* Can we ask what your first name is?"

"You don't want to know."

There was, of course, an uproar from around the table as we all insisted that she reveal her whole name.

"I'd be willing to bet," Dee said, "that it's *Christmas*."

"Now you see why I didn't want to tell you? And why I use my initials?"

"Don't worry, Christmas Carol," Ida said. "My father traveled out west when he was young. He wanted to call me Idaho, but my mother nixed the idea."

Sadie looked at her blankly. "You never told me that."

"Thank you all for sharing," my sister said. "Now Bisque and I don't have to feel quite so weird."

"If the weather ever moderates," Carol said, "maybe I can check out the tombstones before I leave."

"We've got some good ones up there," Rebecca Jo said.

Naturally, we all had to tell Carol about our favorite epitaphs.

"I like the one that says *This ain't bad, once you get used to it*," Maddy said.

"How about *I was not expecting this*," Dave said.

"Or *I Got Ahead, but Now I'm Dead*," Bob offered.

Sadie raised her hand, "I'm partial to the one that says *The Good Die Young*." She paused a moment. "It's on the tombstone of Sam Clough, who lived to be a hundred and four."

"I wonder who ordered that particular epitaph," Pat mused.

"Sam did," Sadie said. "As soon as he turned ninety-eight."

*Nobody is making any sense at all.*

Marmalade, who had installed herself on my lap, yawned through a meow, and I was once again dazzled by the whiteness of her teeth.

"There's a tall monument in the middle of the cemetery," Glaze told Carol, "with a stone wall that runs around the graves at its foot." She looked at me with a grin in her eyes.

"Yeah, right." I couldn't resist poking fun at her. "When Glaze was first learning to dowse, she practiced in the cemetery. Dowsing works on buried bodies as well as on underground water, but Glaze's dowsing rods clicked together when they were right over the wall."

"Don't make fun of her, Biscuit." Rebecca Jo wagged her finger at me. "She redeemed herself when she dowsed out the location of those bodies in your yard."

"This is the second time you've mentioned that," Carol said.

"Later," I said. "We'll tell you later." Maybe after a couple of good stiff drinks. "Tell her about the column, Glaze."

"We have that lovely old church here in town…"

"Yeah," said Ida. "That's why we call it the Old Church."

"Right," I said. "But, as we told you, the beautifully carved front doors were saved from the fire by two brothers, Henry and Jason Martin."

"Martin, as in Martinsville," Pat said, nodding at Carol.

Carol obviously had been listening and absorbing everything. "The Mary Frances Martin letter," she said. "About how the boys died."

"The older of the two boys," Bob interjected, "would have been next in line to take over the chairmanship of the town council after their father died. But as it was, that honor went to the third brother. To the best of my knowledge, it's the only time it hasn't been a first-born son to take the helm."

Dave cleared his throat, but didn't say anything. I wondered what that was about.

"When the boys died," I said, "the town voted to bury them next to Homer Martin, their great-grandfather. He was the first person buried in the walled-off portion of the cemetery—"

"Where Mary Frances sat while the digging was going on," Ida said.

"Right. Although—correct me if I'm wrong here—the monument wasn't raised until a number of years after the church fire."

Rebecca Jo nodded. "That's right."

"I'm not sure about that," Bob said. "That may be just a legend. As far as I know there's nothing that says precisely when the wall and the monument were raised."

"Well, the wall sure was there when Mary Frances sat on it," Maddy pointed out.

"No matter when it was built," Sadie said, "the wall is just the right height to sit on. I often take a little rest there when I'm on my way to visit the graves of my husband Wallace, and my brother Eustace, and …"

Her voice trailed off. Not surprising, I thought. She's lived more than eighty years here in Martinsville. She must have a lot of friends buried in the old cemetery.

"It's a wonder that column has never fallen over in all these years," Father John said.

"It's nearly fallen twice that I know of," Bob told us, "but the town propped it back up both times, once in 1906 and again in 1936."

"I've often wondered why it tipped like that," Tom said.

"Frost heaves," Carol suggested. She looked a bit miffed when we scoffed at her.

"You have to have deep frost for that to happen," Tom said.

"How deep is the frost line here in Georgia?" she asked.

*What is a frawsline?*

Tom pressed him thumb and his index finger together. "About that deep."

"Oh," she said. "In Vermont, it goes down four feet."

*I have four feet! I already told you that!*

Reebok spoke up, surprising us all. He was usually so quiet, but now he had to raise his voice to be heard over Marmalade. "I imagine the column may have some more problems once this storm gets over."

"We'd better inspect it once we can get out and about," Bob said, and Reebok pulled a small pad from his shirt pocket and made a note.

"There's an inscription on the column," Glaze told Carol. "The carving is somewhat weathered, but you can still make it out." She quoted it from memory.

> *Henry & Jason Martin*
> *Heroes in Lyfe, Heroes in Death*
> *The Doors of Heavyn are Open to Them*

I could almost hear the old-fashioned phrasing and spelling in the way she pitched her voice.

## Saturday, 2 July 1814
## Martinsville

**JASON MARTIN KNEW** he was supposed to look up to his older brother, but this evening, after Henry had pummeled him yet again for no reason that Jason could think of, Jason considered ways he could take his revenge. It wouldn't be easy. Henry was so much bigger, for one thing. That was perhaps the reason Henry had been apprenticed to the village blacksmith. He could swing those heavy hammers all day and never seem to tire. But Henry was meaner, too. While Jason could not feel comfortable taking advantage of an opponent who was down, Henry had never let something as mundane as common courtesy stop his hand. Or his fist.

Jason did not have long to think about revenge, though.

The dreaded cry of "Fire! Fire in the church!" resounded through the community, and everyone grabbed their buckets and ran.

They had already formed a bucket brigade—everyone in town was well-versed in the process—when Jason heard his great-grandmother Martin call out, "My husband's doors!" She may have been the oldest person Jason had ever known, and her voice may have cracked a bit with old age, but it rang even above the noise of the fire. "Will not someone save my husband's doors?"

Jason looked at Henry, just in front of him in the line of the bucket brigade. Henry was big enough to wrench those doors off their hinges all by himself, but Jason knew Henry would never do it, would never put himself in such danger. The flames were already licking through the window beside the doors.

He caught his great-grandmother's eye. "I will!" He swung his bucket to one of the small children whose job it was to run the empty buckets back to the start of the line so they could be filled with water from the river. He knew the line would automatically close up behind him once he left his place.

He ran for the doors, shouting back over his shoulder at Henry. "Are you too cowardly to answer such a plea?" He knew full well his brother would never let such a challenge go unmet.

By the time they reached the front of the church, Henry's longer legs had eclipsed Jason's efforts, and he had flung the doors open and jammed his knife into one of the hinges, raising the pin enough for him to grab it between his meaty fingers.

Smoke billowed from the inside of the church, almost blinding Jason, but Henry kept on. "Hold the weight up," he yelled, and reached for the next hinge.

They hoisted the first door to one side and dropped it onto the dirt. Jason was vaguely aware of two men grabbing it and pulling it farther away from the flames.

He turned and saw through the smoke that the back of Henry's shirt had caught fire. Without thinking, he flung himself toward his brother and pounded out the incipient flames, then turned to hold the weight of the left-hand door off its hinges so Henry could force the pins out.

Together they manhandled the scorched door away from the fire as a burst of flames erupted from the opening, enveloping both of them. They staggered a few feet, dropped the door, and collapsed beside it.

Instantly the people in front of the bucket brigade line poured their water over the two, but it was far too late.

The doors may have been saved, but the boys were lost. Men scooped them up and carried them to the closest house, which happened to be Emeline's home, the parsonage at the corner of Fourth Street and Juniper, and laid them as carefully as they could, each on a narrow bed in the back room.

Emeline, Jason's wonderful Emeline, knelt beside him to his left, while Mary Frances Martin knelt on his right, both of them pouring water with their own hands onto his shoulders, his chest, his arms. Emeline sobbed so loudly, she could barely control the tremors running through her body, so a great deal of the water she tried to lave him with ended up on the floor or the bedding.

"I never meant for this to happen," Mary Frances wept. "The doors are not worth enough to make up for this."

Jason would have liked to comfort both of these women he loved, but he found that his voice would not work.

"Still," his great-grandmother whispered to him, too softly for young Emeline to hear through her tears, "I thank you. The doors were the work of Hubbard's hands, the only thing I have left of him."

Jason looked a question at her, but the pain was too great for him to ask it. Great-grandfather Martin's name was Homer. Was she too old to remember that? He closed his eyes. It hurt too much to think.

"The only thing I have left of him? No. That is not so," his great-grandmother breathed quietly. "I have you and your two brothers and three sisters. You are my husband's legacy."

**THEY BURIED HENRY** with one of the hinges from the church door, a hinge that had been so badly twisted by the heat of the fire it could not be reclaimed. They buried Jason with the half-charred remnants of Emeline's blue kid glove that they found in his pocket.

# 2000

**"SOMETIMES THE INSCRIPTIONS** on monuments are somewhat overblown," Carol said, "but it sounds like these two boys really were heroes."

"I think they were stupid," Easton said. "All that waste of life over just a couple of doors?"

Bob broke the incredulous silence that had greeted Easton's pronouncement. "Can we back up a minute, Carol?" He waited for her to turn her astonished eyes from Easton to him. "I'm wondering about something you said earlier. How did you know so much about Willem Breeton and how old Pioneer was when he traveled here?"

"This is really interesting," Pat said. "She told us all about it at Melissa's place this morning."

Carol shifted in her seat. "Not quite *all*. There's still a lot more to tell."

"She shared a lot with us women in the attic," Melissa said, "but I wouldn't mind if you repeated yourself, Carol. I'm not sure I have the names straight."

"I'm not surprised," Carol said. "It took me months—years—to figure out a lot of this."

"So," Bob said, "we have time if you'd like to clue us in."

"Maybe a condensed version," Dave said.

"I'd like to hear the whole thing," Reebok said, and then blushed furiously.

"Me, too," said Doc, ungrammatically but kindly.

"I've known the name Martin ever since I was a child," Carol began, and then proceeded to outline how she'd gotten interested in this search a number of years before.

She pulled a worn and wrinkled hand-drawn map from her

pocket, the same pocket where she'd stored her notebook, and passed it down the table. Pat and Dave barely glanced at it—"We've already seen it"—and the rest of us studied it only long enough to see that it showed the towns along the Metoochie River, with *Enders* written in pencil below where the mile-long gorge spilled into the wide lake below Keagan County on its way to the Chatooga River.

Once the map made its way around the long table, she spread it out in front of her and finally got to the meat of her story.

"As some of you know," she said, "Homer Martin was the leader of a band of well more than seventy people who left Vermont in 1741 and, I'm hoping to prove, ended up in Martinsville." She tapped the name on the map and then pointed to a town farther up the valley. "Calvin Garner headed a family that left with Homer Martin. His older son Nehemiah was nineteen, and there were two girls and two other younger boys. My contention is that Calvin Garner, or one of his sons, could have founded Garner Creek."

She ran her finger northward, toward the town of Hastings. "Robert Hastings was an innkeeper. He and his wife Jane Elizabeth Benton Hastings had either three or four children—I can't remember for sure at the moment. I'd have to look at my notes. Robert ran a very successful public house in Brandtburg, but he must have thought it would be a danger to stay behind with his family."

"Well," Sadie said, "that would explain why a Robert Hastings built this house as an inn."

"Really?"

Sadie nodded at Carol and swept her gaze around the huge kitchen. "Of course. All this space, and all those rooms on the second floor." She ran her hand across her mouth. "That must mean that it was one of their sons who founded the town of Hastings, since Robert was here with his inn."

Carol looked thoughtful. "That would make a great deal of sense. People usually stayed in one profession all their lives back then. None of the job-hopping that happens nowadays. If he ran a public house in Brandtburg, then he probably did the same here." She looked back at the map. "Robert Hastings supported his elderly father and his wife's aged mother, so although those two are not mentioned specifically as having left, they must have gone along with Robert."

She looked around at her rapt audience. "Are you with me so far?"

When everyone nodded, she continued. "Sarah Endicott Russell," she said, "was married to the Reverend Anders Russell, the oldest of the heads of families in the exodus, hence the town of Russell Gap. He had a younger brother Matthew who was a blacksmith, and the blacksmith had two sons Mark and Luke who were apprenticed to him. And then Sarah's sister was in that group as well—Charlotte Endicott Ellis and her two daughters."

Carol looked up sharply at me when I inhaled enough to set me coughing.

Once I had my wind back, I said, "Charlotte Ellis? Like our Charlotte Ellis?" I looked down the table toward Charlotte, but she seemed involved in getting her luncheon meat to stay in between the bread slices.

"Well," Carol said, "as we've already mentioned, names get repeated down through the generations."

I wondered, without saying anything of course, if the first Charlotte Ellis had been as hard to figure out as the current-day one. To be fair, though, ever since she'd shown up here, she hadn't been a bother at all. Just an enigma.

"Sarah Russell," Carol continued, "insisted that their daughter Myra Sue be married to Homer Martin before they left."

Bob looked skeptical. "How would you know that?"

"It was in a newspaper article I found."

Rebecca Jo held up her hand, fingers out-spread. "That can't be right. Homer's wife's name was Mary Frances. Not Myra Sue."

"You're right. Melissa told me the same thing this morning, but I can explain the discrepancy."

"Okay," Bob said, "but first, what about Braetonburg and Surreytown? Where did those town names come from?"

"Well," Carol admitted, "we have to take into account the fact that there wasn't a standard of spelling at that time. Willem Breeton, that's B-r-e-e-t-o-n, was a widower with four young children."

"I already told her B-r-a-e-t-o-n was pretty close," Dave said. He sounded like he was bragging.

Maybe Carol thought the same thing. I saw her eyebrows gather together a bit. "Another family in the group was Call Surratt and his wife Geonette Black Surratt, their four children, Geonette's sister Presila Black, Call's father, and Geonette's parents. Geonette had a younger brother named Sergeant Black."

"Sargent?" Rebecca Jo sounded incredulous. "I never heard of anybody by that name in the town history. At least, not that I remember."

"You would have remembered it if you'd seen it written down anywhere. They used the British spelling of S-E-R-G-E-A-N-T."

Rebecca Jo looked at Sadie, who shrugged. "The name's new to me."

"Sometimes people get lost in the shuffle," Carol said. "It may be stretching the imagination a bit, but Surreytown could have been founded by the Surratts. Maybe it was called Surratt Town to begin with but got shortened over the years."

"I'm trying to add up the numbers," Dee said, "but I got lost somewhere in there. You said more than seventy? What you've listed doesn't sound like nearly that many, unless every family had more than ten children."

"I tried to keep track of it when she told us at the B&B," Pat said, "but I got as lost as you."

"Nobody's sure of exactly how many people left Brandtburg with Homer Martin," Carol said. "There were a number of other families—we know there was a Joseph Everest and his wife. They had at least five children. Peter and Rebecca Fountain had an even larger brood. There was a Timothy Stickney, his wife Adah Kellogg Stickney and five or six children, and the Endicotts. The records aren't clear. They may have dropped out along the way before they reached Georgia, but there were at least seventy in the group to start with, and possibly more that we just don't have names for, and with that many families, it stands to reason that some of the women must have been pregnant. The Endicotts, for instance, only had three children when they left, and families were usually a lot bigger back then. They may have had more over the next four years as they travelled. Then, too, maybe people joined them along the way. We just don't know. Of course, some of the travelers must have died on the trail."

Maddy moaned. "They did?"

"It makes sense," Carol said. "That long a trek, and the usual life spans weren't that long to begin with. If somebody was fifty, they were considered practically ancient." She leaned her elbows on the table and made a tent of her fingertips. "Then, too, there was always the possibility of serious injury. And there were predators."

"Ewww," Dee said. "Like bears?"

"Like panthers—mountain lions. People had to leave the trail to go to the bathroom, and mountain lions roamed those early woods."

I shivered.

Melissa must not have wanted to think about those more gruesome aspects of the journey. "I suggested to Carol this morning that the Endicotts might have founded Enders." She twisted her coffee cup around several times. "Does anybody know for sure?"

I shook my head. Nobody offered any suggestions one way or the other, so Carol finally said, "We do know that Worthy Endicott had four brothers."

I did a quick mental calculation. Four men, four wives, at least two children per couple. "With their families, that would mean at least another dozen people, probably more."

"No," Carol said. "When they left Brandtburg, those four brothers were all unmarried, even though they were adults." She pursed her lips for a moment. "Of course, they could have found wives along the trail, either in the towns they passed through or among the others in the group."

"I've never heard of any Endicotts here in Martinsville," Sadie said.

"Ida's hat," I said, and half the people turned to look at me and the other half to look at Ida, who put a hand up to her head self-consciously.

"What about my hat?"

"Remember the note on the bottom of the box? Sarah said her mom's name was Prissy Endicott Martelson, which meant her grandmother—Prissy's mother—married an Endicott." I looked at Bob with a question in my eyes.

"That's news to me," he said. "I'm with Sadie. I've never come across that name here in town."

"If Prissy lived here when she was a little girl, then that means at least one family of Endicotts owned this house." I thought about it for a moment. "Grandma Endicott didn't necessarily need to live here, though." Somehow I didn't like the thought of Endicotts owning my house. How ridiculous. Just because I didn't like the town of Enders…

*Why do you not like a town?*

Not that I disliked the whole town. There were some lovely people there. I thought about the young man who'd saved my life when I was trapped in the floodwaters so recently. He and his grandmother were from Enders. Okay, so I didn't hate the town.

*That is good.*

"Tax records," Carol said. "Anybody want to investigate the county clerk's files?" She glanced toward the windows. "Once the storm's gone?"

"Dee and I can do that," Maddy said.

"Wait a minute? You're volunteering my time?"

"Yep. You know you'd love to be in on it. Imagine finding the whole history of this house in dusty old tax records."

Rebecca Jo emitted a dry laugh. "It would hardly be the *whole* story."

"What you need," Bob said, "is to find a bunch of old letters."

Maddy made a gagging sound. "So far, it's mostly been hats."

"Watch yourself," Ida warned, placing a protective hand on her white feather.

"Really interesting hats," Maddy amended, and Ida grinned.

The grin transformed her usually dour face. Ida didn't laugh nearly often enough. Come to think of it, she hadn't laughed much ever since her sister was murdered.

"We did find letters," Glaze said. "A whole trunkful almost. Underneath the wedding dress," she added. "But so far we haven't tackled reading them."

"Letters would really help," Bob insisted. "Or maybe some more diaries."

"I'd like to know more about that hobby horse up there," Dee said.

"They must have had some awful experiences," Amanda said. "Can you imagine taking off like that and carrying along only the absolute essentials? They must have had to leave everything extraneous behind."

"They couldn't have left everything extraneous," Rebecca Jo said. "I'm sure the women took their quilting frames and cameos or brooches that were particularly meaningful to them. And the men must have taken, uh"—she looked around the table. "What would men treasure enough to cart along?"

"Their muskets and bullet molds," Tom said, "for feeding and protecting everyone."

"Those would be essentials," Rebecca Jo said. "I was thinking about the, uh, the other things. The things that make life worthwhile."

"I think eating is very worthwhile," Ralph said, and Ida swatted his shoulder.

"Their favorite pipes," Dave offered. "And tobacco."

"If they had playing cards back then," Father John said, "I'd be willing to bet at least one man smuggled a deck along."

"A chess board," Henry suggested.

"Still," Bob said, "they probably had to limit their extras. Those wagons must have been stuffed to the gills when they began." He leaned back in his chair. "I wonder what they had to ditch along the trail."

"I would have made a lousy settler," I said.

Melissa raised one of her dark, expressive eyebrows. "How so? I think you would have done pretty well, as long as you could have a composting toilet."

"I'm serious. I doubt I could have put up with panthers and soggy dresses after a rainstorm and having always to cook over a sooty campfire."

"Tush," Rebecca Jo said. "There's a big difference between not wanting to do something and not being able to do it. You would have made it just fine."

*I would be with you to help.*

I reached for Marmalade and scooped her into my lap.

*Thank you.*

Maybe Rebecca Jo was right.

"I can just see you in a long homespun dress," Dee told me, "cooking up a pot of your eternal soup over a campfire."

"Probably stirring it with a spurtle," Maddy said.

*What is a spurdle?*

"With what?" Dee asked.

"A spurtle. It was a long fat stick sort of thingie used to stir porridge with," Maddy explained. "They used them years ago in Scotland, and I daresay a lot of them crossed the Atlantic with the original settlers."

*Thank you for explaining it.*

Dee looked from me to Maddy. "Why would Biscuit have a spurtle?"

"How should I know? I just like the sound of the word."

"Is it heavy enough to fend off a panther with?" Dave was obviously joking, but I could all too readily imagine one of those enormous cats, claws extended, headed for my throat, and me armed with only a porridge stirrer.

*I will protect you!*

Marmalade let out a growl that practically curled my toes. It was eerie the way she seemed to echo my imaginings.

Maddy waited for Marmy to quiet down. "I doubt a spurtle would work against a panther, but she could always clop it on the nose with a cast iron fry pan."

"Or her soup pot," Glaze said, sounding as dry as Ida usually did.

Dee rubbed her fingertips along her hairline. "Do you think we could look back in the old Georgia census records and find out how many of the original travelers made it this far?"

*What are sin suss rekerds?*

Carol balanced her hands in that universal *maybe-maybe not* gesture. "Probably not."

"Why not? Maddy and I are great at researching." The curl of Dee's lip negated what she'd just said, but then she and Maddy laughed. Some sort of in joke, I guessed.

"Carol told us this morning that the government lost the records from the first three censuses here in Georgia," Pat said.

"That's right." Carol sounded surprised. "You're a good listener. The census from 1820 was reconstructed, but there aren't any official records until 1830. That's almost a hundred years after they settled here, so I doubt even some of the children who made the journey would have still been alive."

"But you said tax records and church records and such..." Maddy's voice trickled off as she appeared to grasp the enormity of the task ahead of us. She shifted in her seat, switching her right leg, which had been curled beneath her, with her left one. "Well, at least it'll keep us out of trouble for a while."

"I don't know about that," Ida said. "You could get in trouble just sitting there."

*CurlUp is not in trouble.*

Carol laughed. Apparently she appreciated Ida's weird sense of humor.

By the time we were ready to leave the lunch table, the sky had turned noticeably darker outside, but that darkness seemed to be offset by the glittering white of the ice that coated everything. The reflected light penetrated the bright yellow kitchen curtains. Even so, we'd put candles in tall holders down the center of the table. It truly was festive-looking. "This is like a holiday," I said, "without all the fuss and bother." I pushed my plate a few inches away—there wasn't much empty room on the table—stood, and walked to the bay window. I didn't want to let in any of the cold, but I just had to check on the Old Forest behind our yard.

Many of the trees in this block had been here since the 1700s. Homer Martin and the other founding families had watched them grow. Someone had refused to let the men clear-cut the land back then. As a result, three stands of old-growth trees graced Martinsville—here in our block, up behind the Old Church, and in back of the library. The air was different underneath them—fresher somehow. I was immensely grateful to the unknown person or people who had saved the trees, in a time when I knew most of the land in and around a town was routinely cleared of trees and underbrush. I couldn't help wondering why these particular trees had been saved.

*I like trees.*

I knew Sadie had been instrumental in protecting a lot of the trees that lined the streets of Martinsville.

*LooseLaces likes the trees, too.*

I'd loved Sadie Russell Masters long before I met her because I'd seen a news photo of her in the *Keagan County Record* maybe fifteen, twenty years ago. The photo showed her only from the waist up, and I couldn't help but wonder, now that I knew her, if her shoelaces had been untied way back then the way they usually were now. At any rate, she'd had her arms wrapped as far as she could reach around one of the big old oaks whose roots were splitting the sidewalk on Juniper Street. She was facing off with a thoroughly disgruntled Hubbard Martin, who held a chainsaw. The look on Hubbard's face was murderous, but Sadie had won the battle, the sidewalk had been re-routed around the tree roots, and Sadie had extended her protection to every old original tree in town, one of the reasons Martinsville was so beautifully shady in the summer. As far as I knew, Hubbard was about the only one now who wanted the old trees cut down. After Sadie's stunt—good for her!—a truce of sorts, hammered out at numerous town meetings, protected the trees officially, not only now but far into the future. In perpetuity, the wording of the official document had stated.

*What does that mean?*

Marmalade hopped up onto the windowsill, purring like a steam engine.

*What does that mean? I am not a steemenjin.*

I stroked her soft back. Ida told me once that Sadie's mother fought off Leon and Obadiah Martin, Hubbard's father and grandfather, to save those same trees. But somewhere, way back when, there must have been someone who started it all.

The window had fogged up the moment I opened the curtain. I traced my initials into the fog, and then rubbed a circle clear so I could peer outside. The thick coating of ice had bent all of the branches, some more than others. "I do hope the trees will be okay," I said.

*They love the winter time. It is their time to rest.*

"Those woods have lasted well more than two centuries," Ida said, "and I daresay there've been other storms as bad as this one."

"You're right, I'm sure." I pulled the curtain back into place once Marmalade jumped down.

"Two centuries?" Carol sounded genuinely surprised. "Are they really that old?"

"Yes," I said. "And possibly even older. Why do you ask?" Silly question. I knew why she asked. She was a historian.

"There are so few ancient trees left in this country," she said. "The early settlers tended to clear-cut the land to make room for growing crops and grazing their livestock."

"And the developers," Pat said. "Don't forget them. Anything left gets mown down to make room for houses. We've seen that happening everywhere we've lived."

"Not here," Ida said. "Martinsville has three huge stands filled with old-growth trees."

"Maybe it's because there was so much land available for crops north of town," Rebecca Jo said. "Up above the cliffs to the west, too," she added.

Carol's forehead wrinkled. "No. They didn't cut the trees just to get land for crops and grazing. The forests were actually seen as a danger."

"What kind of danger?" Maddy asked.

"Enemies could use the trees for cover. There was a risk of fire spreading to the wooden houses if lightning torched a nearby tree. And there was always the risk of predators."

Maddy thought about it. "Yeah. You mentioned them. I guess bears could hide in thick trees."

"From what I know about it," Carol said, "bears weren't usually that much of a problem. But cougars certainly were."

I shivered. Mountain lions. The thought of being stalked by an enormous feline like that brought on goose bumps. And I'd read once about how eerie their screams sounded. I knew they still lived in the forests of the eastern states, but as far as I knew, there had never been any in Martinsville. I hoped that once this storm was over and I started walking to work each day, I wouldn't feel like I was being stalked.

*I always walk with you. I will protect you.*

Marmalade growled, almost as if she were a watchdog.

*Watch dog?*

Or I guess I should say a watch cat.

*Yes you should.*

My miniature mountain lion.

Saturday, 25 April 1741<br>
Day #6 of the journey<br>
Somewhere in the Champlain Valley

**WILLY BREETON HAD** already hollered his head off and whistled as loudly as he could, but Lucky wasn't anywhere to be found. They'd been walking along happy as could be that morning, with Willy throwing a stick ahead and Lucky darting off to scoop it up and bring it back to him, when all of a sudden she'd perked up her ears and run off into the scrub, followed closely by a string of other dogs—all males—from the surrounding family groups.

Willy started to head after her, but MaryAnne came out of nowhere and collared him. "You know better than that, Willy," she scolded. "You get lost in those trees and we will have to stop the whole line of wagons just to try to find you."

"I would not get lost, and anyway, if I did, Lucky would find me and lead me back."

MaryAnne let out one of those sounds she made whenever she was about to say 'you try my patience, brother.'

"You try my patience, brother. Lucky cannot always be hauling you out of mischief."

"But why would she leave?"

MaryAnne may have been only thirteen, but she had a clear-headed way of looking at the world. She knew quite well why Lucky had run away. After all, MaryAnne had been raised in a farming community. So had Willy, of course, but he was only nine, and he tended to be oblivious of what was going on right in front of his eyes between the mares and stallions, the cows and bulls, and of course, the various dogs that roamed the town.

Two days later, as Willy finished the last bite of his evening meal beside the campfire, a rather bedraggled Lucky bounded into the circle of firelight and pounced on her young master, knocking his eating knife from his hand.

"Where have you been all this time, Lucky? You like to scared me to death! I could not hardly sleep the last two nights I was so worried about you." He lowered his voice and whispered in his dog's ear. "I even snuck out of camp to look for you, but I could not find you. Do not you tell MaryAnne what I did or she will tie me to the wagon for sure."

Lucky, in total unconcern for the disruption she had caused, sprawled across Willy's lap, panting, the very picture of doggie contentment. The other dogs, the males, settled around and under their accustomed wagons, but Willy paid them no attention. After all, Lucky was his special dog.

## 2000

**"IT SOUNDS EXCITING** on one hand," Amanda said, "and awful on the other. I agree with Biscuit. I think I would have been a lousy settler. Imagine having to wear those long dresses while you're trying to wade across a creek."

"You're right about the awful experiences," Carol said. "Travel back then was fraught not just with inconvenience, but with danger."

"Like what?"

"Blood poisoning from infection after injuries or accidents, possible starvation, snakebites, and, as I already mentioned, lots of different types of predators." She ticked off the ideas on her fingers.

"Predators!" Dee shivered.

"Yes. Bears and wolves would usually only attack a lone person, but I imagine there were plenty of times when a person had to step away from the trail."

Maddy nodded sagely and muttered something about *potty time.*

"Same with the cougars," Carol said. "They called them painters at that time."

"Painters? How do you get a word like *painters* from *cougars?*"

"It derives from *panther.* Nowadays we usually call them mountain lions." Carol held up more fingers. "Our travelers could have frozen to death or been washed away by a raging river as they tried to ford it. Most people back then couldn't swim."

Dee leaned her elbows on the table and cupped her chin in her hands. "It sounds like it's a wonder they ever made it here."

"I'm sure a great many of them didn't," Carol said.

## Saturday, 27 June 1741

**MARYANNE BREETON'S PATIENCE** had just about run out. She

grabbed her nine-year-old brother by the tail of his shirt as he ran past the wagons that were slowing and pulling into position. "You have your evening chores to do, Willy. I will not have you neglecting them." The almost four-year difference in their ages seemed to her to be more like twenty. Had she not been responsible for all three of the other children ever since her mother died? Was she not tired of constantly hauling Willy out of trouble? Had she not done enough?

"Tomorrow is our day of rest, young man, and you must collect enough wood for the cook fire for this evening as well as enough for tomorrow morn."

The women of each group prepared the evening meal for their own husbands, children, and other assorted members of their extended families. When they had begun the trek from Brandtburg two months ago, the Reverend Russell and his family had invited the newly-bereaved Willem Breeton, MaryAnne, and the other three children into their circle each night. But Mistress Russell and her daughter Ann had both been ailing for three days. MaryAnne hoped it was not serious.

She supposed she should be grateful for the fact that seventeen-year-old Edna Russell, the youngest of the Russell brood, had taken over the care of the two sick women, but it was hard to feel grateful when that left thirteen-year-old MaryAnne and her twelve-year-old sister Susan responsible for cooking for the seven remaining people. Mistress Russell was still grieving the death—the murder—of her daughter Myra Sue as well. It was no wonder she had fallen ill.

"Mayhap Thomas will gather the wood for you," Willy said with an irrepressible giggle.

MaryAnne turned her head to where Thomas Russell had finished maneuvering the horses to pull the wagon into position. She had found herself more and more aware of him of late, of all the little things he did, the movements he made, his smiles, his tone of voice. She did not mind that he sometimes had difficulty beginning his speech. The stuttering quality of his voice made her feel … protective somehow. He was but seven years older than she. She had always liked Thomas. But now she had begun to wonder if perhaps in another two or three years, when it was time for her to marry …

She shook herself. "You know quite well that Thomas"—her voice caught a bit and she cleared her throat—"is busy with his own chores."

Willy laughed up at her, and her eyes softened in response. How did her little brother manage to do that? She was so worried about preparing the meal, and here he was able to turn her dreary thoughts to hopeful ones. One more day, perhaps, and Mistress Russell would be back on her feet to take over the meal preparation once again. MaryAnne was always happy to help, but she knew the meals she prepared were nowhere near as tasty as those that came from the hands of the Russell women. She hoped Thomas remained well. She hoped he did not mind the way she cooked.

MaryAnne straightened her shoulders and cuffed the side of Willy's head softly. "Go on, you young scamp." She lifted her gaze to the tall trees surrounding the clearing. They had been fortunate that Silas had found a space large enough to gather the wagons close.

The first number of nights they had spent on the trail after leaving Brandtburg had been in fields large enough to accommodate the entire group. But the farther south they went, the more the trees seemed to close in around them. They had regularly heard the howls of wolves and the screams of painters and had seen bear scat aplenty. The men had, of course, taken turns guarding the camp at night, and twice MaryAnne had been awakened by the sound of gunfire.

"Take Lucky with you," she told her brother, "and do not go too far from the wagons."

"Lucky doesn't want to go," he complained. "She curled up under the wagon and won't move." He pointed.

Lucky had hardly even waited for the wagon to stop moving. Her advanced pregnancy was obvious. If she had to drop her pups, MaryAnne thought, at least tonight would be a good time for it, and thank the heavens the dog had not chosen to slink away into the woods to find herself a place to whelp them.

The first month on the trail, they had traveled every day of every week, taking only a short time each Sunday for Reverend Russell to lead the worship service. After four weeks without any of the Brandts following them, though, Reverend Russell had insisted that Sundays must be a day of rest. Not that any day was truly restful. There were always the chores to be done, cooking, tending the livestock, mending clothing, repairing wagons. Everyone stayed busy, even on the Sabbath.

MaryAnne thought quickly. If the pups were born tonight or to-morrow, Lucky could ride with them on Monday in the back of the wagon and for the first few days. Puppies slept most of the time any-way—slept and ate—and Lucky would not want to leave them at first. "Leave Lucky, then, but hurry with that wood. Do not go too far." Willy scampered off and MaryAnne headed for the wagon. As she walked, she scanned the skies. The clouds were not thick enough for rain, not yet.

She had just hefted the iron girdle out of the wagon and headed toward where the fire would be—whenever Willy brought the wood—when she heard the first scream. Behind her, the chickens set up a rau-cous chorus of cackling in their cages, and every rooster in the camp began to crow in agitation.

Thomas reached up a hand to reassure the horses, and MaryAnne saw that all around the clearing men had stepped to the heads of their lead horses. "That is a painter for sure," Nehemiah Garner said from the other side of the circle, "but it sounds like it is far off in the woods."

Early in the journey, Silas Martin had told everyone that painters would not attack a large group. But their scream, which sounded eerily like a woman in the throes of a difficult birth, could spook the livestock. It was good, MaryAnne thought again, that Lucky had not crept off into the woods to give birth. She would have been an easy target for an enormous tawny cat.

The woods.

Willy.

"Willy," MaryAnne called. "Willy!"

Thomas stepped toward her. "W-w-where is h-h-he?"

"He went that way"—she gestured with her head toward the trees, toward the source of the painter's scream. "To gather firewood." The girdle clanged against a stone when she dropped it and began to run.

Thomas had his rifle in hand within seconds. Nehemiah fol-lowed, and as the word spread, a dozen men fanned out along the en-croaching edge of the forest, calling her brother's name.

MaryAnne heard her brother an instant before she saw him run-ning down the hill toward her, weaving between the trees, the painter streaking through the woods far behind him, but gaining ground every second. One of the men fired, then another, and her vision was clouded by the smoke from the guns.

"Did you hit it?" "No!" "Hold your fire," someone yelled, "you might hit Willy!"

Their shouts rang out as MaryAnne surged ahead of the men, but she barely heard them. Thomas grabbed at her to stop her, but she eluded him without even thinking about it. She could not even feel her feet pounding into the spongy mold of the forest floor.

She had never seen Willy run so fast. The painter was closer now, far too close. It had been only seconds, but those seconds seemed like hours to her.

The painter bounded onto an outcrop of rock and launched itself toward her brother, its claws extended. MaryAnne threw herself across her brother, crushing him to the ground beneath her. Any moment she expected to feel fangs and claws in her back. Any moment now, she expected to die. "Let Willy be safe," she breathed and turned her head to face her certain death. She watched in disbelief as a dead tree fell across the airborne path of the big cat. The stark leafless trunk shook the forest floor with a resounding crash.

It took her a moment to realize that the woods had gone silent. It took a moment more before the men began to whoop and yell. It took her yet another moment before she felt Willy stir beneath her.

Beside her, Thomas let out a low whistle. "I n-n-never saw anything l-l-l-like it," he said. "That t-t-tree l-l-looked like it w-w-was aiming r-r-right at the p-p-painter."

Silas Martin approached the cat, which had begun screaming again, but this time with the sound of pain and desperation. He was careful to stay out of range of its thrashing front paws, even though it looked like its back legs had been broken when the huge trunk of the old dead hickory tree fell on it. He killed it with one shot through the head. Willy, once he recovered his breath, couldn't stop talking. "I followed a rabbit," MaryAnne heard him say. "Scream…scared…ran…" But she stopped listening and simply gathered her little brother into her arms, where he promptly burst into tears.

Thomas accompanied her as she led her brother to a nearby stream and wet the corner of her apron to wash the mud and tears from his face. Behind them, the other men set to work chopping the dead tree to provide enough firewood for a dozen cooking fires.

The next morning, before the Sunday services, Lucky gave birth to a litter of four puppies. Willy, by that time fully recovered from his moments of terror, named the light brown female with the big feet *Painter*. The gray one with the stumpy tail was *Rifle*. The brown and gray runt was *Branch*. But he saved the best name for the black and white pup, the biggest one, who looked just like its mother. *Hickory*.

## 2000

**"ANYWAY," CAROL WENT** on, "that's why most people have huge lawns today. It's a throwback to when people believed the land around a cabin had to be completely cleared for safety."

"So," Amanda said, "why were these three wooded sections left standing?"

Carol grinned at her. "Another one of those mysteries?"

"I'd like to know why the trees were left, too," Bob said. "Too bad we'll never know the answer. There are some old records that indicate the first thing the settlers built was that big barn-like structure that, as you know, sheltered all the families and some of the livestock."

"They would have had to clear-cut that area," Carol said, "to get the lumber to build it."

"That's right," Bob agreed. "The barn stood at the bottom of Upper Sweetgum Street—I guess there wasn't a street there yet, though. There aren't any really old trees anywhere around that part of town. There's a sketch of the barn hanging in City Hall, not more than"—he held his hands apart, palms facing each other—"say about ten or eleven inches wide and maybe seven inches tall. Once the storm's over with, I'll show it to you if you'd like to see it."

"I'd love to," she said. "Do you have any idea who drew the sketch?"

Bob thought for a moment. "I think there's a name at the bottom, but I don't recall exactly." He looked around the table as if asking for some help. I couldn't even remember having seen the darn thing in the first place.

"Uh, Chief?"

We all turned to look at Reebok, who stood with his back against the door of the walk-in pantry. "There's no name."

He paused.

"But there are some initials."

## May 1745

**"WE FINISHED THE** barn just in time," Silas said as he and Brand walked away from it in the misty light of pre-dawn, up the slope toward the high cliff to the west. Having a shelter from the heavy rains of the last four nights had been a relief after four years in leaky tents and under sodden wagons. It was still early enough in the year to give them time to plant and to build sufficient cabins before winter set in. Everyone said that the seasons would not be so severe here, but Silas had a hard time imagining a winter without the kind of heavy snows that had stalled them for as much as a month at a time during the journey south.

He was surprised that more of the families had not left the company to settle in the various towns they passed on the long journey.

Still, maybe it was not so hard to understand. There was a cohesiveness now to the motley group, a connection that had been forged as they faced the inevitable challenges along their extensive road. He hoped the connectedness would continue now that they had settled, although he knew enough of human nature to suspect that small divisions would begin, small irritations would grow into larger ones, small complaints that had been stifled on the long trail could very likely become major divisions now that the survival of the company seemed assured, or at least less precarious.

Thank goodness they did not have to deal with the Endicotts any longer.

"Will my mother be safe?"

Silas looked at this boy he had begun to think of as his son. He could not lie, for childbirth was dangerous, and Brand would know that. He had stood with the others beside numerous graves along the trail. The survival of the Martin company as a whole may have seemed certain, but the survival of individuals, particularly of women in travail, was never a sure thing. Before he could craft an answer, Brand asked, "Mistress Russell told me it was in God's hands, but how do we know what God intends?"

"Your mother is attended by competent midwives who will know what to do. She is a strong woman, and already knows how to birth a babe, does she not?" He touched Brand on the shoulder. "Fear not. The women of this company will do their best for her. It is not in our hands, for we are but men."

Men. Silas saw Brand's narrow shoulders straighten at that term, and he smiled inwardly, glad that he had given this small gift to the boy, who still had not filled out his lanky, awkward frame. "We can but wait," he told the boy.

"Let me know when it is time," Brand said. "I want to see my new brother." He wandered off along the wide stump-filled meadow the men had created at the base of the cliff. Already there were early wildflowers springing up where the trees used to be. The trees, the ones they had felled for the building of their houses farther down the slope, had been tall and straight, as straight as the cliff beside which they had grown, perfect for house walls and plank floors, for roof beams and doors.

Several men, himself included, had first considered building their houses near the base of the cliff, for much of the land up here was relatively flat, unlike in the rest of the town—or what would one day be the town—which sloped more or less evenly down to the river. The men had been dissuaded, though, when they saw evidence of occasional rock-falls.

Silas sat on one of the stumps they had not yet dug out of the ground. It made for a good vantage point from which to watch the sunrise. This was the day his son would be born. Or daughter. He cared not, so long as his beloved Louetta came through her labour safely. And so long as the babe was safe as well.

He could do naught to help her. That thought bothered him, and he did not know how to settle his unquiet mind. He plucked idly at a small twig that grew from the side of the stump. It had already begun to sprout tiny green leaves. Life kept going, somehow.

The ground was soggy enough now after the rains of the last few days that digging out this stump might be easier than some of the others had been. It would yet be hard work, but well worth it when all this land was cleared for crops and for cabins with their kitchen gardens. He and

Louetta had discussed where they should build their house. Beneath the cliff or nearer the river? They were undecided as yet, but there was time. If they built near this meadow, they would yet have to stay far enough away so that any falling rocks would not harm them. They might choose to be closer to the river—proximity to a water source was always a good thing. He studied what he could see of the placid little river through the intervening trees. Come next spring, the water, so peaceful at the moment, might turn into a rampaging flood. Any house nearby could be swept away.

Halfway up the hill, then. About the same level as the barn now stood. That would be best.

He smiled down at the barn, amused by the exodus from it. He was not the only man who had chosen to make himself scarce while the womenfolk fluttered around his wife and around Constance Breeton. He supposed it would be easier to bring a baby into the world in a dry barn than it had been for the women whose time had come upon them while the company was traveling. He did hope his wife would have an easy time of the birth. She had assured him that her labor with Brand had been mild. Not that there was anything he could do to help other than to get out from underfoot, but he breathed a fervent prayer, just in case.

He pulled a treasured square of paper from the leather satchel he carried with him. He had so little paper left from the ream he had begun the journey with. His brother Homer did not understand how important it was to Silas to record the everyday doings of the journey. The ream had cost him dearly—for Willem Breeton had needed to order it from Boston—but it would have been worth twice the price to him. He had a skin pouch where he kept this treasure at the bottom of a tightly joined wooden box, safe from rain and—so far, thanks be to God—from the gnawings of mice.

Sometimes he drew with a piece of charred twig—he always kept a few with him—in order to save his hard-won ink. Not that the ink was difficult to make, but the effort was time-consuming, and time was something he seemed to have little of on the journey, what with having to hunt, to scout ahead for the best trail to follow, and to try to keep Homer from making any decision that could cost lives. Now that they were finally settled, though, he could take the time to make ink from the abundant acorns in the valley. In the meantime, this charred stick would need to suffice.

He would have to be sure that at least a few of the heavy oak trees were left to live. One oak alone would provide enough acorns for ten lifetimes' worth of ink, but Silas rather thought that if only one oak were left living, it might be lonely.

He lifted his eyes to the dark presence of the trees above the cliffs on the other side of the river, and saw their echo in the leafy bounty along the river and up this hillside to the south of where he now sat. Even with all the cutting they had done so far, there were so many trees left. Enough, he thought, to last many ages of building and firewood and fencing.

Platters, too, he thought with a wry grin. He sometimes wondered how he could have been so bewitched by Sophrona Blanchard that he had entwined his initials with hers on that platter he had made for her. If he had married Sophrona … he stopped that thought and shuddered. If he had already been married on the journey here, he would have missed out on the joy he felt in the wife he had taken to himself just a year ago. And he would not have the companionship of a boy he could call his son.

How close a call it had been, though. He had been overwhelmed by Sophrona's beauty, but now, whenever he looked at his wife, the stark planes of Louetta's face seemed to beg to be sketched. Louetta was so unlike the rounded softness of Sophrona, whose face, now that he thought about it, had held very little strength of character in it.

The pre-dawn light was just strong enough for him to see what he was doing. In the upper left-hand corner of his paper he drew his wife's face, as if she were looking at him over her shoulder, and was delighted when he was able to capture the light in her eyes and the quirk of her mouth, just as she had laughed at him yesterday when she told him that their child would be born soon. He gave up another quick prayer that she would be safe and that the child would live, but he could not remain in fear for long. He wrote her name below the face. *Louetta Tarkington Martin.* She was a masterpiece indeed.

To the right of his wife's face, he sketched what he could remember—and that was a great deal, for his artist's eye paid attention to details. Under his swift fingers, a river ford appeared. Only two months ago, Homer had wanted to cross farther up the stream, while Silas had known from the way the water swirled that a crossing there would cost them wagon axles and would delay the journey for days while they stopped to repair the damaged shafts. He labeled this scene *The Ford, March 1745.*

He gazed through the gradually brightening light, across the river that flowed gently through the bottom of the valley. The high cliffs behind him and on the far side of the river made this place like a natural fortress.

Below the scene of the river ford, he briefly sketched the last camp the group had rested in for any length of time. It had taken him a great deal of time to convince Homer that the group needed to stay in one place for a fortnight. There were so many small chores that needed time to complete, to say nothing of the need for a goodly supply of smoked meat. Homer had finally agreed to stay.

The men had spread out into the surrounding countryside to hunt, and had filled a quickly erected smoking shed with meat that would last them through the rest of their journey, although at the time they had not known they were so close to the end of their long road. Matthew Russell, younger brother to the Reverend Anders Russell, had set up a temporary forge where he and his sons, Luke and Mark, could create or repair the countless iron implements required on such a long journey. *Fortnight for Repairs April 1745.*

The next day, a Sunday, Silas had slipped from the camp following the morning services. "I want to scout ahead," he told Homer as he saddled Devil and checked his weapon to be sure it was primed and ready. But the truth was that he had felt restless and simply wanted to get away from the press of people. "Do not expect me back for a week, perhaps more." He had considered taking Brand with him, but Louetta had asked that he leave the boy with her. "His forehead feels too warm to me, and I would not risk him away from my care."

It was as well, Silas thought, that he had left the boy behind. He treasured his solitude, even though he had been happy to give up much of it to share his wagon and his life with Louetta and her son.

At first he had simply wandered along various deer trails, choosing them at random, knowing that he and Devil could always find their way back. He came to a fork and hesitated until he saw a red-jeweled hummingbird flit past him, almost inviting him to follow. He went that way more from curiosity than from any sense that what lay ahead would betoken the end of their time-consuming travels.

Following the hummingbird had been a matter of mere whimsy. It led him to the edge of a tall precipice. Before him spread a river valley, the trees below him leafy green with early spring growings. "We have time, Devil," he had said to his horse. "Shall we explore this valley in full?"

He and Devil turned left, toward the north, leaving the hummingbird behind, and found a gap in the cliff. Once in the valley, he had known that this would be their place of safety. He turned north again at first and followed the river as far as he could, then backtracked to the south and went on beyond the gap in the cliffs, all the way to a deep cleft where the river left the valley between high bluffs that never seemed to end.

When he returned to the camp just a day before their fortnight was ended, he carried the news that their new home was only four days—perhaps five—ahead of them.

Naturally, Homer had balked at the idea. Silas convinced him to walk away from the wagons so they could discuss the plan in privacy. More than an hour it had taken him before Homer agreed.

Silas was genuinely puzzled as to why the men of the group continued to turn to Homer as their leader, yet he knew that his own actions—his way of hiding the arguments from the others, his way of seeming always to defer to Homer's judgment—helped to bolster his older brother's standing in the community.

The Martin name, too, was still held in deep respect by all the members of their community. Homer benefited, for few questioned the decisions of a Martin.

A scream from the barn caused him to turn his head just in time to see an errant sunbeam—the sun had risen fully without his being aware of it—as it fell on the newly built barn, making the structure glow. He turned the paper over and with a confident eye and sure hand, he sketched the scene below him before it shifted to a more prosaic sight. The sketching took his mind off the fear he had that the scream might have indicated more than just the normal pain a woman felt during a birthing.

As he finished, he heard the cry of a newborn babe. Was it his babe or Willem Breeton's? At least it lived. All was well, then. He sharpened the stick and wrote the year, not that he was liable to forget when he had drawn it. After that, there was only enough char left on the stick to write his initials, and at that, the M was sadly faint.

Ah well, he thought, no one will ever see these except myself, and I certainly know who it is that has done this work.

He heard two babes squalling at one time. He could wait no longer. He had to know. He cupped his hands around his mouth and shouted toward the far end of the meadow. "Brand!" His voice echoed from cliff to cliff across the valley and back. Surely the boy would hear. Then he tucked the drawings away in his leather pouch and ran toward the barn, toward his wife, toward the promise of their newborn child.

## 2000

**"THERE'S NO NAME,"** Reebok said. "But there are some initials."

We waited for him to go on.

"S M," he finally said. "But the M is really faint." After a moment, he added, "And a date."

I hate to sound trite, but this really was like pulling teeth. "What date?" I prompted.

"Not really a date. Just a year."

Ida waved her hand toward the window. "Don't worry, Reebok. We've got all the rest of the day to get the information."

He blushed. "Seventeen forty-five."

"That makes sense," Bob said. "We know that's when the town was founded."

"But it's good to know for sure," Carol said. "It could have been drawn from memory any time, but the date would seem to indicate that the sketch shows the barn newly built, and it's more likely to be accurate, depending on the skill of the artist."

"It's pretty detailed," Reebok said.

"That's good." Carol lifted her eyes to the ceiling. "Reebok, you did say S M, didn't you?"

"Yes, ma'am."

"I wonder if that was Silas Martin."

"Of course," Melissa said. "The wooden plate. He was something of an artist."

*What are you talking about?*

What on earth was she talking about? Apparently a number of people around the table felt the same way I did, and demanded to know more. Even Marmalade added a meow that sounded amazingly like a query.

*It was not a kweree. It was a question.*

"You know that old wooden platter I have that I use for serving breads and coffee cakes?" Most of us nodded. "Carol, tell them what you told us this morning."

By the time she explained about the interwoven initials—SM and SB—we all were eager to study the sketch. If the weather had been mild, we would have trooped the two blocks to City Hall. Of course, if the weather had been mild, we might not have learned all this to begin with. Thank heaven for winter storms.

"I may have to extend my stay here," Carol said. "There's going to be a lot to investigate."

"That's fine with me," Melissa said. "It's not like I'm overbooked."

"Is the barn still standing?"

"Nope," Ralph said. "Marvin Axelrod's funeral home is there now. The barn burned down sometime in the late 1800s."

"Too bad," Carol said.

## 1892

**MORGAN MARTIN, WHO** never woke easily, felt like he was being dragged through a pit of sand. His eyes were practically glued shut with sleep, but he could not ignore the insistent clanging of the church bell. "Why do fires always seem to happen in the middle of the night?" He felt every one of his thirty-seven years, and the broadening expanse of his middle did not help matters, for it made it that much harder for him to reach below the bed for his other shoe.

His wife donned her outer clothing as swiftly as she could, far swifter than her sleep-riddled husband. She seemed to have little sympathy for him, but before she left the room she managed to sweep her foot below the bedstead and extricate Morgan's second shoe.

"If you would lay them out in order before you retire, Husband, you would find them more easily." She swept from the room, no doubt to direct their nine-year-old son Obadiah to watch the younger children.

He took no time to reply. The imperative of the bell swept all other concerns before it.

By the time they reached their front door, Morgan was, if not fully alert, at least fully awake. "Barn," he heard someone yell as a steady line of people ran past, each of them carrying the required three fire buckets.

"Whose barn?"

"*The* barn."

Morgan did not like the sound of that. He grabbed his own buckets from where they sat just within the front door and joined the throng. There was only one barn in town that would be referred to as *the* barn.

Built in the early days of Martinsville—some said it had been the first structure raised in the town, but Morgan could not believe they would not have built the church first—the barn had withstood hail and floods, even the deadly snows of the six-year winter that had so recently been dispelled by the sun. Although it was a sturdy structure, Morgan knew the wood was dry as tinder. Luckily, there was not much stored in it. In fact, the council had talked about dismantling it, for each family now had its own barn, sheds, and outbuildings.

By the time the majority of townsfolk reached the block whereon the barn stood, the entire building was engulfed in flames. There was no hope at all of saving it.

"Thank goodness there is little wind tonight," he heard someone call out.

William Fenton seemed to have taken charge of directing the fire brigade. He had the people divided into three lines, each of them pouring their buckets onto the sides of the houses closest to the barn, and tossing water up onto the roofs as well. William and his wife joined the sparsest of the lines and handed their buckets to several small children who ran them as quickly as they could down to the river so they could be filled and handed from person to person up the line.

**ONCE THE BARN** burned itself out, Bill Fenton approached Morgan's father, Tobe Martin, the chairman of the town council. "Well, Tobe, what say you to this mess?"

"It could have been far worse, had there been a wind," Tobe admitted.

"Do you still insist we do not need a fire engine? Think how much quicker the blaze could have been extinguished had the council seen fit to fund a horse-drawn engine. Even a man-powered pump engine would have been preferable to—" Mister Fenton shook his fist, but Morgan did not think he was criticizing the dispirited people who stood around in small clumps looking at the mess that remained of what had been the largest structure in Martinsville. They had worked hard and long to save the nearby houses. "A bucket brigade has its limits."

A sudden loud *pop* from the fire as a final burning log collapsed and settled into a cloud of ash and steam seemed to emphasize Mister Fenton's words.

"You are welcome to lay your proposition on the table at the next meeting of the council," Tobe Martin said, but Morgan could tell there was a core of steel in his father that would not allow anything proposed by young Bill Fenton to pass without a fight.

Morgan said nothing, for his father was a formidable man, but after he and his wife had retired for what was left of the night, Morgan quietly admitted to her that the idea of an engine that would pump a steady stream of water onto the fire seemed like a fine idea.

"When you are chairman of the council," his wife said, "you will have considerable power, enough to raise the issue and see that an engine is purchased."

Morgan could not place his finger precisely on what his wife's tone seemed to indicate, but she seemed intrigued with the idea of the power he would have.

Now that he thought about it, power was certainly a quality worth having, but Morgan was wary of the idea of that much authority. When he had been but a child, he had thought his father was powerful enough to command anything and have it materialize. But then during the war, his father had promised Morgan that he would be safe behind the battle lines. Morgan had believed his father, until the battle lines overwhelmed them and the lower part of Morgan's face had been torn apart by an errant musket ball. Where then was his father's power?

## 2000

**I RUBBED MY** thighs to bring some circulation back into them. I'd been sitting way too long. "Let's head back upstairs, ladies. I'm dying to know what's in some of those letters."

*I hope you are not dying.*

"I'm anxious to learn more, too," Carol said.

*Oh.*

Pat looked confused. "Shouldn't we clear off the table first?"

"Nope," I said. "In this house, the cook is exempt from clean-up chores. So,"—I looked around the table with a great deal of satisfaction—"all the females, with the exception of you, Easton, since you didn't help us"—I couldn't resist that dig—"can repair to the attic, while all the rest of you can divide the clearing, washing, drying, and putting away chores."

"Fine with me," Bob said. But of course he would, since that had been our arrangement from the very first. I cooked, he washed up, or he cooked and I did the dishes. It made perfect sense to the two of us. Sometimes we both cooked and both washed, which was even more fun.

Tom was the first to stand. "Fine with me, too," he said. "They were the chefs, so we're the busboys, right fellas?" Leave it to Tom to put in into restaurant terms.

Ralph looked for a moment like he was going to complain, until Henry Pursey, in a suitably ministerial voice, said, "That sounds very sensible. And very fair."

Doc Nathan stood, moved Korsi carefully onto the seat he'd just vacated, and picked up his plate. Father Ames blew out the candles.

Easton just sat there with her mouth open.

"We're all so safe here," Sadie said, and I sat back down. So did the men. This sounded like it was leading somewhere. "If they had the barn when they first got here, they would have been protected from the worst of the weather, but what sort of protection did they have while they were on the trail?"

"Good question," Carol said. "We know they had sturdy canvas at the time, so there would have been coverings for the wagons, and some sort of tents, I suppose. That would have been enough for rain—although they probably spent a lot of soggy nights and days. But heavy snow, ice, and especially hail could have posed a much greater problem."

"Auntie Blue," I said, referring to my Aunt Beulah, "told me once about a spring hailstorm in Colorado that she and Uncle Mark were trapped in. The hailstorm came on so unexpectedly, they were caught out in their car. Within what seemed like moments, the hailstones, which were the size of softballs, clogged up the storm sewers and piled up on the streets so high the car couldn't move forward."

"I've never seen hailstones that big." Ida's skepticism was in full flight.

Glaze jumped in to defend me. "It's true. Uncle Mark had his camera with him and he took a picture. The hailstones were bouncing off the hood leaving dents. It's a wonder they didn't break the windshield."

"How long did it take them to get out of it?" Pat asked.

Glaze looked at me and I shrugged. "I don't know," I said. "They had to wait until a snowplow came along to scoop the hail out of the way."

"Thank goodness for snowplows," Pat said. "Not that we have any such things here in Georgia."

"But there wasn't anything like a snowplow back in the 1740s," Melissa said. "Can you imagine what heavy hail could do to a bunch of wagons?"

"And the livestock," Maddy added.

"And the people," I put in.

"Hailstorms, ice storms," Henry glanced meaningfully toward the window, "predators, illness. They must have been sturdy stock indeed to have made it all this way."

"In one way, they were lucky," Carol said. "There were enough of them that they probably had all the skills they needed along the journey. We know they had a cooper and a blacksmith when they left Brandtburg, and there would have been midwives and herbalists, people to tend the livestock, men to hunt, enough willing backs to rescue wagons that got stuck in the mud, someone to scout out the way ahead."

"I thought Homer led the group," Ralph said, astounding everyone. He was usually so quiet I tended to forget he was around. From the looks on the faces of others at the table, I could tell I wasn't the only one Ralph had startled. Even Ida, his wife, seemed a bit surprised.

"Undoubtedly," Carol agreed, "but Homer can't have done it all by himself, and he probably wouldn't have wanted to leave the group to do the scouting. All they knew when they left Brandtburg was that they wanted to go south toward a milder climate."

"So," Doc said, "if they had everybody they needed, it must have created a big problem when any of the families left the company."

"Left?" Maddy sounded incredulous."

"Left," Doc said. "Remember those Fountains and the—what was that other family nobody's heard of since?"

"The Stinkers," Pat suggested, "or something like that."

"Stickneys," Carol corrected.

"Right. Surely the families that left couldn't have had everything they needed—all those skills you mentioned, Carol—when they took off."

"Sometimes," Carol said, her voice sounding sad, "people might have gotten too sick, too old, too injured to travel. Their families might have chosen to stay behind, perhaps in a town they passed through."

"Sometimes," Ida said, "some of them might have been too cantankerous for the others to put up with. I can't believe there weren't some instances of *good riddance.*"

*What is a riddents? Why is it good?*

Carol chuckled when Marmalade meowed. "Even if they were glad to be rid of some folks"—she put a curious emphasis on the word *rid*—"it can't have been an easy occasion to lose people."

Ida raised an eyebrow. "I don't know about that."

I had the distinct impression she was thinking of Hubbard Martin, whom she detested. I doubt she would have actively wished him ill. But now that he was incapacitated, I was fairly sure she was delighted not to have him as the chair of the town council anymore. For that matter, I felt pretty much the same way. Now, if I could just get rid of the library board.

Giving myself a mental slap—I could live with the board's oversight even though it was a pain in the tutu—I leaned close to Bob. "I know you're up to something," I whispered. "I expect a full report this evening."

He grinned at me, but shook his head. What on earth was he hatching? Why had he taken Tom outside for such a long time?

Sadie brought the conversation back on track. "Each family that left the group took not only their individual skills, but took something away from the safety of the group as well."

I wondered what she was talking about, just as Ida asked, "What do you mean?"

"Well, think about it. The larger the group, the less likely those predators Carol mentioned would be to attack, right? There was safety in numbers, wouldn't you say? "

"Safety in numbers," Rebecca Jo echoed, and I wondered what she was thinking. The kitchen had suddenly become very silent.

## Tuesday, August 7, 1928

**"REBECCA JO!" MAMA'S** voice, carried upward on the evening breeze, sounded shrill in the sun-warmed air. "Come inside this instant!"

Oh dear. Rebecca Jo knew she was in trouble, and she couldn't very well blame it on her friends because they'd all gone home at least a quarter of an hour ago, leaving Rebecca Jo wandering along the path at the top of the cliff all by herself. They'd run up here, at the instigation of Eustace Russell after somebody—Rebecca Jo wasn't sure who it had been, but it was probably Eustace— knocked Mama's green vase off the whatnot shelf.

Mama's tone said she'd found the broken pieces in the trash bin, and now there was nobody else to take the blame. Just like Eustace to evade punishment.

It was a quandary all right. If Rebecca Jo told on him, she'd be spanked for tattling. If she didn't, she'd be spanked anyway for letting the damage happen.

"It's your responsibility when your friends come to play with you," Mama would say.

Rebecca Jo wished Eustace had brought his big sister, Sadie, instead of picking up an assortment of neighbor children on his way. Sadie would know what to say to Mama. But Sadie was three years older than Eustace and ten years older than Rebecca Jo—far too old to play with such youngsters.

Rebecca Jo dragged her heels as she headed home to face her punishment. Even if all her friends had been around her, she knew Mama would still spank her as soon as they left. Rebecca Jo had heard once that there was safety in numbers.

Not when you had a mother like Mama.

**THE NEXT DAY, SADIE** Russell jumped when Eustace banged the screen door on his way into the kitchen. "You big oaf," she complained "can't you be quieter?"

"Nope." He scooped up a handful of the cookies Sadie had just transferred onto the cooling rack. "Yum!"

Sadie knew it was hopeless to stop him. Eustace loved her cookies. "You have to be quiet. Mama's got a visitor with her in the parlor."

"The parlor?" Eustace paused, the cookie halfway to his mouth, his eyes growing wide. "Who?"

Before Sadie could tell him that it was his friend Rebecca Jo's mother, Mama called out in one of the sternest voices Sadie had ever heard her use. "Eustace. The parlor. Now."

Her little brother turned to her. "Come with me," he begged. "There's safety in numbers."

Sadie narrowed her eyes and shook her head. "What did you do this time?"

# May 1995

**CHARLIE ELLIS PLOPPED** her load of books onto her desk and gave an exaggerated groan, stopping only when she realized Tricia wasn't back from class yet. Oh well, she thought, groaning feels good anyway, even without an audience. She laughed at herself and started sorting through her book bag, pulling out what she'd need for the paper that was due in three days.

As soon as Tricia walked in, though, Charlie forgot about her paper. She'd never seen her roommate so angry. "What's wrong?" She'd learned early on that Tricia didn't like to be touched, so she stifled her impulse to reach out.

"Halders had the nerve," Tricia said, "the *nerve* to—" She ripped open her backpack, grabbed a paper, and threw it onto Charlie's desk.

Charlie didn't have to look closely to see the comment slashed in bright red ink across the front page of the essay. *HOGWASH!*

Even the exclamation point looked scathing.

"He didn't like it?" Charlie ventured and then could have kicked herself when Tricia glared at her.

"Can't you tell he loved it?" Tricia ripped the first page off the paper and began to tear it in half, and half again, and again. "He loved impressing the whole class with his wit."

Charlie's protective instincts rose. "Surely he didn't show it to anybody?"

"All he had to do was make sure the people around me saw it, and the word spread fast enough." Tricia gritted her teeth as the stack of shredded paper became too thick for her to rip through. "And they all laughed at me."

"My professors always lay our papers face-down when they return them to us," she said in a small voice, but she doubted Tricia even heard her. Charlie had heard often enough that there was safety in numbers, but when a group went along with a bullying professor like that, nobody was safe. Who would he single out for ridicule the next time? Charlie swore she'd never sign up for a Halders class. "I heard that Dr. Halders doesn't have tenure yet. Maybe he won't last long."

"Any time is too long," Tricia said.

**THE DAY BEFORE** the last day of school that year, the HR department mailed a letter to Dr. Halders, congratulating him officially on having been granted tenure. When Dr. Halders died the next day, the victim of a hit and run driver as he walked from campus to his small apartment, many were not aware of his death, for he had already turned in his grades, so his students were not inconvenienced, and his colleagues had all dispersed for the vacation, except those who were teaching summer courses.

The letter was returned a week later, marked *Addressee De-*

*ceased.*

The school held an on-campus memorial service in early September, where a few grad students praised his exceptional teaching. Charlie and Tricia attended, because an announcement said the whole student body was expected to be there, and then they forgot about Dr. Halders and went on with their studies. Charlie had spent most of the memorial service thinking about her dad, anyway, and all the tears she shed were for him. She wished she'd brought her teddy bear to the service with her.

## July 1997

**HENRY PURSEY PUSHED** the draft of his latest sermon across his desk and watched the papers cascade to the floor.

"Safety in numbers," he muttered. "As if there were such a thing." Why had he ever thought to preach about something he wasn't sure he believed in?

It had been a good idea to begin with, all about how people like this congregation gathered together each week to affirm their faith and gird themselves against the operations of a faithless world.

About how communities rallied together when something like this most recent murder threatened to tear at the fabric of people's well-being.

About how families would congregate throughout the upcoming holiday season to cement their connectedness.

And then he thought about all the counseling he had to do every year during the three months at the end of the year and at least two months at the beginning of the next one, as people aired their complaints and frustrations over those very same holidays.

Safety in numbers, indeed.

That saying probably went back to the days of the cave dwellers, when people crowded together to avoid being eaten by a saber-toothed tiger, he thought. Except for the poor yokel on the edge of the crowd.

And crowd mentality so often led to irresponsible behavior. He thought of the ring of boys that had surrounded him that day so long ago when Al Manning was beating him to a pulp in the schoolyard before Mrs. Pollard, the fifth-grade teacher, intervened. He still occasionally had nightmares in which he heard their chanting. *Beat him up, beat him up, beat him up.*

Maybe he'd change his sermon topic. He drew a clean sheet of paper toward him and thought for just a few seconds before he wrote *The Sermon on the Mount.*

# 2000

**I WAS HAPPY** to leave the remains of lunch behind. Twenty-plus people sure could make a mess of a table.

*I am very tidy when I eat.*

Marmalade led the way up the creaky stairs to the attic. We chatted happily about what we'd found and what we hoped to find.

As we began to fan out to our stations around the attic, I took a look in back of the cheval mirror and found an old step stool, its two hinged steps tucked in underneath the seat. "I sure could use this in the kitchen," I said, intending to move it closer to the stairs, but something made me pause. Instead, I hauled it over closer to the front wall, opened the steps, and climbed up to peer out one of the eyebrow windows. Below I could see the area that Carol and Reebok and Tom had disturbed. Everything else glistened under unbroken ice.

I was about to step back down when I saw a movement below me at the edge of the porch. Bob, Reebok, Doc, and Tom. Of course, I'd know Bob anywhere, even from up above like this, but I recognized the other men by the distinctive colors of their parkas. They had just stepped out from under the porch roof. I watched as they slid down the ramp and started across the lawn, breaking the ice up as they went, much the way we'd done this morning when we went out to feed the birds. Where on earth were they going?

Bob must have gotten a phone call for help, but if that were the case, why hadn't I heard the phone ring? No, I thought, I wouldn't have, not with all the chatter of the women behind me. But if it was a police matter, why were they letting Tom go with them? That made sense, though, because Tom had been deputized a couple of times in the past when Bob needed backup. Oh dear, with Doc along, I hoped that didn't mean there'd been a medical emergency.

"What's up, sis?"

I hadn't heard Glaze come up behind me. I didn't want to worry her, so I decided not to tell her what I'd seen. "Nothing, just checking out the condition of the snow out there."

"Frozen, right?"

"Right." I folded up the stool and put it next to the stairs. "Let's get busy."

Maddy handed out a few more hatboxes and we spent time admiring—or groaning about—the contents. "These hats are a lot of fun," I said several minutes later, "but I sure wish we could find answers to our questions."

Ida raised an eyebrow. "Questions?"

"Like who lived and who died."

"I'd say they all died eventually," Ida said, "unless you've heard about some four hundred and sixty-year-old people hanging around town."

"You know what I mean."

Rebecca Jo ignored Ida and me. "I think this means we just have to search harder. I suggest we tackle that trunk with all the cards and letters. We're sure to get some answers there."

"I think," Pat said, "it might be best if we each take an area. We can't all work on one trunk."

Ida studied the trunk in question. "We'll probably get a whole lot more unanswerable questions."

"We could work in pairs." Glaze nibbled briefly on a fingernail. "Two or three people to a trunk. Won't that be easier?"

"If you're asking me to break my back bending into those old trunks," Sadie said, "you have another think coming."

"Let's you and me set up here at this card table, Sadie." I lifted the lid of one of the nearby trunks. It was filled with envelopes. "I'll do the bending, and we can both do the reading."

**THE SECOND ENVELOPE** Sadie opened brought a smile to her lips as she glanced through it. "Eighteen-thirty-eight," she said, "and this one looks like it's going to be good." She took a deep breath. "Melanie Hoskins was the one with the brown lace wedding dress, right? She and her husband Zenus?"

"Right." Dee pulled a folding chair up close to Sadie's side.

"Those were the names on the wedding invitation."

The envelope, which Sadie had set off to her left, was yellowed with age and sported, not a stamp, but an elaborate franking—I think that was what it was called. "When were stamps invented?"

*What are stamps?*

"The eighteen-forties, I think," Maddy said.

I pointed to the markings on the envelope. "So, even if it wasn't dated, this would prove the letter is older than that."

"Not necessarily," Carol said. "Stamps weren't required in the U.S. until 1855. To begin with, people had to lick the little squares on the back to make them stick and to prove that they'd paid to mail the letter."

*Thank you.*

"Thanks for that completely unnecessary history lesson," Ida said.

"Before that"—Carol ignored Ida's acerbic comment—"the postage was paid by the receiver."

"But what if they received a letter they didn't want?" Maddy asked. "Would they still have to pay for it?"

Carol nodded. "You couldn't read the letter first."

"Glad that rule doesn't still apply," Maddy said. "I'll bet they didn't have junk mail back then."

"Listen up," Sadie said. "There's a newspaper clipping in here, too." She read the clipping aloud and then passed it around so we could all get our hands on it.

*Metoochie River Valley News*
21 March 1838

The birth of a son last week to Zenus and Melanie Hoskins on the 13th of March has increased the population of Martinsville by one and the volume of hot air by a noticeable amount. Mis-

<blockquote>
ter Hoskins, according to town leader Jerrod Martin, "near made a fool of himself when he interrupted the town council meeting to brag about his third son and pass out cigars to everyone present — ladies excepted, of course."
</blockquote>

When Sadie read it, I couldn't help but guffaw. "Zenus sounds like something else."

*What does that mean?*

"He's a hoot for sure," Dee said, "but I think Jerrod Martin sounds even better, insulting Zenus like that."

The clipping had reached Maddy by that time. "Don't you think somebody might have sued the newspaper for talking about all the hot air?"

*The air is not hot. It is pleasantly warm.*

"Maybe liability laws weren't around back then?" I had no idea, so I turned to look at Carol, but she just lifted her shoulders.

"No clue," she said.

I began to giggle. "Don't you think whoever wrote that article sounds just like Myrtle?" Myrtle Hoskins was Martinsville's very own—what was the term?—intrepid reporter, except that she was well into her seventies and relished her gossipy "Myrtle's Musings" column in the weekly *Keagan County Record*. I took a moment to explain this to Carol.

Fortunately, Ida interrupted me before the explanation could get too complicated. "What's the letter about, Sadie?"

*Thursday, 22 March 1838*
*Bower House*
*Russell Gap, Georgia*

*Mrs. Zenus Hoskins*
*Beechnut House*

*Martinsville, Georgia*


"Beechnut House," I said. "Do you think that's what this house was called originally?"

"People used to name their houses," Carol said. "I've seen that in a lot of old letters I've researched. The habit of naming one's house was a tradition carried over from merry old England."

"I rather like the name," I said. "Maybe Bob and I can have a wooden sign fashioned to attach beside the front door."

"Maybe we should all name our houses," Sadie said.

"Yours could be the *Hive House*," Maddy said, "what with all your beehives."

"Melissa already has *Azalea House*." Pat turned to Rebecca Jo. "What would you name yours?"

Rebecca thought for a moment. Then she looked at Dee and said, "*The Haven*."

Dee smiled broadly.

Glaze looked at Dee and Maddy, the other two members of what they called their Butterfly Brigade. "Guess we'll need a shingle that says *Chrysalis*."

Carol looked confused so I briefly explained the situation to her. "Sorry for the interruption," I finally said. "Go on, Sadie."


*My dear Melanie,*

*<u>Another</u> boy? Naturally, I am delighted that you came through the birth with no problems, and that your new son seems to be thriving, but really, Melanie, with four sons of my own, I cannot help but hope that you will produce at least a couple of girls after these three boys of yours so that we may marry your daughters off to my sons.*

*I do love my husband, and I have found great contentment here in Russell Gap. The women of the church have, as I have told you before, been most welcoming, but I do miss my old and dear friends from Martinsville. The miles that separate us may as well be as far as from here to the moon, for I despair of ever seeing you again.*

*Of course, if you would agree to birth some girls, then we might contrive to make the journey that they might become my beloved daughters-in-law, although I would hate to have to wait another twenty years for that to happen.*

*In the meantime, continue to write to me often.*
*Your loving childhood friend,*
*Lovina*
*(Mrs. Benjamin Russell)*

"You know," Carol said when Sadie finished reading it, "she's right about that *here to the moon* idea. Although men frequently traveled on business of one sort or another, there were many women back then who never went more than five miles from where they were born, unless"—she pointed to the letter—"it was because she'd married some fellow from another town."

"I do wonder if poor Melanie ever had any girls," Ida said.

"Maybe Lovina should have tried to have some girls herself," Dee drawled.

"Maybe we'll find another invitation," Maddy said, "to the wedding of Melanie's daughter to Lovina's son twenty years after this. Wouldn't that be fun?"

"Or Melanie's son to Lovina's daughter," Dee insisted.

"We'd better keep looking, then." Rebecca Jo headed toward an old chest of drawers. "It doesn't look very imposing," she said, "but you never know what might be in here."

I watched idly as she opened the top drawer, and rummaged a bit. It looked like there wouldn't be anything promising there, so I turned away just as she withdrew a shallow basket. I moved closer. It looked like there was some sort of fuzzy animal curled up in it.

"I haven't seen one of these in years." Rebecca Jo set the basket on the top of the chest and pulled out the furry concoction. She slipped her hands into it.

"Is that a muff? I've only seen pictures of them. Maddy," I called, "here's something you can put in one of your books."

Naturally, everyone came over to look, and Rebecca Jo passed it around the circle.

Glaze held it up to her cheek. "It's so soft. What do you suppose it is?"

Marmalade jumped into her lap.

*I will take it if you do not want it.*

"Rabbit fur, I would imagine," said Sadie. "I had one a lot like it when I was a girl."

Amanda screwed up her face. "Poor bunny."

"Spoken like a true vegetarian," Melissa said, but her tone was soft.

*May I play with the rabbit?*

"This basket is quite a work of art," Rebecca Jo said, and started it around the circle in the other direction.

"Pine needles," Pat said. "The whole basket is made of long-leaf pine needles. This pattern is lovely."

"You can tell it was made by an expert," Dee said. "I've seen baskets like this made by women in the Gullah communities along the coast of Georgia." She handed it to Carol.

"What do you suppose it's doing up here?" Carol passed it to me. "Here. I need a potty break. Wouldn't you like to use it, maybe as a bread basket?"

"Rebecca Jo's the one who found it," I said. "She has first dibs on it."

Rebecca Jo waved a hand at me. "Goodness no. I'm trying to cut down on all my stuff, not add more of it."

I couldn't help feeling relieved. "I'll be happy to have it, then." And I walked it over to where I'd left the step stool beside the stairs so I'd remember to take them both downstairs with me.

"Do you want the muff as well?"

"I can't see myself using it," I told Melissa. "So, unless you want it, I suppose it's up for grabs."

*I would like to have it.*

But nobody wanted to wear a dead bunny rabbit, it seemed. "I'll just put it back in the drawer," Melissa said.

*No!*

Melissa looked quizzically at Marmalade for a second, then shrugged. "You can always find it later if you change your mind."

"I don't suppose there's any sort of label," I thought to say before Melissa closed the drawer.

"I didn't notice one, but let's look just to be sure."

"Sometimes the initials are sewn into the inside lining." Sadie said.

"Aren't linings always on the inside?" Ida's question was a logical one, I thought.

"I mean way deep on the inside, right in the center."

There were initials. M D H.

"Whoever MD was," Rebecca Jo said, "I'd be willing to bet she married a Hastings."

"What makes you think that?"

"Think about it, Melissa. This H was obviously added at a later date. See? It's not quite lined up with the first two initials, and the thread color doesn't quite match. The M and D are a dark grayish thread, but the H is a soft black. And here, can you see this? The H is slightly larger, with bigger stitches."

Melissa took a long look. "Not much bigger."

"Enough to show that a different hand put in that third initial."

"If you say so." Melissa didn't sound quite convinced, but I had to agree with Rebecca Jo. She was an expert at stitchery.

"And if it was here in the attic," Rebecca Jo added, "it stands to reason it would have been a Hastings."

"It could have been a Hoskins," Sadie said. "Anybody know of an M D H?"

*What is an empty aitch?*

Blank looks appeared on everyone's faces. "What a shame," I said. "Somebody lived her whole life and all she left behind was an unidentifiable muff."

"I guess I never thought much about it," Rebecca Jo said, "but you're right. I don't feel much of a connection to my own great-grandparents and such." She set the muff aside, and Marmalade promptly sprang onto it and curled into a tight ball.

*Thank you. Finally.*

I could feel the silver pendant hanging against my chest under my sweatshirt. "I'd really like to know the story behind some of these items we've found up here."

"We need a diary," Ida said. "One where whoever wrote it tells everything she can think of about what was going on in her days."

"Like Faith and Chastity's diaries," Maddy said.

"Only I want ones that are even more informative." Ida looked around the attic. "Information about the stuff up here."

"Well," Sadie said, "let's keep looking."

Carol rejoined us then. "Looking for what?"

"Anything we can find," Rebecca Jo said.

# 1768

**MARGARET DEWITT HAD** precious little to take with her when she married Alonzo Hastings and moved into his parents' house just uphill from the tavern. She and her mother had kept up a running battle for years simply to keep food on the table and were able to accomplish that only because they had such an extensive garden. It filled the yard in front of their small house, wrapped around the shady sides, and over-flowed the area between the back stoop and the privy.

There was no jewelry left, for Father had sold it all off. If her mother's hands had not swollen so badly over the years, making it im-possible for her to take off her wedding ring, Margaret had no doubt that Father would have pried the ring off the old woman's hand and sold it so he could buy more drink. Margaret loved her father and mourned him truly when he died in 1767, but—really—life was so much simpler now that he was gone.

That was the one reason why Margaret had stipulated before she agreed to marry Alonzo that when his father died and he inherited Beechnut House, he would cease the operation of the tavern. "Do you think your father will object?" she had asked Alonzo shortly before they announced their engagement.

"We will simply not tell him of our plans," Alonzo said. "Of course, once he is dead and I have inherited the tavern, he will have nothing to say about the matter."

Margaret was faintly scandalized at his levity, and told him so.

"I mean no disrespect," Alonzo said, "but dead is dead and little we will be able to do about it."

"Will your mother mind?"

Alonzo smiled in the way Margaret loved to see. "Mother will be happy with whatever we decide."

Margaret had her doubts about that, but held her tongue.

"I doubt many of the men of the town will appreciate our closing the tavern, but you know I have never wanted to be a publican."

"You will make a fine schoolmaster," Margaret assured him.

"After all," Alonzo reasoned, "once the tavern is closed, I will need a source of income." Here he kissed her soundly. "For supporting my family."

The position of schoolmaster would not bring in much income, but Margaret had no fear of that, for she was used to scrimping and saving and making do with little.

So, on her wedding day, she had but two linen bags of clothing and three small boxes that her brothers carried to the Hastings house for her. She left her loom with her mother, knowing that once Alonzo inherited Beechnut House, she would invite her mother and any of her brothers and sisters who remained at home to move in with her and Alonzo, and the loom would of course come with Mother. There was no sense in having a fine house with so many rooms and not using them all.

She might not have had any jewelry left to wear on her wedding day, but she did have a fine muff of rabbit fur that her grandmother—her mother's mother—had given her on her sixteenth birthday. For the five years since then she had kept it hidden from her father lest he trade it for spirits. Grandmother had stitched Margaret's initials into the soft lining, and Margaret planned to add the H for Hastings after her wedding ceremony. She had been tempted to add her new last initial almost as soon as Alonzo proposed to her, but she would not do it, lest she somehow call an apoplexy upon her husband-to-be. It would not do to have Alonzo die before they could be wed.

This day, her wedding day, she walked up to the front of the church proudly, with her muff gracing her left arm. With her right hand in Alonzo's firm grip, she pledged to be true to him and he pledged the same to her.

What need had she of gold and silver when she had a fine muff and, even more importantly, the love of a good man? A good man who was not a drinker.

Margaret and Alonzo's first child, born ten months later, was a dark-haired daughter, whom they named Lydia. As Margaret held her that first day, she could almost imagine the child grown and wearing the muff to keep her hands warm in a chilly autumn wind.

They named their second child Reuben, and Margaret wondered if he would follow in his father's footsteps and become a schoolmaster.

# 2000

**REBECCA JO STROKED** the muff one more time, despite the fact that Marmalade was curled up on it.

"You might want to keep it close," Ida said, "if you can get it away from the cat."

*The cat? You know my name.*

Ida waited for Marmalade's meow to subside. "It's still fairly chilly up here."

"Chilly?" I was surprised. It seemed perfectly comfortable to me. Of course, Ida was somewhat scrawnier—scratch that word.

*Why should I scratch it?*

She was somewhat leaner than I, so maybe the chill bothered her more. "I have just what you need, Ida." I scooted down to my bedroom and retrieved a long fuzzy knitted scarf, a soft white with little touches of ginger. It would go well with her rather wan coloring. And it wouldn't clash with her feathered hat.

When I handed it to her, she immediately wrapped it around her neck. "Wow," she said. "This really makes a difference." She lifted one end of it. "This feels different than most wool scarves. What is it?"

*It is me.*

Carol tilted her head to one side.

"You'd never guess," I said.

Sadie and Melissa started to laugh, soon joined by Rebecca Jo. They all knew the story.

"Cat hair," Carol said, without much question in her voice.

"What a lucky guess." I was surprised. Who on earth would have thought of cat hair? "Annie knitted it for me. Annie was the one who owned the herb shop before Pumpkin," I explained to Carol. I knew we'd already told her about Annie, but I thought her memory might need jogging a bit.

"The one who was killed," Carol said. I guess her memory was a lot better than I thought.

"Right. Annie quilted, but she also loved to spin. One day she was talking about all the different kinds of fibers she used in her yarns, and I asked her if she'd ever spun cat hair."

Maddy raised a dubious eyebrow.

"You're right, Maddy. Cat hair is too short to spin well, but I've been collecting Marmalade's hair over the years. Each time I brush her, I put the hair in an old wine bottle that I keep sitting beside my chair in the living room."

*That is where you like to brush me.*

"It's amazing how much hair comes out of a cat," I added.

*I have a lot of hair to share.*

"So," Carol said, "if cat hair is too short to spin …" She left her sentence dangling, the question obvious.

"Annie was delighted to get it. She mixed it in with white angora fibers. That's why the scarf has all those sort of splotches of Marmalade color here and there."

Ida ran her index finger over one of the little tufts of cat color. "I swear it's the warmest scarf I've ever put on, and"—she held one end of it up next to her head—"it goes beautifully with my hat, wouldn't you say? I just love scarves."

Charlie smoothed back her improbably black hair, although it didn't seem to need any straightening. I remembered Sadie mentioning, shortly after Charlie moved back to Martinsville, what a curly-headed little redhead she'd been when she was a little girl. Maybe the hair dying process took out some of the curl as well as all the color? I had no idea. Despite Sharon Armitage and her ongoing drive to dye every head in Martinsville, Glaze and I had both consistently refused her insistence.

"I had a gorgeous bright red and blue scarf when I was a kid," Pat said, "only my Sunday School teacher said I was showing off with it, so I never wore it again."

"Same thing happened to me," I said, "only it was a bright yellow skirt and my seventh-grade art teacher."

Rebecca Jo shook her head. "It's appalling what adults do to children sometimes, tearing them down like that."

Pat rubbed the back of her neck. "Sounds like you had a valid complaint, Biscuit, and a lousy art teacher. But with me …"—she gave a rueful grin—"I was sort of using a scarf to swat flies off the windowsill, and I sort of knocked over a flower vase in the process. It sort of tore the scarf when it shattered."

After we finished chuckling, we all dispersed to our various stations.

Sadie found the next treasure. She held up an envelope along with the letter she'd pulled from it. "This is a wonderful letter," she announced. "I think you'll all want to hear it."

*Azalea House*
*Wednesday 21 May 1890*

*Young Gideon Hoskins*
*Beechnut Lane*
*Martinsville*

"Beechnut Lane," Sadie said. "Surely that must mean here, but I wonder who Gideon Hoskins was."

Dee peered over her shoulder. "And why call him Young Gideon?"

"It must mean he was named for his father," Rebecca Jo said.

"Well, yeah," Dee said, "but why not just call him Junior?"

"I want to know about that Azalea House in the top line," Melissa said.

"That's right," I said. "Could it be the same place as your B&B?"

"I doubt it. I named it Azalea House when I opened it, because of all the azaleas blooming around it."

"Probably just a coincidence," Ida said. "There are azaleas all over this town."

"Yeah, I guess you're right." Melissa sounded disappointed.

"A lot can change in a hundred or so years," I said. "Maybe it started out as Azalea House, lost the name somewhere along the line, and then you picked up on ancient vibrations of some sort when you renamed it that." My reasoning sounded lame even to me, but it was what I wanted to believe.

Sadie handed an old photo to Melissa and kept reading.

*My dear Gideon,*

*Even though we are engaged to be married, my mother informs me that it is not appropriate for me to send you a photograph. 'Not until you are married,' she told me, 'and then you might give it to him.' I was ever one to flaunt the rules of propriety, though, as you know! Herewith is not only a photograph of me—the only one I have ever had taken, so I am sure you will consider it a treasure indeed—but I include as well the story that must accompany it.*

*Mister Morgan Martin has taken up a new pastime, and I know you have seen him lugging that unwieldy camera of his all over town. Only last week he begged me to let him take my photograph. "Portraiture," he told me with great solemnity, "is the up-and-coming art of the future."*

*I do not know whether I agree with him, for holding still so long for the plate to be exposed (he explained these terms to me with great patience, I think mostly to hear himself talk) is most difficult. 'If you twitch, the camera will record the movement,' he warned me, but even his most grave caution was not enough to prevent the corners of my mouth from inching upwards.*

*Consequently, as you can see, my mouth on the enclosed photograph is somewhat fuzzy, for I found it most difficult to keep myself from grinning as I thought about my plans for this masterpiece. I can imagine it even now in your strong and able hands.*

*He wanted me to pose standing stiff and still, with my hands folded (ladylike) in front of me. Nonsense, I told him. I want the photograph to look more natural than that, for I hardly ever stand still.*

*His visage appeared somewhat scandalized when I explained what I wanted, but he agreed to try it my way.*

*Do try to convince him to take your photograph. I would love to hold the likeness of you near to my heart.*

*Are you scandalized as well at the forwardness of my words?*
*Laughingly, I remain,*
*Your Amelia*

*Post Script. I will deliver this letter directly into your hands at this evening's service, for I know full well that your father will likely impound the letter if it arrives by post. Please tell your mother I have set aside two jars of my raspberry preserves just for her. I will bring them with me.*

"There are two more lines," Sadie said, "but they've been thoroughly inked out."

"Probably complaining about Mister Hoskins," I said.

"Sounds like the father—he must have been the original Gideon—was something of a stinker," Dee observed. Her voice held an undercurrent that I doubted many of the others noticed, but I did, simply because Dee told me once, shortly after she moved to Martinsville, that her husband—her former husband, Bob's brother—used to read her letters. The stinker.

"Sons often brought their wives home to live in the family house," Carol said. "I'd hate to think what someone like Gideon's father might have done with someone so full of life as this woman obviously was."

"I love this picture." Maddy seemed unwilling even to think about the obnoxious elder Hoskins. "Can't you just see her laughing like crazy once the photo session was completed?" She handed it to me.

The dark-haired woman appeared ready to leap into life. The camera had caught her looking back over her shoulder, rather impishly I thought. "I can see what she means about the fuzzy mouth, but even so, she looks like somebody I'd enjoy knowing."

Sadie took the picture, tucked it back into the letter, and set the envelope aside. "This is a *to keep* pile."

"I hope we find a lot of things to keep," I said, and went back to taking letters out of the trunk for the next quarter hour.

**SADIE AND I** were nowhere near the bottom of our trunk. Our card table was stacked with piles of letters we'd bundled together according to who the writer was. I had rummaged around in my sewing area and come up with several spools of ribbon so we could easily distinguish between the different groupings. It would take months of work to decipher all the ancient handwriting, but at least we had a plan of sorts.

"Surely whatever's on the bottom has to be older than most of what's on top," I said.

"There's nothing to stop you from looking farther down to begin with," Sadie said.

I agreed readily, since what she'd said mirrored what I'd been thinking. I leaned back into the trunk and pulled out three pasteboard boxes that, from the weight of them, probably contained more letters. My hand brushed across a fabric-wrapped bundle, and I lifted it into the light. Just the feel of it made me shiver with anticipation. I unfolded the layers with care. It felt old for some reason, almost ancient, although I quickly squashed that thought. Ancient meant the pyramids, Indian burial mounds, the Grand Canyon. Still, it felt older than anything else I'd ever handled. The gingham was a blue and white check, worn in places, and faded as if the material had been subjected to sunshine for many years. There was more fabric inside—no, not fabric, but a thin, cloth-covered book of some sort. Beneath it were four more matching volumes. Each one of them couldn't have contained more than fifty or sixty pages. "Look at these, gals. Have you ever seen anything like them?" I sat down, moved aside a stack of letters, spread out the ging-ham, and positioned the books carefully on the table in front of me. Almost afraid to handle any of them, I opened the top book carefully.

The slender volume I'd opened at random was crammed with a spidery, illegible script. Or rather, the letters were fairly clear, although they slanted so far to the left I almost got dizzy looking at them. Wasn't that sort of slant the mark of a highly repressed personality? The words were nonsensical, though. Dee had joined Sadie. They were perched on side-by-side folding chairs nearby, so I passed the first book to them and opened the next volume. It turned out to be equally illegible.

Sadie adjusted the reach of her arm. "Doggone trifocals. Well, I'll be jiggered. I can't make any sense out of it."

"Maybe it's some sort of secret code."

Sadie sniffed. "That's ridiculous, Dee. Those women worked from dawn to sunset. They wouldn't have had time to be fiddling with secret codes."

I opened the third book in the stack. It was just as undecipher-able as the first two.

"But, it makes no sense otherwise." Dee tried to sound out one of the lines. "… riaf a demees ti nwaf a was i dna atteuol revir …" The nonsense words drew the other women around us.

"Let me try." Maddy held out her hand. "I was an English ma-jor."

Dee raised a suspicious eyebrow. "This isn't English, I guarantee it, but you can certainly give it a try."

The book passed from hand to hand on its way toward Maddy, who was by this time ensconced on a pile of puffy feather pillows next to the lopsided hobbyhorse, and everyone had a suggestion.

"Maybe it's French?" "No. Slavic, maybe?" "Unh-uh. Dee's right; it's a code."

When it landed in Ida's hands, she stopped the forward momentum. "Wait, wait, wait, wait, wait a minute. A word just jumped out at me. ATTEUOL. When I was in fifth grade, my friends and I had a good time spelling all our names backwards. I was Adi, my friend Margaret was Teragram. Well, I did my parents' names, too, and my mother Louetta Garner was—"

"You were a Garner?" Carol asked.

"Well, Mom was born a Breeton, but she married Louis Garner."

"Breeton and Garner," Carol mused. "Then you go right back to the beginning."

Ida laughed. "Practically everybody in this town goes back to the beginning one way or another. Except for the newcomers." She looked directly at me, but with no rancor in her voice whatsoever—only a mild humor. Ida had turned out to be a true friend.

I closed the volume I still held and put it back on the small stack. "Some beginnings are more equal than others," I said, thinking of how Clara always bragged about Hubbard's direct line from Homer Martin.

Carol looked at me quizzically, but Rebecca Jo picked up on my oblique referral to *Animal Farm*. "There's always been a sort of Martinsville royal line," she explained to Carol. "There's a plaque in City Hall that lists the chairs of the town council. They've all been directly descended from Homer Martin. You can trace it father to son all the way from the beginnings of the town."

And their wives all think they're the queen bee, I thought, but I didn't say it aloud. Instead, I pushed aside the thought of Clara Martin and took the high road.

*What high road? Are you going somewhere?*

I waited for Marmalade to quiet down. "What were you saying about your mother's name, Ida?"

"Oh, yeah. As I said, she was Louetta, named after one of the women way back when in the history of Martinsville. When we spelled it backwards, her name turned out to be Atteuol Noteerb Renrag. I remember laughing like crazy over that Renrag." She lifted the old book slightly. "I bet this is just written backwards."

"The whole thing?" I asked. "How could she possibly do that?"

"Maybe she was left-handed," Glaze suggested.

*What does that mean?*

"It's easier for us to write from right to left. And she would have been using a quill pen, so the ink wouldn't flow correctly if she were trying to push it across the paper from left to right. Ballpoint pens are hard enough, but a quill?" She shivered. "Can't imagine how hard that would be."

By this time everyone else had gathered around Ida. Sadie's voice inserted itself from behind us. "Maybe she was telling secrets."

We turned the way a school of fish does, everybody at the same time. Ida spoke for all of us. "Sadie, that's brilliant. How did you ever think of that?"

Dee leaned to her right and prodded Sadie gently with her elbow. "Maybe Sadie has secrets of her own."

Poor Sadie looked so distraught at that, I shot Dee a dirty look before turning back toward Ida. "Read it, read it to us, but let's all sit, first." We pulled folding chairs from where they leaned in rows against the wall, and formed a loose circle. Maddy stayed right where she was on her pillows.

Ida started reading at the top of that page on the right-hand side, groping her way from word to word.

*...when we were ... fetching water from the river Louetta and I saw a ... fawn. It ... seemed a fair ... token that we may have a good ... harvest this year...*

"You know," I said, taking up the second book, "This one looks like it might be the first one." Nobody seemed to grasp what I was talking about, so I explained. "The first page in this one looks almost like a title page. Here, Ida. What does it say?"

She hesitated a second before taking it from me, almost as if this was a portentous moment. I found myself holding my breath. Starting again at the right-hand margin, she read, *"This is the personal diary of Mary Frances Garner."* After all the gasps subsided, she added,

"There's something written underneath that, and the ink is a lot darker." She looked at Carol. "Does that mean she probably added it later?"

Carol nodded. "Could be. What does it say?"

"It says *wed to h.m. 24 May 1741.*"

The attic fairly erupted with shouts of glee. We all knew that Mary Frances Garner Martin was the wife of Homer. She was the great-great-grandmother of the two boys who died when they saved Homer's handcrafted doors from the Old Church when it burned in 1814. We were looking at the written history of the founding of our town. Cause for celebration, indeed.

"We know they left Brandtburg in late April," Carol said. "So that means this wedding happened only a month down the road."

"Sure didn't take him long to replace the murdered Myra Sue," Maddy said with a scowl.

Ida turned to the second page.

"Before you start reading," Carol said, "my historian's sensibility tells me I have to warn you to handle the pages as little as possible so the oils from your fingers won't damage them."

"Would gloves help?" Ida set down the book and rubbed her hands along her sweatpants. "I might have a hard time turning the pages, but I could wear my wooly gloves."

"I have something even better." I said. "Something you mentioned a while ago. Be right back."

*I will go with you.*

It took me a while to find the white cotton gloves I'd bought once when I had a rash on my hands. I'd worn them to bed at night after slathering my hands with a special herbal cream Annie McGill made up for me, and after about two weeks, the rash was completely gone. It never came back, but I'd boiled the gloves and kept them around just in case. I sure did miss Annie. I had half a dozen pairs of the things, so I took a second pair just so Ida would have a backup. On the way out of the bedroom, I picked up a box of tissues. We'd probably need them.

"Here you are, Ida!" I couldn't avoid the triumph in my voice as I handed the gloves to her. "They're clean and ready to go."

Carol blessed me with a vibrant smile. "Those are perfect."

I sat, and Marmalade jumped onto my lap.

*I like to curl up here. Your lap is wider than the rabbit.*

Once the gloves were in place, Ida opened to the first page.

*Sunday, 19 April 1741*
*Late at night*
*This journal will be the ongoing story of my marriage to*
*Hubbard Brandt.*

She looked up, eyebrows raised. "Hubbard Brandt? Who's Hubbard Brandt?"

Carol leaned forward in her chair. "He was brother to Ira Brandt, my ancestor. This is the first I've ever heard this part of the story, though. Keep reading. Maybe we'll figure it out."

"Ira's the one who killed Myra Sue," Maddy said, and Carol briefly outlined—for the newcomers—what she'd told us about Myra Sue Russell's murder on the church steps just minutes after she'd married Homer.

"I hate to sound dense," Pat said, "but would you refresh my memory about who all left Brandtburg?"

So she did. I appreciated the repeat, since a lot of those names hadn't sunk in the first time.

Ida went back and repeated the first line.

*This journal will be the ongoing story of my marriage to*
*Hubbard Brandt, which began just after moonrise on Saturday*
*night, the 18th of April. A fortnight ago he gave me five of these pre-*
*cious blank-paged books, asking that I record my innermost thoughts*
*in them. Keep them secret, though, he warned me, although the warn-*
*ing was not necessary, as well he knew, for I had shared with him my*
*way of writing. Several years ago I tried writing from right to left*
*across my school slate, and found it to be so much easier. The true*
*advantage, though, was that the girls sitting near me could not read*
*it and thus could not copy my school notes. It seems a miracle that*
*Master ...*

"The next word starts with what I think is an O," Ida said, "but I can't make it out."

Carol leaned forward. "Maybe I can help." Ida pointed to the offending word and Carol studied it for a moment. "Oh! Ormsby. He was the schoolmaster in Brandtburg. I found him in an old newspaper article. He made quite a splash when he insisted on educating the girls of the town beyond the first grade, which was the usual practice at the time."

Dee drew in her breath sharply. "First grade? That's all they got?"

"They needed enough training to be able to keep household accounts," Carol explained, "but many of the women back then had few skills beyond the basics of addition and subtraction and simple reading, all of which they were expected to learn in just one year of schooling. Ormsby lived with his sister—I think her name was Silva, although that might have been a misprint of Sylvia—and she was a force to reckon with. From what I can figure out, she insisted her brother teach her, and then she extended the crusade to all the other girls in town. But, keep going, Ida."

*Master Ormsby never caught me at it. Sitting as I did at the back of the schoolroom, for I was ever the tallest of the girls, I evaded his inspection, and my dear friend Myra Sue who—*

"Myra Sue?" Maddy interrupted. "Do you think that was Myra Sue who got murdered?"

Maddy seemed to feel a real affinity for Myra Sue, I thought. Maybe because Maddy wrote about murders all the time.

"It's quite likely," Carol said. "I never found another Myra Sue in the records."

*... and my dear friend Myra Sue who shared my desk never*

*gave me away. I told Hubbard to keep all but one of these books, but he said he feared his brother would find them and, seeing no worth in them, would destroy them. At my insistence, he kept one volume for himself.*

"Wait a minute." Melissa pointed to the stack of four more books. "That means we have all five of hers. Check the dates, Biscuit, so we can see how long she wrote."

"The one on the bottom will probably be the oldest," I said. "Let's see."

But when I took that fifth volume from the bottom of the stack, it was in an entirely different handwriting altogether. I quickly checked the other three, and they all had the backwards writing that was almost impossible to decipher, for anyone except Ida, that is. "We have a surprise here," I told the group, and read the first two lines of the fifth cloth-bound book.

*Personal Journal of Hubbard John Brandt 1741 to* ______
*In twelve more days I will take Mary Frances Garner as my wife.*

To say we all looked stunned would be a gross understatement. Then the questions exploded from all sides.

Rebecca Jo: "How did it get here to Martinsville?"

Melissa: "Does this mean he and Mary Frances hooked up somehow?"

Dee: "That's not possible. Mary Frances was Homer Martin's wife—and then his widow—for her whole life."

"No she wasn't," Maddy objected. "Not according to Ida's book. And not this one either."

"But if he came to Martinsville, there would have been a huge scandal," Dee said. "And I don't think the passage of two hundred and fifty years would have covered it up—not in this town."

"We're definitely missing some vital information," Carol said. "Suppose we keep reading—both books—and see what we can find."

"What I'd like to know," I said, "is why there's no end date on that first line of Hubbard's journal. It says *1741 to,* but then it's just blank."

"Maybe he died," Dee said.

"But somebody—whoever saved the diary—would have filled in the year," I said. "The answer has to be in here somewhere. Go ahead, Ida. Why don't you finish your entry, and then I'll read mine. I mean Hubbard's."

"Yours—I mean Hubbard's—starts before this one. Even though that first entry isn't dated, it's pretty obvious he wrote it before she started on her entries. Why don't you read it first, and then I'll pick up with Mary Frances."

"Okay. Sounds like a good plan."

Before I could begin reading again, Maddy said, "It'll be fun following this story from two different viewpoints."

"Spoken like an author." Glaze grinned at Maddy.

I turned over a couple of pages. "It's a really long entry."

Rebecca Jo swept her hand toward the windows, where we could see and hear ice pellets attacking the panes. "Like we don't have the time?"

I slipped on the second pair of cotton gloves.

*In twelve more days I will take Mary Frances Garner as my wife. I would marry her tomorrow—this minute, even—if Reverend Atherton would agree to perform the ceremony, but he is convinced that waiting until just before the Martin clan leaves this valley is a safer alternative. 'If all those people are here,' he told me, 'there will be deep dissension over the marriage, and I fear violence might erupt. If, on the other hand, they are already on their way out of this town before you announce your marriage, they will have little choice but to leave her behind.'*

*While I understand his reasoning, I am not happy with this delay. It will, of course, be a secret wedding ceremony, with only Mistress Atherton as a witness. Before we wed, I wish to record here how and why I came to love Mary Frances Garner with all my heart.*

"Oh," Sadie sighed. "How sweet."

Ida nodded. We all nodded.


*It began when I first saw her ready wit, her vivid intelligence, her willingness to learn. I knew without a doubt that I had met someone with whom I would never grow bored. Even now I can imagine that a dozen years from now—nay, two dozen—I will read this passage to her as we sit, perhaps with our grandchildren at our knees.*

*I had, of course, been aware of Mary Frances for years. I say of course, for who could have missed those bright eyes of hers? With only one schoolhouse in this town, and with Mistress Silva Ormsby insisting that her brother educate the girls as well as the boys, Brandts and Martins alike, it was inevitable that we would know each other.*


I paused in my reading. "You were right, Carol. It was the schoolmaster's sister who was responsible for all this. And he says—writes—Silva, not Sylvia."

She nodded, but motioned me to continue.


*The moment I knew I wanted her for a helpmeet, for my wife, for the mother of my children, was that afternoon I walked back to the schoolhouse to see Master Ormsby and return a book I had borrowed. Although school had long been over for the day, Mary Frances and her friend Myra Sue Russell sat on the front step in avid conversation. They were unaware of my approach, and I listened unashamedly to their argument about the play Master Ormsby insisted we read.*

*'They should have told her father,' Myra Sue said. 'He liked Romeo, did he not?'*

*Mary Frances shook her head and set her young-girl braids to dancing. 'No. The divisions between the two families were far too great.' Her voice carried absolute conviction. 'Mister Capulet would never have approved of the marriage. It was all well and good for him to think Romeo a comely youth, but he would not have condoned a marriage of his daughter to a Montague.'*

I stopped reading. "I wonder how old she was here. She sounds pretty mature for a schoolgirl."

Carol agreed. "Girls had to grow up faster back then in some ways, although they were generally kept fairly uninformed about things that girls today learn about much earlier."

"You mean like birds and bees?"

Carol nodded in Pat's direction. "Remember that a lot of these schoolgirls would be married with children of their own by the time they were sixteen or seventeen."

"Like Juliet's mother," I said grimly. "And just look how that turned out."

"What else does he say, Biscuit?"

I smiled my thanks at Ida and kept reading.


*Just then she looked up and saw me watching her, and a most becoming flush reddened her cheeks. 'Do you always eavesdrop like this?' she accused me.*

*'Only when the conversation is most interesting,' I replied. 'If I may be so bold as to comment?'*

*Her brow furrowed slightly, but she inclined her head in gracious assent, with an assurance that was far beyond her years, and I loved her even more.*

*'I agree with you that the enmity between the two families was, at that time at least, insurmountable. Nothing so slight as the opinion of his daughter—' I broke off abruptly at the fierce look she gave me. 'I did not say I agreed with him, but I feel he would have considered her wishes to be of little importance.'*

*'There may be some matter in what you say,' Mary Frances said. 'Go on.'*

*'Thank you. Nothing that Mister Capulet considered to be of so slight a significance would have swayed his thinking.'*

*'And it took the death of his daughter—'*

*'And the death of Montague's son—'*

*'Before the rift could be healed,' she finished.*

*Our words flowed so easily together, and I suddenly could imagine what it would be like to spend long winter evenings discussing ideas with someone who appeared to hold reasoned thought in as high a regard as I did. A few more years, I determined, to give her time to grow up a bit more, and I would speak to her, and to her father.*

*The fact that she was a Garner from the Martin clan did not at that moment seem to be much of a factor. We could have been a Montague and a Capulet, but I knew even then that <u>our</u> situation would surely end with a marriage, but not with two deaths.*

*That was the day, after Mary Frances and Myra Sue left the schoolyard, that Master Ormsby gave me six precious books of blank paper, one of which I hold now in my hands. 'Record your thoughts,' he told me. 'You have much to learn, but you also have much to share, and I would see you become school-master in my stead when I am no longer here.' The fact that he gave me what amounted to a king's ransom was testament to his belief in me.*

*I never before now, though, wished to write on these in-finitely costly pages. I have given the other five volumes to my wife-to-be—how I love writing that phrase—for I know that my brother would just as soon use the pages to wipe his arse with, and I would find it difficult indeed to forgive Ira if he destroyed even one page of these volumes.*

I'd been leaning forward as I read, so intent on Hubbard's words that I clutched the book more tightly than I should have, considering its age. "Wow," I said after I finished that entry. "Do you think it ended up like Romeo and Juliet?"

"It couldn't have," Dee said. "Mary Frances lived. And she married Homer Martin. We know that from town history. It even says so on"—she pointed to the book Ida held—"on the first page there."

I stroked my gloved hand across the age-softened cover of the book I held. "But what about Hubbard?"

"Is that the end of that entry?" Leave it to Ida to be practical rather than sentimental.

I nodded. "The next one is dated, uh, April seventeenth. And then one on"—I turned the page—"the nineteenth."

"The same day as this entry," Ida said. "So, you read that one, the seventeenth, and then we'll both read the ones from the nineteenth."

I was sure we were all quite capable of figuring out the chrono-logical order, but I supposed Ida needed to clarify it in her own mind. "Seventeen April, 1741," I read. "Friday."

*17 April 1741 Friday. My brother woke me from a sound sleep when he staggered in, shouting, 'Those blasted Martins need to be thrown out of this town! 'Tis a good thing they are leaving soon, or I would usher Homer Martin into the nearest river headfirst! They cannot leave soon enough!'*

*'Can you not leave it be, Ira Michael?' I asked him. 'At least one person in this house would like some sleep.' I was too tired to be civil, to listen yet again to my brother's braggadocio about having expelled the Martins from this valley. They are not gone yet, but I knew if I mentioned that small fact, my brother would rave even longer. Even from where I stood in the doorway to my small room, the smell of Ira's whiskey-laden breath reached me, and I turned away from him. 'Go to bed,' I told him. 'Go to sleep. They will be gone soon enough.'*

*'Not soon enough for me!'*

*I left him fuming and came here to sit and write. Perhaps this will calm me, for I cannot sleep with my mind turning as it now does. Ever since the death of Ira's wife eleven months ago, he has become increasingly obstreperous. My brother has always been one to enjoy his drink, even from the time we were but boys and Ira learned to sneak our father's forbidden whiskey, but something in Ira seems to have broken this past year when Felinda died a-birthing.*

"Did you know that, Carol?"

"I knew his wife died, but I didn't realize his heavy drinking was the result of it."

*Sometimes I miss the continual hilarity of my four nephews and three nieces. They are Ira's offspring indeed, always loud, always ready to poke fun at each other. Sometimes though, I have to admit to myself that the house is considerably more peaceful without their constant clamor. I was against my brother's decision to hand the children over to other relatives, but I know that Ira and I alone could never have cared for such little ones, and Ira has shown no immediate wish to remarry. The four boys, all of them sharing a first name with their father, are now with our sister Catherine, while the girls replaced the three children Edward and Caroline Dillingham lost the past year when their house caught fire.*

"Oh, God," Pat breathed. "She lost three children? How horrible."

"Fire was a constant threat back then," Carol said. "All those candles. All those fireplaces with sparks flying. Often there were highly flammable rushes strewn on the floor. And no smoke detectors."

*Between my brother's shouting and the unwelcome memory of the noise of the Dillingham fire mingling with my remembrance of the screams of the children trapped within, I want nothing more than to go back to sleep, but whenever I think of fire, all possibility of sleep flees from me. It is, perhaps, my greatest fear.*

*Instead, I called to mind the face of the woman I love. Reverend Atherton advised me only this evening to delay the wedding, thinking to first soothe the minds of Ira Brandt and of Homer Martin, who lead the opposing factions, but there is no time for that. I cannot claim Mary Frances publicly without being first wed to her, and that must happen before the Martins leave the valley. One more day to endure. Only one. And then she will be truly mine. Forever.*

## Saturday, 18 April 1741
## Brandtburg
## early morning

**ONE MORE DAY** to endure, thought Charlotte Ellis, *and then we can be rid of this house forever.* She had decided that she would insist on a larger house when they reached their destination, wherever that would be.

It was not fitting that a respectable widow such as herself should have to be immured in such a small room with both her daughters. Surely the girls could be in a room by themselves and Charlotte could enjoy some privacy for once. She knew that both her girls—well, not Martha, perhaps, but certainly Louisa—were curious about the well-wrapped parcel Charlotte protected so determinedly. There would be time, plenty of time eventually, to initiate Louisa as the next keeper of the secrets of the town. But for now, Charlotte wanted privacy.

It would be a long time coming, she feared, for they might be months upon the road ahead of them. At least she would have a project to keep her busy in the evenings. She fingered the white linen she had set aside for a new cap. Shirring around the edges, with the ties shirred as well, although she doubted she would loop them beneath her chin. Ties tended to call attention to the multiple chins she seemed to have developed recently. They could dangle. That would look fetching.

# 1984
## Atlanta

**CHARLIE ELLIS FLUNG** open her mother's bedroom door without knocking. She almost never knocked, even though she knew she was supposed to. "Can we bake cookies?"

Her mother took a bunch of papers that were spread all over the bed and piled them together.

"What's that stuff, Mommy?"

"Uh, just some … some family papers. Nothing very interesting."

Something in her mom's voice made Charlie look closer. "They look old."

"Yes, dear. They are. Very old."

"Can I read them?"

Her mom swallowed and pulled a worn piece of cloth up around the papers. "No sense in doing that now. I doubt they'd be interesting to a fourth-grader. Let's go make those cookies."

"This looks like more fun."

Mom reached out to brush Charlie's red curls off her forehead. "Someday, sweetie. Someday they'll be yours. But for now"—her voice turned all official-sounding—"we'll just put these away and go do the important things, shall we? Why don't you run and get out the bowls we'll need?"

Charlie turned back at the door and saw her mother stuff the bundle into the bottom drawer of her dresser. Charlie wasn't a snoop. She really wasn't. But she sure was curious about the funny writing on those old papers.

# Saturday, 18 April 1741
# Brandtburg

**AFTER THE EVENING** meal, Myra Sue Russell and Mary Frances Garner retired to the room Myra Sue shared with the two other Russell girls. Myra Sue was several years older than Mary Frances, but she and Mary Frances had been the best of friends for as long as either of them could remember and had often slept at each other's houses. This was a special night, for it was the last time she and Mary Frances would be girls together. On the morrow, Myra Sue would wed Homer Martin. It was Myra Sue's mother's wish that she be wed before the journey began. Myra Sue tried not to think about it. Homer Martin was well respected by the men of the town. Myra Sue hoped she would come to love him after they were married.

The light of the candle threw the shadows of the four young women across the log walls and onto the door between this bedroom and the large room where they had eaten so recently. Nineteen-year-old Anne crawled over the large wooden box that held extra quilts and all their clothes, except for the ones they would need tomorrow for the wedding. Once she reached the wide bed, she clambered in next to six-teen-year-old Edna and pulled the quilts right up to her chin. The April evening had been fairly mild, but once the sun set, cold drafts drifted in between the logs of the outer walls. Over the winter, some of the chinks of wattle had loosened, but the men had not wasted time repairing the leaks this spring, knowing that they would soon leave this house behind.

Myra Sue knew they faced weeks, possibly months of sleeping even colder on the trail, nights when she knew she would miss the comfort of this cabin, the only home she had ever known. She and her sisters and mother had spent every night of the autumn and winter knitting and quilting, ever since the men declared their intention of leaving the valley, so they would have ample warmth when they left Brandtburg.

Of course, Myra Sue would no longer share a bed with her sisters, for she would travel in Homer Martin's wagon and then later—perhaps a year from now—at the end of their journey, would live with him in a house. She hoped and prayed she would be a good wife to him and a good mother to the children she felt sure they would have. When Father joined her to Homer in holy matrimony tomorrow, Myra Sue prayed that the union would be blessed.

She briefly reviewed what she knew of other marriages in Brandtburg. There were many husbands and wives who seemed genuinely fond of each other, such as her parents were, but there seemed to be far more others who simply—for want of a better word—endured. She shook her head as she thought of one of her favorite aphorisms. *What we fear in ourselves, we accuse in others.* She sincerely hoped she could avoid seeing misery elsewhere, for she did not want such misery for herself. Homer was surely not an unkind man, even though she knew he was overly fond of strong drink. He was, she knew, well liked among the men of the town, although sometimes Myra Sue wondered if that was simply because of the mystique around the Martin name.

"Come to bed," Anne whined. "The candlelight keeps me awake."

Myra Sue knew that was not so. Once her sister—both her sisters—were sound asleep, it would take far more than the light from one feeble candle to disturb them, but Myra Sue knew not to argue the point, for that would simply delay the onset of sleep, and Myra Sue wanted her sisters to sleep well this night, for she had much to discuss with Mary Frances. She also knew enough not to speak of anything she wished to keep private during the first few minutes after her sisters retired. Anne and Edna both loved to ferret out Myra Sue's secrets. But once they had been sleeping for a short time their limbs relaxed into unmistakable deep slumber. That probably came from their having learned early on to sleep through their father's snoring.

She smiled to herself. Myra Sue's parents slept in the largest of the three bedrooms, and Reverend Russell's snores resounded all night through the thin interior walls of the house, so there was no chance of her conversation with Mary Frances being overheard, particularly since her brothers Thomas and Abner, sleeping as they always did on pallets before the large hearth, had begun to develop snores almost as loud as their father's. The third bedroom in the house held Myra Sue's widowed Aunt Charlotte and her two daughters, but Myra Sue knew they all three slept like the dead, which she sometimes wished they were. Myra Sue did not like either her busybody aunt or her two useless cousins. She would miss the constant loving presence of her immediate family when she was wed, but she would not miss Aunt Charlotte, Louisa, or Martha. Why did they not stay in Brandtburg and bedevil the Brandts?

Myra Sue removed her cap, set it aside, and picked up the brush her brother Thomas had made new as a wedding present for her from the bristles of a hog they had slaughtered last autumn. She turned to Mary Frances. "Will you brush my hair one last time?"

Neither of them spoke as Mary Frances began the soothing motions, first smoothing out the inevitable tangles from the ends of Myra Sue's long black hair, and gradually working her way up to the crown. They did not speak right away, although both of them were bursting with the need to share their thoughts. Eventually Mary Frances set aside the brush, and she and Myra Sue crept to the bed to peer through the gloom at Anne and Edna. The curtains surrounding the bed had already been packed away. Their even breathing and the lax way in which their mouths hung slightly open assured their sister and her friend that they both slept soundly. They tiptoed away, and Myra Sue asked quietly, "Are you still determined to follow this course?"

"I will miss you dearly," Mary Frances told Myra Sue in tones so low Myra Sue could barely hear her, "but I must do this."

Myra Sue wiped at the tears she had been trying to hold back. "I understand how you love him," she whispered, "but I do not understand how you can bear to be parted from your entire family."

"Hubbard is more to me than brother, sister, mother, father." Mary Frances tended to be a bit dramatic, and Myra Sue knew it, but this sounded like Mary Frances really believed it.

"The Brandts are our longtime enemies," Myra Sue hissed, "and you will have to live among the Brandts if you marry him. How can you bear to do that?" She tried to soften her voice, and the way her friend gently braided her hair helped to soothe her somewhat. She could not completely set aside her worries, though. "Are you not frightened of what may happen?"

"If there are none of our Martin families left in the valley," Mary Frances reasoned, "the fuel for the anger will be gone. That is why Reverend Atherton insisted we wait to wed until the very last moment." She gave one final stroke through her friend's hair and laid the brush on the table.

"*You* will be in the valley."

"But I will be the wife of Hubbard Brandt. As his wife, they will not harm me." Mary Frances removed her own cap and began to unbraid her hair. "I will pray for you every night. And I will miss you. But I will proudly stay here in this valley to be with the man I love."

"I hope you do not regret your decision." Myra Sue picked up the brush and lifted her friend's light brown curls. "A marriage seems to me to be more than simply wishing to be together. I look at my mother and how tired she is after each baby is born, and all the last five children born dead, and I wonder if love is enough."

"Is he not wonderful, though?" Mary Frances asked, a dreamlike expression on her face.

Myra Sue thought for a moment before answering. Hubbard Brandt, the younger brother of the often drunken Ira, was a young man of mild looks and tall stature. He was soft-spoken and of graceful carriage, even considering his somewhat lop-sided gait, the result of a childhood accident that had left one leg slightly shorter than the other. She knew that Hubbard not only could read, but he enjoyed doing so, which was something important to Mary Frances. "Yes," she said. "Of all the Brandts, he is perhaps the least objectionable."

Mary Frances turned on her stool, striking her knees against the table with enough force to jar it. Myra Sue grabbed for the candle before it could tip. Both of them froze, waiting to see if the noise had awakened anyone. When they were sure they were safe, Mary Frances hissed, "*Least objectionable*? That is not a rousing statement of approval."

"What would you have me say? That I delight in your staying behind while the rest of your kin take a dangerous and unknown road to a land that we hope will be less harsh and that will have no enemies in it? Did you expect that I would applaud your staying here? Do you think your father will not object, that he will not haul you away with him?"

Mary Frances pulled back from her friend's true anger. "I will not be within reach for him to pull me away," she said. "He knows I am here with you tonight. He and my mother will not look for me until tomorrow when I do not appear at church for the services. By that time I will be Hubbard's wife and our marriage will have been con..."—she stumbled over the word—"consummated. I am going to Hubbard tonight. He has arranged for Reverend Atherton to marry us and I depend on you to keep my secret."

Myra Sue's eyes went wide in disbelief. "Tonight? You cannot do that!"

"I can and will, Myra Sue. I have spoken with the Reverend, and he told me he hoped our marriage would heal the anger between the two families."

"Why bother with healing anything?" Myra Sue did not try to hide her disgust. "We leave the valley in two days' time."

Mary Frances lowered her gaze. "I wish we had married weeks ago, or months ago."

"Or years ago?" Myra Sue's voice had an edge to it. "You could have wed him when you were but a babe. Think of the healing that would have happened then."

"I know you are angry with me"—Mary Frances apparently chose to ignore her friend's derision—"but I fear you do not understand how much I love Hubbard." Mary Frances reached up to put her hands on her friend's shoulders. She squeezed gently, and Myra Sue could sense that Mary Frances was trying to transfer all her compassion through her fingers. "I think *you* do not love *your* intended."

Myra Sue stepped away from her friend's embrace and even more so from her words. "Homer Martin will provide for me and will give me children." She thought briefly of the way her parents sometimes looked at each other, and a twinge of regret pulled at her heart. "I ask nothing more from marriage."

"Oh, Myra Sue. Can you not be happy for me?"

"Happy? Happy that my dearest companion is leaving me at the time when I need her the most?" Myra Sue shook her head. "How can you leave tonight? You must be at my wedding on the morrow."

"Oh, my dear, I did not think of that." Mary Frances picked up the brush again and passed it back and forth from one hand to the other as she thought quickly. "Of course. Of course I will be with you. But I have no way to get a message to Hubbard tonight, so I must meet him. Reverend Atherton expects us soon after moonrise. I will tell Hubbard that I must return here well before dawn. And then I will slip away from the church tomorrow after your wedding is complete." She gazed at her friend from childhood, and Myra Sue could see that Mary Frances almost lost her resolve.

"You must be with me on the journey south," Myra Sue urged. "You must be there to help me when my first child is born." She watched her friend's jaw soften. "You must be there to cook and sew with me, to help me plant my garden when we reach our new home."

But Myra Sue could tell, even in the wavery light of the candle, the moment when Mary Frances thought of her Hubbard. Myra Sue saw that her friend's determination had hardened again.

"I will go to Hubbard tonight." Mary Frances gathered her hair around her head and tucked the ends into her cap. "I will marry him tonight, but I promise to return long before dawn." She paused and touched Myra Sue's cheek. "I wish with my whole heart that you could be with me tonight when I wed, but I know that is not possible. I will be with *you* when you are wed tomorrow."

Myra Sue was not happy with that answer, but she knew now that she could not change her friend's mind no matter how long she argued or how much she reasoned.

Shortly after the moon rose, Mary Frances and Myra Sue opened the creaking shutter, both of them cringing at each sound it made. Then Myra Sue helped Mary Frances slip out the window. Hubbard appeared out of the shadow of the barn, his uneven gait only barely discernible. Myra Sue watched as the two joined hands and glided out of sight, like two ghosts flowing at the whim of the nighttime breeze. She shuddered. It would not do to think of spirits, for fear that her thoughts might somehow summon evil beings.

## 2000

**WITHOUT WAITING FOR** our murmurs to die down, Ida began to read, running her gloved index finger along under each line as she scrutinized the backwards writing.

*I almost wrote my name on the first page as Mary Frances Garner Brandt, but feared to do so lest my sister Constance see it.*

*She knows too well my habit of writing backwards. 'Do not let anyone see you write this way' she has warned me again and again, 'lest they believe you to be a witch.'*

"Wait," Rebecca Jo said. "I'm confused. What day is she on here?"

"This one is Sunday," Ida said. "April nineteenth in 1741. Remember? We backed up a couple of days when Biscuit found Hubbard's diary."

"This is the day Myra Sue Russell was shot," Carol said. "Go on, Ida."

*Why do I write thus of inconsequential matters when my heart is breaking in twain? First, for the death this morning of my dearest friend Myra Sue, as much a sister to me as Constance has ever been. Second because I cannot yet see how to escape and find my way to Hubbard's side. My mother dragged us all home immediately after the killing, and barred the door while we huddled in the middle of the innermost room. Father appeared hours later with a monstrous wound in his leg, which Mother bound tightly. Almost as soon as we finished our evening meal, my father—despite his wound—and my brother*

Again, Ida paused and held the book out so Carol could look at it. "Nehemiah," Carol said. "He was a year older than Mary Frances, nineteen when they left Brandtburg and she was very nearly eighteen."

*... my father and my brother Nehemiah drew lots to see who would stand the first watch in case the Brandts chose to attack again. Mother objected, for his wound is deep, but Father was insistent that he would guard us. When I brought a candle, which I had lit at the fireplace, into my room after Constance was well asleep, Nehemiah came to my window and berated me through the shutters. So the*

*candle is out. Once he walked away, though, I opened the shutters as wide as possible and now I write by the light of the thin unhappy moon.*

*When we leave tomorrow, I will allow my steps to linger behind the others. I must arrange to walk in the very back and then to drop far enough behind so that Hubbard and I might steal away in the confusion. I know he will be watching for me. This means I will not be present when Myra Sue is buried far from Brandtburg, but I feel fair certain she will forgive me, for she knows—she is the only one who knows—of my secret marriage last night to Hubbard Brandt.*

**The End**
*Not quite*

Thus ends RED AS A ROOSTER. This ongoing story will be continued in BLACK AS SOOT, PINK AS A PEONY, and WHITE AS ICE. Please read them in order.

## Fran's Gratitude List for the four volumes of *White as Ice*

As far as I know, there is not, nor has there ever been, a Carol Mellinger teaching at any Vermont college. The name flew out of the air one day, and I chose to hang onto it. I am eternally grateful to my muse, whatever she may be.

A lot of the highly unlikely names in the history of Martinsville and Brandtburg (such as Cleusa, Presila, Rhoda, Tobe, Irraiah, Sophrona, and Virgil) did not come out of the air, however. I found them in census records from 1790 through 1830, and (quite a few of them) from old Stewart family diaries.

For those diaries, I must thank the late **Mary Nell Stewart Bowen**. In and around 1992, my Aunt Mary transcribed diaries that were kept by her parents and her grandmother, covering almost all the years from 1910 through 1967. She then had the entire collection printed and distributed to her parents' children and grandchildren, of which I was one. These records have proved invaluable, both as family history and as a source for many of the stories I developed for *White as Ice*. The story of Nancy Geonette Harrison Hoskins and her account book in Black as Soot, for instance, came directly from my great-grandmother's 1910 account lists. I changed her last name, but nothing else. And she really did support a family of six by selling butter and eggs (and hens and geese and dresses and milk), losing only $28.42 over that entire year, which included her purchase of an organ for $37.50. That organ had pride of place in my grandmother's dining room and was a source of happy childhood memories. Please know that I did not intend to imply any resemblance whatsoever between my relatives and the characters in this book. The names were just too good to pass up, though. Tobe and Morgan, for instance, were not father and son, and my Uncle Morgan was not even alive during the timeframe I gave them here.

My beta readers, **Diana Alishouse, Darlene Carter,** and **Millie Woollen,** read (without complaint) through thousands of disorganized pages and helped me mash it all into a semblance of understandability. If you get confused, believe me, it is not the fault of these three phenomenal women. Millie insisted I let everyone know what happened to Babylon in Black as Soot; Darlene suggested that a little bit of chronological order would help, and Diana let me know every time my writing confused her. Diana is also the one who asked, "Why don't you have Hubbard keep a diary?" That one question changed the scope of the entire book, solved a lot of logistical problems, and let me into Hubbard's thoughts in a way I hadn't come anywhere near to before that.

**Bill Fenton** kept me well supplied with pithy sayings that his grandfather (also named Bill Fenton) passed on to him when he was a youngster. My favorite—*chew the grass and spit the sticks*—was too good not to use, and I just had to put an otherwise totally fictional Bill in there as a character.

**Dottie Morefield** found a type(writer)-written journal from 1926 at the bottom of a box of old papers she picked up at a flea market. She asked if anyone from Sisters in Crime wanted it, and I was the lucky first responder.

**Jean McCandless** and her husband **Chris** were the original perpetrators in the elephant poop story at the Big Apple Circus in Red as a Rooster, although I've changed a few of the details (mostly because I couldn't remember them exactly!)

My niece, **Erica Jensen**, gave me the "moment of nature" idea in Pink as a Peony – only the time she first said it involved a vibrant red fox we saw in the middle of a country road.

I must thank my dear friend **Peggy Dixon**, who showed me an antique brown wedding dress wrapped in linen, and the matching hat, which you'll find described in the wedding dress story in Red as a Rooster. Peggy shared her mountain cabin with me numerous times as we spent days working separately but together—she making designer jewelry while I wrote. Why she ever put up with me—"Listen to this one, Peggy!"—I'll never know, but I am eternally grateful to her.

**Charlotte Ellis**, whom I met several years ago when I spoke at the Tallapoosa Public Library, won the chance to have her name used in one of my mysteries. As you can see, I liked the name so much, I used it for two separate generations.

**Liz Waisath:** I was at a FedEx one day some time ago to make some copies (dead printer at home) and happened to notice a stack of large photographs the woman next to me was making copies of. "A family reunion," she told me. "I'm making copies for all my brothers and sisters and cousins." Her grandmother, the woman wearing the muff, was so stunning, I had to ask permission to describe the muff—and the hat—in my upcoming book. The woman in the photo was Mabel Moran White, who lived from 1895 to 1927. Marmalade, as you have seen in Red as a Rooster, was extremely grateful for the muff idea.

Finally, my deepest thanks to **all my faithful readers** who kept emailing or messaging me to ask, "When will the next Biscuit McKee book be ready?" This book—or rather, this quartet of books—may have been long in coming, but is my heartfelt gift to you.

And one more note: There are a few more little mysteries I've not been able to solve. If you have any clue what *rubnomes, blewen,* or *44B dom* (from the 1910 accounts list in Black as Soot) might refer to, please message me through my website (FranStewart.com) or my FB author page (FranStewartAuthor).

# Author's Note

Dear Reader,

All along, I've been promising you that I would end the Biscuit McKee mystery series with *White as Ice*. Until fairly recently, I thought that end would be a long time in the future. I came up with 31 different titles, all involving colors of course, although some of them (such as Pink as Bubblegum and the one with Puce) hit the trash can early on. Because all the colors of light combine to create white, though, I always saw *White* as the final book.

I began writing *White* in 2004 (when *Yellow as Legal Pads* was still just a baby) with a rough draft of what has turned out to be the chapter about the historian Carol Mellinger looking out her window in Melissa Tarkington's *Azalea House Bed and Breakfast*. I knew Biscuit's attic would be an integral part of the story, so, over the next few years, I played around with various chapter ideas. In 2006 or thereabouts, I wrote a very rough draft of an ending, in which I revealed how Martinsville was founded and where the other towns along the Metoochie River got their names. It explained why the street names in Martinsville don't sound like good old Georgia names—there's not a Peach anywhere in the town—and why Sadie always wore yellow.

Over the next couple of years, other chapter ideas showed up as brief outlines in various computer documents or scribbles in spiral notebooks or on yellow legal pads.

I researched the first World's Fair of 1876, which was put on in honor of America's first centennial celebration; I looked up "woolgathering," which came from the aimless appearance of people who roamed around meadows gathering tufts of wool caught on shrubs after sheep had passed by; and the powerful solar storm of 1859, which set telegraph offices on fire. I looked into the gas-rationing program of 1942 and the origin of the straw boater.

There the book sat until February 8, 2016, which is the day I woke at four-thirty-nine a.m. with this book in mind. Not my original idea of *White as Ice*, you see, but the idea of what you're now holding in your hand (or on your e-reader). I ditched a number of the themes I'd researched. I practically began anew. I had a good reason to do so.

You see, in early 2015 I came within a heartbeat of dying, and the following eleven months were a time of deep contemplation for me, as well as a time of great joy, as I rediscovered how important it was to me to be alive. It was also a time of reorganizing my priorities, and I found that my "mystery-writing time" was almost over. I was still under contract to Berkley Press for the final two books in the ScotShop series, featuring ScotShop owner Peggy Winn and Dirk, a fourteenth-century Scottish ghost, but I deliberately wrote that third book, A WEE HOMI-CIDE IN THE HOTEL, knowing full well that I wouldn't write a fourth one. I put in as much of Dirk's story as I could—his centuries-old rela-tionship to Peggy, for instance—and the resolution (almost) of Peggy and Harper's ongoing attraction. I hope you'll read the three ScotShop books, and understand that my decision to end both of these series was one deeply grounded in my belief that there is still something—some-thing else—for me to do, to be, in this lifetime. Do I know what that something else is? Not yet. That simply means the years ahead will un-fold (as all my previous years have) as a marvelous adventure.

And so, I give you *Red as a Rooster, Black as Soot, Pink as a Peony,* and *White as Ice*—my gift to you, my faithful reader. This four-volume book may not be wrapped with quite the sort of ribbon you expected, but it comes from deep in my heart.

From my house beside a creek,
on the other side of Hog Mountain,
--Fran

# A Necessary Note About History

I've stayed as close to actual historical events as I can, although I must admit I cheated a bit on two of the stories. The first is the story of the hidden room in Black as Soot. The name of the town of Hephzibah was just too good to pass up. The town was, as Dolly mentions in her letter, originally called Brothersville in honor of the three brothers who founded it, but the name wasn't changed to Hephzibah until 1870 (rather than 1856 as I wrote it). If your historical sensibility is offended, I do apologize.

The other change of dates, also in Black as Soot was in the letters from Lydia to Astaline. The grand old Dakota Hotel on West 72ⁿᵈ Street in New York City was built between 1880 and 1884. I changed the chronology of the hotel's construction by 78 years so I could have a letter about the "year with no summer" written from there in January of 1816.

The rules that little Alfred Finlay Hastings had to copy out for his school lesson in Pink as a Peony came from Education World ([http://www.educationworld.com/a_lesson/lesson166.shtml](http://www.educationworld.com/a_lesson/lesson166.shtml)).

If you choose to scoff at the idea of cat communication, I will not be offended, but I should warn you that Carol's description of her sister's experience with a woman who could speak with cats (in Black as Soot) was taken from my own experience. I wouldn't have believed it if it hadn't happened to me (and to Miss Polly, a slate gray cat who complained about the "red furniture" and who served as my alarm clock until the day she died at the happy old age of sixteen).

As to the possibility of six caul births in one family, which comes near the beginning of Red as a Rooster, I stretched it a bit—quite a bit. The actual statistics are something like one in 180,000. Suspend your disbelief, please. I couldn't think of anything more likely to instigate suspicion on the part of the Brandts.

I leaned quite heavily on my own family's genealogical charts, borrowing names (particularly last names) with gleeful abandon. My Surratts in these four books have no relationship whatsoever to the Surratts on my family tree. Ditto for my various aunts, uncles, and grandparents—Myra Sue, Morgan, Call, Ketchum, Tobe, Nell, and even Mary

Frances, herself.

Finally, please believe Carol's story of the music of Comet Kohoutek in Black as Soot. I lived in Vermont in 1973 when the comet appeared, and, except for the identity of the person next to me, I might have been Carol herself, for I have described "the music of the spheres" just as I heard it (although Carol's and my description falls sadly short of the majesty of the event).

# The Original Families on the Trek

**MARTIN**
(descended from Albion & Lucelia Sabriss Martin through their son William)
Homer (marries 1. Myra Sue Russell / 2. Mary Frances Garner)
    John (born to Mary Frances on the trail)
Silas (marries widow Louetta Washburn Tarkington)
    Brand Tarkington (son of Louetta)
    Louise (barn baby, daughter of Silas and Louetta)

**BREETON**
Willem Breeton & 1. Mary Surratt Breeton / 2. Constance Garner Breeton)
    MaryAnne (marries Thomas Russell)
    Pioneer (marries Bridgett Hastings)
    Susan (became a spinster)
    Willy (marries Nell Surratt)
    Parley (barn baby, born to Willem & Constance) (marries Brand Tarkington)

**GARNER**
    Calvin Garner & Augusta Hastings Garner
    Nehemiah
    Wilbur
    Mary Frances (married to Homer Martin on trail)
    Constance (marries Willem Breeton on trail)
    Able (marries Anne Russell)

**HASTINGS**
Robert Hastings, innkeeper & Jane Elizabeth Benton Hastings
    Charles (marries Edna Russell)
    Bridgett (marries Pioneer Breeton)
    Lucius (marries Fionella Surratt)
    Clarissa (born on the trail)
    Cordelia (born in Martinsville)
Robert's father Richard Hastings (the original innkeeper)
Jane's elderly mother

**RUSSELL**
    Reverend Anders Russell & Sarah Endicott Russell
        Myra Sue (marries Homer Martin)
        Thomas (marries MaryAnne Breeton)
        Anne (marries Able Garner)
        Abner (bachelor)
        Edna (marries Charles Hastings)
    Matthew (blacksmith) & Abigail Downes Russell
        two sons, Mark and Luke, apprentices

**SURRATT**
    Call Surratt & Geonette Black Surratt
        Nell (marries Willy Breeton)
        Fionella Surratt (marries Lucius Hastings)
        Edward (bachelor)
        Barnard (barn baby)
    Widow Black and Geonette's siblings (Sergeant & Presila)

**ENDICOTT**
  Chauncey (elderly brewer) & his wife
    Worthy Endicott & Eunice Surratt Endicott
        Isabelle
        Jonathan
        Rufus
        Ellen (born on the trail)
        Herman (born in Enders)
    Charlotte Endicott Ellis, widow (first daughter of Chauncey)
        Louisa (unmarried)
            Jane (born on the trail)
            Adele (born on the trail)
        Martha (unmarried)
            Alice (born on the trail)
            Tansy (born on the trail)
    Sarah Endicott Russell (Rev. Russell's wife)
    Sayrle (bachelor)
    Joel (bachelor)
    Daniel (bachelor)
    Sanborn (bachelor)

**EVEREST**
Joseph Everest & Arinda Surratt Everest, with five children

**FOUNTAIN**
Peter Fountain, wife, and eight children
Marcus Fountain (marries Juliana Stickney)
Orra Fountain (marries Colton Shipleigh on trail)
Alan Fountain (fiddler)

**SHIPLEIGH**
Elias Shipleigh & Anthina Surratt Shipleigh
Colton (marries Orra Fountain on trail)
and six daughters

**STICKNEY**
Timothy Stickney & Adah Kellogg Stickney with various children
Juliana Stickney (marries Marcus Fountain on trail)

==============================================

**BRANDT**
Ira Brandt & Felinda Merchant Brandt (deceased)
Ira Marcus
Ira Alonzo
Ira Prentiss
Ira Samuel
& 3 daughters
Hubbard John Brandt

## Children of Beechnut House

**Robert & Jane Elizabeth's children:**
1. **Charles** m. Edna Russell
2. Bridgett m. Pioneer Breeton
3. Lucius m. Fionella Surratt
4. Clarissa (born on the trail)
5. Cordelia and Emmeline

**Charles & Edna's child:**
**Alonzo** m. Margaret DeWitt

**Alonzo & Margaret's children:**
1. Lydia m. Curtis Sheffield
2. **Reuben** m. Astaline Shipleigh
3. Ethan m. Naomi Russell

**Reuben & Astaline's children:**
1. Mary Etta
2. Electa
3. **Rose** m. Baxter Hoskins
4. Emma and Caroline (twins)
5. Lilian
6. son
7. son

**Rose and Baxter's children:**
1. Zenus Hoskins m. Melanie Surratt
2. Kathryn
3. **Arthur** Hoskins m. Grace Surratt (sister to Melanie, Elspeth
   & Delilah "Dolly")
4. Euston
5. Timothy

**Arthur & Grace's children:**
1. daughter (stillborn)
2. **Gideon** Zenus Hoskins m. 1. Leonora Martin 2. Eliza Russell
3. daughter
4. son
5. son

**Gideon & Leonora's children:**
1. son
2. Ellen
3. son
4. Rachael
5. **Young Gideon** m. Amelia Stockwell

**Young Gideon & Amelia's children:**
1 - 4. daughters
5. **Perry** m. Elizabeth Endicott
6. Myrtle m. Frank Snelling

**Perry & Elizabeth's child:**
Lyle

# Town Council Chairmen

Homer Martin (b. 1721) m. Mary Frances Garner
John (b. 1742) m. (wife's name unknown)
Jerrod (b. 1772) m. Betsy Surratt
Ketchum (1800-1893) m. Janet Russell
Tobe (1822-1912) m. Irraiah Garner
Morgan (1851-1924) m. (wife's name unknown)
Obadiah (1883-1946) m. Irmagarde Hoskins
Leon (1915-1979) m. Matilda Shipleigh
Hubbard (1940- 2000) m. Clara Black

# Owners of Beechnut House

Robert Hastings, builder of Beechnut House, m. Jane Elizabeth Benton
Charles Hastings (son of Robert) m. Edna Russell
Alonzo Hastings (son of Charles) m. Margaret DeWitt
Reuben Hastings (son of Alonzo) m. Astaline Shipleigh
Rose Hastings (daughter of Reuben) m. Baxter Hoskins
Arthur Hoskins (son of Rose) m. Grace Surratt
Gideon Hoskins (son of Arthur) m. 1. Leonora Martin 2. Eliza Russell
Young Gideon Hoskins (son of Gideon) m. Amelia Stockwell
Perry Hoskins (son of Young Gideon) m. Elizabeth Endicott
Biscuit McKee and Bob Sheffield

# Who's in Biscuit & Bob's House

**Biscuit** McKee, librarian & her husband **Bob** Sheffield, town cop
and, in alphabetical order by first name:
**Amanda** Stanton, neuromuscular massage therapist
**Carol** Mellinger, visiting professor
**Charlotte** Ellis, relative newcomer to Martinsville
**Dee** Sheffield, employee of M'ville Fdn., Rebecca Jo's daughter-in-law
**Easton** Hastings, redhead
**Father John** Ames, priest at St. Theresa's, brother to Maddy
**Glaze** McKee, Biscuit's sister, head of the Martinsville Foundation
**Henry** Pursey, minister at The Old Church
**Ida** & **Ralph** Peterson, grocery store owners
**Madeleine** "**Maddy**" Ames, would-be thriller writer and employee of
M'ville Fdn.
**Melissa** Tarkington, owner of *Azalea House B&B*
**Nathan** Young ("Doc"), town doctor, and **Korsi**, the office cat
**Pat** & **Dave** Pontiac, guests at Azalea House
**Rebecca Jo** Sheffield, Bob's mother
**Reebok** Garner, Martinsville Deputy
**Sadie** Masters, widow and role model to Biscuit
**Tom** Parkman, restaurateur and Glaze's fiancé
*and me! I'm Marmalade*

## Latecomers:
**Frank** & **Sylvia** Parkman, Tom's parents
**Esther** Anderson, Tom's grandmother
**Ivy** & **John** ("Mom" and "Dad") McKee, Biscuit's parents

## In Matthew's House:
**Matthew** Olsen & his parakeet, Mr. Fogarty
**Hubbard** and **Clara** Martin
**Nick** & **Anita** Foley